HIGH VALUE TARGET

HIGH VALUE TARGET

A NOVEL
BY ANDREW SLOUGH

"AFTER THE FIRST DEATH, THERE IS NO OTHER."
DYLAN THOMAS

MILL CITY PRESS

Mill City Press, Inc.
212 3rd Avenue North, Suite 290
Minneapolis, MN 55401
612.455.2294
www.millcitypublishing.com

ISBN-13: 978-1-936780-80-8
LCCN: 2011912302

Printed in the United States of America

Chapter 1

C linging to a red plutonic spine above Afghanistan's dry Ganjgal Valley, U.S Marine Firebase Saker confronted the cedar-covered northwest border of Pakistan's Federally Administered Tribal Area. During the day, hot desert winds lifted a corundum of granite sand and crushed obsidian that, given sufficient time, would reduce sheer cliffs and forged armor to gray dust.

At night the winds reversed. Descending from the twenty-one thousand-foot summits of Kuh-e Shashgal and Kuh-e Tuioksa, the winds whipped the gray silt across Firebase Saker's sand bags and stone parapets. Once becalmed in the personnel bunker's dark silence, the dust settled onto the Marine's bivy sacks, packs and M16s.

Saker. Named after Afghanistan's Peregrine Falcon, the Coalition's most eastern outpost snagged July 15th's first light.

The shadowy edge between dawn and day crept onto the reinforced concrete bunker where it touched the M2 fifty-caliber machine gun before spilling down the rocky west slope to the valley floor.

Six Marines squinted toward the rising sun. Afghanistan's jagged eastern border was silhouetted against the bright yellow orb.

A Marine Sergeant shielded his eyes against the glare. Two months had passed since the SEAL team killed Osama bin Laden in Abbottabad, Pakistan. If the Marines hoped bin Laden's death would accelerate rotations home, they were wrong.

"Another blistering mother fuckin' hot day in paradise!" He forced

1

an oiled patch into the breech of his M16. The Marines hated the dawn when their NVGs faded and the Taliban finished their prayers and opened fire from the surrounding high ridges.

Under ideal conditions--no wind, rain or incoming fire--Saker's Marines took three minutes to clean and oil the M16's breech, bolt and magazine. Then the hard winds would rise, filling the machined slides, hinges and pins with the same tenacious, abrasive grit.

"Fucking dust," the Sergeant looked around the dim bunker. None of the six Marines bothered to glance up from their weapons. Dressed in dusty desert camo pants, faded olive green T-shirts and worn, dun-colored boots, they worked cleaning patches down the barrels of their M16s. To a man, the Marines refused to bitch about Saker. Not about the gritty MREs, the stink of shit, piss, sweat, the water rationing or the fact that the Taliban had the crapper's coordinates dialed in.

Two days earlier, the Moolies had fired three mortars off Mind Bender Ridge. The 82mms arrived with shrieks, punctuated by the crack of high explosive. The mortars blasted three shattered bowls into the hard rock, two outside the perimeter, one next to the plywood shitter.

"Maybe mortaring the doogey pit is a kind of Moolie joke!" a PFC remarked as he heaved the shattered frame onto a burn pile.

The Sergeant shifted his M16 to the crook of his arm. "Private, you're more fucked up than the Taliban."

"Yes, Sir," the PFC tossed a fragment of shit-splattered plywood onto the foul smelling pyre.

Straddling a major infiltration route, Saker's mission was to observe and interdict, not capture and hold. As such, the weapons were mobile small arms, AT-4 shoulder-fired rockets, M252 81mm mortars and one M120 millimeter mortar.

Built of bunkers blasted out of the base rock and supplied by helicopter alone, Saker was hot. The Taliban constantly probed it with small arms, mortars and rocket-propelled grenades. Two weeks before, the outpost had come within twenty meters of being overrun. It was the fourth time in the last nine months. Saker suffered six casualties. One dead, five wounded. Of the five, one would later die at Landstuhl. The Firebase's annual death toll eclipsed eight times that number.

The Marines posted to Saker were convinced the U.S. Army riflemen spent too much time glassing the surrounding hillsides and not enough searching the local village compounds. The mission, as the Marines interpreted it, was kill Moolies, kill Moolies, and if you can't kill Moolies, then drive them back into Pakistan. Contact, however, bred casualties and the American taxpayers had grown weary of hometown boys dying in unpronounceable places.

Including the six Marines, Saker was manned by thirty-two regular Army; two Afghan National Army; and three officers--a captain and two lieutenants. With few exceptions, the Firebase's contingent was tough and highly motivated.

A Solifugae scuttled across the bunker's dirt floor. Six million years of Afghanistan's blistering days, freezing nights and prolonged droughts had sculpted the six-inch Camel Spider into a brittle mix of speed, armor and firepower. Little wonder the Marines respected them. Cloaked by the shadows, the Solifugae were drawn to heat and movement. An Army PFC used his M9 bayonet to herd a six-inch Camel Spider into a cardboard box then tossed in a scorpion. The spiders and scorpions instantly morphed into tiny gladiators, circling fangs against arching stingers, in a gladiatorial fight to the death.

Blocking the Camel Spider with the M9's blade he looked up. "Gentlemen, place your bets." The game was an old one.

The Sergeant's oily patch hesitated on the trigger guard. "Private, turn that fucking spider loose." After PFC Howard-Smith got bit in the hand, the Captain issued an order against pitting spiders against scorpions.

Prior to Howard-Smith's bite, the most reckless of Saker's defenders bet a week's hazard pay on the winners. Ninety percent of the time, the spider killed the scorpion, forcing the PFC to offer odds. The fights ended when Howard-Smith was bitten while trying to separate the combatants long enough to close the bets. Examining the PFC's hand, Saker's medic told him camel spider venom wasn't fatal, and treated the draining blister with an antibiotic cream. Covering it with a large band-aid, he advised Howard-Smith to walk it off.

The PFC, however, proved to be allergic to Camel Spider venom. By that night his arm had swollen to twice its normal size. When blood stopped flowing to his forearm and hand, the medic tried to reduce the PFC's compartment syndrome. The skin ripped open across his bicep, and he was helivacked to Khost where surgeons performed an emergency fasciotomy. He was then evacuated to Landstuhl, Germany. Last anyone heard Howard-Smith was on his fifth skin graft and could still lose the arm.

Camel spiders were as aggressive as abused pit bulls and, like the Taliban who ringed the rocky hills above Saker, would attack whenever the odds tipped in their favor. Still, the Marines rarely killed them. The camels kept Saker's plagues of mice in check.

The smell of sweat mingled with the reassuring chemistry of Hoppe's cleaning solvent and gun oil, eddied through the square, concrete bunker. Metal slides traced metal grooves with coldly efficient tolerances that projected Saker's boundaries out to five hundred meters. The solvent reminded some of pheasant season in South Dakota, others of a screaming drill instructor.

The Marines could recite the Sergeant Instructor's warnings in their sleep, "A fucking grain of sand can cost you your life. Treat your weapon like your dick. Protect it! Honor it! Keep it clean! Don't let Homos touch it! And don't take the safety off until you're ready to rock and roll!"

After nine months in Afghanistan, the Marines knew if you didn't keep the M16A2 cleaned and oiled, you were fucked. Fire six clips on full auto and the barrel turned red-hot seconds before the slide jammed. It was predictable. Between the dust and heat, nothing worked in Afghanistan.

To prove a point, the string of overhead bulbs blinked out. The bunker pitched into deep darkness. It took three seconds for the Marines eyes to locate the thin ray of dusty rose light that speared through a tiny hole in the canvas door. The men listened.

"Anyone gas the generator?" the Sergeant glanced over his shoulder at a PFC. The generator was flown in on the last supply Chinook three days before. Taliban mortar attacks destroyed the last two. After the last direct hit, Saker's Captain ordered it fortified with sandbags.

"Yesterday afternoon," a PFC shifted under the Sergeant's glance.

"Check it again!"

The PFC rose, crossed the room and exited into the dusty light. Three minutes passed before the generator coughed to life, then settled down into a constant, calm hum. The lights blinked on and the PFC parted the blanket that served as a door. "The generator had gas," he stepped into the bunker. "The air filter was clogged." He sat down on his cot and returned to his M16.

As the Marines cleaned their weapons, the shadowy edge between dawn and day flowed west across the remnants of an ancient road that divided the dry valley. Four kilometers out, the mud brick compound of Turah Tizhah lay broken on the valley floor. Two years had passed since the Taliban used it to attack a supply convoy to Saker. During the firefight that followed, a B-52 dropped a single, five hundred-pound bomb that reduced a central compound to shattered piles of brick and earth.

Twenty kilometers further west, the road skirted the villages of Zherah Ghar and Dehi Ghar that squatted upon the dusty, desiccated plain. In the eight years since the last significant rain, Dehi Ghar's poppy fields and scattered fruit trees had withered and died. Deprived of water, the thin soil boiled away in Afghanistan's raw winds, leaving only the land's red bones to bleach beneath the desert sun. Dehi Ghar had since shrunken to a few families clustered around a salty well.

Eighty kilometers beyond Dehi Ghar the rough road joined the AO1 Kabul-Jalalabad Highway northwest to Kabul. What the harsh winds and endless drought spared, the goats finished, browsing away the foliage until the valley resembled an ancient, scarred anvil. The hammers came later. First as conventional bombs dropped by B-52s, then 120 mm artillery shells and later, when Coalition's armored vehicles rolled through, mortars arced onto attacking Afghani Taliban.

Aji al Swardi, the Firebase's Afghani interpreter, claimed that Alexander of Macedon's legions marched down the road into the Hindu Kush. In 325 A.D., Alexander attacked the ancient cities of Ora, Bazira and Massaga. Six enlisted men listened to al Swardi recount that upon the death of Massaga's chieftain, his aged mother, Cleophis, assumed command of the army.

Seeing the old woman lift her son's spear in defiance of the vast horde, Massaga's women joined her on the walls. When Alexander's siege failed to conquer the city, he negotiated a treaty. Cleophis opened the gates, and the Greeks marched in and promptly slaughtered every man, woman and child.

"Fucking smart," one of the PFCs observed. "Too bad the Moolies won't suck on the same dick."

The Coalition could secure and hold the tortuous road to Dehi Ghar during the day. The Taliban, however, owned the night. Working in the dark of a new moon to compromise the NVGs, the bomb-makers buried a Russian 105 millimeter shell between the rough, four-wheel tracks. Triggered to a remote detonator, the IED flattened an armored personal carrier. When the dust cleared, three soldiers were jack-strawed into a tangle of scorched limbs, blackened heads and naked torsos. A paragraph appeared on the second page of the L.A. Times. Brass blamed it on Iranian-shaped charges…and the war raged on.

A distant muzzle flash summoned a return burst from the M2 .50 caliber machine gun.

Captain Richard Heinson, Saker's Officer in Charge, scanned the hillside with his armored binoculars. "Hit anything?" he asked the gunner.

"No sir! Not that time."

Hidden within the north slope, Deodar cedars, which the local villagers logged for pocket money, the Taliban swept the parapet with harassing small arms. When AK-47 rounds splintered against the stone parapets, Saker's Marines would pound back with the .50 caliber. Returning fire held the insurgents a distance. Sooner or later, when bad weather prevented air support, they would assault the rock walls.

Afghanistan's high mountains and narrow valleys, vast deserts and deep gorges, rocks, insects and thin, weak soil had forged the Taliban into a hard, resourceful force, ready to die for their beliefs. Lacking airpower or mobile artillery, armed only with light and heavy mortars, rocket propelled grenades, a few inaccurate rockets, small arms, Browning Automatic Rifles and .50 caliber machine guns, the Moolies had forced the world's best-equipped army onto a series of besieged outposts supplied solely by Chinook helicopters.

Heinson turned and stepped down into the bunker. All water was helicoptered onto the isolated spine. None of Saker's contigent had bathed or shaved for ten days and the strong smell of men accustomed to living in sweat-stained uniforms filled the twelve by twelve rock enclosure. The captain was the lone exception. Though he had shaved that morning, his face was already dusted with Saker's gray talc. The Marines sitting on the bunks acknowledged him with nods.

Looking around the dim bunker, the Captain advised them, "Predator INTEL reports a company-sized contingent of Taliban have gained the ridge."

The Marines stopped cleaning their weapons. The closest to the exit stood up. "Sir, is that a full company?"

"Three hundred, give or take," the Captain nodded toward Mind Bender Ridge.

"Did the Predator catch anything else?"

"Two dozen dead Moolies strung across the valley floor and up the east slope of the pass."

"Fuck, yes!" a Marine Sergeant released the slide on his M16. A round slid home. "Any idea who's responsible?" He set the safety. "None," the Captain noted the action. The Marines were well trained. No way could he could hold Saker without them.

"What's next?"

"We check our weapons and ammunition and prepare for contact."

The M2 gunner leaned into the bunker, "Sir, there's something you should see!"

The Captain crossed to the armored observation point, where a spotting scope pointed toward the distant ridge. Adjusting the focus, Heinson watched a figure run down the trail that descended from the pass into the shadowed cedar forests. From the distance of a thousand meters, something wasn't right. No rifle, no turban, short hair, a pistol gripped in his right hand. A bright red stain covered his salwar kameez blouse, torn izar pants. The sound of automatic fire reached the Firebase.

"The Moolies are doing their fucking best to kill him!" the Sergeant raised his M16 and checked the safety. "Wonder what he did?"

"Held hands with the Mullah's daughter," a PFC appeared next to him.

"Or got to second base." A second PFC looked across to the forested hillside, "Sir, we should save them the trouble." He rested his M16 on the wall.

Watching the Taliban run full tilt down the trail, Heinson said, "Private, you couldn't hit a moving target at that distance with all the ammunition in Afghanistan. Save the round, you may need it."

Two hundred meters behind the running figure, a dozen men

7

with AK47s raced to close the distance. One stopped and raised his rifle. Sharpening the scope's sixty-power optics, the Captain saw muzzle flashes. A second later, the sound of automatic rifle fire floated across the valley to the Firebase. The figure kept running.

Standing behind Heinson, the Marine Sergeant tracked the lead figure with his M16. Just short of pulling the trigger, he set the sights ahead and above of the runner's head. At that distance, a killing shot was luck alone. "That Moolie's a fucking Marathon Man." He held his fire.

"The enemy of my enemy is my friend," Heinson silently recited the ancient Arab proverb.

Attracted by the rapid small arms fire, soldiers materialized on the parapet. In a minute, twenty men, including the six Marines, were scattered behind the sandbags. The two Lieutenants glassed the sheer, rocky face.

One turned to the riflemen, "Back to your posts!" he shouted. One 82mm Russian mortar would devastate Saker's crowded defenders.

"Sir?" the Marine Sergeant continued to track the runner. "We could drop the 120mm on that first group...we've plotted the coordinates."

"Where?" Heinson searched for the impact zone.

The Sergeant pointed to a glade, a thousand meters and three quarters of a mile up the forested face. "Locate the clearing where the trail crosses!"

The Captain swiveled the scope. The lone figure was still far above them, running fast. "How long to target impact?" Moolie or not, Heinson admired the insurgent's stamina.

"Fifteen seconds--give or take."

"Hold your fire until I give you the signal!" the Captain rapidly calculated the distance between the runner and the pursuing Taliban.

The Sergeant erected the M252 mortar on a fixed-point concrete slab, dialed the coordinates and glanced at the Captain.

Heinson waited until the running man crossed the clearing, then counted down twenty-five seconds. "Fire!" he commanded.

The Taliban reached the clearing a second before the mortar rocketed in. Three heard the incoming whistle in time to dive for cover. Six others were a second late. Two bodies tumbled downhill out of the explosion's gray smoke and disappeared into the dense cedars. The remaining seven were either killed instantly or were mortally wounded. Five would die within minutes.

The Private pumped his M16 above his head. "GET SOME!" he yelled.

The Captain's scope traced the trail uphill to the pass. He counted twenty Taliban running through the green cedars. Roughly fifty more cleared the ridge and took a lower, more direct trail that led down through the cedars and into the narrow valley. During the next minute the Captain watched a hundred and fifty men cross the pass.

"Sir, I've got Tactical Air Control on the radio," the Sergeant held the radio out to the Captain. "They say it's a slow day at the office and can deliver a load in, uh, three minutes."

"We'll keep them advised of our situation."

From over two kilometers away the scope magnified details: beards, caps, the color of a disdasha, AK47s, mortars and RPGs. Utilizing the terrain for cover, the running man sprinted through the clearings and slowed when the cedars closed across the trail. The Captain watched him stop, turn, take aim with the pistol, and fire. The distance to the Taliban was far beyond the pistol's maximum accurate range. Watching from two thousand meters away the Captain judged it was a wasted round. Then, the lead pursuer suddenly staggered off the narrow path. His gray turban spun away. Gathering speed, it launched off a cliff then floated for a hundred meters before it disappeared onto a shadowed scree slope.

The Captain could only guess at the lone runner's crime.

Following four decades of war, the Moolies had refined guerilla tactics to fine art. When confronted by overwhelming firepower, they never exposed themselves in large numbers. An attack averaged less than a dozen men. Even then, the insurgents maintained their spacing. Ten years combating the Russians and now more than that fighting the Americans had taught them that the Coalition wouldn't waste a fourteen thousand dollar cluster bomb on one man.

"Captain," the Sergeant was standing behind and to his left, "What's up with the Marathon Man?"

"Something critical," the Captain looked away from the scope to rest his eye. Marathon Man could possess valuable INTEL.

"If the Moolies close with us, TAC won't drop."

The rules governing CAS, Close Air Support, were modified after four Canadian Light Infantry were killed and eight wounded by a friendly-fire laser-guided bomb. The Captain was well aware of the minimum distance required before a pilot could drop. No close-in bombing runs were authorized, no matter how loudly Coalition troops were screaming for help.

"Sir, we've got maybe twelve minutes before Marathon Man reaches us. Another three or four before the Moolies hit us with everything they've got. Much closer and they'll overrun us."

"He could have INTEL about HVTs."

"Or be wrapped in C4 and ball bearings," the Sergeant watched the running figure. "No Moolie Intel is worth the risk of significant casualties. Sir, I suggest we call in the strike."

The Captain returned to the scope. Marathon Man appeared to be tiring. The Taliban were closing the distance. Seventy meters now separated him from the pursuers. The sound of repeated automatic bursts reached the Firebase. The Marathon Man turned, fired one shot, and instantly returned to full stride. A second pursuer crumpled.

"Fuck me!" the Captain whispered.

"Sir?" the Marine Sergeant turned from the hillside.

"Can you light up that pursuing group without killing the Marathon Man?"

"Doubtful! A mortar is chancy. We can harass them with the .50 cal and M16s."

"Then harass them!" In seconds thirty automatic rifles and the .50 caliber machine gun raked the pursuers. "Stay off the Marathon Man!" the Captain ordered. "Can you reach them with the M107?" he turned to the Sergeant.

"Sir, it's a kick in the ass to shoot but worse than inaccurate on moving targets."

"What about that surplus LAW?"

"The 72? It's designed to take out tanks."

"It's been gathering dust for two years. Use it!"

The Sergeant retrieved the short tube from the ammunition bunker, set the sights on the trail and cleared the area. A second after the rocket exited the tube, six fins extended. A screw of smoke raced toward the rocky hillside.

The detonation killed three of the pursuing group. The survivors dove for cover among rock outcrops and rotting cedar logs. The LAW bought time enough for Marathon Man to reach the rocky slope that rose a half mile from Saker. Descending the loose shale in long windmill strides, he fell once, rolled and was on his feet, running across the dry, flat valley to the Firebase.

Puffs of dust on the valley floor marked the AK rounds. Saker's combined force was now on the trench walls. Thirty-eight M16's returned fire with a steady, sharp chatter. Two more Taliban crumpled. Distracted by the incoming small arms fire, thirty Taliban switched their fire to Saker's defenses. AK rounds rang off the armor plate, chipped at the mud walls and thudded into the sandbags. An incoming mortar landed long, sending a fountain of broken rock and dust rolling over the riflemen. The next would fall six meters short. The third would land on their heads.

"Take out that mortar," the Captain yelled.

The mortar team rapidly swiveled the 81mm and fired. The explosion was long. Still, it was close enough to send the Taliban mortar team scrambling for cover. The second rocket landed closer. The Moolies' fire faltered.

The lone figure reached Saker's slope transition. Rising four hundred vertical feet above the dusty plain, on a good day it was a hard climb. Using the terrain for cover, he sprinted up a steep trail that clung to the shadows, away from the incoming small arms fire. The slope turned vertical and the figure slowed to a walk. Exposed on the vertical face, the next mortar could take him out. The Captain had too much invested in the Marathon Man to let him die on the lee slope. He turned to the Marines. "I need two volunteers to bring that man in!"

"Sir?" The Marines were shocked by his request. They wouldn't hesitate to rescue a wounded, or even dead Marine. But risk their lives for a Moolie? Two reluctantly stepped forward.

"Sir, he could be packing!" one noted for the record.

Heinson watched the runner falter. "He has INTEL! Take water! He'll need it!"

One Marine glanced at the other then dodged between the bunkers and slipped onto the exposed slope. Marathon Man had ground to a stop. Running downhill, the Marines reached the man. He was on his hands and knees, his head down, facing the shale. The Marines patted him down. He was clean.

When one tried to take his pistol, the grip tightened and a dry, barely audible voice issued from the dusty face. "Negative," it croaked. In the second before the shock wore off, the exhausted runner identified himself, "Major Jack Hull, Marines…" he stated his serial number, and then grabbed the water bottle. He drank, hurried, desperate gulps. His breathing slowed and the strength flowed into his arms and legs.

Two Taliban had worked into a position that offered a clear shot. Rounds cracked off the surrounding rocks. Major Hull's voice was clearer now. Staggering to his feet he ordered, "Move!"

Ducking the incoming rounds, the Marines exchanged a single, amazed glance and started to climb.

The Captain was huddled against the bunker when Hull and the two Marines dived over Saker's perimeter wall. Hull's eyes were bloodshot, his manjammies were filthy and stank of sweat, urine and death. Catching his breath, he identified himself.

The Captain straightened. "Major Hull? Where's your uniform? What happened to your unit?"

Hull shook his head. "No unit. My spotter's dead," his breath came in deep, distorted gasps. "Where's TAC?"

"On standby!" Heinson glanced at the Sergeant. TAC was waiting for coordinates.

"You should have called in a mission when you had a chance!"

The Captain struggled to adjust to the new chain of command. "An air strike would have wasted you along with the Moolies, Sir!"

"You should have taken the shot," Hull cut him off. Small arms fire was increasing. A mortar landed down slope, shaking the ground. When the dust cleared, Hull crossed to the parapet and reached for the Barrett M107.

The Sergeant moved to stop him.

"Sergeant, stand aside!" the command clear in his voice, Hull squared himself to the M107.

Captain Heinson's nod served in place of a direct order.

The Sergeant stepped to one side. Hull shifted the M107 .50 caliber to a sand bag on the parapet wall. Placing the stock against his shoulder and opening his eye to the scope, he asked, "Sergeant, are you worth a shit as a spotter?"

"Fair, Sir!" the Sergeant reached for a loaded clip.

Watching Hull settle the butt stock against his shoulder, one of the Marines whispered, "Fuck, that's Jack Hull!"

"The Sniper?" The other ducked as a fresh burst of small arms fire raked the bunker. "He's real? Fuck! I thought he was a comic book hero!"

Small arms fire intensified as the Taliban registered the distance. Focusing the spotting scope as he scanned, the Sergeant said, "You've got a mortar eleven o'clock, four degrees, nine hundred meters!"

Hull exhaled and squeezed the trigger. The white puff of a shattering .50 caliber round appeared below the mortar.

"Twelve up, six left!" the Sergeant barked the coordinates.

The Major spun twelve clicks of elevation into the scope and six clicks of left windage. The next shot cut the loader in half. Hull was waiting when the panicked aimer rose in confusion. Traveling at 1900 feet per second, the heavy 709-grain ball split his upper body in two. The Sergeant watched as the aimer's chest came apart, his head disappeared in a puff of red and gray vapor as his arms spun away in opposite directions.

"Sergeant! Stop rubber necking!" Hull yelled. "This is a target-rich environment! You're falling behind!"

The scope swept the steep rock face. "Two RPGs, eight o'clock, eight hundred meters, five degrees!" the Sergeant reported. The thirteen-kilo M107 swung smoothly to the left, hesitated and then recoiled. Hull found the next target, hesitated and squeezed again.

"Seven o'clock six hundred meters..." the .50 caliber's thunderous report cut him off.

Hull's next round hit a man sprinting across a shale slide. Two Taliban tried and failed to improve their firing position. A new mortar position opened up, an RPG flew from a cedar grove. The heavy caliber replied with a diesel's heavy steady rhythm. Shot followed shot, followed shot. Each shot, unhurried, exact--mortal.

For all the expression that crossed his face, Hull might have been a champion skeet shooter breaking clay pigeons. A tribal sense of purpose filled the defenders of Firebase Saker. The Marines rapidly loaded the massive .50 caliber brass into the steel clips then handed them to Hull, who shoved the heavy boxes home, racked the slide and selected a target. Fighting for the field glasses they watched the attacking Taliban fall. A dozen crumpled before the survivors searched for cover on the bare surrounding hillsides. When the .50 caliber continued to decimate their ranks, they started to retreat. At first in singles, then pairs and finally, as the .50 caliber sucked them out from behind rocks, cut through cedar trunks and picked off exposed legs, arms, chests or heads, the reluctant retreat turned to a rout.

None of the Taliban that the .50-caliber hit survived. Hull was still swinging on figures struggling toward the pass when the LRSR jammed. He squeezed the trigger then racked the bolt. Again he squeezed the trigger and yanked the slide. And he continued to cycle through the loading and firing sequence until the Sergeant emptied his water bottle onto the breech. Steam flashed off the black metal. "Sir, it's overheated. A round jammed!"

Hull jerked slide again and then again, before he looked up with a dazed expression. Staring toward the rocky pass, he took a deep breath and struggled to gather himself. Thirty seconds passed before he nodded and slowly released the M107.

Few men could shoot more than four rounds through the massive rifle. Now the ground around his feet glistened with a two-inch deep layer of brass casings. The butt of the M107 was tinted red. The heavy recoil had bludgeoned his right shoulder. He could not feel his right arm.

Saker's riflemen lowered their rifles and stared at Hull. To a man they recognized the difference between a trained sniper and one bred to the profession.

"Captain!" the waiting Sergeant held the radio to his ear. "Tactical Air Control says they're waiting to hump the load!"

Captain Heinson looked away from Hull's bloodied Afghan shirt.
"Sir?"

The Captain turned to face the Sergeant, "Advise them to bring it. West side of the pass. Sergeant, relay the coordinates."

"Yes, Sir!"

Two minutes later an F-18 screamed low over the ridge. From that distance the captain could see the 500-pound cluster bombs tumble onto the ragged horizon. A minute later a B-52A dropped two more from 30,000 feet. Firebase Saker's defenders watched in awe as rolling fire swept the ridge.

Chapter 2

A CH-47D Chinook swept over the shattered Afghanistan compound of Turah Tizhah. Rotor roar filled the cockpit as the pilot moved the cyclic in time with the collective, throttle and anti-torque pedals. The CH-47D was beyond maximum limits yet the pilot still kept the throttle pinned against the stop. Checking his gauges, he held the nose hard down, the twin rotors spinning at max pitch as he jinked and dodged down the narrow valley. Flying between the rock walls made his skin crawl.

Still three kilometers out, the pilot had no way of telling if the Taliban were now tracking the lumbering Chinook with one of Charlie Wilson's Stingers. Two weeks earlier he'd watched a Blackhawk Helicopter auger into a rocky east face above the remote firebase. A thin contrail of smoke had rocketed up from an adjacent ridge shattering the Blackhawk's fuselage, below the tail rotor. The spinning rotor froze; the helicopter commenced a rapid spin, nearly recovered, and then exploded in a ball of orange flames and broken rotors. A team from Firebase Saker had fought their way through small arms and RPGs to the wreckage. All knew it was a body recovery mission.

A kilometer south of Turah Tizhah's collapsed walls and ruined fields, the pilot exerted left pressure on the yoke and the large helicopter banked east toward Saker. The short preflight briefing detailed how the Firebase had been attacked by a company-sized group of Taliban. Casualties needed to be evacuated. From three kilometers away the Firebase looked untouched but as the distance closed to a kilometer and then to five hundred meters, the pilot started to pick up mortar craters on the slopes below. Hundreds of bullet holes pockmarked the reinforced bunkers, mortar pits and machine gun emplacements.

Triggering his microphone he raised the Firebase, "Saker this is Domino One, we're one seventy en route. What's the LZ's SITREP?"

Ten seconds passed before Saker's Marine Sergeant filled the pilot's headphones, "Domino One, Saker. LZ is Cherry."

"Say Again?"

"LZ is Cherry. We're taking small arms fire!"

"It's never fucking ICE, never," the pilot looked at his copilot.

At two hundred kilometers per hour it was difficult to estimate how many corpses lay scattered across the hillside—a hundred, possibly more. Their bodies were sprawled in a fan pattern rising to the ridge; it was clear they were in full retreat when they died.

" Fuck...Saker served up some serious hurt!" The pilot pushed the cyclic far left. The Chinook banked in a tight, counter-clockwise turn. "Saker, can you suppress the incoming?"

"We're suppressing now."

As the CH-47D swept over the surrounding forested gullies and flared toward Saker's landing zone, the pilot gritted his teeth and braced for small arms fire. Saker was hot. A second before he flared for the landing zone he dumped the ramp. He had forty seconds to drop the two replacement Army PFCs, ammunition, water and food, and load the wounded before the Moolies lobbed a mortar onto the LZ. Rotor spinning at max RPM, the pilot watched the FB's .50 caliber dust a distant cedar grove. Saker's PFCs hit the ramp at a run, heaved the ammo onto the deck, then turned their attention to the walking wounded. The first had been hit in the bicep, a second took shrapnel in the calf, the third was shot through the hand.

A Navy medic checked the PFC's bleeding bicep and yelled, "Where's the Major?"

"That's him," the bandaged private nodded toward what looked like a Taliban insurgent walking out of the mid-day glare and up the ramp.

Hull dropped into one of the canvas seats that were anchored to the fuselage. The Chinook's rotors hammered as the pilot pulled pitch and Hull watched Firebase Saker drop below the closing ramp. The pilot moved the

16

cyclic, left, right, forward and back, trying to anticipate RPG's arcing up from the ridge outcrops below. The Chinook hit dead air. The riveted metal floor dropped beneath Hull's boots and he took a deep breath and thought about the members of Seal Team Six who died when an RPG exploded against their Chinook in the Tangi Valley. It was night. The Moolies got lucky. Of the thirty-eight who died, twenty-two were Seals. Command claimed none participated in the Abbattobad raid but Hull knew a dozen of the dead Seals had gone over the wall. Command would never admit the Taliban had avenged the killing of Osama bin Laden.

Hull gripped the seat and opened his eyes. The wounded were secured to the floor; the medics changed IVs, checked vital signs. A PFC stood against the opposite fuselage staring at the Major.

"Something on your mind, Private?" Hull yelled above the rotor roar.

"Sir, we've never flown a mission solely to retrieve a Moolie!" the Private ventured.

"You're evacuating these wounded." Hull yelled back.

"Sir, we had the room, they needed stitching up!" the Private braced himself against the rolling fuselage. "Our orders came from General Petraeus himself. With all due respect, Sir, any idea why he sent this thirty-four hundred-dollar per-hour stretch-limo to pick you up?"

Hull's glance ended the conversation.

Seventy-two hours and thirty kilometers separated Major Jack Hull from the goat trail that snaked across the high pass above Sherghatu, Pakistan. Hull had been ordered to wait on an exposed ridge for a High Value Target. This was the dragon's tail of the Himalayas--high enough at 4000 meters to suck the power out of his lungs, low enough to spare the blinding headaches triggered by a rapid ascent to altitude.

Beneath him, a trail wound down a sheer face that in turn funneled into a rocky defile. A young Afghani would need two, maybe three minutes to run from the pass to the cleft. A middle aged Moolie in good shape might add another minute. The faint track was one hundred and thirty meters from the blistering, rock point. Hull's laser range-finder recorded exactly 128.498 meters—a no-miss guarantee for the Scout Sniper's magnum rifle.

The lofty ridge's strategic advantage was compromised by a lack of cover. Without the Ghillie suit's twisted cords of beige, rose and brown colored yarn he would be visible from any one of six surrounding ridges.

Hull forced a voice up his dry throat, "Anything?" He moved the Ghillie yarn to face Bauldaire, his spotter.

At six-two and a hundred and seventy-five pounds, the lean, twenty-four year old Lieutenant was tough beyond measure. "We got spit," Bauldaire squinted through the Swarovski spotting scope. Able to gather light at the limit of dawn and dusk, the thirty-five hundred-dollar scope could magnify a dirty thumbnail or facial scar at two hundred meters. As soon as the stars appeared, Bauldaire attached NVGs to the eyepiece. INTEL believed the Taliban cadre would move at dawn of the second day. INTEL was wrong.

"Don't talk about spit or piss," Hull checked his Seiko chronograph. Six o'clock, first light--fourteen hours until sunset.

To ensure lethality, standard operating procedure dictated the deployment of three teams. Three teams, however, would guarantee detection. This time, it was one team consisting of two Marine Scout Snipers. Silent, hidden, and out of water.

INTEL insisted it would be one day--max. Hull and Bauldaire were now pressing six. The five gallons of water the two Scout Snipers had humped seventeen hundred vertical meters and six kilometers from a faint spring had lasted until dusk of the third day.

Even if the Scout Snipers had known the INTEL was faulty, they could not have packed a third water bladder. Not in the frayed Afghani packs. Hull had divided the loads. Three point seven kilos per gallon, times two. Seven and a half kilos of water. Add four fragmentation grenades, a kilo of MREs, eight clips, or forty rounds for the .338...another ninety for Bauldaire's M4A1. Throw in a kilo plus for the Ghillie suit, half a dozen rounds for the M4A1 grenade launcher, a satellite phone that doubled as a GPS, a digital camera for the Swarovski. Grams added to kilos, and kilos bred pain.

When the bladders ran dry, the Scout Snipers struggled to avoid obsessing about liquid. Sucking on a smooth stone helped but there were lapses. After two days without water, Hull dreamed about Gatorade: lemon lime, orange and cherry, primary colors filled with thirst-quenching electrolytes. On the second afternoon he imagined a cold beer, and that evening could not take his eyes off the dark blue glaciers of the high Hindu Kush. Like a melody from a haunting song, the image played endlessly through the night and early morning.

As Pakistan's July sun climbed toward its zenith, temperatures within the Ghillie suit's overlapping cords soared above 116 degrees. Hull prayed through cracked lips that no part of him, not a foot or elbow, finger or rifle barrel had slipped outside the Ghillie suit's sweltering camouflage. Lying motionless among the plutonic rocks, sand, dust and scorpions that covered the exposed ridge, he had held his water for twenty-two hours against this eventuality. He knew growing dehydration would compromise his accuracy and he now licked his blistered lips. He had no choice but drink his own piss.

Hull had read about people who brewed piss tea. Fuck knows why. He could even diagram the chemistry. Urine was composed of two percent uric salts and ninety five percent water. The water went down without protest. It was the salts that made him puke. His abdominal muscles tightened at the remembered bitter taste of his own hot stream and he nearly wet his reeking sweat and urine-stained Ghillie suit. It would not be the first time in the five days he had gritted his teeth on the exposed, plutonic knife-edge.

He was torn between duty and survival. Drink pee, or back off the exposed ridge and report the INTEL was faulty. The HVT had canceled his journey or had chosen a different trail. He could have passed at night to their south below the intervening outcrop.

The ridge raked light from the sun's first rays, casting the goat trail in a muted, rose glow. Studying the rugged northeast horizon, Bauldaire whispered, "Bliss was it in that dawn to be alive. But to be young was very heaven!"

Unable to stop himself, Hull whispered, "Fuck this motherfucking country!" A serpentine rivulet ran from his cropped black hair down his cheek. He was surprised he could still sweat.

"Is that Iambic pee, I mean pentameter?" the Lieutenant quietly laughed.

Hull couldn't help but admire the young Lieutenant's sand. Out of water, twenty-five kilometers inside Pakistan, surrounded by the Taliban, with their odds at best fifty-fifty of humping it back to Firebase Saker, Bauldaire was quoting Wordsworth and diagramming profanity. It was no coincidence the two Marines had both majored in English literature.

On the strength of his past service, Hull could have chosen any spotter in the U.S. Marine Corps. He picked Bauldaire specifically on the basis of his performance in graduate-level Lit classes. Literature studies bred creative thinkers. Bauldaire's emphasis was 19th Century English Poets, a pantheon of writers he resurrected during hard contact. Hull preferred 20th Century American Novelists and, while he was well-read, following a second Scotch he would readily confess his admiration for Hemingway's hunting and fishing stories--"Death in the Afternoon", "The Old Man and the Sea" and "The Snows of Kilimanjaro".

Holding his voice to a dry rasp, the Major recited, "Count it a quirk, that Wordsworth never remarked how it hurt to lie face down in the dirt!"

In return Bauldaire responded, "With respect, Sir, Wordsworth valued, 'The earth, and every common sight, did seem appareled in celestial light."

During the past year, Hull had repeatedly advised Bauldaire that he could drop the "Sir." The Marine form of respect rang falsely in Afghanistan's bombed out buildings and blistering hides. The Major preferred "Hull" or even "Jack" but four years at Annapolis had ruined the Lieutenant. It was "Sir" when Hull and Bauldaire first met in Bagram, and "Sir" on that dry Pakistan ridge.

There was another thing. General James F. Amos, the Commandant of the Marine Corps sent a message outside of channels advising Hull that the Corps was fast-tracking Bauldaire. While General Amos would not venture how high the Lieutenant might rise, he reminded Hull that Bauldaire needed combat experience to validate future command. Scout Sniper in Afghanistan danced too close to the edge but it was the Lieutenant's decision, and Command vacillated just long enough to block Bauldaire's acceptance to the 3rd Marine Division SSBC on Ford Island in Honolulu, Hawaii. When he graduated at the top of his class, the Corps could only try and protect him.

"You will not lose Lieutenant Bauldaire, Major Hull. Is that clear?" the Marine Commandant demanded.

"Yes, Sir," Hull promised.

If Hull had been ordered to baby-sit Bauldaire, Annapolis had trained the Lieutenant to lead from the front. For the past year, Hull fought to shield the Lieutenant from errant AK-47 rounds and RPGs. General David

Petraeus' Special Ops mission into Pakistan blindsided them both. The Four Star should have detailed an Army Delta team but the INTEL was perishable, and the ranking Delta team was off the grid in Helmand Province.

Hull's rasp sharpened as he stated the obvious, "We're fucked if our HVT doesn't show today."

Bauldaire's Ghillie suit shifted to face him, "Sir, in case you hadn't noticed, we reached that exalted state around noon, yesterday." Though Bauldaire's face was hidden beneath the yarn, Hull heard his faint laugh. Bauldaire never swore...no "Fucks," "Goddamns," or even "Shits." He was an Eagle Scout packing an M4A. Hull could never have predicted how much he would come to care for and respect the Lieutenant.

Operating out of Bagram Airbase, Kandahar, and half a dozen isolated Firebases, for the past seven years teams of Scout Snipers had conducted counter-insurgent operations across Afghanistan. Officially, they did not take orders from NATO and rarely coordinated their operations with the Afghan National Army. Surprise was critical and the fewer Afghanis and Pakistanis privy to perishable INTEL, the better. Hull knew that if the Coalition could not win the covert war in Pakistan, it would never prevail in Afghanistan.

Following the US-led invasion of Afghanistan in October of 2001, the Taliban armies collapsed. Special Ops' coordinated attacks with the Northern Alliance but Mullah Omar, Osama bin Laden and the majority of senior al Qaeda and Taliban leaders escaped to Pakistan.

Relying on a labyrinth of trails pitted with caves, forests and village compounds, once the leaders crossed the border, they took refuge in Pakistan's FATA--the Federally Administered Tribal Areas--that straddled 1,000 kilometers of the 1,600-kilometer Afghan-Pakistan border. The Pashtuns, who claimed the high mountain valleys, made up 42% of the population of something less than twelve million in Afghanistan. More than twice that number lived in Pakistan. Pashto was their language, Pashtunwali their legal code, and all shared a fierce hatred of foreign invaders. The British fought to subjugate the Pashtuns for two centuries. The Russians followed. Now the Americans believed they could turn FATA tribesman for the cost of better roads and mud-brick schools. If they succeeded, they would be the first in nearly two hundred years.

ISAF had lost faith in the Pakistan Army's ability to stop the Taliban from re-crossing the border. U.S. Command in Khost believed that the Taliban were supported by elements within the Pakistani government. Worse, the recent attack on Mumbai and Pakistan's resulting shift of troops from FATA to the Indian border had freed the Taliban to reinforce its presence in Afghanistan.

Hull and Bauldaire had watched more than a hundred Taliban insurgents follow the faint trail into the dry valley below. Locked to the camouflaged Swarovski, Bauldaire had tracked each cadre as they negotiated the exposed track and disappeared into the shadows. As columns of Afghanis, Pakistanis and Iranian mercenaries passed beneath their rifles, Bauldaire had repeatedly cautioned Hull to hold his fire.

According to available INTEL there would be a signal but, as day bled into night into day, none appeared. Surrounded by al Qaeda recruits and Taliban tribesmen, if either of the Scout Snipers as much as took a piss in the open they would certainly die. Yet, unless they pulled off the ridge, their chances for survival were equally bleak.

Hull had made a career out of volunteering for brutal assignments. Two months before Iraqi Freedom launched across the southern deserts, he was ordered to neutralize Saddam Hussein. INTEL got most of it right. Right car, right route, right time. The third story window offered a clear angle. The .338's sights were tack at three hundred meters. INTEL could not know Hussein would use a double that day.

Al Jazeera published a photo of the body. The 250-grain Lapua slammed into the back of the skull. Entry was the size of a dime. The Spitzer's exit removed the face. Identification was impossible.

Hull harbored few illusions about snipers. The Russians claimed Vasily Zaytsev was the best ever. Using a standard-issue Russian Mosin-Nagant rifle, between November 10th and December 17th, 1942, during the Battle of Stalingrad, Zaytsev reportedly killed two hundred and twenty-five German officers and soldiers. Most impressive, the figure included eleven opposing snipers. Hull knew the numbers were fiction. Zaytsev was a very good, but not a brilliant shot. During the bleakest days of Stalingrad, Russia needed a hero. The Commissars picked Zaytsev.

Hull briefly wondered why Command hadn't used a Predator to take out the target. The Predator could stay aloft for days then kill on command.

Invisible, accurate, lethal--the lone disadvantage was misidentification. Prior to the Abbottabad raid, video pilots in Las Vegas believed they'd killed Osama bin Laden three dozen times only to discover they'd taken out a funeral procession, a wedding party or an Afghani family on the way to market. For that reason alone, the Pakistani and Afghan tribes both hated and feared the Predators.

Even then, thirty thousand feet above, a drone was monitoring the Scout Snipers' fading heat signature. Nothing--neither success nor failure, bravery or cowardice--would go unrecorded.

To avoid dwelling on his thirst, Hull meditated on why only goats, spiders, scorpions, the Taliban's turbaned soldiers and Afghanistan's Commander of International Security Assistance Force coveted this scorched corner of Pakistan.

Sanctuary.

Following four tours in Afghanistan, Hull respected the Pashtun tribes' fitness, determination and fighting spirit. The Coalition had only begun to understand that if they escalated the war, they would further alienate Pashtuns living in Pakistan. The result would be further instability or the total collapse of Pakistan.

The history of the Taliban was brief, devout and brutal. Inspired by Saudi Arabia's conservative Sunni Islam, the Taliban had emerged from religious Madrassas to fill the political and military vacuum created when the Soviets withdrew from Afghanistan. Promising peace and security, these bearded Pashtun tribesmen attacked corruption, enforced laws, patrolled the roads and provided a safe environment for trade and commerce. One result was the Taliban soon controlled ninety percent of Afghanistan. Linked to that peace, however, was a strict interpretation of Sharia Law that dictated traditional Islamic punishment--public executions for murderers and adulterers, amputations for thieves, canings for violations of strict dress codes, which dictated beards for men, burkas for women.

"Got a silhouette!" It was Bauldaire. "He'll skyline in a second."

A figure appeared, hesitated then quickly crossed. Another hurried along behind him. Hull centered the crosshairs. Built by Sako, his TRG-42 bolt action Magnum .338 weighed five kilograms and had an effective range of 1500 meters. Charged with Lapua's 250-grain B408 Lock Base round and traveling at 760 meters per second, the fully jacketed bullet would decimate the target.

In compliance with the Geneva Convention's mandates dictating the military use of jacketed bullets, the Lapua's 250-grain Spitzer-boat tail's ton and three-quarter foot pounds of energy would blow through military grade body armor a millisecond before it crushed the heart, lung and liver.

Under ideal conditions Hull could have increased the distance by another thousand meters. At that range a bullet drop of 2.45 meters and the fact that he would only have time for two shots, left the Scout Snipers stranded on the exposed ridge. One hundred and thirty meters guaranteed the shot. Detection, however, was also assured. The first round would betray their position. By the second, the Taliban would have them in their sights.

"Any signal?" Hull held the crosshairs on the leader's temple.

"Negative."

Hull watched the two men cut across the slope and disappear into the rocky defile. The sun lighted the rocky ridge. He thought of the Tehrik-i-Taliban, the preferred name of the Pakistani Taliban who had allied with al Qaeda. Translated it meant "Freedom Fighter" which lent legitimacy to the Pakistani and Afghani cutthroats. He tried, and failed, to summon enough saliva to spit.

Hull could no longer even think "Freedom Fighter" without prefacing it with the alliterative "Fucking." He shook his head at the soft, self indulgent, stupidity of stateside talking heads. The nightly news commentators wouldn't recognize an Afghani "Fucking Freedom Fighter" until he thrust a Karud Dagger through his crisply pressed shirt, past his bright knotted tie, beneath his rib cage and into his heart.

"Taliban Jihadist," "Muslim Extremists," "Pashto Freedom Warriors." "Freedom Martyrs for Allah," traveled less well, though Hull agreed there was a certain suicidal romantic aura affixed to the last. He preferred to keep it simple.

The most descriptive prefixed sand. "Sand Flea" was shortened to "Flea." "Sand Kisser" alluded to a believer's five daily prayer prostrations to Mecca. Echoing the United States' racially confused rules governing political correctness, "San Niggah" was reserved for use solely by black troops. "Sand Scratcher" spoke to the Afghan soldier's habit of itching their eternal infestations of fleas, ticks and bed bugs.

Hull's favorite was "Moolie" which bastardized Mullah, the Afghan religious teachers. Few Coalition soldiers researched the origin. Bauldaire had. The Lieutenant traced the root slur to the Italian "melanzane" or black-skinned "eggplant." Bauldaire had not discovered whether Moolie stopped at Mullah or included Mujahid, the singular of Mujahideen. Mujahid described a struggler who volunteers for a jihad. English- speaking Coalition troops had shortened it to simply Moolie, which stripped out the religious call to Allah. Though Bauldaire's definition of "Moolie" wasn't technically accurate, for Hull it described a bearded serial killer in Michelin all-weather sandals, nothing more.

Hull did not hate Afghanis. On some level, he knew their ingrained lack of compassion in battle was irrevocably linked to Afghanistan's brutal geography, harsh climate and long, bloody history. From the Achaemenid Empire under Darius the Great through Alexander the Great, to the Mongols and Abdur Rahman Khan, Afghanistan's history had been marked by conquest, war, institutionalized dislocation, torture and genocide. After four tours, Hull clearly understood the challenge of winning Afghanistan's national hearts and minds. While ISAF might hand out cash, radios, food and schoolbooks to buy the Afghani villagers' loyalty, the Taliban were far more efficient. If they suspected a man was collaborating with Coalition forces, they gouged out his eyes, ripped out his tongue, or beheaded him in front of his family.

None of it shocked Hull. Not anymore. He had witnessed the worst, some of it by his own hand. Ensuring loyalty by gouging out a man's eyes, however, resonated on CNN. He was not stunned or even surprised when Sayaed Ghulam's bloodied face filled his computer's nightly news. Ghulam described how three men broke into house, jammed a Kalashnikov into his mouth, and dug out his eyes with a knife. Sobbing from empty sockets, the illiterate farmer insisted he only raised wheat and popcorn. He always believed he had no enemies. He did not know why he'd been attacked.

"The fuck you don't," Hull had commented over CNN's Wolf Blitzer's outraged commentary. Ghulam knew. Just as Hull knew it was to ensure loyalty. Innocence or guilt made no difference. In time, Sayaed Ghulam's blinding would be attributed to a greater, historical "good."

In his dark soul, Hull admired the Taliban's penchant for cruelty.

There were no democratic niceties such as extenuating circumstances or the promise of rehabilitation. During August of 1998 the Taliban attacked the large northern city of Mazar-i-Sharif. Using pickup trucks as light armored personal carriers, the Taliban thugs shot everything that moved; men, women, children, shop owners...dogs, goats and donkeys. Eight thousand noncombatants died in two days. When the automatic weapon fire ceased, the Taliban left the corpses to rot in the streets as a lesson for those who opposed their rule. For the Taliban there was simply a strict interpretation of Sharia Law and Infidels—there were Patriots, Martyrs and the Coalition Invaders. The Taliban had a far clearer situational perspective than ISAF. And in the coming years, that clarity would oust the Coalition, just as it had destroyed the Greeks, Mongols, Indians and most recently the Russians' will to fight and die in this dusty, medieval land. Little wonder Afghanistan was known as "The Graveyard of Empires."

Hull had long since stopped judging or, for that matter, noticing the men's black, rust and white robes, turbans, black beards, and undecipherable eyes, or the women's anonymous burkas. To him, the Afghanis had morphed into a race of Falcons. Peregrine, Saker or Kestrels--they were defined only by variations in color and size.

Four tours had taught him that like Falcons, the Afghanis were fiercely independent. They could be taught to build bridges or kill Taliban, but ISAF, the International Security Assistance Force, would never buy their loyalty. Not with schools, roads or flush toilets. Hull knew you could share your dinner with a Sergeant in Afghan National Army, or at the risk having your throat slit, sleep with an Afghan whore. Loyalty, however, was defined by a daily obeisance to Allah, fealty to your tribe, and a ferocious devotion to honor and family. The ISAF could dress the ANA in new uniforms, give them M16As, teach them how to use a latrine, pay them $120 per month and transport them in Armored Personnel Carriers. But if you questioned their honor, or touched their sister they would happily cut you in half with an M16. Hull had seen it happen.

Bottom line was--working with Afghanis had taught him never to handle a Falcon without a thick leather glove.

"Sir, who do you think it is?" Bauldaire crushed a scorpion that sought refuge in his Ghillie's cords.

"The Target?"

"Yes, Sir."

"Fuck if I know! It could be Mohammed Omar."

"He's a member of the Hotak, an ethnic Pashtun." The Lieutenant flicked the scorpion's crushed carcass out of the depression. "Lost an eye in the Battle of Jalalabad."

"INTEL says he cut it out himself, then sewed the socket shut." Hull shifted among the scorching rocks. "Schwarzenegger plagiarized his big scene in that first Terminator movie."

"Sir, credible CIA reports say he had it surgically removed at a Red Cross facility near the border." He looked through the scope at the distant goat trail. Nothing. "Omar is over fifty years old, has been wounded four times and reportedly doesn't travel well. I don't think it's him. But if it is, do you think Command will give us the ten million dollar reward?"

"Bauldaire, you're dreaming." Hull blew dust out of the Sako's bolt then lifted the lever. It was clean. "When we make the shot, and if we make it back to Afghanistan, we'll rate basic hazard pay and an extra week of leave."

"That's a disappointment--what about OBL?"

"Bin Laden?" the Ghillie yarn moved as Hull shrugged. "SEAL Team Six killed him in Abbottabad.

"You believe that?"

"The President promised they had genetic samples, pictures, eyewitness reports from the operators."

"But no body. No published photos."

"Bin Laden was shot in the face. The SEAL's 5.56 round took everything from his ears back. You show that photo on the evening news and you'd have half of America puking into their pasta."

"Every bearded Moolie with his eyeballs laying on the cheeks, looks pretty much like every other head shot Moolie. They didn't bring back his body."

"Bauldaire, he's dead."

"Then someone obvious-- Hakeemullah Mehsud?"

"The head of the Pakistan Taliban?"

"He took over when Baitullah Mehsud was killed by a US air strike in 2009."

27

"Baitullah Mehsud? Benazir Bhutto's assassin?"

"The same."

"I'd rather eliminate Omar," Hull scoped the trail. Nothing

"I'm guessing it's Malawi Jalaluddin Haqqani."

"Charlie Wilson's go-to guy?"

"Reports claim the Congressman once referred to Haqqani as 'goodness personified.' That was then, this is now," the Lieutenant raised the Swarovski and swept the surrounding ridges. "A 2008 air strike just missed him. It took out his house in Dandy Drape Hail, killed twenty-three of his relatives, one of his two wives, his sister, sister-in-law, and eight of his grandchildren. Unfortunately, it missed his son, Sirajuddin Haqqani."

"Jalaluddin Haqqani must be close to sixty years old!"

"Which is why Intel believes Sirajuddin now controls the Haqqani network. Recent reports claim he forged new financial and political alliances with al Qaeda."

An imperceptible movement of Bauldaire's Ghillie yarn served as a nod. "INTEL reports Jalaluddin Haqqani may have helped Osama bin Laden cross the border into Waziristan. He's been linked to both Pakistan's ISI and Hamid Karzai.

"Karzai?" Hull tried to spit. "That corrupt fucking bastard…"

"Yes, Sir," Bauldaire agreed. "Seems that Karzai offered to make the elder Haqqani Prime Minister--if only to protect himself from Haqqani's suicide bombers. You knew Haqqani imported the tactic into Afghanistan?"

"Not until now."

Bauldaire swiveled the Swarovski and adjusted the focus. "That hasn't been completely proven, but Haqqani is the prime suspect. He was also implicated in the Indian Embassy Bombing in Kabul. In spite of a touch of Parkinson's, he stays on the run and never sleeps in the same bed."

"If that's true, then it shouldn't be hard to ID him," Hull lowered the Sako. "We'll just take out the old guy with a bad shake and a cane."

The Lieutenant stifled a laugh. "At his age, he'd have to be packed up here. Recent INTEL rates his twenty thousand fighters as utterly devoted to him. Zealots!" He focused the Swarovski. "Careful!" he cautioned, "We've got targets! Five, just crossing the ridge!"

Hull put the cross hairs on the lead figure. The shimmering heat waves obscured features. Other than counting from front to back, there was no way to identify a target. "Any signal?"

Ten seconds passed. The five Taliban moved quickly down the trail. "Nothing," Bauldaire lifted his eye from the scope.

Hull held the crosshairs on the leader's chest. He calculated the rising thermals and descending crosswind would push the 250 grain two clicks right, and one click down. Employing a minimum of movement, he tracked the leader until the five Taliban disappeared into the rocky defile.

A sharp rock was digging into his hip. He shifted imperceptibly, dragged his tongue over his dry lips and thought of a proverb from Ecclesiastes, "If thine enemy be hungry, give him bread to eat...and if he be thirsty, give him water to drink. For thou shalt heap coals of fire upon his head." Applied to their particular situation, "coals of fire" served as a fair definition for the Lapua's 250 grain FMJ.

Taking care to avoid resting the scope, muzzle or breech in the red dust, Hull confessed, "Lieutenant, we're both out of the loop. My best guess is Omar...but who the fuck knows? Kill him and the coordination crumbles. It'll take years to reorganize."

"And if the target doesn't show?"

"Command will raise hell."

Chapter 3

General David Petraeus, Commander of International Security Assistance Forces in Afghanistan, wanted this High Value Target-- wanted him so badly he jerked Hull and Bauldaire out of Jalalabad within a day of a two week leave and helied them to Kabul.

Graduate of West Point, U.S. Army Command and General Staff College, Ph.D. in International Relations from Princeton University, Master Parachutist, Associate Professor at West Point, writer, philosopher, potential future presidential candidate, Petraeus commanded the 101st Airborne Division during V Corps' race to Baghdad. He then led V Corps into Karbala, Hilla and Najaf where he secured a reputation for judicial use of force. A classic soldier--scholar, Petraeus would have continued to lead U.S. Central Command if Four Star General Stanley McChrystal hadn't run off the tracks.

McChrystal and Petraeus were close. West Point, Iraq, Counter Insurgency Planning; a staff officer who had served under both noted they were woven from the same ballistic-grade Kevlar. Allowing reporter Michael Hastings unlimited access to McChrystal's staff was a total FUBAR. Petraeus had heard the details from McChrystal himself. The Rolling Stone article would have amounted to little more than a rehash of old press releases if the ash from Iceland's Eyjafjallajökull volcano hadn't stranded Stan, Hastings and Team America, McChrystal's general staff in Paris.

Stan had been working eighteen-hour days for five months to drive the Taliban out of Marja and Kandahar. Team America absolutely deserved a few days rest and recreation—just not in front of a reporter. If Stan believed he and Hastings shared an understanding, the Four Star would later pay dearly for allowing Hastings access to his inner circle. Rolling Stone had an agenda. McChrystal's failure to read one or two of the magazine's Vietnam era issues represented a severe lapse of focus. The drinking, dancing and alcohol fueled jokes about President Obama, Vice President Biden, U.S. Ambassador Karl Eikenberry, and Special Representative to Afghanistan, Richard Holbrooke, should have never happened. Rolling Stone's reporter should have been restricted to limited one-on-one interviews in Kabul.

Stan McChrystal got fucked. Pasted up by the writer and Rolling Stone's New York editors, the resulting story was a sensationalized hatchet job that destroyed the Four Star's career. The editors cherry picked the tape recordings, pulling one-liners out of typical staff officer bitching, they then used to anchor the piece. By the time it hit the stands, half a dozen off the cuff sound bites framed the story. Given the President's shrinking approval numbers, it was enough. McChrystal's resignation nearly destroyed ISAF's command structure. Afghanistan Command would have suffered far less damage if the Four Star had simply run over an IED.

Petraeus blamed McChrystal's lapse on exhaustion and the demands of running the Afghanistan war. The only line that resonated was his confession, "All these men…I'd die for them. And they'd die for me." But then, swaddled in an Army issue kevlar helmet and flak jacket, Michael Hastings never came within twenty kilometers of dying. One thing was gospel. Imbedded reporters were history. If the press wanted to get up close and personal with the Afghan war, they could hire their own bodyguards.

Petraeus did not seek the job of Commander of U.S. Forces in Afghanistan. A prostate problem and the vertigo that appeared in front of the Senate Armed Services Committee, had taken half a step out of his stride. At fifty-seven he feared he lacked the necessary strength and energy to pursue the Afghanistan campaign. But when President Obama came hat in hand, begging for his help, Petraeus had no choice. One saving grace was he quietly rehired many of McChrystal's staff. Those who had been specifically tainted by the Rolling Stone disaster, he replaced with officers of equal intelligence, experience and ferocity.

A Captain on Petraeus' staff led Hull and Bauldaire to the General's spartan office where they had less than a minute to study the group photos of the General and his troops before the door swung open. The two junior officers locked to attention.

Petraeus once ran five miles every morning, but a fractured pelvis from a hard parachute landing while commanding Eighteenth Corps at Fort Bragg now limited his distance. The General typically stuck to two meals a day, abstained from alcohol, didn't smoke and slept fitfully at night. He was well read, articulate and, as he crossed the room, under enormous pressure to reverse the course of the war.

ISAF's mission had always been to capture, or kill, one high value target. Now, within weeks of the General's return to Washington D.C. to head the CIA, the actionable INTEL was unassailable. During his years in Afghanistan Petraeus had struggled with a ratio of one hundred and fifty soldiers pulling triggers and two people gathering intelligence. He would now lead a hundred and fifty people gathering INTEL and two men pulling triggers. The General had personally selected the two Scout Snipers standing in front of him.

"At ease," the Four-Star shook off what was troubling him. Gentlemen, I'm sure you're wondering why I brought you here, so I'll keep this short." He opened a file. "Hull, I see you graduated from VMI with a degree in English Lit?" he looked up.

The Major nodded.

Petraeus skimmed the page. "You then joined the Marines, excelled in Basic and subsequently distinguished yourself in the four phases of Marine Corps Forces Special Operations Command. Scout Sniper Team Leader Course, first in class at Quantico. Top grades at SERE, U.S. Army Airborne Jump School and Marine Corps Combat Diver Course. Number one at the Intra-services Sniper Team Competition four years running at Fort Benning, Georgia."

"Served in Iraqi Freedom. You held off 30 Republican Guards, Iraqis...with uh, a .338 Lapua...the enemy took a dozen casualties, all head and chest shots...before they broke and ran." The General turned the page, read for a moment, then proceeded, "You saved three wounded. Battlefield promotion for bravery. Sniper in Baghdad and Fallujah...forward observer for the Marines, coordinated air strikes and artillery--with maximum effect to insurgents, and minimum civilian casualties. There are other details in your file that are classified…you wouldn't care to comment?"

"No Sir," Hull replied.

"I didn't think so. You speak Farsi?"

"Passably, Sir."

He paused at the page bottom. "I see your last two spotters were killed in action."

Hull blinked. "Sir…that's correct." He took a shallow breath. "Millard died when OP Saker was overrun. Baran was hit by mortar shrapnel outside of Sursurang. Two dozen Taliban ambushed us. They held the high ground."

"Sursurang?" Petraeus glanced up from the file. "That's thirty clicks inside Pakistan."

"Twenty-five clicks, Sir."

The General accepted Hull's statement without comment. Turning the page, he continued, "Sixty-two confirmed kills in Afghanistan. Hull, you had significantly more than that in Iraq. General Joe Osterman of 1st Marines believes that total puts you ahead of Sergeant Adelbert Waldron's hundred and nine confirmed kills in Vietnam.

"Sir, I wasn't aware of that honor," Hull neither denied nor acknowledged the compliment.

"I confirmed it with your last three commanding officers. To a man they agreed you were among the finest they'd had an opportunity to command."

"Thank you sir," Hull wished he'd get to the point.

Opening a second file, the four-star inquired, "Lieutenant Bauldaire--what nationality is that?" It was a rhetorical question--the file held all the facts. Top five at Annapolis, number one in his Scout Sniper class, following a tour in Iraq, Bauldaire had graduated with honors from the Corps' Advanced Linguistics Course. He now spoke Farsi, Dari and Pashto almost without accent.

Bauldaire's first name and middle initial R, for Remarkable, honored his Romanian heritage and the love of his mother. Bauldaire was French, from his father, a Harvard Professor of Philosophy who vehemently objected to Adorean's choice of the Naval Academy.

The general continued to read. "I see you graduated fourth in your class from Annapolis with…" he paused, "A degree in English Lit? Gentlemen, literature majors would not be my first choice for a sniper team—why not first?"

"Sir?"

"Why not first in your class at Annapolis?"

"A little weak in math sir." Marine-proud, Bauldaire was tempted to ask where the Army General had ranked at West Point. Raising his eyes, the General would have noted 43rd. The Lieutenant wisely held his tongue.

"I see. In all honesty, number one would never be picked for this mission." He nodded, "SEAL training, Scout Sniper, top 5 of your class, M16 and M4 Distinguished Rifleman. Teamed with Major Hull a year ago this October. This is your first tour, his fourth. It appears you're on some kind of fast track, Bauldaire."

"Yes, Sir. Major Hull has taught me to play well with others."

"That's also noted. Together you've accounted for thirty-eight confirmed kills this tour. You both play exceptionally well with others. However, I guarantee you won't enjoy the next seventy-two hours."

Petraeus studied them for an instant more then confessed, "I have an assignment that requires you surpass what you consider your best effort." He walked over to a high-resolution map of the Afghan-Pakistan border, and pointed to a jagged ridge seventy kilometers east of Jalalabad. "I don't need to tell you that, following the SEAL raid in Abbottabad, a joint agreement between the U.S. and Pakistan President Zardari has suspended Predator flights over the Federally Administered Tribal Areas."

"The collateral damage was unsustainable," Bauldaire noted.

The Lieutenant's intellectual sugar prompted Petraeus to glance up from the file. "It was an unmitigated FUBAR….those joy stick jockeys at the C.I.A.'s Counterterrorist Center in Virginia pulled the trigger without accounting for the women and children in the surrounding blocks," Petraeus paused. "The real cost of neutralizing a dozen mid-level Taliban commanders are the video clips of dismembered six year-olds on prime time Pakistan News. Our reliance on Predators has shaken Zardari's government. Intelligence believes a resurgent al Qaeda's primary goal is to destabilize Zardari, force new elections and in the confusion of the campaigns, attack Pakistan's nuclear repository."

"Yes, Sir," Hull was well versed in the politics behind the decision.

"Despite what CNN reports, we've been forced to restrict our armed flights over Pakistan's airspace. The Taliban now move without restriction. Mohammed Omar has achieved a huge, tactical superiority in FATA. We lost forty-six men last month. That's the second straight month of higher casualties than Iraq. This year will be the war's costliest. Our strength now totals one hundred and twenty thousand Coalition troops and we're still being driven back into a defensive posture." The General unnecessarily added, "Sending forty SEALS into the Federally Administered Tribal Area is no longer an option."

"The Vice President doubts an increase in the size of the Afghan National Army or our plans to involve civilians in our efforts to dislodge the Taliban will succeed. We're facing a twenty-five percent attrition rate in the ANA and the cost--the pencil pushers put it at two hundred and fifty billion--I believe that's unrealistically high. Then there's Karzai!" He stopped before he said something that might be misconstrued. There were major political risks to revealing his personal feelings about the Afghan President, even in front of the two Scout Snipers.

Shifting to the reason behind his summons, he admitted, "Special Operations has killed too many civilians. Night attacks, faulty INTEL, targets who surround themselves with women and children--accountability is a critical problem!"

Bauldaire held the General's glance. "You have a question, Lieutenant?" Petraeus asked.

"Sir, with all due respect, doesn't Special Ops report directly to you?"

The General's demeanor hardened. "Lieutenant, I'd advise you to stop reading the New York Times! The Times, the Post, Mohammed Iqbal Safi, head of the Afghan Parliament's Defense Committee and Sayid Mohammed Mal, Vice Chancellor of Gardez University, have all demanded clarification concerning Special Ops chain of command. For the record, there are no rogue operators in country."

Returning to subject, he stated the obvious, "The Taliban are committed to exchanging casualties for gains in world opinion. We've got to stop their momentum, stop their initiative."

Petraeus continued, "In the past eight months al Qaeda and the Taliban have captured ground in central and western Afghanistan. They've tightened their control of the roads in and out of Kabul. The Taliban can come and go at will within the city. A major result is IEDs are increasing, suicide bombings are on the rise." His expression hardened.

Studying the two officers standing in front of him, the General revealed, "Karzai is rapidly being confined to a small safe area in the capital."

He turned to the large detailed map and traced Afghanistan's eastern border with a laser pointer. "Our greatest tactical problem is Pakistan has failed to halt the flow of militants across the passes into Afghanistan. Estimates continue to shift, but Taliban activity in Kunar Province has increased sixty percent in two years! The primary result is U.S troops KIA during the last year increased fifty percent. Support for this war is rapidly eroding. The President, Vice President and Congress are demanding to know…how long and how much?"

"We have INTEL detailing Pakistan's peace deals with the militants. Since then the cross border attacks have doubled. We need to take the fight to FATA. We need better short-range surveillance--and a way to disrupt the Taliban's command structure."

The two officers understood what the euphemism described.

"Gentlemen, we're in the midst of a strategic crisis that we must rapidly address or lose the war," he paused. "We've got 98,000 American troops trying to control a country the size of Texas--a country that speaks a fragmented, ancient language that varies from village to village. Despite our best efforts, the Taliban is growing stronger, not weaker. The situation is deteriorating on all fronts."

Petraeus retrieved his glasses from the desktop. Leaning on his clenched fists, his frustration was evident. "Our tactics are outdated. We cannot continue to depend on air superiority or unrestricted bombing of rural compounds. Ample evidence exists that those strikes simply exacerbate hostility toward Coalition forces." He paused to consider the consequences then added, "Following the raid on Abbottabad we're getting minimal assistance from the Pakistan Military. Analysts at Langley believe that, in exchange for a cessation of attacks within Pakistan, a separate peace was negotiated with the Taliban. Once the insurgent's bases are secure, we'll witness a Civil War managed by the Taliban and al Qaeda."

"The bottom line?" The General rhetorically asked. "Pakistan's sixty nukes. That's minimum. With Zardari's national government weakened by his devastated economy and a growing opposition within the military and the ISI, we're off balance! I have no doubt, I repeat, no doubt, that the Taliban plan to capture Pakistan's nuclear arsenal. When that happens, it's a given they'll detonate at least one--simply as a demonstration of their ability to incinerate their enemies. No national capital will be safe. Two bombs, two cities...Washington DC, New York, London, Paris, Tel Aviv.... Casualties will climb into the tens of millions." He looked from Hull to Bauldaire.

Both were aware of the consequences of a nuclear al Qaeda. Bauldaire kept his eyes forward. Hull held his thoughts to himself.

Petraeus leaned over the desk. "We cannot lose this war! We need to stabilize this region. And to do that, we need to adapt our tactics. We need to return to what we should have done all along. We didn't need to invade Afghanistan to neutralize al Qaeda. We only managed to drive them into secure strongholds."

"Look at the hills around Kabul. Every one of them is crowned by fortifications. And look how many of the armies who built them remain. None! The Taliban, Mullahs, Jihadists, al Qaeda, the weather, dust and the Afghani people themselves are breaking us down."

"The Taliban are using FATA as staging areas. We've got to take the fight to their leaders, and we can't do it sitting on our asses inside of fortified compounds!"

The laser pointer illuminated a remote ridge deep inside the Federally Administered Tribal Area. "Gentlemen, we need a victory. We need a predator on the ground."

Bauldaire turned to face Petraeus. "Sir, pardon my interruption, but OBL's death was a major victory. Scuttlebutt says we're going home."

"The General appeared momentarily troubled. "Lieutenant, I suggest you ignore the scuttlebutt."The light wavered down the ridge to the valley. "I cannot order you into Pakistan. If you're wounded, it's doubtful we'll be able to extract you. If captured alive..." he did not need to state the obvious; capture was unacceptable. "You'll carry no identification. Serial numbers and labels will be removed. Succeed or fail, your reward will be the same.

There might be a promotion in the future….no note, however, that alludes to this mission will be attached to your records."

"Sir," it was Hull who addressed Petraeus first. "Is this a rogue mission? These orders do originate in the chain of command?"

Petraeus was surprised by the question. He realized it originated from Hull's years in Special Operations. When he answered, he promised, "Absolutely, Major, directly from the Principal's Committee. It originates with the President's top National Security and Foreign Policy advisors. Considering the timing and origination of this INTEL, I'm surprised they turned it back to us this quickly."

"General?" it was Bauldaire, "Why Marines? Joint Special Operations has Delta covert anti-terrorist teams."

"Simple answer, Lieutenant Bauldaire, you're here. You're familiar with the terrain. If we don't move tonight, the window closes."

"Sir, what's our ETD?" It was Hull, rising to his full six-foot height.

"2300…"

"Do we have a code name for this operation?" Hull inquired.

"How does Viper sound?" Petraeus clicked off the light pointer.

"As good as any," Hull replied. "Your name sir?"

"Hell no," Petraeus shook his head. "The White House loves this cloak and dagger shit."

Command issued Hull and Bauldaire clothes that were stripped off dead Taliban. The stinking pants, dirty salwar kameeze and vest remained unwashed. Only the bloodstains were removed and the bullet holes sewed shut. The INTEL Quartermaster traded their helmets for keffiyeh turbans.

"Sir, you know how to wrap one of these?" he asked

"It was required dinner dress at Annapolis," Bauldaire replied.

Returning a gratuitous smile to the Lieutenant's joke, the Quartermaster handed them each a tube of walnut stain. "You'll need this," he said. Despite their dark tans from exposure to Afghanistan's summer sun, the stain turned their faces a deep brown.

"And, sir, I'll need your boots," he held out a pair of the cheap black broughams.

"Negative to that, Sergeant. I can't pack forty kilos uphill in ballet slippers. I'll stick with my Danners."

"Sir, with all respect, the Moolies will kill you for those boots..."

"I'm keeping my boots," Hull cut him off.

Hull and Bauldaire were helicoptered to Jalalabad, where they were met by an Afghani Special Forces Commando in a heavily dented white Toyota Hilux pickup. Armored vehicles signaled the Coalition. The two officers understood that a night flight onto the Afghan-Pakistan border would have compromised their mission. The safest route was through Jalalabad north along the braided Kunar River Valley past Kuz Nurang to the Naubad Bridge. Once across the Kunar River, a rough road followed the east bank, past the intersection for the Chartni Ghasay Pass that crossed a rocky saddle into Pakistan. Chartni Ghasay offered speed at the cost of detection. Beyond the road to Chartni Ghasay, the track continued to degrade until it was barely better than the ancient trails that spider-webbed out of the Kunar Valley and across the high ridges into Pakistan.

It was 23:15 when the Toyota turned east along a rocky streambed. Two kilometers later the track started to climb, forcing the pickup toward the high ridge that served as the Afghan-Pakistan border. The rough road switched across a rocky face that slowly degraded into a boulder-studded track, which gradually narrowed to a goat trail. At that point, the four-wheel-drive Toyota could climb no higher. At 23:55, five minutes before midnight, the wheels spun in the loose shale. The Afghani Commando yanked on the emergency brake and slipped out of the driver's seat.

"Watch closing the door," Hull cautioned. "Noise will travel in this cold air." Working by night vision, they shouldered their packs, loaded their weapons and nodded their thanks to the driver.

"Anshalam," the Commando climbed back into the Hilux. It was critical the truck leave immediately. A set of headlights passing in the night would send an alarm through the villages they had skirted. Even then a local Taliban soldier might be alerting his superior. Hull wondered if the Commando would make it out alive. His chances were no better than even. The Afghan knew better than to be captured alive.

In front of them the track turned to a trail that led uphill into the dark foothills. No words were exchanged as they started to climb. Four tours in Afghanistan's high mountains had taught Hull to move like one of the

Himalayan Palais Cats. Six feet tall, with strong legs, hips and chest, for much of the night he led the way up the dry stream which faded into a gray escarpment. The Scout Snipers had twenty-four hours to reach their objective. It was shortly before dawn when they crossed the border into Pakistan. At their backs, the Kunar River Valley stretched north in a dry brown ribbon. The Valley may have supported crops--before the Soviets--poppies, but four decades of war and eight years of drought had flattened all vegetation, leaving only a few, stubborn yellow grasses and scrubby thorns to support the flocks of goats that infrequently skirted the shadowed cliffs.

Dawn lit the distant Hindu Kush with a faint Alpenglow. Ringed in white glaciers and blue ice, Tirich Mir, the major peak, rose to 25,233 feet. That dawn Tirich Mir stood as a rose-tinted sentinel, guarding the gates to the distant seven-thousand meter Pamir and Karakorum Mountains.

Seeking a lee below the windy ridge, Bauldaire turned to the north. "Look at these mountains! Nothing has changed in two millennia. We could be fighting for Alexander, the Mongols...."

"Or the Soviets...or Taliban." Hull shifted the Sako rifle strap on his shoulder. "Lieutenant, the General didn't order us into harm's way to enjoy this view."

"Yes, Sir," Bauldaire lowered his pack to the ground. "General Petraeus' intent not-with-standing, we need a photo!" He took a Nikon digital camera from his pack. Turning toward Tirich Mir he recorded a panorama of the towering mountains. Next, he took one of the Major. Dressed in a patched, salwar kameeze and dusty pants Hull looked like a Taliban insurgent.

Setting the timer, the Lieutenant pre-focused on Hull, then placed the Nikon on a rock, and hurried to stand next to him. "Sir, this will be worth something to you one day," he said. He took two more frames then repacked the camera in his bag.

Traveling by night vision and hiding during the day, the Scout Snipers covered thirty kilometers in twenty-four hours. According to the GPS they were less than six kilometers below their coordinates when they rounded a corner and encountered a young shepherd who had bedded down a flock of two-dozen goats in the rocky ravine.

Hull made him to be fifteen, maybe sixteen. Black hair, the first thin evidence of a coming black beard sprouted from his square chin. He had a thin, hawk nose and fierce dark eyes that took the two men in a single, suspicious glance. His gaze lingered for a second on Hull's face, his clothes and his pack. Hull saw him glance at his boots and the Sako slung over his shoulder. The boy did not recognize the make.

"A' salaam aleikom." Bauldaire touched his right hand to his forehead. The MARSOC Advanced Linguist Course had drilled timing, pronunciation, and gesture. Bauldaire now spoke Pashto almost without accent. Almost.

Tradition forced the teenager to reply, "Salaam aleikom," He continued to study Bauldaire's face. There were two major tribes that occupied these high, remote mountains and this tall, powerfully built man was not of either. He was well fed, a shade too dark and he was carrying an M4A rifle. The Taliban would not carry this rifle. The Coalition's ammunition was impossible to find. A second later, the shepherd's curiosity faded to an undecipherable blank façade.

"Hale´ shoma khub e´?" Bauldaire forced a polite precision into his question.

"Alhamdollah," the shepherd replied, forcing his sheep around them.

Bauldaire tried to engage him, "Praise to Allah, your goats are thriving?" he asked in Pashto.

The young shepherd struggled to place Bauldaire's faint accent. "As much as Allah permits. It has been dry," A ewe was slow to rise and the young shepherd hit her hard across the back.

"And are you many days from your family?"

"A day, at most." He dropped eye contact and struck the trailing goats with his staff.

"In the valley…?" Bauldaire persisted.

"There," the boy waved to the east, in the direction of Dag, Pakistan.

"With your family?"

The briefest nod. He continued to push the sheep. By now he was past the two Marines, moving down the track toward a dogleg in the rock trail. Only the sheep, looking over their withers at the two men, saw Bauldaire pull a Colt 1911 .45 pistol from his vest and with the slightest, sad hesitation shoot the young goatherd in the head.

"Fuck!" Hull exhaled. From the moment they encountered the young goatherd he had hoped for a different ending. Since taking command, General

Petraeus had ordered his command to avoid, at all cost, killing civilians.

"Sorry sir! There was no choice," Bauldaire returned the .45 to the shoulder holster.

The blood drained from the boy's shattered head, staining the red dust black. "Goddammit!" the Major reached for the herder's right hand.

"Sir, if he wasn't Taliban, he was related to Taliban. He would have betrayed our position within the hour." Bauldaire grabbed the boy's dirty left hand.

"Lieutenant, I'm aware of the reason," Hull shouldered his Sako.

They dragged the goatherd's body into a side canyon where they covered it with rocks and scrub. Then they swept their tracks and buried the bloodstains. The cairn would hide the body for two days--any longer was left to luck.

They followed a thin streambed a thousand vertical feet to a cleft in the rocks where they waited for night. As soon as true dark crept into their hide, they started up a steep, shale slope. Overburdened with forty kilo packs, they took most of the night to reach the ridge designated by General Petraeus where they excavated two shallow depressions among the rocks. From there they could see the pass where INTEL promised the target would appear at dawn.

Hidden in their sweltering Ghillie suits, the following day the two Marines watched columns of Taliban slip beneath their rifle sights that morning and afternoon. Once the first evening stars rose in the east, Bauldaire screwed the night vision to the scope. Still the target failed to appear. Nor did he appear the next day, or the day after. Neglecting to ration their water was based partly on bad INTEL, partly on bad tactics. Remaining awake and hydrated in the crippling Pakistan heat required they drink. They had no way of knowing the two day window would stretch to five—or that mid-day temperatures would rise above one hundred and fifteen degrees.

Chapter 4

Hull moved the Ghillie string to check the time. The Seiko on his wrist had been a gift from his ex-wife. She had given him the watch as a talisman…a combination "Think of Me," "Come Home Safe," "Remember I Love You!" amulet. Her email appeared with two months down and seven to go on his fourth tour. Seven months later he could not remember it all. Just the bullet points.

Cheryl's renewed dependence on anti-depressants came as no surprise. He guessed it was either a choice between Zoloft or vodka martinis. The martinis improved their sex life, but Zoloft had zero calories.

"Cannot handle the stress," she started. "Have insomnia. Health suffering. Started purging again. Doctor prescribed antidepressants. Can't go on this way. Moved your things out of the house. Hired an attorney. Please forgive me. Cheryl."

Drafted by an attorney in Upland, California, the divorce papers split the checking and savings, the furniture and crystal. Cheryl kept the silver from her mother; she would store Hull's personal things, CD's, books, wall art, clothes, and shoes in his locker in Riverside.

Hull signed the papers and dropped them in the mail. It took a week to reach L.A. Ten days later he was divorced.

After nine months in Afghanistan's wind-driven sand, the Seiko was junk. The numerals were polished to shadowy divots in the titanium case. The sand had buffed the crystal and its hands now appeared as faint lines beneath an ice gray fog. Hull would be the first to acknowledge that Afghanistan was tough on both men and machines. When the spring-loaded titanium band fell apart, Hull replaced it with a Velcro strap salvaged from Millard's pack.

Five days into a twelve-hour stakeout, the distance between a rock and a hard place had evaporated. Dehydrated and fighting the onset of hallucinations, Hull swallowed hard and reached for his camouflaged water bladder.

"Careful," Bauldaire scanned the cleft where the Taliban soldiers would first show themselves. "In two minutes it'll be light enough for the Moolies to see you."

"We need to decide how many more hours we can survive without water." Hull raised his head off his pack, "You need to tell me, straight up."

"To have the strength to hike out? Without water?" Bauldaire took a deep breath, "Tonight, at the latest. If we can hang here until dark, I'll hump a gallon up from the spring."

The head of Hull's Ghillie suit moved emphatically no. "That's six clicks and twelve hundred meters vertical. If you reach the spring without taking a 7.62 round, you won't have time to return before dawn."

"Next option?" The Lieutenant failed to suppress a dry laugh.

"I'm going to piss in my camelbak and then drink it."

"Sir, you sure we've come to that?" the Lieutenant's Ghillie dread locks shivered.

Hull carefully rolled on his right side and dragged the camouflaged water bladder into his Ghillie suit. "Without water neither of us will last through the day!"

"You need water, not urine, to make the shot."

"I can make the shot today," Hull slipped his penis into the bladder neck and started to piss, "Tomorrow, there are no guarantees." Hull's Ghillie strings shifted. "If he doesn't show by dark, we beat feet back to the spring. We'll decide there if we hump it back to base or climb back up."

"Ten minutes after we back off, he'll cross the ridge."

"We'll be worth shit when he does." The bladder was a quarter full.

Bauldaire coughed to clear the dust out of his throat. Then from within his Ghillie's tangled knots, he produced a quart bottle of Evian water. "Sir, I rationed this in case things got tough. It appears we've reached that demarcation line. You need it to make the shot." He slid the bottle to Hull.

Hull parted the curtain of Ghillie Thread. The clear bottle lay among rocks between them. It was as close as Hull had ever come to a mirage. His body burned for a sip. "No way," he finally refused. "...you humped it, you drink it. I'll drink piss and make the shot."

"Sir, with all due respect, I haven't cooked on this ridge for six days to watch you choke. You make the shot and we fly home First Class. You miss and our leave is just a blip in the rearview. Drink the water. That's an order!" his laugh was a childish croak that caused Hull to laugh with him.

"Bauldaire...you take the first sip."

"Negative there. One sip and I'll drink the whole bottle. Urine will force me to self-ration."

Raising the bottle, though Hull barely wet his lips his mouth wrapped around the wet liquid. He fought the desire to drain the bottle in four, desperate gulps. Instead he took another faint sip. Looking at the dry Lieutenant, he regretted he hadn't drunk his piss. Faint as it was, the Evian cleared his head and sharpened his vision. He took another sip at ten and noon, then two and four, until half the bottle was gone. At that point, Hull ordered Bauldaire to drink a quarter of what remained.

By 19:30, deep shadows had settled upon the goat trail when a lone figure silhouetted on the ridge.

Bauldaire twisted the scope's focus ring. "Moolie," he noted. "AK47, scoped. Two bandoliers. Binoculars....can't make out the manufacturer, but the shape, could be Steiners.....damn," he froze. "Don't move, he's looking this way!" The figure spent five minutes glassing the ridges, rock faces and valley. Then he scanned it all again before giving a quick hand gesture behind. A second figure appeared, then a third, moving quickly downhill.

"This could be our boy," Bauldaire froze. Four more figures hurried through the gap. The light degraded. Less than fifteen minutes until full dark. The Cadre was cautious and precise. Four more crossed. Then six. Which one....if any? Watching through the riflescope, Hull saw one in a white turban, third from the front, bend to tie his shoe.

"That's the signal!" Bauldaire remained locked to the Swarovski. "Our boy is in the house!"

"Which one?" Hull swung the cross hairs down the line. At a hundred-thirty meters the twenty-power scope revealed facial features, jaws, eyes, broken teeth and scars.

"Wait." The group hurried downhill. Bauldaire had forty seconds before the column disappeared into the cleft. The Swarovski scanned the column. Even at the scope's maximum magnification, there were no insignias, variations in clothes or colors to pick commanders from soldiers. It was critical to the Taliban's camouflage they all appear the same.

"Give me the number."

"No can do! No distinguishing features!"

Hull had to think fast and act quickly. He had two shots. At a hundred and thirty meters, bullet drop was negligible. The target would not be the first or last but somewhere among the middle six.

Bauldaire screwed the camera to the Swarovski.

Hull needed to take a shot. He took a breath, exhaled half then set the cross hairs. The target was middle-aged. Black beard, erect, dressed in the dusty robes of an Afghan peasant. Hull did not rush the shot. He and Bauldaire had suffered on the ridge too long to jerk the trigger. His index finger touched the curved lever. He had shot a thousand rounds through the Lapua and knew the exact, six-pound trigger release point. As always, the recoil surprised him.

The 250-grain FMJ hit mid-level on the left side, exploded through the man's hips, busted both sockets, shattered his pelvis and shredded his bladder and large intestine. Hull intended that the wound would be horrifically painful. The Jihadist's high-pitched scream erupted into the gathering dark.

A man in dun colored robes lunged to help the screaming target. Hull knew what came next. His scope locked on eight men who shouldered their AK-47s and surrounded an erect lone figure who stood three below the last man.

Bauldaire caught the same movement. "That's our boy." Bauldaire switched the camera to video and touched the release button.

Hull centered the cross hairs, took a breath and synched to his heartbeat. The scope twitched with each contraction. In the instant before he squeezed the trigger he wondered why Petraeus had insisted on a body, and not a headshot. He did not need to feel the recoil to know the bullet hit low

46

in the throat. He heard a confirming "THWACK" as 250 grains bisected the man's carotid arteries then simultaneously fragmented the second and third vertebrae. The shot nearly beheaded the target—who staggered in mid stride then pitched face-first onto the rocks below. He began to roll and as his body gathered momentum, his arms and legs flung wildly about.

Magnified by the Swarovski, the video picked the scene out of the growing shadows. Bauldaire watched eight men pitch downhill to stop the spinning tangle of clothes and arms, before the body tumbled off a two hundred-foot cliff. At the last instant, the target folded around a protruding boulder. The turban ripped off, exposing a braided knot of gray hair.

The point man quickly flipped the body onto its back. Held in place by two tendons and a single muscle, the gray head, rolled loosely downhill. The Taliban jerked upright, his back arched, his arms thrown wide, his mouth open. His scream reached them a second later. It was as much plea as promise. "ALLAH!!!!!! Lotfan Ni-toonid na ra rah-nama i konid?"

Bauldaire translated. "He asked Allah to guide him."

"I heard," Hull lowered his head.

"Full dark is twelve minutes away..."

Less than forty seconds had elapsed since the first shot when a rock exploded a meter to their left. Hull's second muzzle flash had betrayed their position. A second bullet shattered in front of the .338's barrel, blasting bits of plutonic debris into their faces. The ridge suddenly danced with incoming small arms rounds. Both men backed away from the crest. The short retreat lifted a foot of rock between the Taliban and themselves.

"We've got a minute lead—maybe. We've got to move." Slowed by his Ghillie suit, the Lieutenant grabbed his pack and started down hill.

An RPG skimmed the ridge and exploded twenty meters down slope. A second RPG crashed into the ridge. The third exploded to the right ten feet away from Hull's head. The concussion sucked the air out of the Major's lungs, lifted the yarn away from his Ghillie suit and flipped him onto his back. When his eyes focused the Lieutenant's boots were churning through the loose sand and rock. Bauldaire's left hand was locked in Hull's collar, his right dragged his pack downhill. An incoming mortar drove the Lieutenant face first into the rocks then showered them with debris.

"They're guessing!" Bauldaire jerked the dazed Major to his feet. A mortar screamed in ten meters behind them. The shock blasted them off their feet.

Bauldaire guessed they had two minutes before the first Taliban reached the ridge. The Scout Snipers were a hundred meters below the ridge when a swarm of 7.62 mm rounds ricocheted around them. Hull shouldered his pack and the .338. Running downhill he jacked a round into the .338, turned and fired offhand. The closest Taliban piled up. Seconds later, four others took his place.

Hull's cross hairs hesitated on each of the four robed silhouettes. He did not need to watch them crumple. Keeping the scope raised to his eye and his cheek on the stock, he estimated, "We've got three minutes till full dark. I'll hold them here. We'll meet at the spring."

"Negatory Sir. Your bolt action against assault rifles is a bad bet."

"Hand over the M4!"

"No can do! A team is only as strong as its weakest member."

Despite Bauldaire's refusal to follow orders, a smile flickered across Hull's dusty face, "When this is over, I'll have your bar!"

"When this is over, I'll wrap it for you!"

A figure skylined. Hull's 250-grain solid core hit the Taliban soldier square in the chest pounding him down the shale slope and off a cliff. "We just bought thirty seconds!" Hull turned and ran downhill.

The Major was wrong. A bearded figure crawled over the ridge. Using a rock outcropping for cover, he loosed a three round burst from his AK47. The bullets splintered against the surrounding gray rocks. Bauldaire raised his M4. "Save it," Hull shouldered the Sako. When the Taliban soldier rolled to trigger another burst, Hull's .338 smashed through his right eye.

A second turban crawled behind the corpses. Hull had always admired the Taliban's readiness to trade casualties for a few miserable yards. He now hoped for an equal measure of cowardice. The turban peeked above the dead Moolie. The corpse would absorb the Sako's 250 grains. "Use a grenade," Hull ordered.

Bauldaire touched off a 40-millimeter fragmentation that cut the corpse in half. The shell-shocked Taliban was crawling on all fours when Hull shot him through the lungs.

He swept the dark ridge with his scope. No silhouettes showed above the ripsaw of red rock. Grabbing his pack he warned Bauldaire. "They're establishing a crossfire, we need to move."

Scrambling across the scree slope, their boots dislodged loose rocks that clattered downhill. Alerted to their position, two dozen orange flashes sparkled off the ridge. The two Marines dove into the rocks. Small arms were steady and closing. Four more 7.62 rounds chattered off the ridge, splintering the rock into shards that sliced into Bauldaire's face. Drops of blood speckled across his forehead and right cheek. A second later, a mortar blew the exposed slope into a fountain of crushed rock and splintered steel. The next mortar was four meters closer.

Bauldaire's reaction was instantaneous and accurate. The M4 grenade launcher coughed three times. Deep screams echoed down the canyon. The grenades bought them fifteen seconds. "GO!" He pushed Hull toward a deep gully that bisected the slope. The two Marines were three meters from the gulley when a sixth mortar dropped in.

The explosion flipped Hull end for end. When his head cleared, he was face down in the rocks. His ears were ringing when he reached for the .338, cleared the dirt from the breach and searched for Bauldaire.

The Lieutenant was sprawled against the far wall, the M4A lying across his lap.

Chapter 5

Bauldaire's pack had ripped open, scattering its contents down the rock filled gully. It took the Lieutenant a second to regain his feet and locate the fragmentation grenades, the MREs, medical supplies and spare ammunition. If any chance existed of escaping in the dark, they would need to lighten their loads.

Small arms fire increased to steady staccato bursts. The buzz and hum of AK47 rounds pulsed above the depression. A mortar round exploded above the gully, the shrapnel hissing above their heads. The light was fading. Soon their field of vision would be limited to NVGs.

"You OK?" Hull crawled over to the Lieutenant.

"No problem," Bauldaire's voice was a shade too hoarse.

"Dark is ten minutes away." Hull dumped his pack and stripped off his Ghillie suit. "Keep the fragmentation grenades. Save your M4 ammo. Hold three MREs, one water bladder, your Quik-Clot and WoundStat, Night Vision and batteries, knife, spare socks."

Bauldaire dumped his tangled Ghillie suit then inventoried the ammunition, food and medical supplies, scattered the rest and shouldered his pack.

Still a degree too light for night vision. Hull could see the Moolies scrambling through the shale slides toward the gully. Sliding a round into the chamber he held the cross hairs on a shadow and squeezed the trigger. The Sako's recoil produced a shriek. A silhouette of knotted robes and an unraveling turban tumbled downhill. The light continued to degrade until it was impossible make a clean shot. Facing two-dozen insurgents, a wound was better than a kill. He shot another silhouette before the light disappeared and the shale face faded to true dark.

Hull slipped on his Night Vision. Thirty-plus Moolies were creeping across the shale. Deprived of light-enhancing technology two stupidly turned on flashlights. The faint pool of light illuminated them for Hull's .338.

Shouldering their packs, the Major and Lieutenant traced the steep gully until it dropped into a dry stream. From there they continued silently downhill, following the rough streambed to a distant confluence with the valley floor. They had covered two kilometers when an AK47's three round burst sang around them.

"Night Vision." Hull dropped to a kneeling position. His NVG revealed a figure creeping on bare feet across the rounded boulders. Despite the NVG's ghostly, inaccurate lighting, the .338 round exploded the shadowy figure's femur. The insurgent's screaming held the panicky edge of impending death.

A hundred vertical meters below, they cut a trail that descended west along the escarpment. Hull estimated it would take twenty-four hours to reach the Afghan border. That night they slowed only long enough to fix a trip wire to a fragmentation grenade buried in a rock cairn. The wire was stretched across the path and anchored to a stick. Hull hoped for one leg. Minimum. Better, both legs and a scattergun of shrapnel into the hips and abdomen. The unstated corollary of war--a crippling wound was more valuable than a kill.

They were four hundred meters away when the grenade detonated. The first trap bought them half an hour. Long enough to fill their jugs at the spring.

Hull and Bauldaire ran in the frayed pants and loose blouses for most of the first night. By dawn of the seventh day the twenty-kilometers had taken half a step out of Bauldaire's long stride.

The .338 ran out of ammo in the late afternoon. Without ammunition, the fiber-stocked Sako was dead weight. Hull reluctantly smashed the scope, broke the stock and trigger and dropped the bolt into his pack. After flinging the useless breech and barrel far from the trail he conducted a quick inventory. Sixty rounds for the M4A, four 40mm grenades, two fragmentation grenades, two Night Vision, medical supplies, 3 MREs and two gallons of water.

The Swarovski showed the Moolies were a half a mile behind, still coming. The GPS calculated eight kilometers to Firebase Saker. It would take six hours to reach the ridge.

Hull shouldered his pack. "Time to move!"

Bauldaire took a second to rise.

"Everything copasetic, Lieutenant?"

"Never better!" Bauldaire broke into an easy lope. They were a kilometer east of the valley that led to the high pass into Afghanistan when the Lieutenant piled up. One minute he was running at his steady, kilometer-eating gait, the next he was sliding cheek-down in the dust.

Hull was on him in a second. He put his arm around Bauldaire to help him rise and felt the damp shirt beneath. He prayed it was sweat but, a second later, saw the blood on his hand.

"When did you get hit?"

"Caught a piece of the mortar…at the gully."

"Shit," Hull swore to hide his fear. "How bad?"

"Survivable," Bauldaire's knees buckled.

"Hull removed the Lieutenant's pack and lifted his filthy salwar kameeze.

The mortar's steel shard had hit Bauldaire mid-back above his left kidney. The entry wound was an inch and a half long, three-eighths wide. The trickle of dark blood revealed the steel had nicked his liver. It was a miracle Bauldaire had run through the night. Hull reached into his pack, pulled a drain and a strip of medical tape, sterilized the tube with an alcohol rub then threaded it into the gaping wound. The steel shard had broken the rib and Hull could only guess about internal injuries. Bauldaire sucked up the pain with steady, shallow breaths as a stream of black bile laced with clotted blood poured upon the ground. Hull handed him his water.

"Negative, Sir," Bauldaire panted through the pain. "We'll need to ration for the climb."

"We're not climbing. I'm calling the cavalry."

"Sir, that may not work. We're still five clicks inside Pakistan."

Hull dialed the satellite phone and waited for the connection to Kabul. Instead he reached Langley, Virginia. A female voice answered. He rapidly stated his name, rank, serial number and mission. "Viper," he repeated.

"You said Viper?" the voice was southern.

"That's affirmative. Viper, I need Medivac!"

"And your rank and serial number again?" she inquired.

"Goddammit, Hull, Marine Corps, Major," he spit out his serial number.

"Sir, I don't have a record here…" she paused. "I think I need to connect you to my superior."

"ASAP!" Hull barked.

"Ok, I'm just going to put you on hold." Muzak filled the earpiece-- Barry Manilow's "Can't Smile Without You," minus the words. Two minutes passed during which the recording advised him how important his call was. He would be answered in order. Four minutes later a male voice answered. "Hello, Major Hull…..did I pronounce that correctly?"

"Who is this?"

"Colonel Mike Tamas. I'm attached to Afghan Intelligence. Major, first of all how did you get this number?"

"The satellite phone automatically dialed it."

"I see…and where did you say you were calling from?"

"Eight clicks due east of Firebase Saker, Afghanistan. I need a Medivac, now!"

"Firebase Saker? Uh, I'm not familiar…."

Hull cut him off. "Kunar Province, Jalalabad. Pakistan border…!"

"Yes of course," Colonel Tamas agreed. "What was the name of your operation?"

"Viper. Contact General Petraeus in Kabul. He'll confirm…"

Tamas interrupted him, "Major, we have no record of Operation Viper. Nor can we locate your records. I'm sorry, but without records or a verifiable operation name, we can't order a Medivac Helicopter into Pakistan. You're aware of the No Fly restrictions? For all we know this could be a prank call. You understand. Perhaps you should contact your Base Commander? He might be more familiar with your situation and could offer help."

"GODDAMMIT!" Hull yelled. "I've got a man down. I need a fucking Medivac!!!"

"Major, I should remind you that satellite protocol clearly forbids profanity. I'd refrain from the use of the F….."

"Fuck you, Tamas!" Hull slammed the phone shut against his thigh.

Fifteen seconds passed before Bauldaire noted in a dry whisper, "Pretty much burned that bridge. Looks like the way home is over that ridge." Two rounds splintered the rock ledge above their heads.

Hull waited until the drain slowed to a black drip, then covered it with a quick-clot. He wrapped Bauldaire's broken rib and added the contents of the Lieutenant's pack to his own. Three AK-47 rounds cracked three inches above their heads.

"I'll hump the M4." Hull hefted the pack's heavy weight.

"We'll need the scope," Bauldaire saw it lying in the dust next to the trail.

Hull hesitated then rescued it from the abandoned gear and strapped it onto the pack.

A round ricocheted off the ledge. Reacting out of a reservoir of white anger, Hull flipped the M4s safety to fire, held above a dark spot far out on the plane then squeezed off a round. Two arms flailed for an instant above the spot, before slipping beneath the shimmering heat waves.

A wet cough echoed from Bauldaire's chest. "Two thousand meters?"

"Not that far," Hull shouldered the pack and placing an arm around Bauldaire's waist, lifted the Lieutenant to his feet. Bullets rang off the surrounding boulders as Hull half carried, half dragged Bauldaire up the faint rocky trail that led to the rapidly fading escarpment. The Taliban took advantage of the slower pace and closed the distance to three hundred meters. Hull stopped to pick off the Taliban's point man then handed Bauldaire the water bladder.

"We need to ration what's left," the Lieutenant objected.

"Fuck that noise." Hull unscrewed the cap. "Lieutenant, I'm repaying a debt. You'll never know how fucking good that Evian tasted."

"You made the shot."

"We made the shot," Hull corrected him. He waited until Bauldaire finished a deep swallow, replaced the cap and stored the bladder in the pack. Then, pulling the Lieutenant's arm over his shoulder he started uphill.

They managed to hold a steady pace for the first hours after dark. By midnight Bauldaire had slowed to a high altitude climber's labored step, pause, step. His breathing was deep and damp and he was now coughing, a deep, wracking convulsion that expelled thin, pink phlegm.

Hull stopped and raised the bladder to the Lieutenant's mouth.

"How many clicks to the ridge?" Bauldaire drank deeply.

"Two, three...not far," Hull waited until he finished, then set the last fragmentation grenade. By now the Taliban leader sensed the closing distances and sent two of his point men to Allah in exchange for a chance to close the quarter mile. Hull's Night Vision batteries were fading. Dark shadows were creeping into the scope. Their ammunition was almost gone.

It was five past one when Bauldaire's weight dragged Hull down onto the trail. Taking deep, labored breaths the Lieutenant began to crawl up the rocky incline. Hull dumped the pack and helped Bauldaire to his feet. "Leave me," the Lieutenant gasped.

"No chance," Hull opened the medical pack and stuck him with a syringe of morphine. He then hit him with a milligram of adrenalin. "Shoulder the pack! I'll carry you!"

"You need to get this back to Kabul," Bauldaire held out the camera's memory card.

Hull slipped it into his left pants' pocket. He then dumped all but the water, first aid and ammo from the pack and threaded the Lieutenant's arms though the straps.

"No can do, Sir," Bauldaire gasped.

"I'm getting tired of your disobedience Marine!" Hull squatted slightly. "I didn't suggest, I ordered you to climb aboard." Bauldaire swayed, then slumped forward. Hull grabbed Bauldaire's knees, braced into the load and took his first step uphill.

"One," he counted silently to himself. He refused to think about how many other steps stood between him and the ridge. Number Two stood as a sheer obstacle that he surveyed and then surmounted. Three appeared dark and ominous in the fading night vision. And so the dark hours passed. One foot in front of the other, his knees, hips and back straightening to the load, Hull believed the first fifty vertical feet would kill him. When they didn't, he bent to the next fifty vertical and then the fifty after that. In time, a saving numbness crept into his extremities and he experienced a deep gratitude that he was packing Bauldaire. They would reach the ridge at first light. He would find a way to attract one of the patrolling Blackhawks. And if he couldn't, he would die before he left Bauldaire behind.

Hull estimated three hundred vertical-meters to the ridge. He could have calculated the number of steps but feared the total would defeat him. Instead he took it one step at a time. During the night he spoke to Bauldaire. He told himself it was to boost the Lieutenant's morale, but he knew he spoke as much to himself as the man on his back. "I'll get you out..." he took another step..."if you can hang on another hour, the heli will pick us up. By this time tomorrow they'll have dug this piece of shit out of you, sewed you up and set you on clean white sheets. Give you a day to gain strength and you're on a Medivac Flight to Landstuhl in Germany. In ten days, you'll be on the East Coast....Purple Heart, Silver Star, your Captain's bars....Adorean, you're a hero." It was the first time Hull could remember calling him by his first name.

Bauldaire roused himself. "Jack..Sir," he whispered, "I'd prefer to rehab in Kabul." The word sagged out of him as Bauldaire slipped into unconsciousness. Hull could feel the Lieutenant sag against him and though the Major's arms were in spasm, he took a harder grip on Bauldaire's legs and bent to his load.

Slumped onto Hull's back, the Lieutenant slipped in and out of consciousness. When Hull sensed the Moolies were drawing too close he would carefully lower Bauldaire to the uphill slope. Then he would shoot as many as he could locate in the failing Night Vision. He did not shoot to kill. He shot to maim, to set the Moolies screaming in the night. He would be fucked if he offered them a quick flight to Allah. He knew human nature. Praise Allah, waiting Paradise or not, their screams would terrify their brethren.

Experience told Hull that, in light of the Taliban's casualties, they should have quit the fight. Something else was driving the insurgents. Revenge. Hull killed a dozen that night. He was now down to six rounds. Counting one grenade and his M1911 Colt side arm, he had enough for one determined stand. He would make the Moolies pay, but he had no doubt that he and Bauldaire would be overrun. He did not tell this to the Lieutenant. Instead he spoke of the books he'd read, recalled English and Dari poems, and promised that he would deliver the young Lieutenant safely back to his family and fiancée.

"How is Angela?" Hull took a step, paused then took another. He felt Baudaire's wet cough on his cheek.

"Not sure, now. This tour soured her on the profession."

"Roger that. Stay single long enough and you'll learn to enjoy this old toast. It speaks to a sad truth...." Hull took a step and started. "There is a tavern in the town. And there my true love sits him down. And drinks his wine with laughter and with glee, and never, never thinks of me." Staggering under the weight, he stepped up onto a ledge that angled across the trail and almost dropped Bauldaire.

"You say it's your favorite?" the Lieutenant's head sagged onto Hull's shoulder.

"It makes more sense after three double Glenfiddiches."

"Most things do," Bauldaire slurred. "I'll buy in Bagram."

"I'll hold you to that promise." Hull replied, his boots slipping in the gravel.

Hull made slow time to the ridge as the Lieutenant drifted in and out of consciousness. He ignored the rising dawn at his back and refused to think about the ridgeline. The light continued to improve and the Moolies' 7.62 rounds rang closer. Lit by the rising sun, Hull summoned his last shadows of strength and surged forward. The grade flattened and a cleft appeared. Bullets splintered off the rocks above them as Hull staggered toward the rocky pass that marked the border.

Two steps short of their goal the Major was slammed forward onto his knees. The Lieutenant landed hard on the trail. Turning to face downhill, he saw Bauldaire was conscious. It took Hull less than a second to discover the gaping wound high in Bauldaire's back. A ricocheting 7.62 slug had shattered his C5 vertebrae. The Lieutenant was paralyzed.

Bauldaire's eyes searched for Hull.

The Major was prone in the red dust, returning fire. The M4's last grenade blew four Moolies off the trail. Hull rolled to face the Lieutenant

Bauldaire took a shallow breath, "You must do me a favor."

"I'm not leaving," Hull rose to one knee and shot a turbaned figure who stepped around the rock outcrop.

"Sir, you need to get the memory card back to Kabul."

"Negative! Not without you."

"We're out of ammo, I'm shot to shit." His pain edged through the morphine. "You've got to leave me. That's a direct order." The least humor caught the edges of his mouth.

"Negative, Lieutenant."

"We have…no choice. Take the card and run."

When the next Moolie rushed around the rock outcrop, Hull deliberately shot him in the femur. "Bauldaire, stow it!"

The Lieutenant started to hyperventilate. "Riding a wheelchair for forty years is not an option…you can't hold them off and you can't pack me any further."

"Negative!" Hull shot another of the Taliban running up the trail.

Bauldaire pressed him, "I would be grateful if you did your duty. Take the card to Kabul. Help me die with honor." He tried to raise his head. "I can't move my arms or I would do it myself. You know what the Moolies will do if they find me alive."

Hull knew.

"Remember Kipling's poem? The honest one?" Bauldaire struggled to gain a breath and then started strongly, "When you are wounded and left on Afghanistan's plains…And the women come out to cut up what remains. Roll to your rifle and blow out your brains…."

"And go to your Gawd like a soldier," the Major finished the line. Raising the M4 he shot two more Taliban. The clip ran dry.

"I wouldn't ask anyone but a friend to help me." Lying in the trail's goat shit and sand, his young face covered with dust, sweat and blood, he managed a smile, "Sir, I'd count it an honor…"

Chapter 6

A Captain on Petraeus' staff was waiting on the flight line when the CH-47D landed at Bagram. He was early thirties, a little over-weight, a facilitator who caught the meaningless but important details others let slip through the cracks. The Captain led Hull to an armored Humvee then drove to a small single bedroom apartment. Crude by state side standards, after eight months of firebases, it was luxury. The Captain had pulled Hull's records and now handed him newly pressed BDUs, shampoo, toothbrush and paste, a razor and small can of shaving cream. "Sir, if you need anything else, please don't hesitate to ask."

"Thank you Captain, I won't need anything else..."

"Yes Sir. General Petraeus would like to debrief you at 14:00. He asked me to wait."

Hull opened the bathroom door, stepped inside, and stripped off the stained shirt. A bloody purple bruise radiated down and out from his right shoulder, around his ribs and across his right pectoral muscle to his sternum. His toes, the balls of his feet and heels were blistered. Multiple falls had marked his legs with scrapes and bruises. A hematoma swelled on his left hip.

Stepping into the shower, his internal thermostat swung wildly between hot and cold. One second he scalded his back, the next he shivered in the icy spray. He squeezed a quarter sized drop of shampoo into his hand and massaged it through his inch-long black hair. The dust and grit sucked the suds dry and he rinsed and shampooed again until the rivulets ran down his face. He soaped a washrag and washed his legs, crotch and arms then repeated the process again and again until the soap's floral scent replaced the smell of old urine and dried blood. Hanging the cloth on the faucet, he soaped his hands and moved the suds gently across his shoulders, arms, chest, and ribs.

Hull realized he'd broken too many promises. In the depth of his desperate thirst he promised never to waste a drop of water and yet now let the shower run. He had promised Bauldaire he would return him to his family. A single sob choked out.

Gritting his teeth until the muscles quivered in his jaw, he dug his nails into his scalp and pressed his head against the wall. He remembered lying in the sand, scorpions and rocks, waiting for the target. Bauldaire was alive.

"That's the signal." Bauldaire stared through the Swarovski. "Our boy is in the house!"

Locking his arms around his chest Hull shivered uncontrollably in the warm water. No other sound slipped from his throat.

He eventually stepped out of the shower and toweled off the mirror. A single glance at his face told him more than he needed to know. The fixture's harsh light accented the faint crows feet that radiated out from his dark eyes.

He shaved, brushed his teeth, and ran a comb through his hair. The Captain had fixed clusters of rank and a name patch to his BDUs. Dropping Bauldaire's memory card into his left breast pocket, he stepped into the living room where the Captain was waiting with a pair of fresh socks and a new pair of Danner boots.

"Sir, the General is waiting," he held the door.

The Captain led Hull down the Bagram Headquarters' hallway and knocked once on General Petraeus' door. "It's open!" The General rose from his chair and circled his desk. "At ease Major." He took Hull's right hand in a firm grip that lingered a moment beyond what protocol required. During those few extra seconds, he studied Hull's dark eyes and sunburned face.

"I was briefed on Lieutenant Bauldaire…" Petraeus struggled to form a proper, consoling phrase. "I wanted you personally to know how saddened I am by his loss. There is no honor this country can bestow that speaks to his heroism," the General too a few seconds to compose himself, then continued. "He will be remembered by a grateful nation."

Hull fought the emotion rising in his chest. "His middle name, Remarkable, described him best."

Petraeus turned to his desk. "Two Unmanned Aerial Vehicles have been transmitting 24/7 for the past eight days. Your movements have been monitored by this Command and the First Committee. The President asked to be kept abreast of last week's events."

"Sir," Hull interrupted the General. "If we were monitored, why didn't you send help when Bauldaire was wounded? A single Blackhawk could have smoked the Taliban and Medivaced the Lieutenant."

"Major, following the raid on Abbottabad, helicopter flights over FATA are not permitted. Not while the President was privy to the video feed."

"The President?" Hull remembered Bauldaire's last seconds. Had the President watched the Lieutenant die as well?

"He sends his repeated, heartfelt thanks for your service…and profound regrets for Lieutenant Bauldaire's sacrifice." Petraeus retrieved a small, square box off his desk. "In light of your efforts to ensure the success of Operation Viper, the President asked me to present you with these." The box contained a Lieutenant Colonel's silver leafs. "The President has also ordered that Lieutenant Bauldaire be promoted posthumously to Captain."

The promotion left Hull numb. His training forced a salute but he took no pride from what their mission had accomplished. He had survived. Bauldaire had not.

"I cannot acknowledge the location, or purpose of your mission," the General reminded him. "But for your leadership in the face of overwhelming odds at Firebase Saker, I'm also nominating you for the Navy Cross."

Hull studied Bauldaire's captain's bars.

"Colonel, your promotion originates from the President. Saker rated a Silver Star, you earned the Navy Cross for Viper."

"And Bauldaire?"

"The President regrets a posthumous Distinguished Service Medal will be presented to Captain Bauldaire's mother and father. In time, it could be attached to a Medal of Honor."

"Thank you, Sir."

Petraeus offered his hand. "Colonel, you're owed two weeks of leave. When you're rested, we'll go over the details."

Hull nodded.

"Colonel, one more thing. Before you catch a flight, one or two of the base medicos asked to debrief you."

Hull felt the memory chip's hard, square shape pressing into his chest. Retrieving it from his pocket, he held it for a moment. "Captain Bauldaire asked me to give this to you," he handed the chip to the General.

Hull did not sleep that night. He waited. On a quiet night in the States, a dog would bark, stop, and bark again. Sleep was postponed, anticipating the next bark. In Afghanistan, Hull waited for the LCDB explosions. Kabul's sporadic small arms fire no longer disturbed him. It was part of the city night's white noise, vaguely reassuring that life pressed on in the surrounding, dark streets.

As soon as he closed his eyes the dream coalesced. Khost's dirt street slowly materialized in dawn's first light. He and Bauldaire waited on a rooftop. The target was in range. His eyelids twitched. The field of fire ranged across two streets. One led to the base, the other to Khost's central commercial district. The target was loaded with thirty pounds of plastique encased by rusty nuts and bolts—all wired to a dead man's trigger. He knew this dream. It did not end well. He forced his mind through the aching exhaustion that filled his body. His eyes opened and he stared into the dark. Experience taught him he could hold his exhaustion at bay until dawn. Daylight would then take over.

At 0200 a rocket exploded in Kabul. Deep thunder rolled through the capital city. Two minutes later, another exploded a few degrees further south. He could not guess how far away—two kilometers, maybe more.

Radar would pinpoint the launch site flash. Depending on potential collateral damage, TAC would vector an F-18 with a single five hundred pound LCDB, a concrete-filled Low Collateral Damage Bomb. The Taliban had learned to launch from residential neighborhoods where Coalition high-explosive JDAMs would level everything within a twenty-meter radius. Men, women, children, dogs and goats. Guaranteed, the blackened corpses would make CNN, NBC and Fox.

Lying on the firm bed, he remembered the Special Forces screw up in Gardez. Fire fight, dark night, busting into a room, someone cut loose, and Special Forces returned fire. Somehow three women ended up dead. Two of them were pregnant. One was the mother of six, another of ten.

Hull tried to think of something else but the memory was stronger than his will.

The Operators said they found the women bound, gagged and repeatedly stabbed. Command took the story and ran with it. Later they discovered the Operators had swept the evidence.

It got worse.

Eyewitnesses contradicted the Operator's story. Neighbors said twenty members of the same family had gathered for a baby shower. When the Operators took positions on surrounding rooftops, the father and his brothers ran out with weapons drawn. The Operator's automatic weapons put five down. It was unknown how the police chief and the prosecutor got caught in the crossfire.

The surviving family members claimed the Operators dug the bullets out of the dead women and walls, then wiped it all down with alcohol. Hull didn't believe the Operators could be so stupid as to dig 5.56x51m NATO rounds out of the women.

Whether or not the Operators tried to sanitize the scene, killing the family wasn't deliberate. Bad INTEL sent Special Forces to the house. When the men burst out with AK-47s, one of the team opened up, the women bolted through the door, and before they could shut their M4s down, two mothers and an eighteen-year-old daughter were screaming on the ground. The Operators did not want this to happen. No one wanted to return home with memories of pregnant women and children dying by their weapons.

Hull listened to Afghanistan's dry July winds swirl around the block building and whistle at the windows. A mortar exploded at 0230. Two minutes later, base sirens screamed. He closed his eyes. The dreams started seconds after he fell asleep. He withstood them as long as he could, and then forced himself awake. Hoping Radio Afghanistan's nightly soft rock would help dull the memories, he turned on the clock radio next to the bed. He was still awake 0300, staring at the ceiling, wishing morning's first light would rise in the east-facing window.

The Captain was thorough. A pint of Glenfiddich Scotch waited on the kitchen table. Hull rose at 0330, emptied a quarter of the bottle over three ice cubes in a rocks glass and turned the television to CNN. At the same time the U.S. was retrograding into a depression, fiscal brinkmanship between Democrats and Republicans had driven the country to the edge of default. Federal bailouts, bank foreclosures, growing unemployment and the homeless had replaced a decade of trophy homes, thirsty SUVs, younger women, larger paychecks, and exotic vacations. While the Army, Air Force, Navy and Marines fought to keep Afghanistan from degenerating into a Bronze Age fortress from which al Qaeda could launch further attacks, America's best and brightest could not name two Afghan cities, Afghanistan's President, its form of government or predominant cultural groups. Worse, the talking heads that imperfectly chronicled America's Perfect Union were more influential than the President and Congress combined.

Hull was showered, shaved and dressed when the Captain arrived at 0700 carrying a cup of black coffee and a breakfast roll. "Sir, I hope you slept well."

"Well enough," Hull accepted the coffee and roll with a slight nod.

"Sir, you're scheduled for a medical exam at 0730. I reserved a seat from Kabul to New Delhi, connecting through London to Los Angeles at 0100. Twenty-three hours total. It was the shortest flight I could find. I tried to book you First Class, but it was full. I've got you wait-listed from New Delhi."

"Thank you, Captain," Hull said. "I appreciate your help."

"In light of your efforts..." unable to discuss, or even name the mission, he paused, "I'm grateful to be of service."

The Captain drove across Bagram to the base hospital where Hull signed in at the front desk. He was then led down a polished hallway to an examination room where a young Major saluted. Noting the Silver Leafs on his collar, he saluted, "Colonel, I'm Doctor Bob Gagne. I'll need to give you a quick physical before you meet Doctor Rogers, who will debrief you.

"Doctor Rogers is a shrink?"

"Yes Sir. It's SOP..."

"Major can we expedite this, I've got a flight to Delhi at 1300," Hull stripped off his shirt, boots and pants.

Gagne made a rapid visual inventory of Hull's scrapes and the deep purple bruise that covered his right shoulder. He checked his blood pressure, listened to his heart and checked his pupil responses. "BP one hundred and five over sixty-five, resting rate forty-eight, except for the trauma, you're in great shape," he recorded the notes on the chart.

The doctor next examined Hull's chest. "How did this happen" he inquired, gently probing the purple edges which were beginning to transition to a bright yellow.

"On-the-job injury."

"On the job?"

"I failed to snug an LRSR against my shoulder."

"That would explain it."

A PFC led Colonel Hull through a series of hallways to Dr. Harlow Roger's office. A single glance gave Hull the basics. Two diplomas, one from Northwestern, another from the University of Chicago flanked Dr. Roger's desk. A full colonel, Rogers outranked Hull. He was also twenty years older; mid fifties, gray haired, paunchy, slightly wrinkled uniform shirt. Rogers returned Hull's salute and gestured to the chair across from his desk.

Hull sat, erect, squared to the desk waiting for Rogers to begin.

"I understand you've had a difficult week," the Colonel began.

"Depends what you mean by difficult," Hull replied. Rogers could do him a major favor if he cut the debriefing to five minutes.

The Colonel studied him, and smiled. "OK, Colonel Hull, we'll skip the pleasant, introductory chit chat. You spent a week with little food or water in an area neither of us can talk about. Your spotter was left behind. You killed or wounded roughly a hundred men in three days. According to Dr. Gagne's report," he gestured to the open folder on his desk. "You're beat to hell. You're clearly not sleeping. I'd say we've got some things to talk about." He paused, "But--if you prefer not to, I can admit you to the PTSD ward. I'm not sure if you're familiar with the protocol. Morning begins with breakfast followed by an hour and a half of encounter group. In session, you'll be required to share your feelings about what bothers you. I'll be leading those sessions--you need to know, crying is totally acceptable. In fact, before

65

you're released, it's required. Then we'll start an antidepressant protocol, it'll take time to balance the dose…followed by another hour of therapy in the afternoon or…until you feel well enough to answer my questions."

Hull resisted the urge to glance at his frosted Seiko. "Understood, Sir."

"Let's begin again. You spent the last eight days under extraordinary circumstances. How do you feel?"

Hull took a breath, "Exhausted, sore, tired…" he bargained with the smallest insight into his emotions. "I would have gladly died in Bauldaire's place."

"Totally understandable," Rogers assured him. "Do you want to talk about how it happened?"

"Sir," he hesitated. The mission was still classified top secret. Hull, however, knew Rogers possessed the major details filmed by the UAV. "The Intel was faulty. It hung us out to dry for six days. Bauldaire acquitted himself with honor. I could never have completed the mission without him. He was hit by mortar," he paused. "I was carrying him when he took a 7.62 round in the spine. Captain Bauldaire was dead when I left him."

The Colonel nodded. "Do you blame yourself for his death?"

Hull's abdominal muscles tightened but his expression did not change. "I was the Senior Officer."

"I'd be concerned if you felt any different. About your actions at Firebase Saker-- any regrets about the number of Taliban you killed?"

He shook his head. "No Sir. I've seen mutilated Afghan women and girls splashed with acid to prevent them from attending school. I don't need further beheadings or stonings or suicide bombers to motivate me. The lines are clearly drawn between our goals and theirs!"

"And what would those goals be, Colonel?"

Hull held his gaze. "Peace, freedom and prosperity versus a feudalistic, Islamic dictatorship based on Sharia law."

"You seem pretty clear about that."

"Sir, aren't you?"

Rogers searched for an answer then clasped his pale hands on the desk. "For the time being, neither of us can discuss the details of your mission. In the future, in case something unravels, or you still can't sleep, I'm putting you on a maintenance dose of this antidepressant." He scribbled on a prescription pad, ripped off the top sheet and handed it to Hull. "Unfortunately it will kick in about the time your leave ends." He scrawled "Fit for Duty" on Hull's chart and closed the file.

Hull stood to leave.

"Have a safe trip home." The psychiatrist rose from behind his desk. "And, Colonel, we're all very grateful to you and Captain Bauldaire."

Hull followed the hallway back to the waiting room. Rising quickly to his feet the Captain lifted a duffle and crossed to open the door. "Sir, we took the liberty of packing clothes and a Dopp kit from your quarters in Jalalabad. It was helied up here while you were with Colonel Rogers. The Captain drove Hull to Kabul's International Airport. He handed him his tickets and passport. "Sir, I'll park and wait in case the flight is delayed."

"Not necessary," Hull saluted the Captain. "I appreciate your efforts." He collected his duffle and walked into the rough terminal.

Chapter 7

Security at Kabul's Khwaja Rawash Airport was a strained mix of Afghan National Army, Afghan National Police and ISAF. Each side watched the other while they double-checked all passengers. Three hundred people waited in a long line to be scanned. Hull joined the Afghan business men in dark suits, women in burkas, children in brightly colored dresses and pants, young men in black pants and white vests. He knew it was only a matter of time before the suicide bombers stopped risking the metal detectors, scanners and pat downs and attacked the crowds waiting nervously in line.

It took two hours to clear security, board the Indian Airlines 737, and find his seat over the wing. A year had passed since Hull had waited three days for a space-available seat on a C-19 Medical Evacuation flight to Ramstein, Germany. He was grateful to Petraeus' staff for the confirmed commercial itinerary: Kabul, New Delhi, London, Los Angeles.

He watched the Afghan civilians struggle to jam large suitcases into the small overhead compartments. Those who failed nervously belted their bags and children to their laps. The flight attendants fought to bring order to the blocked aisles, and the Indian Airline's Flight 844 finally departed, a half-hour behind schedule.

He felt the 737 pull off the taxiway and accelerate down the runway. The nose wheel lifted and Kabul's dusty streets and interlocking compounds, courtyards and wrecked planes, tanks and trucks silently slipped beneath the Indian Air jet's wings.

He refused to give into his exhaustion. Instead he fought sleep during the three hour flight between Kabul and Delhi. For him, sleep summoned death. Everyone died in his dreams.

In the hour between flights at Delhi's Indira Gandhi Airport, he slipped into the men's room where he traded his fresh BDUs and Danner desert boots for dark wool slacks, a blue cotton shirt, a tie, dark blue jacket and polished black loafers that the Captain had packed in his duffle. The cracked mirror reflected the dark circles around his eyes and the fifteen pounds he had dropped during his nine-month tour. He combed his cropped hair, brushed his teeth and walked through the crowded terminal to the British Air gate. An attractive Indian gate agent took his passport and military ID.

"You're traveling from Kabul to Los Angeles?" she inquired. "Let's see, first leg to Heathrow."

"Correct," He said.

She studied his ticket and observed, "You have a long journey...a full day en route."

"With luck, twenty-three hours."

"Our Kabul office requested a special priority upgrade." The agent noted his jacket and tie, then took his boarding pass and tore it up. "We have an empty seat in First Class." She handed him a new pass. "Enjoy your flight."

Hull nodded his thanks. Two tours in Iraq and four in Afghanistan had elicited similar acts of gratitude. Wearing his uniform in a stateside restaurant virtually guaranteed someone would pay for his dinner but his years as a sniper made him wary of attention. Even anonymous gratitude now made him uncomfortable.

He purchased the International Herald Tribune and chose a seat against a wall from where he could watch the room. Half a dozen U.S. troops waited around the gate. Darkened by the Afghan sun, hardened by long marches, burdened by the dead, after nine months they only wanted to see their families, hold their children, sleep with their wives. The problems would come later.

He opened the paper. His eyes stopped on a heavy headline banner that screamed, "Parliament Leveled!" "Hundreds Dead!"

The three-quarter-page photo showed Pakistan's devastated National Assembly Building. The facade had been blown away, reducing the interior offices and walls to an empty cardboard box. Hull opened the second page. The Taliban had packed an ambulance with 1800 kilograms of RDX and TNT.

Hull was trained in the use of RDX. Known also as Hexogen, Cyclonite and Cyclotri-methylene Trinitramine, the explosive compound had an extremely low volatility. The military grade was a white solid with a density of 1.806 g/cc and nitrogen content of 37.84%. Composition B, the castable mixture of RDX and TNT was easy to shape, transport and trigger.

An ambulance driver and EMT had arrived with sirens blaring, red lights flashing. Dressed in white uniforms with red crosses, the driver yelled to the front gate guards that a Parliament member was experiencing chest pains. It was a busy day at the National Assembly; the guards waved them through.

A second before the blast erased the building façade, a security camera focused on the driver. His expression was calm, even serene. Linked from the concrete column to a computer housed deep in the Assembly basement, the feed recorded his last seconds. The driver looked first at the two guards stationed on each side of the Assembly entrance then directly at the camera. In a clip that would run repeatedly on international news, he raised his right hand. It held a metal toggle--the trigger. A last smile, his thumb moved, the feed switched to static. The blast could be heard thirty kilometers away. When the dust cleared, an eighty-meter wide by ten-meter deep crater replaced what had been the Assembly entrance.

The initial explosion killed more than four hundred people. Officials feared the toll would rise as teams of men working with dogs, cranes and earthmovers fought to remove collapsed concrete pillars and floors. In addition to the Assembly, the bomb severely damaged the Secretariat building, the Supreme Court building, and stores a kilometer away on Ataturk and Khayaban-E-Quuaid-E-Asam Avenues.

An anonymous caller claimed the attack was a response to the Special Forces mission within the Federally Administered Tribal Areas. The caller hung up before the line could be traced.

An ISAF spokesman stated, "In accordance to the agreement with Pakistan President Asif Ali Zardari, no Special Forces have crossed from Afghanistan. No missions have been sanctioned within Pakistan and we are not in possession of any intelligence that would indicate ISAF has ordered any operation within FATA!"

Hull briefly wondered if Pakistan's Inter-Services Intelligence Directorate had prior knowledge of the attack. Would the ISI blow up it's own National Assembly to force Pakistan closer to an Islamic autoracy?

"Speaking from Aiwan-e-Sadr, the President's official residence, President Zardari described the bombing as a cowardly attack on Pakistan's sovereignty and promised to bring the terrorists to justice. "This is a deliberate attempt to destabilize Pakistan's legally-elected government! We will do everything in our power to hunt these animals into their holes!"

The Pakistani Foreign Minister, Shah Mehmood Qureshi, had left the National Assembly Building ten minutes before the blast. In a statement broadcast on Pakistan TV News, Qureshi said, "Pakistan has not been advised, nor are we aware, of covert operations within the Federally Administered Tribal Areas. If evidence proves otherwise, Pakistan will act accordingly."

"Leaders from the U.S., Germany, France, Italy, Russia, China and many other nations have angrily condemned the bombing and have pledged their nations' intelligence-gathering operations to help bring the planners to justice. Though India also offered help, Pakistan's Army has moved to high alert along the two countries' shared border."

Page two continued, "The Pakistani Army launched an attack on the Tribal Areas bordering Afghanistan. In an attempt to weaken the Taliban leadership, they struck at suspected strongholds. Backed by tanks and heavy artillery, fighting is reported to be heavy. At this time numbers of the killed or wounded are not available, but sources claim Army casualties are moderate. Government officials say the outcome of the battle and the speed with which the Islamabad planners are brought to justice will determine the strength of the FATA militancy and the government's ability to control it."

Hull tried to tie the story's loose ends into something that approximated the truth. The caller to the newspaper had singled out "Special Forces" operating within Pakistan. Hull knew the caller's reference to "Special Forces," could only mean Operation Viper. Neither Hull nor Bauldaire had guessed the target's value. Whoever he was, it explained the promotion and the medal.

Hull looked up from the paper. Two Indian Army Corporals had stopped to flirt with two college coeds returning to London. Dressed in

71

polished black boots, green camouflage uniforms and black berets, as long as the Corporals focused on the coeds, they would overlook potential threats.

Hull scanned the other passengers. Indian businessmen, students, families, British tourists--something was out of place. The attacks at the Mombai Taj Mahal Palace had taught National Security Forces a dozen bloody lessons. The Corporals continued to focus on the coeds. Hull knew that long hours and repetition dulls senses. He studied the short BREN machine pistols hanging from their shoulders.

The loud speaker announced, "British Airways Flight 142 to London, now boarding First Class passengers."

Hull lifted his carry-on and walked to the agent who took his ticket and compared his passport to his face. "Welcome aboard, Major Hull," she said as she returned his documents.

He stepped through the cabin door and followed the purser's directions to aisle Seat 1B, behind the cockpit bulkhead. He stored his carry-on in the overhead and slipped in next to the aisle. A flight attendant offered him a glass of orange juice. He nodded his thanks and emptied the glass. She returned a moment later with the carton.

"Push back will be in ten minutes," her accent was English. She was pretty in a pale, Midlands country girl way.

Flight 142 rapidly filled with businessmen, tourists and families with children.

The terminal's glass walls faced the jet. Hull watched the gate agents scan tickets. The Indian Army corporals were still distracted by the coeds. A peripheral movement appeared in front of the double doors that opened into the jet way. The gate agent was trying to detain a young man in levis, a dark shirt and small carry-on. The thin, uniformed agent suddenly grabbed the man's dark shirt and, as Hull watched the two went over backwards in front of the double doors. The corporals hesitated as the gate agent fought to keeping the young man from regaining his feet

Rising from 1B, Hull turned toward the open cabin door.

The flight attendant moved to block his way. "Major Hull, please return to your seat!"

Hull pushed past her. He alone knew what a Glock machine pistol and half a dozen fragmentation grenades would do to a fully loaded passenger plane. If the young man forced his way on board, the horror would begin.

Why had the terrorists picked that flight? Hostages? To trade for prisoners? And if India stonewalled? Methodically kill the passengers as the negotiators tried and failed to establish a dialogue. Burn the plane. Let the national press film the horror. The vast armies that projected a nation's immense power could not protect its citizens. The target? It made no difference. In the end, no one was safe. All travel was dangerous when young men and women joyfully embraced death.

Shouted orders echoed down the jet way into the cabin. Pushing past the flight attendants, Hull slammed and locked the cabin door then scanned the cabin for a secondary escape. If the hijacker breeched security, he would blow the door.

The purser was in her mid thirties, slender, dressed in a blue pants suit, crisp white shirt and a tie. She had no training, no preparation for a terrorist attack on the ground.

Hull pointed to the three exits. "Prepare to open the emergency exits and trigger the slides!"

Keeping her eyes on him, she ordered the six flight attendants to station themselves by the rear, wing and front exits.

Four security agents sprinted to the gate where they repeatedly swung lacquered clubs into the melee. The young man ceased struggling. The agents grabbed his arms and jerked him to his feet. He was twenty, thin, dark hair, a twin to the Mumbai attackers. A wound on his skull was bleeding onto his face. His ear was torn, his cheek misshapen. Dragging him away down the causeway, security guards continued to beat him. Something had gone wrong. Security had failed. Somehow the young man had slipped through. If the gate agent hadn't tackled him, he would have boarded. Someone would have to pay.

Security banged on the main cabin door. The pilot demanded identification which was shouted through the closed door. The pilot requested confirmation from the tower before he allowed the purser to lift the latch.

Security quickly unloaded the British Airway's 747, then escorted the passengers to an isolation room where armed agents checked passports, place of birth, destination, reason for travel, and all hand-held luggage. Bomb-sniffing dogs then swept the cabin. All seat backs, the galleys, toilets, food carts, stainless storage areas and overhead bins were searched. When nothing was found, they unloaded all baggage and inspected the 747's cavernous belly compartments. Security routed all passengers through visible body scanners. A dozen were strip-searched when the detectors indicated anything remotely suspicious.

Hull was led into the Office of Airport Security off the main concourse. Dressed in a crisp blue uniform, the head of security was studying Hull's passport and Military ID. He was late forties, graying around the temples. The officer turned the card and read the back. "Major Hull," his military ID had not yet been updated. "Why are you are traveling in civilian clothes?"

Holding the Head of Security's skeptical gaze, Hull replied. "I'm on leave, flying on a full fare ticket. I'm not required to wear a uniform."

"The flight attendants said you closed and locked the airliner's main cabin door."

Hull nodded.

The officer looked up. "That wasn't wise. Since you were not wearing a uniform, tell me, how could the attendants know you weren't one of the hijackers?"

"They couldn't."

"Your actions were rash."

"But necessary."

The officer nodded without commitment. "Locking the door was the right decision, of course, but you were the wrong person…"

"The cabin was vulnerable. The flight attendants failed to secure it."

He placed Hull's military ID on his desk and reached for his blue, U.S. Passport. "And where are you stationed?"

"Afghanistan," Hull revealed the required minimum.

"Unit?"

"Marine Corps, reporting to General Petraeus."

"And your assignment?"

"Marine."

"But specifically?" The questions were a necessary formality.

"Marine is specific enough. If you need further clarification, you'll have to call ISAF Headquarters in Kabul. I'll save you the trouble. They won't offer any more information than I have."

"I see. Final destination?" He opened Hull's passport.

"Los Angeles." Hull watched him study the stamped pages. U.S., Iraq, Switzerland, Israel, Vietnam, Costa Rica, Chile, and Argentina. South Korea, Germany, Germany to… no stamp. Scattered randomly through the passport were four pages of expired visas. The passport tracked Hull's life but revealed nothing about the owner. What could the official hope to learn that wasn't already in the national computer? What did he hope to catch? A brief lack of eye contact revealing Hull had something to hide?

The officer opened the final page. Only room for three more stamps remained. "You travel a great deal, Major Hull. Your passport is almost full. I doubt, however, that it records the full sum of your destinations." When Hull failed to answer, he persisted, "Would you agree that not all your entry or exits were stamped?"

Leaks or confessions of any gravity risked a court marshal. The nature of his missions prohibited the disclosure of specifics. The entry and exit stamps served as grave markers in his dreams. The memories would sicken the agent. Best to say nothing at all. Point the official toward Kabul.

Hull straightened. "If you require further clarification, you'll have to contact General Petraeus' office."

The officer continued to study Hull. "And what will General Petraeus add to what little you've told me?"

"Nothing more than what you have on your computer and the passport."

"I see. Can you at least reveal the purpose of your travel?"

"Leave."

Returning his ticket, passport and military ID, the officer said, "Further questions will only waste our time, Major Hull. I can only guess at what you do. I'm glad it's you and not me. Have a safe trip. And Major Hull, if there's a next time, I'd advise you to remain in your seat."

"I'll keep that in mind," Hull replied.

It was 8:00 PM, seven hours behind schedule, when British Airways Flight 142 New Delhi to London made a slow right hand turn onto the runway. Hull settled back into Seat 1B and closed his eyes. The massive jet engines wound up, the Captain released the brakes and the huge plane began to accelerate. Forty seconds elapsed before it reached rotation speed. The nose lifted and the 747 quickly climbed away from the runway. The vibration from the spinning wheels stopped, the gear folded into the wells and the doors snapped shut.

A middle-aged Indian gentleman seated in 1A ventured in Hindi-accented English, "Appalling development in Pakistan. I thought once Osama bin Laden was dead, these terrorist attacks would end."

Hull opened his eyes. The bombing was a Taliban response to Operation Viper. Who was the telltale that took the bullet through the hips? And who was the gray-haired target? CENTCOM knew, but no one was talking. Not even Petraeus. Hull had been paid to keep his mouth shut. Colonel, future Navy Cross. Leave, First Class flights. Who was the gray target?

"Terrible," the Indian man observed as the engines throttled back. "Of course, it is a great worry to all my countrymen. It is only a matter of time before Pakistan blames India for this tragedy. It will not be good for either of us! Not good at all!"

The flight attendant leaned down and handed him a folded slip of paper. "Colonel Hull, our co-pilot took this message."

Inside the slip, a rapid, masculine handwriting recorded. "Regret incident and delay at New Delhi airport! With all gratitude and sincere wishes for a safe journey." It was from General Petraeus.

Hull had slept less than three hours in the last fifty-six. He anticipated the drop in cabin pressure, but could not resist it. His eyes closed during the Captain's announcement. "On behalf of British Airways, we sincerely regret the unexpected delay. Our 747 has been thoroughly searched and you should look forward to a safe, smooth flight to London. We will be serving complimentary drinks in Cabin Class and will do our best to make up time. For those of you making connections in London, our agents are working to rebook you on other flights..."

Hull dozed and dreamed of Roxana.

Chapter 8

R oxana appeared at Chapman Airfield a month after her father died. The Taliban had yet to target the gate with female suicide bombers, but Chapman Security was convinced it was only a matter of time. Four U.S. soldiers trained their SM16s on the day workers who lined up waiting to clear security. Searching local workers was a dangerous, thankless detail. It wasn't a matter of if, but when, the next eighteen year-old Madrassa student would attempt to punch through Chapman's Main Gate into Paradise.

The stress of waiting for a bomb blast took a toll. If they survived, the soldiers counted their blessings. None lasted long. Simple machismo helped some stick it out for a week but few played Chapman's Main Gate game of Russian Roulette for longer than ten days. After a month in Afghanistan, all knew that high explosives were the ultimate horror. Sooner or later they would be called to secure a bombed market where bodies lay like curled jackstraws, dead Afghani civilians mixed with police cadets. Coalition soldiers quickly learned there was little difference between charred men, charred women, Iraqi, American, Canadian, Pakistani, Taliban or al Qaeda. Later, even battle-hardened surgeons stood silently, their hearts aching for the shattered bodies with unfocused eyes…wondering where, or if, to start.

Stopping in front of the blast barriers, Roxana called in accented English, "I am Ajmal's daughter. I wish to speak to someone about work."

Protected by interlocking blast walls, the guards pointed their M16s at her.

A column of Humvees slowed for the main gate. Returning from a three-day patrol, Lieutenant Bauldaire was riding shotgun in the point vehicle. He was tired, dirty and in need of a shower. The Main Gate Guards were negotiating with a burka-clad Afghan woman.

Leaning out of the Humvee, Bauldaire said, "Sergeant, let's expedite this...."

"Yes, Sir," he tried to hurry the woman along. ISAF orders forbade touching her. Bauldaire's Humvee slowly moved forward

"Step out of the way," Bauldaire ordered in Farsi.

"I only need one minute!" An English speaking voice within the burka hurried to explain. "My father worked at Chapman's motor pool. "His name was Ajmal, it translates to...."

"Handsome in Farsi," Bauldaire interrupted her.

"You speak Farsi." The Burka's crown nodded with gratitude. "That will make it easier. My father greased the trucks and the personnel carriers."

ISAF mechanics hated the filthy, dull monotony of greasing hundreds of zerk fittings. After ten hours spent crawling under the trucks and armored personnel carriers, Ajmal turned his attention to a small garden he cultivated next to the garage. He enriched the dry soil with sludge from the base sewage plant then planted the seeds in precise rows. Because Ajmal was well liked, during the following weeks, the motor pool mechanics looked the other way when he attached a water hose to a spigot and watered the tiny plants. The vegetables ripened in late May. Ajmal was arranging his tomatoes on a small table at the local market when a car bomb ripped through the rough stalls, killed fifteen people and maimed thirty-three. What was left of Ajmal barely filled his basket.

Traffic was piling up in front of the Main Gate. The guards saluted Bauldaire for a second time and discretely signaled him to drive on.

"Corporal, give me a second here," the Lieutenant would not be rushed.

"Winter is approaching!" Roxana reminded him. Deprived of her father's income, Roxana, her mother and four sisters would surely suffer.

Exhausted, haunted by images of the day's running firefight with two-dozen Taliban, Bauldaire listened while the Humvee continued to creep forward. He handed her a small card with a phone number. "Come back tomorrow, I'll see what I can do."

The motor pool vouched for her father, Chapman security checked her family, cousins and uncles. A week later Roxana joined the hundred other Afghan day workers who passed through the Main Gate.

Bauldaire and Miller hired her to clean their quarters on Mondays and Thursdays. The two Lieutenants understood that they could not be at home and if either ever touched her, she would never return. Bauldaire honored their agreement. Each week the two Lieutenants left two tens on what served as a kitchen table. When he and Miller returned to their bunks, desks and shared shower were spotless. They found the bathroom clean, floors swept and mopped, fresh towels, windows washed, flowers in a chipped vase. They never saw her without a burka. The truth was, they never saw her at all.

A month passed before Bauldaire was visiting Hull's hooch. Studying the Major's dusty apartment he observed. "Sir, with all due respect, your place could use a little sprucing up."

Roxana appeared two days later behind a soft knock on Hull's front door. Opening it, he faced a blue burka that fell in a cascade of lace and embroidered silk to the ground. An unescorted Afghan woman was rare on the air base. When Hull stepped outside, Roxana backed discreetly away.

"Assalam u alaikum," he said in greeting.

"Assalam u alaikum," Roxana replied. In accented English she asked, "You speak Farsi?"

"Not well," Hull said. In Afghanistan, only educated men and women spoke English. The vast majority of Afghanistan's women were cloistered behind the high mud brick walls of residential compounds. Eighty seven percent of Afghan women were illiterate and if they studied English, they could only practice with a female teacher. Little wonder Hull was surprised by this Afghan woman, covered in a crown-to-ground burka.

"Esmam e' Roxana," she started to translate. "My…"

"Your name is Roxana."

"Your accent is excellent." To compliment a man other than her husband, no matter how innocent, was forbidden. That she was talking to Hull at all violated dozens of social codes. In Afghanistan, women were often treated as property. Seventy percent were forced to marry against their will. Thirty percent were victims of physical and sexual abuse.

79

Half of Afghanistan's women prisoners had been convicted of running away, adultery, or being in the company of an unrelated man. Roxana could not leave the house without the permission of her father, husband or male relative. If she was raped, she could be sentenced to prison or stoned. During the past year, a hundred and eighty women had set themselves on fire. Her compliment on Hull's accent arose from desperation. Under the Taliban women had been forbidden to work, forcing professionals--doctors and teachers--to beg, or in the most desperate cases, prostitute themselves to survive.

"Bebakhshid," she apologized then continued in Farsi. "Your friend, the young Lieutenant Bauldaire...I clean his and the other Lieutenant Miller's rooms. He said you often work together and perhaps you might wish your rooms cleaned as well?"

"Lieutenant Bauldaire spoke of you."

"The Lieutenant Bauldaire and Lieutenant Miller are very kind." The voice within the burka betrayed her nervousness. "I work very fast and I do not charge excessively!"

Hull sensed she was young but the burka left few clues as to her age, and none at all as to whether she was married. Her hands were covered with cotton gloves and she wore traditional black shoes. Only the lace opening that covered her face allowed the afternoon light to silhouette her profile.

"What is not excessively?"

"One dollar per hour and you must buy the cleaning supplies." She gestured in the direction of the front gate, "I have clearance from base security but can only work when you are not home." At the risk of her life, they could not be discovered alone together.

Hull noted her accent and her occasional reversal of syntax, but those mistakes were insignificant. She was fluent. "Where did you learn to speak English?"

"I do not speak it well." She tried to dismiss his compliment. "When my mother was young, before the Mujahideen fought the Russians she received a scholarship to Iran. She studied English and French. She spoke English to me when I was growing up. When I attended school, I read and listened to improve my accent. The Coalition soldiers came and I listened to the English radio. When the war is over I hope to study abroad."

A week passed during which Hull and Bauldaire waited in Kandahar for a Taliban leader who never appeared. Hull was sunburned, dusty and hungry when he unlocked the front door to his apartment. The floors were washed, there were fresh sheets on the bed and the refrigerator was defrosted. On the top shelf he found a plate of Chabli Kabobs, Challow white rice and Salaata spinach covered with cellophane. He reheated the dish in the microwave, opened a beer and settled at the small table. A vase of flowers had started to wilt in the heat. The Chabli's ground lamb, green onions, cilantro and green bell pepper patty offered a welcome change from Marine chow. He was grateful to the young woman in the blue burka. That night before he fell asleep he researched the meaning of her name.

Roxana came from the Persian, Roshanak. Translated to "luminous beauty," the earliest reference was to the young Afghan girl Alexander the Great had taken for his wife.

Because Roxana worked around Hull's schedule, two months passed before he saw her again. When he returned on Tuesday and Friday evenings, the apartment would be clean, his sheets and towels washed and folded, dinner waiting in the refrigerator. When he tried to raise her pay to ten dollars per day, she returned the extra five dollars with a brief note. Her precise, feminine cursive said, "Dear Major Hull, Our agreement was a dollar per hour for a total of five dollars per day. The food is my mother's thanks for your help."

Roxana continued to clean his quarters after he left and disappeared before he returned. It was early February when he forgot to reinsert a back plate into his body armor. The sound of the vacuum hid the door's opening creak. In the seconds before she saw him, his mind locked upon details. She was in her late teens, twenty at most. She was wearing an aqua perahan tunban, a scalloped, thigh length dress over white cotton pants that did not hide her narrow hips, small waist or full breasts. It was clear she owed her dark eyes and thin strong arms to ancestors who had occupied the land since Alexander's cohorts crossed Afghanistan.

Cat quick, she lunged for her burka hanging from a hook on the door. Hull was blocking her way. She covered her face with her hands and turned her back to him. "Please, don't look at me!" she begged.

Holding his hands up he apologized, "I forgot something."

"My burka!"

Hull lifted it from the hook and handed it to her. As she reached to take it, her black hair fell in glossy ringlets across her shoulders. He had seen such curls on three thousand year-old Sumerian bas-reliefs.

Luminous Beauty. It was an injustice. In the second before she slipped beneath her burka, Hull recorded her eyes, mouth and jaw. Her face would haunt him afterward. "I'm sorry, I should have knocked before I entered."

"I must go."

He turned toward the door. "No, that's not necessary. Finish your work..."

"I can't now. If I am seen...." She straightened the long gown and hurried toward the door. "I cannot be alone with you. I would be accused of..." she struggled to say the word. "Zina," sexual intercourse outside of marriage, was punished by public execution.

"If that is true, why do you risk coming?" he asked her.

The burka's lace panel moved with her breath. She was terrified to be there alone. "To survive...if I was unable to clean this house or the Lieutenant's, my mother, sisters and I would be forced to beg. If we could not beg, we would starve." She placed her hand on the doorknob.

"I'm leaving," he said. Retrieving the ballistic plate, he stepped around her and closed the door behind him.

In the weeks that followed, she continued to clean his house. Hull wished they could have met at another time, somewhere outside of Afghanistan.

Except for stray dogs slinking among the shadows, the streets of Khost were empty. As dawn crept over the distant Torah Bora Mountains, the ancient city came awake. Shop owners unscrewed the broken sheets of plywood guarding their storefronts, swept the sidewalks and stacked their displays. Traffic increased. Vortexes of dust lifted from the pot-holed street.

An informant had betrayed a suicide bomber. The target was Chapman Field, Main Gate. Details of when and where were coalescing. Hull and Bauldaire were ordered to occupy a Crow's Nest overlooking the intersection of two main streets at 0400.

CENTCOM's Crow's Nests encompassed one small facet of its strategic vision for Kabul and to a larger extent, Afghanistan as a whole. The role of armored boxes came under the general heading of "Secure and Serve."

It was CENTCOM's phrasing, targeted more toward the American press than at the Afghans. General Petraeus believed victory required that the army live among the people rather than remain hidden in fortified barracks.

"You can't commute to this fight!" provided a favorite stateside sound bite.

Double-rotor Chinooks ferried the armored boxes to strategic rooftops. The operation depended on precise timing. For safety and maximum psychological effect, the Chinooks lifted off at 0200. The arrival of the Crow's Nest at 0220 approximated the voice of Allah. Seconds before the Chinook's rotor wash blew in the windows and doors, a ten thousand-candle power light turned early morning to midday. The armored box landed with a thunderous bang on drying laundry and charcoal ovens. The pilots laid the cyclic over and went to full throttle before the sleeping Taliban could shoulder their RPGs.

If America needed a symbol for an invading super power, dropping a Crow's Nest on a sleeping family equaled raising the Stars and Stripes above the ancient Khost Mosque. Manning the Crow's Nests was guard duty, eight hours of boredom sandwiched between sudden, fierce firefights. The Crow's Nest destroyed any element of surprise. Every Moolie within a twenty-block radius could plot the exact coordinates.

Hull never, never, traded stealth for armor plate. Moving through the predawn dark, he picked a position that looked down the central road leading to Chapman's Main Gate. A hole in a parapet wall offered a clear shot without exposure to a Taliban sniper.

Half an hour passed. Hull and Bauldaire waited.

Turning a suicide bomber marked an extraordinary stroke of luck. CENTCOM went even further. Intelligence believed it signaled a major change. Following a decade of hard work and bloody sacrifice, perhaps the Afghans were beginning to trust the Coalition; General Petraeus hoped so. Any positive turn of events would play well in Washington.

Keeping his eye pinned to the Swarovski, Bauldaire glassed the surrounding rooftops. Nothing. Chapman Intelligence would ID the target "The Taliban claim they don't target civilians," the Lieutenant whispered.

"Tell that to the four thousand men, women and children they killed last year." Hull remembered the teenager who triggered a BBIED--Body Borne Improvised Explosive Devise--in Khost's crowded Central Market. The blast killed three police, seven civilians and maimed forty others. What was left of the boy was dumped in the graveyard for suicide bombers on the outskirts of Kabul beneath Kol-e-Hashmat Khan Mountain. Ringed by junkyards and guarded by two Afghan National Police, the graveyard was patrolled by packs of starving dogs that fed on the unclaimed corpses.

Bauldaire lowered the scope. "Sir, there's a perverse truth to the Taliban's claim that their primary target is the Afghan National Army, the Afghan National Police and the Coalition. If they can't hit their primary targets, they bomb civilians as a distraction and then wait for the ANP to show up. The second and third bombs take out the ANA. Did you watch the YouTube video I forwarded?"

"About the Australian photographer who was covering poppy eradication?"

Bauldaire nodded. "Saving the world from heroin, keeping the junk out of the pipeline plays warm and fuzzy back home."

"Until that twelve-year old paper boy walked into the crowd of elite Afghani police and touched off a BBIED."

"The ANP said the kid's Mullah triggered him with a garage door opener. His head and half his left hand was all that remained."

"The young, devout, impoverished and dead," Hull observed. "A hundred and eighty-seven suicide bombers this year alone. Three a week."

"Were you here when the bomber hit Bagram's Main Gate?"

"Cheney's deal?"

Bauldaire raised his eye from the scope reticule, "Vice President Cheney was the primary target?"

"Cheney barely heard the blast. He was never in any danger but nuts, bolts and ball bearings embedded in the high explosive shredded everyone within twenty meters. Two Coalition soldiers, a U.S. contractor and twenty Afghan locals looking for jobs stopped the shrapnel. The bomber wasted twenty bystanders to kill two ANA." Hull stared down the dusty street.

"Takes unwavering commitment."

"Or terrified teenage boys." Hull added.

"After the SEALs killed OBL, suicide bombers hit that paramilitary academy in Peshawar. The first rode his motorcycle into the crowd and triggered a body born. The second suicide biker hit when cadets were cleaning up the mess. Eighty dead, 40 crippled. Headquarters claims the numbers will rise." Bauldaire worked the math. "Figure a BBIED kills eighty people while a vehicle borne improvised explosive device wastes a hundred. Trucks are expensive and obvious but detonating a Body Borne in a crowd gets up close and personal--it breeds universal mistrust." The Lieutenant scanned the early morning street. Still nothing. "Suicide bombers are cheap. INTEL figures it costs the Taliban less than a hundred and fifty dollars per. That's compared to the four hundred thousand al Qaeda spent to destroy the World Trade Center," Bauldaire settled back against the mud wall.

"Four hundred thousand? Is that all?"

"The U.S. took the major financial hit. When all the bills are totaled, 9/11 will cost fifteen billion for reconstruction alone. No one can put a price on the dead." The Lieutenant lowered his helmet to shield his eyes from the rising sun. "Too bad we didn't listen to Ahmad Massoud."

Massoud was the Commander of Afghanistan's Northern Alliance who warned of the 9/11 attacks. His Chief of Security had no reason to suspect the bogus passports that identified two Tunisian al Qaeda operatives as a Belgian news team.

Massoud had just started the interview when camera operator Bouraoui el-Ouaer touched off the five pounds of high grade RDX hidden in his Sony. The blast took Massoud out along with the cameraman. Massoud's men shot the other reporter while he was attempting to flee.

"The State Department believes Osama bin Laden had Massoud killed to secure his Afghan base. It was a miracle that Massoud reached a hospital. He died two days before the Towers fell."

Hull's headset came alive.

Chapman's Security Officer reported, "Here's what we know! The bomber will appear at 0755! Target is the Main Gate Guards clearing day workers. The device is an explosive vest wired to a hand held Dead Man detonator. As soon as the clip is released, it triggers the explosive. The bomber must be stopped no less than eighty meters from the main gate. Repeat, she cannot be allowed to approach the gate! Is that clear?"

"She?" It was Bauldaire.

"Affirmative! The bomber is a woman." Hull and Bauldaire exchanged a glance.

Hull's first word was a profanity. He checked the Sako's safety.

Bauldaire triggered his mike, "Say Again?"

"The Target is a woman!"

"Chapman....how will we recognize the target?"

"Our informant will identify her."

"What are your informant's credentials?"

"Impeccable. He's given us detailed information about three other operations. Time, place, type of explosives, target, casualties," there was five seconds of silence.

Bauldaire checked his M4's safety. "We'll stand by."

At exactly 0755 a woman appeared on the dusty street. She was walking quickly. Erect. Alert. Her burka swinging an inch above the broken tarmac. She looked straight ahead and kept to the right side of street as she made her way to Chapman's Main Gate.

Bauldaire kept the Swarovski focused on the blue burka. Her face was hidden, her body a shapeless column, her stride unwavering. A Body-Borne Improvised Device strapped to a woman had Taliban written all over it. Coalition soldiers couldn't or wouldn't search her. Bauldaire refined the focus onto her hands. He tried to locate the trigger switch.

"Anything?" Hull inquired.

"Nothing," Bauldaire squinted into the reticule. "Her hands are covered."

"Can you see a belt or vest through the burka?"

"No, Sir, no VPLs," Bauldaire replied.

Their headsets crackled with Base Intelligence. "Major Hull, we have confirmation. She is our bomber. Repeat--the woman in the blue burka is our bomber. Wait until she clears the crowd, then take her."

Hull centered the cross hairs two inches below the burka's crown. Mid-forehead. He pressured the trigger just below release. His sight picture revealed black ringlets of hair and skin the color of shattered marble. He knew the woman beneath the burka. He stopped tracking.

Roxana cleared the small crowd and without checking for traffic, started across the road.

"Major, you have permission to take her out," the INTEL Officer advised him. A second passed. Hull set the crosshairs below the burka's crown. "Major," there was concern in his headset, "You have permission…."

"Sir?" Bauldaire swung his M4 and took a rest on the wall.

Tracking Roxana with the cross hairs, Hull knew what had driven her to that moment. An unending war that forced honest people to commit desperate acts. The death of her father, cousins, uncles, aunts and friends who had fallen to bullets, mortars and mines. Desperation. Constant fear.

Hull thought of Roxana's pitiful, dangerous job. It offered access to the base. The guards wouldn't search her. How had the Taliban broken her? By holding her mother and four sisters? Their offer was irresistible. Deliver the bomb, or her family died.

"Sir?" Bauldaire switched the M4A's safety to off.

Roxana closed to within seventy meters.

"Major?"

Hull gritted his teeth. His finger pressured the trigger.

Bauldaire set his cross hairs on the burka and triggered a burst. The Lieutenant never heard the .338's report. The heavy slug exploded out the back of Roxana's burka. Bauldaire's half a dozen rounds only made a mess of her corpse.

They waited for the blast. Nothing. A crowd gathered around the corpse. None bothered to lift her veil. Life was cheap in Afghanistan. The bystanders turned toward the rooftop that held the Crow's Nest. It was empty. Seconds later Chapman's bomb disposal team appeared. Using a remote robot's arm, they checked the burka for an explosive vest. She was clean.

"Fuck!" Chapman Security swore. "Goddammit! Our INTEL was unassailable! Our source wouldn't set us up! She was wired!"

"Sir?" It was a woman's voice.

Hull's eyes opened. He came awake quickly. The dream was always the same. One time, once, he hoped he'd miss--or an explosion would follow--anything to alter the ending.

The flight attendant was standing above him. "Major Hull…do you care for dinner? It's quite nice tonight. You have a choice of fish or beef." She opened Hull's tray and set a white cloth and silverware in front of him. "I'd stick with the beef," she whispered, setting a glass of water on the white cloth. "India's fish is always a little chancy."

Chapter 9

I t was ten past midnight when British Airways Flight 142 touched down at London's Heathrow International Airport. The 747 took ten minutes to taxi to the gate where it finally shuddered to a stop. The passengers rose stiffly, crowded into the aisle and dragged their carry-ons from the overhead bins. The purser announced that the gate agents were working to re-book connecting flights. They would find the Flight Services' desk in Terminal Five. He did not reveal that nothing departed Heathrow at one AM. Transferring passengers were facing a long, uncomfortable night.

The jetway telescoped against the Boeing, the cabin door opened and, as the passengers filed out, the flight attendants straightened their uniforms and forced a cheery, "Goodbye, thanks for flying with us."

Hull was one of the last passengers to leave. He was walking down the aisle, close to the exit when the First Class flight attendant handed him her card. "...I wanted to thank you for your assistance in India. If you ever have a layover in London, give me a call." She stepped between the seats to give him room to pass. "Colonel Hull, have a safe flight home."

He took the card, glanced at the name, "Linda... thanks for your quick reaction...and the flight." He knew he'd never call.

Passengers hurried past him to stand in line at the flight services desk. It took twenty minutes to reach an agent.

"Name?" she keyed her computer.

"Hull, Jack," he scanned the empty terminal.

She typed his name, "Yes, Colonel Hull," your reservation has been updated. "We apologize for the delay…"

"I understand. When is your next flight out?"

"That's the problem," she scanned the screen. "Our first flight to Los Angeles departs at 6:30 AM."

"Book it," he said.

"Unfortunately it's a Northwest flight that returns to Amsterdam for," she checked the screen, "…a four hour and fifteen minute layover. You'll arrive in Los Angeles at 3:20 tomorrow afternoon for a total flight time of seventeen hours. British Airways leaves a bit later…10:15 AM. It's a significantly shorter total time. Eleven hours and ten minutes puts you in at 1:25 AM."

"What about connections through New York, Chicago or Denver?"

She checked. "I'm sorry, it gets worse. No flights depart after eight PM or before six AM. The layovers add hours to your total flight time." She waited. "You could get a room--perhaps one of the airport hotels."

He glanced at the Seiko. Nine hours. An hour to clear customs. Another hour to the hotel room, with check-in…three AM. An hour to wind down…four AM. If he set the alarm for 6:45 to make the 10:15, he'd have two and a half hours net. A hotel didn't make sense.

He said, "Book me on the 10:15."

Hull had bivouacked in far worse places than Heathrow's Terminal Five and now walked slowly past the closed stores and tried to readapt to life in the West. The windows were filled with Philippe Patek watches and Mont Blanc pens, Waterford crystal and ruby earrings that would feed an Afghan family for five years. Silk scarves, Cristal champagne, Godiva chocolates, Cuban cigars, Bally alligator shoes, ostrich purses…he struggled to decompress.

A television monitor was tuned to Skye TV. A late night fashion show focused on Italian designer, Enrico Giarretto. Enrico's designs ran to wide, floating hats done in primary colors, ruffled dresses and transparent tops. The models were beautiful and boyish with athletic hips and small breasts. Hull watched the thin dark Somalis, the emaciated French and pouting Italians strut imperiously down the runway.

Surrounded by riches he could not afford, Hull recognized the West had traded love of God for a love of luxury. Or perhaps they'd just made a

God of luxury.

While he hated the Taliban's use of suicide bombers, their conservative, Sharia religion, their institutionalized brutality…. he admired their loyalty to tribe, family and Allah. He tried not to think about the dismembered bodies ….the innocent wives, children and parents of Taliban soldiers killed by errant bullets, artillery and bombs.

The airport was silent. He walked the length of the concourse before he settled on a shadowed bench behind a partition where he lowered his head onto his carry-on and closed his eyes. He was exhausted. He prayed he wouldn't sleep. He would close his eyes for one minute. No more. His eyelids twitched. A dream formed.

Eight months had passed since Hull and Bauldaire led a column of Humvees, south out of Khost. The column was bait for renewed Taliban activity along the Shimal Khwar valley. The Taliban would be found when terrain and numbers favored the Taliban. Of far greater concern than an ambush were the buried IEDs that could easily turn an armored vehicle into a melted coke can.

In the last six months, Coalition casualties had increased twenty-four percent. Seventy-five NATO and American soldiers were killed in July alone.

Twenty kilometers outside of Khost on the main A-1 Highway, the Humvees crossed the dry Arghandab River where the road continued south toward Sorkh Doz and Qowyrsh. An hour later Hull's lead Humvee stopped next to a rough foundation. A Mosque was being rebuilt out of a pile of dun colored rubble. That afternoon the new construction amounted to a few mud bricks set on uneven footings.

"This rubble once served as al Qaeda's primary training camp." Hull told Bauldaire as they climbed out of the Humvee. "The Coalition bombed the compound a few weeks after 9/11. When the JDAM leveled the mosque, the Coalition figured game over. Osama was in Paradise working through his forty virgins….we were ready to declare victory and go home." Hull skirted a pile of broken bricks. "Unfortunately, that's not the way it played out. Forty al Qaeda were praying when a five hundred pound laser guided hurtled through the roof. The explosion killed all but six."

"I heard bin Laden was wounded." Bauldaire followed Hull up the dirt path.

"Bin Laden was either smart, lucky or had left the building. An unverifiable report claimed he was wounded by shrapnel. Either way, that day, Allah proved to be on OBL's side." Hull surveyed the devastation.

"It would have saved a world of hurt if OBL died. Too bad the JDAM missed him."

"Locals living in the town nearest the mosque hated al Qaeda because they were outsiders--Arabs with a few fundamentalist Afghanis and Pakistanis thrown in. All that changed after the bombs leveled the compound. It was bad timing that the JDAMs hit on the second day of Ramadan. Death converted the al Qaeda trainees into saints."

An Afghan elder was sitting on the uneven wall. Fifty pilgrims crowded the enclosure and he greeted each new arrival. Most were ill or served as caregivers to a sick son, daughter, wife, uncle, parent—the devotion to family was strong when life was fragile. The elder stared at Hull and Bauldaire as they stopped before what was left of the mosque's entry.

A car arrived. The driver stepped out, stared blankly at the two Scout Snipers and opened the back door. The man was old and grimaced as he lifted a young woman off the rear seat.

Hull looked into the face of the ancient Afghan's daughter. She was wasting. Cancer, tuberculosis, hepatitis, she stared with undisguised hope toward the graves. Hull watched until her father stepped around him and laid her next to a marker.

Hundreds of pilgrim's scarves fluttered on lines above the graves. A dust cloud rose on the desert. Hull raised his ballistic goggles, "In death the al Qaeda recruits became Shaheeds--Islamic martyrs who died fighting infidels. This is Afghanistan's Lourdes. Afghanis, Pakistanis and Iranians bring their diseased and wounded, even their infertile wives from Kohat… Kabul, Kandahar."

"Devotion is tricky," Bauldaire turned to check the Humvee. Two Corporals stood guard. "Mother Teresa spent her life caring for Calcutta's poor, sick and dying….these thugs only had to die in the right place at the right time."

Hull watched a man lead his autistic son to the graves.

"If the cure works, their deaths will accomplish more for Afghanistan than two centuries of fighting the British, Russians or Coalition." Noting at an approaching truck, Bauldaire pointed out, "Sir, we're exposed here."

Hull looked at the ragged sedans, trucks and aging four wheel drive Russian jeeps. "Lieutenant," he said. "Even the Taliban won't bomb pilgrims. Allah would never forgive them."

Hull turned from the al Qaeda graves. He knew the Coalition would lose the war. The West would grow war-weary. Politicians in distant parliaments would rise to rail against the cost in men, materiel and crushing deficits. Another two years, or perhaps five…. in the scheme of things, the number wasn't significant. Sooner or later was more accurate. This harsh, dry land and fierce people would drain the youth and wealth of the U.S., Britain, France, Canada, Holland and Germany.

He did not speak of this to Bauldaire. The Lieutenant was young, patriotic and convinced he was fighting the right war in the right land for the right reasons. Hull dared not question his devotion to duty or love of country. He took a last look at the ragged pilgrims praying over graves of men they once hated. Lowering his dark, ballistic goggles, he climbed back into the Humvee.

Hull's eyes opened. He checked the Seiko. One thirty a.m. He'd slept for fifteen minutes. Rising from the bench he knew it was going to be a long night.

British Airways Flight 279 departed on schedule at 10:15 AM. Hull was seated in First Class, row five, on the aisle. Fifteen minutes after the wheels came up, the flight attendant rolled a periodical cart up the aisle. "Something to read, sir? We've got the International Herald Tribune…and if you speak German, Bild Zeitung, …" she checked the stack, "and we have one last Wall Street Journal."

The papers were laid one on the other. Irrespective of language, each paper bore the same front-page photo. Taken with a digital camera mounted to a Swarovski spotting scope, the image framed a man's upper body from waist to turban. A gray beard covered his throat. His eyes were open. Surprise was frozen on his face. His head was cocked at an unnatural angle to the right.

The photo was of Osama bin Laden--two months after he was reportedly killed by the SEAL team in Abbottabad. The front page framed the man Hull shot on the ridgeline. Bauldaire's camera chip had frozen bin Laden just before he pitched face-first into the scree. For the second time in as many months, bin Laden was dead on his feet.

The WSJ headline declared, "Osama bin Laden Killed--Again! President Calls Photo a Fake! Senate and House Republicans Demand Investigation.

The promotions, medals, VIP flights now made sense. It was all part of a President's extraordinary gratitude. And a clear message to reveal nothing about the mission. Ever. What difference did it make when or where bin Laden was killed. He was dead. The President could spin it any way he wanted but he couldn't be caught in a lie.

The WSJ continued, "Since no pictures of the corpse of Osama bin Laden had been released publicly, this photo was the first to surface. It appears to suggest that Al Qaeda's leader was fatally wounded a full two months after the President went before the American people to announce the top secret SEAL mission to Abbottabad had succeeded."

Straightening in his seat, Hull skimmed the second paragraph. "Speaking on behalf of ISAF and NATO commanders in Kabul, Brigadier General. Eric Tremblay denied any knowledge of a second Special Ops team. "We stand by the President's statement. Osama bin Laden was killed in his Abbottabad compound. The photo is fake."

The Herald Tribune declared, "Bin Laden Rises from the Dead! Obama Asks Press Restraint." Hull now knew why Petraeus had ordered them into Pakistan, in Taliban manjammies at night. And why the General had stipulated no headshots. Osama bin Laden. The SEAL raid was too big to keep secret. Someone tipped Pakistan's ISI, who had warned bin Laden. The message was succinct. Get out now. Tonight. Bin Laden had escaped four hours before the raid.

The London Times was equally skeptical of the Abbottabad Raid. "No evidence exists that bin Laden spent all of the last five years in the Abbottabad compound. Reliable intelligence describes him as someone who constantly altered his disguises, surrounded himself with extremely loyal aides, never allowed strangers to approach him, and regularly changed safe houses."

"Unconfirmed sources claim Osama bin Laden was warned by Pakistan's ISI hours before the SEAL team attacked the Abbottabad compound."

"An un-credited video has surfaced of this latest operation. It appears to have been taken on a ridge in Pakistan. After reviewing the footage, intelligence experts from the U.S., Great Britain, and Canada conclude the target was undeniably bin Laden."

The Times story continued, "Of equal importance was the death of Siraj Haqqani, the Taliban battle commander for the Haqqani group. Rumors had circulated that Haqqani had died from complications of diabetes. Intelligence agencies now believe his purported death was a diversion. Frames from the digital video reveal the Pashtun leader was shot through the hips on a mountain trail. While the wound did not immediately kill Haqqani, experts reviewing the footage believe massive internal hemorrhaging and the distance from medical treatment guaranteed death."

A half page photo of Haqqani confirmed he was the telltale Hull shot first. The Times had gotten one detail right. Haqqani had not died quickly. He was still screaming when Hull and Bauldaire backed off the ridge.

Shortly after receiving the news of bin Laden's alleged second death, President Obama released a statement to the American people. "I stand by my statements of May 1st. Osama bin Laden was killed by a Navy SEAL Team acting on years of painstaking work by our intelligence community. The team was helicoptered into the Abbottabad compound where they surprised bin Laden in his bedroom. Bin Laden was killed while reaching for a weapon. In light of the role Osama bin Laden played in planning and financing the attack on the Twin Towers, this nation continues to honor the men of SEAL Team Six who risked their lives to eliminate this international terrorist."

When asked if he had sanctioned any other missions into Pakistan, the President replied succinctly, "I did not. SEAL Team Six killed bin Laden." With that the President ended his statement and exited through a single door.

David Cameron, Prime Minister of Great Britain, carefully admitted, "I'm sure President Obama is correct. The photo is a fake. Bin Laden died two months ago. On that subject, the world's spirit has been lifted by the deaths of these terrorists. We are indebted to the U.S. Navy Seal Team who ended bin Laden's life in Western Pakistan.

France's Sarkozy was more specific, "The French people have suffered terrible losses as a result of Osama bin Laden's terrorist attacks on New York, Spain, Kenya and Tanzania. I do not care if he was killed two months ago, or last month, or yesterday. He is dead. Though the world had hoped to bring bin Laden to trial for orchestrating the brutal attacks on 9/11, it is grateful to the men who administered this rough justice."

Hull skimmed the rest of the carefully worded statements. Leaders representing Colombia, Argentina, Brazil had released measured statements. All were notable not for what they said, but what they didn't. Which story was true. And which wasn't?

Hull wondered who leaked the photo? Someone in Petraeus' office? One of McChrystal's remnant staff who, as payback for firing the General, wished to embarrass the President? Washington ordered the chip burned an hour after its contents had gone viral.

The conflicting story would destroy President Obama's soaring popularity. Which story was true? One that produced no photos and no body. Or one that captured a video freeze frame of bin Laden's head snapping back as bits of bone and flesh exploded out the back of his neck? Had bin Laden truly died two months before?

Hull knew exactly what had gone down.

The four helicopters and forty Seals were four hours too late. They found Bin Laden's wife, his son and a double in the third floor bedroom. All resisted. The wife took a bullet in her tib-fib. The son and double took 5.56 rounds to the face. The SEALs could not afford to disappoint the President. One bearded shot to shit face looked pretty much like every other. The SEALs took blood, skin and brain samples from both corpses, cleaned out the computer files and helied back to the Carl Vinson. Once over the Gulf of Saudi Arabia, in accordance with orders, they kicked the double's body out of the Blackhawk. Osama bin Laden was dead. The President was grateful for their heroism. "Medals?" he answered a reporter's question. "They can pretty much name what they want."

"Hell of a story," Hull's seatmate noted.

Hull looked up from the paper.

"Osama bin Laden," the seatmate leaned over. "I believed the President when he said the SEALs got him last May. Now this comes out. I don't know who to believe. I wonder who shot him this time. What ever, he's a hero. My guess is he'll be on the front page of the New York Times by this weekend."

Hull turned the page.

"I work for an investment firm in Los Angeles. Are you in the market?" The trader wanted to talk. If Hull encouraged him, he'd spill his life story. Ten hours, nonstop.

"No. I don't have time to follow stocks."

"Sorry to hear that. Whether the first time, or second, bin Laden's death is good for the market. It'll be up today."

"Shame to miss that opportunity," Hull tried to end the conversation.

The trader was encouraged. "The seat phones don't work worth a damn over the Atlantic. My only hope is we catch a tail wind and the market opens when we're within range. I need to balance buy and sell orders before it breaks out!" He looked anxiously out the window. "At this point I don't know what to believe. Dead? Alive? Who knows?" He nodded toward the front page. "That photo is worth a thousand words."

At that same moment, the Private First Class who witnessed the firefight at Saker was being interviewed in Jalalabad by an embedded BBC reporter.

"What was the sniper rifle's caliber?" the reporter pressed for details. "When did the battle start? How long did it last? How many Coalition soldiers were killed? How many wounded? Were they regular Army? Marines? How many Taliban were killed?"

Everyone hopes for five minutes of fame and the Private basked in the spotlight. Two minutes into the interview the BBC reporter learned a lone Taliban had appeared on the pass like some avenging Afghani angel.

"His manjammies were torn to hell, turban gone! He was on the run!" the PFC recalled. "The Moolies were no more than a hundred meters behind. Only weapon he had was a pistol with a single bullet left. The Moolies knew it too. Fucker was saving it for the first Taliban to reach him!"

"We went over the wall to save him."

"You personally?" the reporter asked.

The PFC shook his head. "I was ready but the Captain sent two Marines. Then the beat-to-hell-manjammie-Afghan Ghost spoke English! He was a Special Op's Major! A Scout Sniper. Hull. Major Hull. We'd all heard of the Major, but no one had seen him. He was a myth, maybe real, most likely not. Yet there he was coming over the fucking parapet, kicking ass, handing out orders. A real warrior hero!"

"Once in the bunker the Major shot the shit out of the attacking Moolies. The .50 cal lit them up. Heads, chests…he didn't miss. A hundred rounds, a hundred dead. The hillside looked like the killing room in a slaughterhouse! Fucking awesome!"

"Hull?" the BBC reporter scribbled on a spiral pad. "And he's a Major?"

"That's correct, Sir."

"And a Scout Sniper?"

The PFC nodded, but barely. Aware that he might have said too much, he suddenly said, "but that's off the record."

"Private," the BBC reporter replied in a cool British accent, "In war, nothing is off the record. If you don't want me to use your name, that's your option. But Major Hull is definitely on the record!" He continued to write in his notepad.

The story didn't require confirmation from General Tremblay. It grew legs on spec alone. The reporter filed with BBC's Kabul office an hour later. Senior Army staff in Kabul were asked to verify the story. "No comment," was taken as "Yes." Kabul forwarded the story to London, and while half a dozen senior editors were fact checking, a Pakistani copyeditor forwarded the story to Al Jazeera.

The death of bin Laden and Haqqani had dealt a severe blow to al Qaeda and the Taliban. At heart, the Muslim extremists were simple people. They would seek to avenge bin Laden's death. Hull's name, his location, his family would be worth a great deal. Al Qaeda would soon have his address, phone numbers and the names of his closest relatives.

Chapter 10

Qari Yousuf Azad was the fifth son of Jahid Azad, an illiterate farmer who cultivated poppies on ten acres south of Kunduz. Raised in a three room stone hut that had sheltered five generations of Azad's ancestors, Qari Yousuf's early years were defined by periodic starvation, winter's bitter cold and summer's scorching heat that left him with a single change of clothes and no knowledge of life outside his small valley.

While he was still quite young, it became clear that Qari Azad possessed a remarkable intelligence.

He was six when he knocked on the Mullah's gate. Unflinching beneath the old man's dark gaze, he asked, "Will you teach me to read?"

After some minutes of thought, the Mullah said, "If we begin, you cannot stop, even when you want to play, eat, or work in the fields. Do you understand?"

Qari Yousuf Azad was honored.

Sitting on a bench in the Mullah's courtyard, the ancient, henna-bearded man and the young, black-haired boy opened the village's only book--the Koran. This first introduction to Islam colored Qari Azad's life. Everything he subsequently read or learned was filtered through that holy religious text. The Mullah soon wondered if his first name "Qari," or "One who had memorized the Koran," was divinely inspired.

Qari Azad quickly learned to recognize words and sentences, paragraphs and pages. And, when he wasn't reading, he proved to be a gifted mimic.

During the Russian occupation, on the occasions when their convoys passed through the valley, Qari Azad listened to their shouted orders and private conversations. He then exactly repeated their words, the movement of their hands and their facial expressions. The young boy with the opaque eyes amused the Russian infantrymen. A few spoke to him. Others wasted a few minutes correcting his grammar. In this way he memorized phrases that would serve him well.

Foreign armies had hammered Afghanistan's borders into their modern shape. Starting with the Greek invaders and later the Mongols, Indians, Pakistanis, British and Russians, three centuries of war bred fierce marksmen. By the age of twelve, Qari Azad could empty a full AK47 clip into a target at two hundred meters.

It was three months after his thirteenth birthday when the Mujahideen dragged a Russian captive into his father's compound. Bloodied and frightened, the young soldier's hands were tied behind his back. Qari Azad judged he was close to the same age as Hamad, his older brother.

Brushing Azad's father and brothers aside, the Mujahideen Commander kicked the Russian to the dirt floor. "Which of you speak Russian?" the Commander demanded.

A few seconds passed before Qari stepped forward. "I speak a little," he replied. He had begun to show the first dark shadow on his jaw.

"A little is enough," the Commander pulled him in front of the Russian.

The young soldier was a conscript who told Qari that he only took orders--when to rise, when to move, when to eat and when to shit. He knew nothing, had never seen a map, and couldn't read one if he had. The Mujahideen cared little for the truth. As a matter of revenge, they tortured him. Starting with his feet, they worked up his body while the teenager screamed his ignorance. Qari knew more Russian than he revealed. The soldier was telling the truth--he was not privy to the Russian Army's plans. Tiring of his shrieks, the Mujahideen Commander honored Qari Yousuf Azad.

"Finish him the halal way!" the Mujahideen Commander ordered.

To his lasting credit in the fighter's eyes, Qari did not hesitate. On the Commander's signal, he drew a knife through the young Russian's throat. He felt no remorse, only surprise when the soldier's carotid arteries fountained

99

blood onto his right hand.

One at a time, the Mujahideen soldiers nodded to the twelve year old. It was the ultimate gesture of respect.

Word traveled about Qari Azad's fluency in Russian. Two months later a Mullah from the Kunduz Madrassa presented himself at Jahid Azad's door.

A traditional cup of tea offered by Qari's father preceded the purpose behind his forty-kilometer journey. "It is said you have a son who is in possession of a remarkable talent," the Mullah set his empty cup on the rough table.

"I have been blessed by Allah. I have many sons," Jahid Azad signaled his wife to remove the cup. He leaned back against the mud brick central wall and waited for the Mullah to get to the point.

"As I can see," the religious teacher nodded politely. "They are all strong and devout?"

"Praise be to Allah," Jahid Azad straightened his robe.

The Mullah smiled. "I am interested in the son who speaks Russian."

Jahid Azad nodded with sudden understanding, "Allah has blessed him." How Qari had learned the Russian's language was a mystery. As with his dark hair and dark eyes, it appeared to be first nature.

The Mullah had no doubt Qari could be of use. A student who spoke Russian would be a valuable addition at the school. "His talent requires attention."

"Yes, his ability is rare," his father signaled for Qari to join them. "But he is needed at home." Perhaps there was a way to profit from his fifth son's strange talent. Mullahs were wealthy. Qari's talent for language could be worth as much as twenty thousand afghanis. Jahid Azad had five other sons. Shouldn't the youngest help the oldest?

The Mullah frowned at the ensuing silence. The father had removed his teacup. He was well aware of what Jahid Azad desired. He could not afford to pay what the farmer wished, and instead, in the way of Afghanistan mountain tribes, began to bargain. "An education is valuable. Plant the seed in fertile ground and the tree will bear fruit. Cast it among rocks and it will die."

Jahid Azad was less concerned about Qari's education than making enough afghanis to pay for a dowry, or the spring planting. "He will be my light in my old age, which now rapidly approaches." The passing years had stiffened his limbs and it was with difficulty that Jahid now drew his heels closer to his body.

"I do not doubt that is true, but would you not want him to defend Allah?" the Mullah glanced at the dark eyed boy.

"Perhaps we could agree on a figure to serve Allah. I am thinking of twenty-five thousand afghanis."

"That is impossible."

"But, if as you say, Qari's talents could be of service to Allah, perhaps a figure could be agreed upon that would benefit one of his devoted true believers."

Qari Asad never learned what amount the Mullah and his father agreed upon—but he knew a stack of afghanis was exchanged, not insignificant, as an advance, with a promise of further payments when the boy proved his worth. Three days later Qari Yousuf Azad was assigned a desk at a madrassa in Khost.

The Mullah could not know that, despite Qari Yousuf Azad's humble beginnings, he was a direct descendant of Ahmad Shah Abdali, the first Pashtun king of Afghanistan. On Qari Yousuf's second day in the Madrassa, the Mullah described how Ahmad Shah was born in Herat to the hereditary chief of the Abdali tribe. Within months of his ascendancy Ahmad Shah Abdali had changed his name to Ahmad Shah Durrani. In Persian, it meant "pearl of pearls." During the course of Ahmad Shah's reign he founded the Durrani Empire and between 1747-67, looted the treasures of the Mogul Empire from Delhi and captured the Golden Temple in Amritsar. After slaughtering the Hindu's sacred cows, Ahmad Durrani dumped their carcasses into the temple's well. For a year afterward, the holy water tasted of their blood. The desecration enraged Marathas' Hindu chiefs who launched a holy war against Ahmad Shah. Laughing at the Indian armies, he fought on. It took a decade for the Sikhs to drive his cohorts out of Punjab. Not, however, before he established a dynasty for his son, Timur.

Qari Azad had studied at the madrassa for less than a year when the Russians came for him. Azad's kidnapping, like all things of the Soviet Union, was brutal but effective. Armed with AK-74 Kalashnikovs, the

5.45 millimeter paratrooper assault rifles, four Russians paratroopers in camouflaged battle fatigues stormed the school.

The Russians knew who they wanted. Given the choice of standing by while tanks bulldozed the madrassa, the Mullah reluctantly led them to Azad's classroom. Qari Azad was practicing the Cyrillic alphabet, when the Paratroopers kicked open the classroom door. Panic eddied through the students. One stood and started to run.

"Nyet!" Sergeant Vladimir Yezhov was low-level KGB, a tall, close-cropped, thickly muscled man who regarded his posting to Afghanistan as a sentence worse than a Siberian factory town. Yezhov slapped the boy back into his seat.

Sweeping the room with his dark eyes, Yezhov demanded, "Which one of you filthy little bastards is Qari Yousuf Azad?" His accent mangled Pashto, turning the lyric language into a guttural snarl.

Azad remained sitting, his face impassive, third from the front in the second row.

"Qari Yousuf Azad, stand up!" Yezhov roared in Pashto. He produced a 6P9 Pistolet Besshumny, a crude but effective Russian silenced pistol. Waving the 6P9 above the student's heads, he repeated, "AZAD! Who is AZAD?" Still, Qari Azad did not stand. Yezhov calmly pointed his pistol at Muhammad Qasim Jangulbagh, who sat in the last desk in the central row and pulled the trigger. The cross-eyed boy toppled backward out of his seat. Yezhov's expression did not change. "Qari Yousuf Azad--you will stand!"

Two seats behind him, Arash, a fragile boy who was ill-suited to the madrassa's religious discipline, wet his pants and stared unblinking at Qari Azad. Yezhov followed Arash's stare and crooked a thick finger at the implacable dark-eyed boy. Azad surveyed the room for an escape, and finding none, stood. The Russians led him from his seat to an armored personnel carrier. The boy quickly realized that there was little hope of resistance. Instead, he asked in roughly accented Russian, "Where are you taking me?"

"You'll learn soon enough," Yezhov growled in primitive Pashto.

Qari Azad was driven to the Kunduz airport where he and a dozen other students were shoved into a Russian military cargo jet. In the future he would equate the engine roar, rush of power and shrinking ground with losing his family. The Russians believed the Mujahideen had used Azad's village as a base to attack supply convoys. Two months after he boarded the jet to Moscow, soldiers leveled the stone compounds. The commanding Russian Colonel dismissed the deaths of Azad's father, mother, four brothers and thirty other villagers as collateral damage.

The day he arrived in Moscow, Qari Azad was driven to Lubyanka, the monolithic yellow brick building that housed the KGB National Headquarters. Located on Lubyanka Square in downtown Moscow during Stalin's rule the prison was a staging station for deportation to the Gulags. Few who passed through its thick walls survived and thousands were executed in Lubyanka's dungeons for real or imagined crimes.

Run by Chekists, of whom one Vladimir Putin, would later become President of Russia, Lubyanka terrified Soviet citizens. In thousands of unrecorded cases a simple summons offered sufficient reason to commit suicide.

The square facing the yellow building was dominated by a fourteen-ton statue of Felix Dzerzhinsky, who headed the Soviet Secret Police, GPU, OGPU, NKVD and KGB. Qari Yousuf Azad was dragged from a rusting van through a side door into a poorly lit hallway. Led to a concrete cell, he was issued a uniform, a toothbrush, a cup, a thin blanket and roll of toilet paper.

The boy soon learned that the Russians harbored a deep hatred for all things Afghan. They used a Russian synonym for the English "Nigger" to describe Afghans.

The KGB Director arbitrarily changed Azad's first name to Rostislov. He laughed when the young student translated it aloud in Russian.

"Usurp glory!" Qari Yousuf Azad nodded with a faint smile of gratitude. Because he was able to pronounce "Azad," the Director let his last name stand. It was a small concession, but a foolish decision. In the coming years, his last name would provide hope and a promise to the Pashtuns.

Two weeks after Qari Rostislov Azad entered Lubyanka, Yezhov dragged him from his cell. The massive Sergeant was holding a white Alsatian puppy by the scruff of her neck. The puppy squirmed with pain until Yezhov thrust her into the boy's arms. A recessive white German Shepherd, she was six weeks old, had an intelligent black nose, black gums and black roof of her mouth. Azad held the puppy awkwardly against his chest. The young Alsatian smelled his face then gently licked his ear.

Yezhov proved to be unrelentingly brutal. The boy was not permitted to speak and learned to trust no one, to bring a deep suspicion to any gesture, sadistic or otherwise. He did not trust Yezhov, and the gift of a puppy confused him.

"You will train the dog to obey," The massive Sergeant ordered. "For now, she will serve in place of the men you will ultimately lead. In a year, I expect her to learn every voice command, every hand signal, and every expression. You will feed her, train her and test her. And, you will be judged by her behavior," Yezhov stared at him.

That night Rostislov Azad found a cup for water and partially chewed the gristle from his dinner to soften it for her. The hungry puppy sniffed and took it from his hand. From that moment on the smell of Rostislov Azad was linked to her food.

That night, one minute before lights out, Yezhov entered Azad's room. The Sergeant smelled of vodka. He glanced at the puppy and pointed to the damp concrete. "The dog sleeps on the floor. You will be punished if I catch her on the bed."

Flipping the rusty light switch, Yezhov locked the door. The puppy started to whimper. Her cries quickly increased to a loud, mournful howl. In an attempt to quiet her, Rostislov Azad made a thin bed from his jacket. The puppy howled disconsolately. Desperate to silence her, Azad squeezed her muzzle. The puppy yanked free and doubled her volume. If Yezhov heard the howling he would return. Shivering on his bed, he did not doubt the massive Russian Sergeant would exact a painful punishment. Rostislov Azad knew the dog could not sleep on the bed and carefully pulled his blanket off the thin mattress and spread it on the damp concrete. The puppy curled against him and quieted. For that night, and every night for the next eight years, Rostislov Azad joined the dog on the cold floor.

He named her Sacha, or "Protector of Man." The white puppy grew to honor the meaning. At eighteen months, she stood fifty-eight centimeters at the withers and weighed thirty-four kilograms. Sacha was extraordinarily intelligent. By the age of four months, Azad had taught her signals for sit, down and come. At night, with his face buried in her thick coat, her soft growl alerted him to footsteps in the hall. Azad groomed her each morning, brushing her thick white coat free of the soft insulating fur that lay beneath the strong guard hairs. He fed her the best food he could bribe from Lubyanka's cooks and used his own toothbrush to clean her long, white teeth. He checked her ears for fleas, and walked her each day.

Together for twenty-four hours a day, Azad was convinced Sacha could read his mind. When they were alone in the cell and he kneeled on the concrete and turned toward Mecca, she settled next to him, her head resting on her paws, her breathing steady, patient, as she waited for him to rise. At night, when he whispered memorized passages from the Koran, her tongue touched his cheek.

He trained her to alert him to the presence of enemies, of booby traps and the wounded. Bomb detection, search and rescue, the pure white Alsatian exceeded the KGB's highest standards. Azad took extraordinary pride when she bested Lubyanka's other Shepherds during the quarterly trials run between other, captive Afghan boys. After his mother, he loved only Sacha--her dark eyes, her intelligence, and long forgotten within Lubyanka's stone walls, her loyalty.

Her single flaw was her hatred of Yezhov. Azad lived in constant fear of a confrontation and when it appeared in the guise of Sacha's deep growl and bared teeth, the boy realized he was powerless to affect the outcome.

Gesturing to the white dog, Yezhov said, "The next time she exposes her teeth to me, she dies."

Of all the lessons learned in Lubyanka, Yezhov's warning burned into Azad's heart.

A year after Qari Yousuf Azad arrived, two hundred angry Russian citizens surrounded Dzerzhinsky's statue. Chains snaked from the crowd up and around the hated monument, and as Azad and his white Alsatian watched from a third story window, the statue was ripped from its pedestal.

Sacha was constantly at his side as Azad memorized the details of Lubyanka Square, every window, every drunk slumped in every doorway and every gray bureaucrat plodding to work. Over the course of eight years, ninety-six months, twenty nine hundred days...he would come to know the exact number of tiles in Lubyanka's parquet floors and the precise shade of pale green that colored the walls. He would study the history of the Palladian and Baroque architecture, the importance of the classic Russian palace façade and the accuracy of the central clock that marked the passage of the days, weeks and years. As the years passed he focused less on his family in Kunduz and more on Sacha.

By the time he was twenty, Rostislov Azad spoke Pashto, Dari, Russian, English and Spanish, nearly without accent. He had a working knowledge of French and could speak it well enough to pass through the European Union border controls. He was highly intelligent, read constantly—books on Western History, culture, art, music—studies which convinced him the West was rotting from the core outward. America, Great Britain, France, Italy, all would soon fall to Islam's holy warriors.

The KGB taught Rostislov Azad battlefield first aid and basic battlefield surgery. KGB operatives knew that saving one, or half a dozen soldiers would generate the respect and devotion to duty that the Afghan Mujahadeen revered. Rostislov Azad had a working knowledge of the Physician's Desk Reference and was well-versed in the effects of psychoactive drugs Ethanol, Scopolamine and Temazepam. The best drug was developed for the KGB. Known as SP-17, it had no taste, smell, color, or immediate side effects. It simply loosened the subject's tongue. One critical advantage was that subjects had no memory of the interview. They could only recall falling asleep.

The KGB injected Rostislov with SP-17 twice. His Russian instructors needed to know if he harbored secrets, plots or smoldering anger against the Soviet Union, the KGB, or any of the handlers who had monitored his waking and sleeping hours. They administered the maximum dosage of SP-17, but discovered nothing that triggered alarms. Rostislov could recite his lessons with photographic clarity. During interviews conducted under the effects of SP-17 he conversed about the day, poetry, geography and Marxist-Leninist philosophy, but never, ever revealed a private thought. Rather than alarming his handlers, it reassured them. They would far prefer an agent who had dutifully recited and honored the book than one who read it and then applied it in a haphazard and dangerous manner.

Yezhov had one final test.

It was early morning, still dark when the Sergeant opened Rostislov's door. Sacha had alerted him seconds before Yezhov's hand touched the handle. When Yezhov opened the door, Rostislov was fully awake, sitting on the edge of the bed, his right hand clamped firmly around the Alsatian's muzzle.

Yezhov's eyes flicked from the dog to Rostislov's naked, muscled body. "Get dressed," he ordered. He watched until Rostislov stood fully clothed, then led Sacha down the hallway to a staircase that descended to Lubyanka's catacombs. Fear eddied through Rostislov as the Sergeant led him deeper into the damp basement. Many of the bulbs had burned out and the hall alternated bright pools of light with black shadows. Yezhov stopped in front of a steel door. There had been many other nights when drunk on vodka, Yezhov had dragged the terrified boy into other rooms. Yezhov, however, was focused on Sacha, not Rostislov.

Opening the door he pointed toward the dark interior. "In!" he ordered. Rostislov hesitantly stepped inside. Sacha followed obediently at heel. Yezhov turned on the light, a single, hundred-watt bulb glowing from a broken fixture. Rostislov's eyes swept the room. A hemp rope, tied in a slipknot hung from a rusted pulley, was anchored in the concrete ceiling. Nodding to the rope, Yezhov ordered, "Tie the dog's rear legs."

For once, Rostislov hesitated. Fear gripped him as he asked, "Why?" Eight years had passed since Yezhov dragged him from the madrassa. Rostislov again searched for an escape. The concrete room revealed no exit other than the door behind the Russian sergeant.

"I said, tie her!" Yezhov yelled, his voice bouncing between the damp concrete floor and ceiling.

Sacha curiously watched as Rostislov, slipped one, then her other hind leg in the noose.

"Now raise her," Yezhov ordered.

When Rostislov hesitated, the Sergeant drew a 6P9 Pistolet from his leather holster.

"I said raise her," Yezhov's tone allowed no objection.

Tears swelled behind Rostislov's eyes as he forced his hands onto the rope. His biceps locked, his forearms clenched, the pulley moved. Sacha struggled to walk on her front legs, and then swung free, her alert ears brushing the concrete.

Her head was a foot off the ground when Yezhov pointed to a turnbuckle mounted on the wall and ordered, "Secure her!"

Rostislov realized there was no turning back. His fingers resisted double knotting the rope. Her eyes locked on Rostislov's face. Sacha turned in slow, three hundred degree circles. She whined softly.

He knew it was a question. She was curious. What did he require? If he would show, or tell her, she would be happy to obey. He only needed to teach her.

Long before Yezhov lifted a lead-weighted whip from a hook on the wall, Rostislov understood what came next.

The Russian held the whip out. The handle was worn. It had been used for years. "This is a final test of loyalty--yours and hers."

"And if I refuse," Rostislov made no move to accept it. Hanging by her heels, her ears and eyes alert, Sacha watched the two men.

"Then neither of you will leave this room alive. You, the dog, it makes no difference to me."

A muscle quivered in Rostislov's jaw. His hand closed around the coiled whip. He fought to erase memories of his years with the dog. The months he had devoted to teaching her, the food they shared, the uncounted hours he had confessed his hopes and fears as she listened, her eyes unblinking, her ears erect on her beautiful head. He thought of the thousand of nights they shared the concrete floor of this cell and how she warned him when Yezhov approached the door. For one, desperate moment, he wanted to bring the weighted whip across Yezhov's face, grab the Pistolet and empty it into the massive Sergeant's chest.

But Rostislov knew killing Yezhov would trigger his own death. There was no escape from Lubyanka. Sacha would never leave the concrete bunker. Rostislov would suffer for weeks until he too died. He took a deep silent breath and unrolled the whip. His first stroke hit Sacha once, lightly, across the withers. He had never hit her before and now the Alsatian looked at him, curious, trying to understand the point of the painful lesson.

Yezhov looked at the whip, then at Rostislov and the dog. The arms of his shirt bulged with massive knots of muscle as his hand closed around the whip. "You misjudge me," he muttered. Yanking the whip away, he brought it savagely across Rostislov's back. Yezhov watched the glistening leather slash through Rostislov's cotton shirt. The powerful stroke raised a bloody stripe from shoulder to hip. Rostislov did not shrink away. He would gladly accept a severe beating in place of the dog.

"Your caress served as a lesson--mine tested loyalty," Yezhov explained the difference. Pointing the Pistolet at Rostislov's forehead, he ordered, "Test the dog's loyalty!"

Rostislov would never forget the following hour. No dog had ever survived Yezhov's test for more than fifteen minutes. Sacha endured for fifty-seven. Three minutes short of an hour, in the last seconds of her life, the red stripes had changed her thick white coat into a bloody rag. Whipped to the edge of death, the blood dripped from her teeth as the Alsatian swung toward Rostislov's legs. Sacha closed her powerful jaws an inch from his leg. Once. It was her last act, the wild animal trying to save its life.

Tears locked behind Rostislov's eyes. He would have welcomed her bite but Yezhov refused to permit it. Pointing his Pistolet at Rostislov, the Sergeant snarled, "You owe her nothing. It is a dog! Expendable! Soldiers, family, women, children, the old and young--all are expendable! Your loyalty belongs to your leaders alone, no one--nothing else." He squared to Rostislov. The Pistolet's circular black muzzle was still trained on his face. "Your life belongs to the Motherland! Nothing else, no woman, no man! Only the Motherland! The Motherland! Do you understand?"

Rostislov understood the consequences of a wrong answer. He looked from the dog to his blood spattered arms and from the whip to the Pistolet and Yezhov's square, vodka-veined face.

"Who owns your loyalty?" Yezhov pressured the Pistolet's trigger.

No emotion crossed Rostislov's face as he answered. "Our Leaders."

Yezhov's heavy voice detonated through the square room, "Say it with conviction!"

"The Great Leaders of the Union of Soviet Socialist Republics," Rostislov Azad raised his voice.

Behind him Sacha began to spasm. Her quivering legs and belly muscles swung her in a slow arc that brought her muzzle in contact with his leg. Facing Yezhov, Rostislov felt her tongue touch his calf. In the years ahead he would try to convince himself that she was dead. Hanging limply from her mouth, her bloody tongue had simply brushed against him.

Yezhov lowered the Pistolet and looked as the swinging dog continued to slowly circle past Rostislov. Jerking the whip from Rostislov's clenched fist, he ordered, "Get out."

Rostislov looked at Sacha. Dark eyes open, bloody ears brushing the concrete floor, the dog was still.

Yezhov read little into Rostislov's slumping shoulders. Nor could he detect the deep hatred that burned behind the Afghan's black irises. In time that hatred would grow to encompass sex, women and the reach of national governments.

Rostislov Azad reappeared on a crowded street in Kabul four months later. He was twenty-two, weighed 77 kilos and though he had a powerful chest, arms and legs, was not heavy. He had let his glistening black beard grow which fell onto his upper chest. His black hair descended to his shoulders. He wore a black turban and was fastidious in his dress and bearing. He was neither handsome nor unappealing. He was anonymous. Shave his beard, cut his hair in a short Western part, dress him in a good suit, designer tie and shoes, and he could have easily passed for European. He was an expert in the use of Russian and NATO small arms, possessed a genetic, almost rat-like ability to cross borders, board planes and slip past local police and national security. He also harbored a deep hatred for all things Russian.

Walking into dusty Central Kabul bus station, Rostislov Azad had the finest education the USSR Secret Service could provide. Russian by education, killer by profession, he was KGB-trained to organize Mujahideen cells against the Russians themselves.

He boarded a bus to Kandahar and kept his distance from the other passengers. He looked Pashtun, dressed Pashtun and spoke a Pashtun dialect. Even his mission matched his heritage. The Mujahideen were shooting Hinde helicopters down with CIA-supplied Stinger Missiles. The KGB instructed him to contact Mujahideen cadres. They were confident that through Rostislov, the cadres could be secretly controlled by Moscow. What the KGB never realized was that within days after Rostislov Azad contacted the Mujahideen, he led the cadres on double blind missions--raids against Bagram Air Base, Kabul weapons depots, and Russian collaborators. The cadres took enormous pleasure in torturing Russian soldiers and Afghan traitors. The methodical dismemberment played well on videos they would later deliver to the Russian compounds.

The Russians never discovered that while Rostislov Azad's mission was to generate Anti-Soviet opposition through ineffective, compromised Mujahideen political and fighting units, he used his training and links to the

Russian High Command to counter troop movements and alert Mujahideen commanders.

Searching among his fighters, he would promote a weak, rank and file soldier. Weeks later he would then betray him to the Russians. Compared to the millions of Afghan civilians who died during the Soviet occupation, one poor rifleman was a minor martyrdom that honored Allah. Like a suicide bomber, one life, or later two dozen, bought credibility, trust—if such a word could be applied to his KGB handlers.

By the time the Russians withdrew in February of 1989, Rostislov Azad commanded two thousand Mujahideen warriors. In the months that followed he transferred his allegiance to the Taliban Militia and was on the front lines in late September of 1996 when the Taliban captured Kabul from the Northern Alliance. Present at the public execution of deposed President Najibullah, he pushed his way forward to thrust a knife into the terrified leader.

Along with lessons detailing the placement of PW-5A Plastic Explosive, his years in Lubyanka infected him with remorseless sadism. Eight years of beatings and rapes in Lubyanka's dungeon fueled his hatred for Yezhov, the Russians and, because he was forced to serve as a whore, the weakness of women who were put on earth to serve men.

Rostislov was not raised around women. He had no sisters, and as the years passed, could barely remember his mother's face. Yezhov had violated Rostislov for years, and he now equated sex with torture. He prayed, one day, to capture the Sergeant, castrate him and watch him bleed out.

Rostislov had never been with a woman, knew of their nakedness only through books on anatomy that split them like hogs, head to toe, to display the brain, glands, cavities and folds. Lacking a man's parts, they were inferior, worthy only to prepare food and bear children. The thought of sex with a woman, thrusting himself into their dark recess, filled him with disgust and a faint, inexplicable fear.

Women could not be trusted. Girls, wives, mothers—all needed to be controlled. He rejoiced when the Taliban imposed an extreme interpretation of Sharia law. Women were to remain covered in public. None could appear on the street without a male relative to escort them. Education was forbidden.

Women's crimes included speaking to unrelated men, laughing, clapping, listening to music and exposing any skin. Rostislov never lost control, even when he joined the Mullahs who whipped women with thin, heavy cables. His devotion to Allah deafened him to the women's cries of pain as his slashing cable raised bloody, crosshatched stripes across their burkas.

To Rostislov, the punishment matched the crime. Disobedience, infidelity, sex, all cried out for public stoning.

In the summer of 1998 Rostislov stopped on the outskirts of Mazar-i-Sharif in northwest Afghanistan. A millennium old, and populated by three hundred thousand Uzbeks and Tajiks who lived alongside the Turkmen, Hazara, and Pashtun minorities, the city was famous for the Blue Mosque. Religious scholars believe the mosque was built over the tomb of Ali ibn Abi Talib, the cousin and son-in-law of the Prophet Muhammad.

In 1998, Mazar-i-Sharif was the last major city controlled by the United Front. The year before, two-thousand Taliban fighters had died at the hands of General Malik Pahlawan. Soon after Pahlawan negotiated a treaty, the Taliban turned their backs on the agreement and began to disarm local Hazara Hizb-i Wahdat fighters. The Hazara retaliated and, during an ensuing battle, the Taliban were decimated by General Pahlawan's superior forces.

Rostislov believed the Taliban's account. The Hazaras executed two thousand Taliban prisoners then left the bodies to rot.

Marked by ancient ruins and broad streets, Afghanistan's fourth largest city offered few defenses. When the avenging Taliban appeared on the main road into the city, General Abdul Malik betrayed the local governor Abdul Rashid Dostem, and fled.

No warning was raised, no threat noted. Mazar-i-Sharif's women walked along the road. Men drank tea in crowded cafes. Cart drivers whipped donkeys through traffic. Caravan traders rode horses to the open-air markets. Children played in the alleys.

Standing in the beds of Toyota Hilux pickup trucks, the Taliban entered Mazar-i-Sharif from the west. Rostislov stood in the third pickup in a convoy of thirty. The Hazara were easily recognizable. Facial features carried south from the steppes of Russia and Mongolia's fertile river valleys marked them for death.

The first two Toyota pickups entered without firing. Then Rostislov's heavy machine gun opened up, smashing men, women and children against storefronts. Shooting Hazaras sharpened the skills Rostislov had been taught beneath Lubyanka Square. The pickups raced through the city, machine-gunning any man who bore the distinctive features of the native Hazara. He watched his bullets rip through the Hazara women who shunned the burka and walked the streets in headscarves, exposed faces and bare arms. Turning at the Mazar-i-Sharif's central market, Rostislov made a second pass, then a third. During the next two hours he took pleasure in the power of the machine gun, and how the stream of heavy slugs devastated the Hazara.

In time Rostislov abandoned the heavy machine gun and walked down the side streets, searching for the wounded. Tracking blood trails that crawled into alleys, shops and houses, Rostislov dispatched survivors with his dagger's straight blade. His signature Halal-slash across the jugular bore little difference from how Rostislov killed goats. The Hazara were not worthy of the word "enemy." They were vermin who deserved extermination.

On the second day Rostislov went house to house. He kicked open the first door and a Hazara holding a knife lunged toward him. Rostislov's Kalashnikov stopped the squat, solid father and his two brothers before they reached him. The heavy, jacketed rounds drove them back against the wall.

He then turned to the daughters who huddled behind their terrified mother. Offering her own life in exchange, she begged him to spare her children. In the end success and failure served as life's most consistent promise. Some succeeded, some failed. He remembered Sacha. He had tried and failed to protect her. Watching Sacha die, Rostislov had silently promised never to fail again. Never.

The Hazara woman's life amounted to little more than her birth, a lifetime of struggle and then death. Why should she now be allowed to trade a life of so little value for her daughters? Why should she succeed where Rostislov had not? If she saved her children, her death could be viewed as a victory.

There was nothing remarkable in how the mother accepted his dagger. In the seconds before the terror faded from her eyes, Rostislov read the question. It was always, the same, fragmentary lament, "My children?"

Without their mother's protection, the daughters would survive her by days, no more. Rostislov's dagger offered the gift of peace. The girls died with one thrust. The youngest first, then the older, they felt only the briefest pain. The mother would be grateful.

For three days the Taliban leadership refused to allow relatives to claim or bury the dead. The corpses were left to bloat in the blistering summer sun where the dogs gorged on the exposed muscles and the vultures tore at the intestines, stomachs and livers. By the third day the vultures and dogs were stuffed with rotten flesh. Then the dogs went mad and attacked the vultures that were too heavy to fly.

The stench finally overwhelmed the Taliban commanders who allowed the widows and children to drag the mangled corpses to shallow graves.

In total, over eight thousand Hazaras and Tajiks died in Mazar-i-Sharif. Rostislov believed it was the beginning of a Holy War. When he relived those six days, the steady hammering of the heavy machine gun as the women and children scattered screaming before him…he believed the hand of Allah had guided him.

Chapter 11

R ostislov Azad met Osama bin Laden in 1996, four months after the Saudi was driven from the Sudan. No one recorded the exact day bin Laden arrived in Afghanistan. What was known is that he quickly caused trouble. Even as he used his millions to build a training camp outside Kandahar, he alienated Taliban leaders with declarations of war and Fatwa murders of real, or imagined enemies. Within weeks of bin Laden's scheduled extradition to Saudi Arabia, he arranged the marriage of his eldest daughter to Taliban leader Mullah Omar's son. The resulting political alliance earned the Taliban's protection and despite continued Saudi demands for bin Laden's extradition, Mullah Omar allowed him to remain in Afghanistan.

Washington had overlooked a critical reason behind Mullah Omar's support for bin Laden. The Pashtun concept of hospitality is revered in Pushtunwali--their code of honor. Based on sanctuary and revenge, the Pashtun belief system commands that they provide protection to those who seek refuge among them. The Pashtun tribal belief in sanctuary explains why they refused to betray Osama bin Laden for America's fifty million-dollar-reward. Money had nothing to do with their support. Honor was wedded to their culture and religion.

Word of Osama Bin Laden's arrival in Afghanistan traveled quickly. Rostislov was in Khost when he learned of the Saudi's planned jihad. Like many young Afghanis, Rostislov was drawn to bin Laden's intelligence, self-denial and devotion to Islam. It took Rostislov a month to find the messianic leader of Al Qaeda. Bin Laden, in turn, immediately recognized the value of Rostislov's education and experience. Observing Rostislov at prayers, bin Laden invited him to join his Koran study group.

For Rostislov it was an honor beyond measure.

Two months later he was selected to serve as one of bin Laden's bodyguards. When seventy cruise missiles exploded across Afghanistan on August 20 of 1998, Osama bin Laden survived in large part because of Rostislov's medical training.

In gratitude, bin Laden asked the young Afghan to lead a company in the O55 Brigade. While the Taliban fought with worn out AK-47s, bin Laden's millions supplied the 055 Brigade with new assault rifles, satellite phones, Night Vision goggles, and on occasion, airplanes.

Though numbers in the 055 Brigade were rarely less than one thousand or more than two thousand, it suffered significant losses in the 2001 war with the United States. With the skies controlled by the ISAF Jets and helicopter gun ships and the ground swept by armored personnel-carriers, the survivors retreated to the Afghan-Pakistan border, where they joined bin Laden for what promised to be a long, bloody campaign.

It was bin Laden who planned the assassination of Northern Alliance leader Ahmad Shah Massoud but it was Rostislov who trained the Saudi bombers traveling on Tunisian passports, and Rostislov who built the camera bomb that killed Massoud.

The KGB had taught him well. Torture, dismemberment, blinding-- nothing, including savagery of the most violent form, bothered him. He owed a debt to Mongols who swept out of Asia in 1219 to raze the ancient cities of Balk and Heart, burning and killing until bodies rose above the stone walls. In a strange paradox, Rostislov Azad became more devout as he grew more savage.

Bin Laden selected Rostislov to lead the cadre who flew the commercial airliners into the Twin Towers. It was Rostislov who taught the hijackers how to cut the flight attendants throats with box cutters. He knew the women's screams and bloody deaths would freeze the panicked passengers in their seats. As September 11, 2001 approached, bin Laden changed his plans. Rostislov was a fire-and-forget weapon who could be aimed from a great distance years before the target appeared, and still accomplish his mission. He was too valuable to martyr. Others would take his place.

Following the collapse of the Twin Towers, bin Laden and the surviving al Qaeda retreated deeply into FATA caves where the Taliban kept them supplied with food and arms. In return, bin Laden's wealthy relatives and sympathetic associates found ways to smuggle cash to keep the Jihadist's struggle alive.

Rostislov fought beside bin Laden for five hard years. In that time the unmanned Predators exacted a terrible price; few houses escaped their infrared cameras, few movements went unnoticed. Bin Laden never traveled in groups. Two intensely loyal bodyguards accompanied him whenever he moved from a safe house, cave or mountain stone hut. Rostislov was always one of the two. As they moved from safe house to cave, bin Laden gradually took the place of Jahid Azad, the father Rostislov lost to the Russians.

Rostislov was never surprised. An instinctual ability to ferret out traitors and avoid ambushes was a birth gift from Allah. Even during fierce firefights with the Pakistan Army, he maintained an icy, unshakeable calm.

It was late evening in the early winter of 2010 when, seated cross-legged on his prayer rug, Rostislov looked up from the Koran. Osama bin Laden was standing above him.

Guerilla war was physically ruinous, and bin Laden was no longer young. Years on the run had exacted a heavy physical toll, and the Saudi now appeared far older than his forty-nine years. Deep wrinkles framed his eyes, and his hair had faded from dark brown to gray. Winter nights spent sleeping on the freezing ground had pierced his knees, hips and elbows with slivers of arthritis. He now walked with care, setting his feet precisely and relying on a staff that slowed his pace.

Bin Laden knew time was running out. Driven from the warm beds of his wives, he periodically traded his comfortable compound in Abbottabad for cold floors in mountain caves. Soon one of the unmanned Predator's Hell Fire missiles, a cluster bomb, or super-accurate Excalibur XM982 artillery shell would find the entrance, sending a killing concussion deep among the rock passages. Bin Laden sensed death was near. Before he entered Paradise, he wanted to once again see the Americans mourn.

"Qari," bin Laden called him by his childhood name. Its use filled Rostislov with an intense loyalty. "I have a mission for you." That night in the Abbottabad compound, bin Laden spoke and Rostislov listened. When

117

the gray-haired leader finished, Rostislov asked his only question, "When?"

"Immediately," bin Laden answered. "We know the West's agents have bribed members of our brotherhood. It was bound to happen. In the end we could fight the Western soldiers, but not the rewards."

Rostislov stood and walked to the closest wall. Lifting his Kalashnikov from a wooden stand he said, "Give me the name of the traitor, I will make an example of him for anyone who would betray you."

Bin Laden settled his aching legs into a more comfortable position. "I would, but you cannot kill my family, my advisors, or the faithful who supply us with food and ammunition. I do not know who it may be, but we will find out. When we do, you will be in America."

Rostislov did not immediately object, only listened.

"After the victory of the Twin Towers, it has become more difficult to enter America," he hesitated. "It is still possible to travel to Mexico. You should not have trouble entering the U.S. through its southern border." He managed to straighten his back with great difficulty. As always, that night bin Laden changed locations. This time Rostislov Azad did not guard his route.

It took Rostislov a week to reach Delhi, where he connected to London and a direct flight to Mexico. He spoke Spanish, and while Mexico's custom agent was curious about his accent and his well-traveled Swiss passport, he took Rostislov at his word. He had come to Mexico for the culture, the Mayan Peninsula, the Caribbean beaches and to improve his accent.

"It is not hard if you only speak Spanish," the customs official counseled him. "But you cannot speak English--that is your native tongue?"

"Swiss Deutsch," he replied and listened politely while the official butchered a German greeting.

He passed through customs without notice, and proceeded to the domestic terminal where he caught a flight to Cancun. There he purchased a ticket on a bus south to the popular Caribbean resort, Playa del Carmen. He booked a bungalow at Casa Mara, a small hotel half a block off the Quinta Avenida, the main street that paralleled the ocean. During the next two days he bought a white embroidered shirt, a pair of sandals, shorts, and a high-resolution map of Mexico. He ate dinner alone, avoiding anything that might make him sick.

During the day he walked the beach. He hated the naked French and Italian girls at the Mamitas Club. Their suntanned breasts and shaved pubic mounds screamed for the attention of men in small swimsuits that barely covered their manhood. Rostislov choked down his rage. In Afghanistan the beach whores and their pimps would be stoned. Here debauched Western Infidels paid little attention to the naked women's appraising glances.

He watched the cruise line passengers unload at Playa del Carmen's long dock. Gorged from a week of buffet breakfasts, lunches and dinners, the passengers could barely walk the few blocks into town. Afghanistan was starving while the obese American beasts on the dock left food to rot.

Osama bin Laden had arranged for Rostislov Azad to meet a boat on an isolated beach south of Playa Del Carmen's main hotel district. He had been told the boat would appear at two AM. The message did not specify the night, only one of three. The first night, Rostislov waited in the jungle on a small hill above the beach for a signal. He ignored the mosquitoes that landed on his arms and neck as he monitored the calls of geckos and Yucatan parrots. A change in their rhythm would signal the approach of another man. Small waves broke on the sand and an early morning breeze moved the trees. Rostislov waited exactly one hour but the boat did not show. Nor did it appear the second night. On the third night he detected the signal from half a mile off the beach. Two quick blinks. He returned four. Seconds later he counted the answer. Three.

He waited in the shoreline trees until the boat scraped into the white sand. Two men stepped quietly ashore. One held the boat's bow rope. The other carefully carried a black, stainless steel suitcase up the beach. The two men were Mayan. Born in Chiapas, Mexico's desperately poor southern state, they were raised in poverty. Following years of discrimination, they converted to Islam as had many others in their village and soon ranked among the sect's most radical members.

The closest man offered a faint bow of respect then handed Rostislov the suitcase. The Afghan was not surprised by the eighty-pound weight. He had been trained in the handling of its contents and repeatedly warned about the consequences of a mistake.

"Con cuidado," the Mayan released the suitcase and returned to the boat. "Es muy peligroso!" He pushed the bow out of the sand.

"Sí, entiendo," Rostislov did not wait for the fishing boat to disappear out into the dark sea. Climbing up from the beach he followed Quinta Avenida to Casa Mara.

At six AM he boarded a bus to Cancun, where he purchased another ticket on an express to Mexico City. Thirty-six hours later, he was in the border town of Nuevo Laredo at the corner of Monterrey and Anahuac Streets in the heart of La Zona de Tolerancia. The four square blocks were known by a variety of names: Boys Town, La Zona Rosa, the Red Light District. Young prostitutes loitered outside the strip clubs where they flashed their breasts and brazenly lifted their dresses on the sidewalk that fronted cheap bars.

Rostislov entered a bar named El Cielo del Muerto and inquired in Spanish, "Conoces a Hugo Magana?"

The bartender ignored the question until Rostislov dropped twenty dollars on the bar. Slipping it into his shirt pocket, he admitted, "El señor no esta aqua--por que lo busca?" the bartender's sarcasm weighted the proper, "El Señor."

"Es un amigo…" Rostislov replied.

"Seguro," the bartender dipped a dirty glass in cold water, wiped it once then refilled it with ice. "Como puede ver, el Señor Magaña no está aqua."

Rostislov dropped another twenty on the bar. "Voy a preguntar una vez más, ¿sabe usted dónde está?"

Six years tending bar in Boys Town had taught the bartender more than he needed to know about black haired gringos asking questions in Spanish. Other than that he was a man of consequence who spoke with a classic accent, there was nothing he would remember about the man except that further delay would likely be dangerous. He owed no loyalty to Hugo Magana. "Es posible trovarlo en Los Tres Reyes Bar." It would be better for business if this gringo left.

Half a dozen young prostitutes were seated at the Tres Reyes Bar when Rostislov entered. His eyes swept the shadowed room. Except for the young girls, it was almost empty. The prostitutes appraised the Afghani and smiled. Rostislov looked past their low cut dresses and exposed thighs to Hugo Magana who was smoking at a dimly lit table facing the door.

Rostislov crossed the room and quietly asked, "Hugo Magana?"

Magana's dark, Indian features were deeply pockmarked. The night's third tequila sat half-finished on the table. "Puede ser que sea. ¿Quién quiere saber?" Magana appraised him.

"Un profesor ser desea ser su estudiante para obtener una mejor educación." Rostislov's accent suggested he had been born in Spain, but educated elsewhere. The teacher the Gringo alluded to had paid dollars, half again Magana's usual fee. It was clear the Gringo standing in front of him was no honest student looking for a better education across the border.

"He oído que usted sabe un camino hacia el norte seguro." The exchange was a formality. Magana knew the way north.

"Es posible." Magana lit a cigarette, inhaled and held the smoke.

"For now, possible will do." Rostislov continued quietly in Spanish. "I need to cross undetected into the United States."

"As does everyone."

"You received the payment."

"As well. Your patron is generous," he took a drag on the cigarette. "Unfortunately, the Gringo Border Patrol has closed all but a few routes to the North. The risk is high. The guards have stopped returning Coyotes to Mexico. Now they lock them in jail."

A muscle twitched beneath Rostislov's left eye. "If you require more money…"

The bar was too dark for Magana to notice. If he had looked at Rostislov's face, instead of signaling the waitress for another tequila, he would have returned the payment and disappeared. "Como ya he dicho--the way has become more dangerous."

"Your fee was ten thousand dollars—four times what is typical." Magana failed to read Rostislov's expression. "But you are not--" he threw back the last of his drink, "...typical."

Rostislov's fingers closed around the Karud's bone handle. The Tres Reyes catered to cheats and whores whose lives were of no importance. Under different circumstances Magana would now be dead. The Coyote, however, could lead him across the border. "I will pay you another five thousand dollars, in addition to the ten thousand you have already been paid." An indecipherable emotion flickered across his face. "Is this figure agreeable?"

Magana nodded, "When do you care to leave?"

That night the Coyote's Ford pickup followed Highway 2 northwest along the Rio Grande. The Department of Homeland security had invested millions in Arizona and California, but little in Texas. Beyond Rancho Bonito near Arroyitos, Magana unlocked a steel gate and followed a series of dirt tracks three miles through the thick mesquite to the Rio that flowed with a cold, reptilian silence. Magana scanned the dark far shore with Night Vision goggles for five minutes before he climbed the fence and descended the steep bank to the water. No sounds issued from the thick scrub. A barbed wire fence intended to keep the cattle out of the river guarded the border. Hugo Magana unloaded a camouflaged zodiac from the pickup. "The water is deep. Many drown here and upriver. No one can cross without a boat," he whispered.

Exercising extreme caution, Rostislov settled the suitcase in the inflatable boat. To prevent capture by the border patrol, a thirty-horse out board was mounted on the stern. Magana had no intention of starting it unless the border patrol was waiting on the far side. He pushed off, and the current dragged the rubber boat downstream. Fixing two oars to the felt wrapped locks, Magana quietly rowed toward the far bank. He had crossed many times before and knew the rate of drift and the landing. It took six minutes to cross. He tied the boat and quietly led the way across a pasture to a remote country road where a second pickup truck was waiting.

"This is where we part," Magana said. "My cousin will drive you to the next town where you will catch a bus north. Now amigo, the final payment." Magana produced a .38 Smith and Wesson. The revolver guaranteed he would be paid.

Rostislov glanced at the revolver. A second later, a Karud dagger whispered through the darkness.

Magana suddenly felt incredibly tired. His knees buckled and he sank to the dirt road. A thin red line bisected his throat. His carotids pumped onto his shirt. Magana was slipping into a deep well when Rostislov pried the .38 from his fingers.

"You should have honored our agreement," the Afghani said.

Magana's cousin tried to beg for his life. "Señor, tengo una esposa, hijos y padres." Unmoved, Rostislov put a bullet in his head. Dragging the body out of the truck and off the road, he belted the suitcase onto the pickup seat and followed the dirt track until it intersected Texas's Ranch Road 1472 through the dark rangeland north.

Chapter 12

B ritish Airways Flight 279 landed at Los Angeles International Airport twenty minutes late. Hull collected his carryon and followed the signs to Customs. The agent was young and despite the long lines, diverse nationalities and foreign languages, thorough. He opened Hull's passport and compared it to his military ID. "Where are you presently stationed?"

"Jalalabad, Afghanistan," Hull waited.

The agent thumbed through his passport. "Anything to declare?"

"Nothing."

The agent stamped his passport and waved him through. Hull retrieved his duffle, followed the "Nothing to Declare" line and slipped past the crowd waiting in the arrival lobby. He hoped his return to L.A. would be painless. In the ten years since the first Abrams Tanks raced across the deserts south of Baghdad, the numbers of returning soldiers and waiting families had waned. During those first heady months when President George W. Bush declared "Mission Accomplished" on the USS Abraham Lincoln's flight deck, Hull had endured a multicolored wall of "Welcome Home" signs, balloons and confetti. Americans had become accustomed to the wars and the exuberant reunions had thinned to anxious wives, children, mothers and fathers who were unable to contain their tears when their sons and daughters walked into the lobby.

Other meetings occurred on the East Coast, in Walter Reed Army Medical Center where soldiers with missing limbs, surgically repaired stomachs, lungs and livers embraced families who fought to act as if nothing had changed. In truth, everything had changed.

By now the U.S. Marines would have notified Bauldaire's father and mother of his death.

As the number of Hull's tours increased and the months bled into years, he wished he could disappear. Skirting the crowds in Arrivals, Hull knew no one was waiting for him. His parents were dead, his divorce was final, the single USO volunteer was waiting for soldiers in BDUs. He exited through the automatic doors onto the sidewalk where he boarded a red and white bus that dropped him at an offsite Avis counter. The desk agent typed the information from his Wizard Card and asked if he'd be interested in a Hummer. "Avis wants to introduce our Wizard Members to its functionality," she offered.

"What's functionality cost?" Hull had slept fewer than four hours in the last seventy-two.

"An extra fifty-five dollars per week but Avis will pick up the insurance, and you don't need to fill it up before you return."

Four tours in Afghanistan had taught him the Humvee's truck chassis and four-wheel drive would take a pounding. It was a tactical decision. Reliability versus visibility. Pulsing through L.A.'s interlocking concrete arteries, commuters were focused on their cell phones and would give a shit about another Humvee. Hull dropped his credit card on the counter.

The midnight blue Hummer was parked midway down the second Avis aisle. Hull dropped his bag in back, climbed into the driver's seat and started the engine. He made a right turn on Aviation, followed the freeway to the Imperial Highway, crossed under the 105 and picked up the on ramp.

Accelerating onto the freeway, he hit the radio's seek button. The electronic cursor searched, stopped then searched again. Trapped within the L.A. basin's vast acoustic bowl it skimmed America's music. Gangsta Rap, Reggae, Soul, Muzak, Big Band, Country, and Blue Grass, peppered with 24-hour news, weather and listener call-ins. A thousand pulsing signals choked the airwaves. It had been two decades since the tenths between the station markers had been claimed, nearly six years since the hundredths had closed the last hole in a surrounding wall of sound where dead air was as rare as fresh air.

Hull could not tell whether the radio mirrored the Los Angeles Basin's unrelenting pace or was responsible for it. He hated the radio's mechanical repetition of the same songs, the same time of day, the same screaming announcers, screaming singers and mindless commercials.

He was merging onto the 605 when the ringing returned. The Marine Ear Nose and Throat specialist diagnosed the sound as acute tinnitus--an injury common to Formula One drivers, heavy metal band lead guitarists, and men who shoot high-powered rifles without hearing protectors. "You might notice some upper-range hearing loss." The specialist handed Hull a prescription for eardrops.

Hull accepted the tinnitus just as he accepted Post Traumatic Stress Disorder. Hull preferred the term "Combat Fatigue" to the acronym PTSD.

Hull hated PTSD's touchy-feely, empathetic, feminine rhythm. It sounded like PMS. Combat Fatigue belonged to his father's generation, when soldiers sucked up the horrors of World War II and Vietnam and returned home to start businesses and raise families. No matter what acronym he settled upon, the first weeks home were always a bitch.

Army shrinks claimed roughly fourteen percent of all troops returned home with some form of emotional trauma. In some respects, Combat Fatigue and malaria were comparable. Both caused recurring episodes of fever, shakes, insomnia, liver damage--he was surprised the shrinks hadn't recognized the similarities. Instead of Quinine, Chloroquine or Primaquine to kill spirochetes, Hull took tetra-cyclic anti-depressants. Known by the brand name Remeron, Mirtazapine was easily obtained on the streets of Tijuana, and if he didn't dwell on the side effects--the hallucinations, irritability, dizziness, aggression or the sexual issues, Senor Mirtz held his demons at arm's length.

The dreams he killed with Haldol, Vitamin H. Five milligrams, orally. Just below the threshold for Parkinsonism. Compared to Gentleman Hal, Thorazine was a sugar pill. He'd read the psycho-pharmacology reports. Vitamin H was a highly potent neuroleptic prescribed for use against hallucinations and delusions. Side effects? Shit loads. Tics, dry mouth, tremors, skin rashes, photosensitivity, weight gain...compared to the alternative, Hull would risk a few extra pounds.

After his third tour in Afghanistan, even a mix of Glenfiddich, Haldol and Mirtazapine could not prevent the dreams. On some nights, turbaned men took 250-grain bullets in the throat. On others, children were burned into blackened bows by errant JDAMs. Severed arms and crushed heads, bloated bodies and grimacing, accusatory skulls filled his nights. It was a miracle Hull hadn't been shot, crushed or blown up in the dark hours between two and five AM. He knew, given enough time, no one walked away alive-- everyone died in his dreams.

The Marine shrinks were a waste of time. They asked questions, nodded, took notes as Hull revealed the minimum required to remain on active duty. The shrinks were required to report war crimes. Problem was, what did the shrinks know about Scout Snipers or where duty ended and war crimes began? Scout Snipers never spilled their guts. Not to the shrinks, wives, spotters, parents, or friends. Hull never spilled. Never. Not to save his marriage, or his life.

The word "Afghanistan" broke into his thoughts. He turned up the radio volume.

"...video attributed to Afghanistan's Taliban was released to al Jazeera, the English version of the Arabic language news station based in Doha, Qatar." The news announcer read the wire service's raw feed. "The video purports to show the head of one of the Scout Snipers who allegedly killed Osama bin Laden. The head is displayed on a table behind which five men in turbans and masks hold AK47s across their chests. There is no way to determine which of the five served as spokesman."

Hull was stunned. "The cowardly assassin of the Holy Martyrs Osama bin Laden and Commander Siraj Haqqani was beheaded as punishment for his crimes against the people of Afghanistan and Pakistan. The United States Special Forces infidel martyred the leaders Osama bin Laden and Siraj Haqqani, as they traveled to pray for the souls of the civilians who died in the U.S. bombing of Hindi Khel of Bannu. Osama bin Laden and Siraj Haqqani were martyred while they paused for prayers in the course of their journey."

"While the al Jazeera footage shows the skull of a young male Caucasian," the commentator continued. "It is impossible to know whether the locale is Afghanistan or Pakistan. No identifying dog tags or insignias are visible and the Taliban did not reveal his name."

"A spokesman for ISAF in Kabul said it had no reports of missing U.S. or Coalition soldiers."

"The lack of information raises questions concerning the team's identification. Queried in Kabul, Afghanistan and at the Pentagon in Arlington, Virginia, military spokesmen refused to confirm or deny other details."

"The video closes with a final statement from the masked Taliban spokesmen. 'May Allah condemn his soul to Hell."

Hull remembered Bauldaire lying on his back in the dusty trail above Saker. Bauldaire's face was cut, his blouse bloodstained, his head supported above the goat dung by Hull's pack. The Lieutenant was panting in short, labored breaths, "The chip...." Six Taliban had closed to within thirty meters. Hull had no way to prevent their next assault. Bauldaire could hear the AK47's rapid fire. "Sir...deliver the chip to General Petraeus!" Hull's last grenade landed among the Taliban. The explosion killed one, wounded three. It bought thirty seconds.

Annapolis, Marines, Sniper School, Advanced Language School, Special Ops ...Bauldaire had moved resolutely toward this moment on a high pass in Pakistan and Hull, for all his years of training, could do nothing to prevent the inevitable.

Adrift in L.A. traffic, Hull felt a massive pain explode through his chest. He tried to steady himself against the wheel. The Hummer blundered slowly across two left lanes. Drivers frantically locked their brakes, beat on their horns and screamed soundless insults behind the hermetically sealed safety glass.

Hull had fought to save Bauldaire--he had fought to return him safely to his family. His vision blurred and he racked the steering wheel left, then right, spraying traffic with gravel and dust.

The V-8 pulled blindly toward the massive center abutment of an approaching overpass. In seconds the Hummer's blue hood, fenders and engine would flatten against the reinforced concrete. The abutment swelled in the windshield. Hull refused to join the ranks of soldiers who had blown their brains out, over-dosed, or ran a garden hose from the family sedan's exhaust into the interior. He was stronger than suicide, would not seek a dishonorable escape. Osama bin Laden, Bauldaire, the dead and maimed, the dreams, his divorce, he would survive it all. He had to survive. Suicide killed only weak soldiers and terrified children, the desperate, the weak and damaged. None were like Hull. None had his strength, purpose, experience, will...a keening tore from his chest as he braced for the impact.

An instant before the Hummer slammed into the concrete pillar, Colonel Herbert Nash Dillard, VMI's long dead Professor of Literature filled Hull's mind.

"What though the field be lost?" Colonel Dillard greeted him in a deep voice. "All is not lost: th'unconquerable will, And study of revenge, immortal hate, And courage never to submit or yield." The quote was from "Paradise Lost", John Milton's complex epic poem detailing Adam and Eve's fall from grace.

Hull did not know how the H3 missed the pillar. One second the boxy SUV was racing toward the concrete abutment, the next it was sliding sideways down the gravel shoulder, his driver's window inches from a tangled wall of Oleander shrubs.

"No sense in behaving rashly. At least, not until you take a moment to think." Colonel Dillard continued. "Perhaps you should return to the main road."

Hull had experienced hallucinations before but never one that took the form of a long dead professor of literature. Though he had never met Colonel Dillard, all graduates of VMI knew Dodo Dillard. The witty, empathetic veteran of World War II and friend of Dwight D. Eisenhower, Dillard had influenced decades of VMI corps. By the time Jack Hull entered VMI, the professor had been dead for eighteen years but his picture still hung in VMI's English Department. Perched high on the wall, he still presided benevolently over the passing cadets.

If Hull never met Herbert Nash Dillard, Phil Gioia Hull, his father, had. Phil Hull was VMI class of 1966--a mechanical engineering major who enrolled in Dillard's sophomore literature class.

At the end of the term, Dillard scribbled a note on a poem Phil Hull composed, "Hull, you may have the gift," he wrote beneath the grade A+, only one of two he awarded.

In spite of a two-decade gap, Hull's freshman English Professor venerated Herbert Nash Dillard as an example of what could be achieved if a white hot intelligence was shaped upon the anvil of hard work. Standing in front of VMI's Rats, he remembered, "Colonel Dillard was a savant! A genius who accurately summoned lines from classics; books, poems, hieroglyphics, tombstones and even menus. His legacy serves as a standard for us all."

In the summer of Hull's sophomore year at VMI, a heart attack dropped Phil Hull in the back yard of his Riverside Home. Hull reached him a second before he died. Lifting his father's head, Hull heard him whisper, "What would Colonel Dillard say?" His father never had time to add, "I love you son."

For a dozen years afterward, Dillard, the friend of Eisenhower, quoter of tombstones, literary savant, had been forgotten, free to wander through Jack Hull's mind, examining the particulars of his life like a house guest who feels too much at home.

Before Colonel Dillard materialized, the Scout Sniper regarded mental breakdowns as a weakness of the rich--a type of just desserts for dissolute life styles. The appearance of Dodo Dillard's extinct face, quoting Milton's "Paradise Lost", approximated taking a 7.62 round to the chest.

The next in a series of concrete pillars grew in the H3's flat windshield. Colonel Dillard reminded him, "The First Step Toward Madness Is To Think Oneself Wise!" He smiled at the beauty of the phrase, and then credited the author, "It's from Fernando de Rojas. "La Celestina", Act II."

The line was an old one that appeared at odd times. Accelerating off the gravel shoulder into the fast lane, Hull realized that Rojas' "First Step Toward Madness," had a distant echo and like a Gregorian chant, returned repeatedly to a single dark theme.

Chapter 13

It took Hull an hour to drive from LAX to Riverside. Swept along in a river of moving cars, trucks and motorcycles, Hull tried to dismiss Colonel Herbert Nash Dillard as a rare hallucination--a fleeting neuro-chemical imbalance brought on by jet lag, sleep deprivation and stress. If he could capture four hours of uninterrupted sleep, the venerable professor and his encyclopedic literary recall would fade back into history from whence he had so unexpectedly appeared.

Hull had discovered Dillard's obituary among his father's effects. The yellowed newspaper revealed he was born on September 22, 1913 in Rocky Mount, Virginia. Upon his graduation from high school, he stood first in a class of forty-five. He was sixteen when he entered VMI and by the end of his Rat year, again led his class.

Upon his graduation from VMI, Dillard entered Harvard to pursue a PhD. in English Literature. He served as a communications officer in both the Atlantic and Pacific Theaters during the Second World War, and was awarded an Alhambra Citation for his service in Kwajalein, Saipan, Leyte Gulf, the Philippines, Okinawa, Japan and China.

He then returned to VMI where he assumed the role of Professor of English with the rank of Colonel in 1950, a position he would hold for the next quarter century.

Colonel Dillard was lecturing a class of VMI freshman on Expository and Argumentative Composition when he excused himself, took a few steps toward the exit and collapsed. VMI students and the Institute's physician were unable to revive him. He was pronounced dead at Stonewall Jackson Hospital.

Recalling the death of Colonel Herbert Nash Dillard did not make the professor disappear. The Humvee continued east and Colonel Dillard stood in his classroom, 308 Scott Ship Hall where, surrounded by his books, blackboard, drawings by William Blake and a poster from London's Victoria and Albert Museum announcing an exhibition of Lord Byron, he waited. In life, Dillard abhorred silence and applying a World War II Zippo to an unfiltered Camel cigarette, he noted, "Men are never more frightened than when they are convinced beyond doubt they are right."

Hull had had enough. Summoning the focus that ensured success as a Scout Sniper, he sought to drive the Colonel from his mind. Dillard, though, proved to be far stronger and would neither be hustled away nor silenced. He was still standing just off center, in front of the blackboard, when Hull stopped in front of his storage unit.

The lot was empty. It took Hull two tries before the rusty combination lock reluctantly opened. He raised the metal door then crossed to a gray file cabinet where he found a small cardboard box in the top drawer. Opening the lid, he retrieved a full bottle of Haldol and a half bottle of Mirtazapine, 15-milligram pills, left over from his past bout with CF. He had bought both medications in Mexico. The date was expired but the chemistry still worked. Senor Mirtz was for depression; he hoped the Haldol would evict Colonel Dillard. Tapping one of each into his right hand, he washed them down with the last of the Avis coffee and spun the combination on the gun safe.

He knew that now that his identity was public, al Qaeda would come for him. They would pick a professional. It would be one man, a sniper, with skills in bomb making. Where the terrorist would enter the U.S. was unimportant. Mexico, the Canadian border, he might have already slipped into the U.S. and was waiting for a signal. Hull would not see him. Or her. Al Qaeda would not make it quick or painless.

Alert the L.A. Police? Not likely. If 120,000 trained ISAF couldn't stop the Taliban or neutralize al Qaeda, what chance did L.A.'s Police have? When the ambush came, L.A.'s finest would be little better than neatly uniformed janitors called in to sweep up the pieces.

The M249 Squad Automatic Rifle was as he'd left it two years earlier, clean, oiled and protected by a canvas case. The safe's air seal had protected the metal from the Pacific's salt air. He lifted it from the rack, worked the breech and felt the round slide home. Capable of firing standard M16 ammunition, the SAW was fed by 200-round disintegrating belts. He set a metal ammo box of 5.56 x 45mm NATO rounds to one side and selected an M40A1 scoped sniper rifle. Lastly, he removed a Colt Commander 1911 and two boxes of 185-grain .45 calibers. Checking the alley that fronted the storage unit, he loaded all but the .45 into a canvas duffle. Storing the green duffle behind the back seat, he covered it with a brown plastic tarp. He then locked up the storage unit, tossed the plastic drug vials into the jockey box, started the engine, and turned toward University Avenue.

Colonel Dillard chose that moment to return. Across a VMI black board he had written in white chalk, "Heroes are created by popular demand, sometimes out of the scantiest materials, or none at all." Then, in a clear, legible script, he credited the author, "Gerald White Johnson, 'American Heroes and Hero-Worship.'"

Hull waited for the Haldol to kick in, forcing Dodo Dillard and 308 Scott Ship Hall into an opaque white fog.

A Verizon outlet appeared in a shopping center on the right.
A minute later Hull was standing in front of a young sales clerk. "I need to upgrade my phone," he said.

"Can I have your number please and the last four digits of your social?" the clerk replied. Hull gave her both. She typed his information into a computer, waited a second then without looking up said, "Major Hull, you haven't used your phone in more than a year."

Preferring to skip the pleasant small talk, he told her, "I need a new unlisted number, a GPS connection, Internet access and a good camera...with video." He scanned the multicolored models behind her.

"Of course," she replied. "The new Apple iPhone...

Hull interrupted her. "No, not the Apple."

"Alright...well, the BlackBerry includes those features. If you renew your two year contract, with the rebate it will cost you one hundred..."

"Let's keep it month to month. I'll pay the difference."

Habit brought Hull back to L.A. In the past he would return to Cheryl and their apartment where he would try to knit the marriage together long enough for it to survive the next tour. Now divorced, he had no place to stay. He was bone-tired and heartsick and drove past the faded motels advertising forty-nine dollars a night, free Internet connection, and HBO on University Avenue in Riverside.

Thirteen months in Afghanistan's dust, heat and blood drew him down Lemon Street where he pulled to the curb in front of the Mission Inn's adobe façade. The historic landmark hotel's arched columns and fountains, the ancient wooden beams and tile patios, the leaded glass windows and antique furniture offered a quiet refuge. Hull wanted to soak in a clean tub and shave in a porcelain sink. Most of all, he wanted to sleep without dreaming.

The Mission Inn's front desk clerk's eyes flickered across her computer. Looking over the screen at him, she shook her head, "I'm sorry sir, we're fully booked. We have the Bonsai Club of California staying with us."

"The Bonsai Club?" he inquired.

"Dwarf trees…dwarf trees in pots--this is one of their displays," she pointed to a stunted Monterey Pine on the counter. "Unfortunately, the only room we have open is the Alhambra Suite." Her hands paused above the keys. "It's eight fifty-five a night," she said, looking up from the computer monitor at his two day growth, blue jacket, wrinkled shirt and tie. "But it's our low season and I can take a hundred dollars off that figure."

Seven hundred and fifty-five dollars would feed an Afghan family for a year--but L.A. wasn't Kabul, and he was exhausted and needed a place to sleep. He hoped for days without dreams. Handing her his American Express he replied, "I'll take it." He signed the receipt, and crossed the courtyard to the staircase.

To the north, four arches supported a cantilevered second story where three sets of arched windows opened onto the court below. On this wall a white cameo depicted the angel Gabriel. His hands were clasped and his large wings were partially hidden by the flowing folds of his tunic and his shoulder-length hair. To the left of Gabriel, a Madonna sat on a small bench. Her eyes were downcast, a book open upon her lap, a white halo floated above her head, and her left hand rested in supplication on her upper chest.

Climbing the stairs toward the Alhambra, Hull encountered other statues. Viewed from the depths of jet lag and lack of sleep, Jesus appeared as a Northern European of pronounced effeminacy. Hull noticed the lack of strength in his face, a vacancy that belied the passion he summoned to drive the moneychangers from the temple. Loaded on Mirtazapine and Haldol, Hull's mind wandered through dark alleys. If God existed, such mundane matters as adultery, theft or lying would not concern him. It was murder God abhorred. "Thou shalt not kill" made sense when slaughtering one's neighbor could trigger war.

Hull remembered bits and pieces from an upper division class on the History of the Bible. Hull had read the Bible, more than once. After each reading he could not decide what to believe and what to dismiss and in the end simply set it aside for that moment when personal revelation might reveal the truth.

It was the Bible's drafters, John, Paul, Peter and Isaiah who exorcised God's demons on sheets of papyrus. Centuries later, monks transcribed and edited the fragile manuscripts, adding a clarifying comma, a participle, phrase or paragraph, until the New Testament bore little, or any resemblance to the original. In the final printed copy, "Thou Shalt Not Covet" rang less like a commandment and more like a confession.

Now he slowly climbed the stairs that switched back upon themselves until he reached the top floor. Rounding a corner, he frightened a dozen pigeons off the wrought-iron railing. Launching themselves into the evening light, they swirled around the upper floor's minarets, descending into the inner courtyard on V-shaped wings. Below, a small statue of Saint Francis of Assisi stood atop a stained glass dome. In his right hand Saint Francis held a book; his left was gone, having broken off when the statue was shipped from Europe. Giving life to the legend, the pigeons landed on the statue's head.

Opening the door to the Alhambra Suite, Hull was physically exhausted and emotionally bankrupt. He dropped his duffle in the closet, called bell service and ordered a fifth of Glenfiddich eighteen year-old, single-malt Scotch. He kicked off his shoes, stripped off his sour shirt, walked out of his wrinkled suit pants and fell on the bed. He lay for some minutes, staring up at the heavily beamed ceiling and listening to the pigeons, then touched the television remote.

The Weather Channel appeared. "Hot and dusty for the 33rd day in a row." The announcer continued, "Highs in the 80s, humidity 10%, zero chance of rain, brush fires in the Santa Monica Mountains still out of control; flames have now consumed thirteen houses. Officials believe the fire is the work of arsonists. In Kabul the forecast calls for Highs of 110 with zero humidity, winds light to moderate."

Hull punched the remote. The screen switched to MTV. Dressed in a low, loose fitting top and low slung jeans painted onto her boyish hips, a brainless VJ introduced a singer Hull didn't recognize.

He remembered Shaima Rezayee, an Afghan VJ on Kabul's "Tolo TV." Shaima's show, HOP, was popular with Kabul's youth--too popular for the Taliban Mullahs who banned all women from Afghan television. Bowing to the AK-47s pointed at their chests, the Afghan TV owners fired Shaima. It was not enough. The un-Islamic values of her show continued to haunt the Taliban leadership who gunned her down in the living room of her home.

Hull switched to CNN. "...and in France an argument in a no smoking section of a suburban Paris train led to a stabbing." The anchor looked from the script into the camera, "The argument broke out after three smokers were confronted by a non smoker. One of the three stabbed him in the leg and fled."

Wolf Blitzer appeared. In the past year he'd grown less aggressive, grayer. Facing the camera, Blitzer said, "Today's major story concerns a video delivered to al Jazeera. If you have young children in the room or will be offended by graphic violence please leave the room or turn off the T.V."

Hull struggled to turn away from the al Jazeera feed. The masked figures stood behind a rickety table. Blackened by death, his jaw dislocated, one eye open, Bauldaire's head faced the camera. Hull squeezed his eyes with his thumb and forefinger until the tears spilled onto his cheeks. He remembered Bauldaire looking up at him from the dusty trail. He should have stayed with Bauldaire. If he had fought the Taliban until they were overrun, he would now be dead in Afghanistan instead of crippled in L.A.

Hull fought sleep by sitting in the suite's enormous tub. He had filled it with cold water. The water was a luxury. It was one major difference between L.A. and Kabul; clean water--enough to waste in a tub. He thought of the six days of aching thirst on the ridge. Now he could drink the whole tub if he

136

wanted to. He had drunk far worse than cold tub water. Irrigation ditches, cattle troughs, even pee. He took a sip from the glass of amber Scotch in his right hand and remembered the battle for Kandahar.

CENTCOM deployed Special Operators in the early morning. Hull and Bauldaire had established a position on the second floor of a bombed-out shop. Two, eighty millimeter artillery shell holes faced a secondary intersection. Unless someone knew the Scout Snipers were occupying the abandoned second story, no one could see them. The closed walls muffled the report. Target selection was straightforward. Kill anyone carrying a Kalashnikov and let Allah sort it out.

Kandahar was Indian Country--the Taliban's heart, soul and testicles. Planners believed if Kandahar presented similar challenges to Iraq, similar tactics should work. In the month prior, US CENTCOM had tried to buy information from Kandahar tribal leaders. It was a disaster. Sell out the Taliban for a new road and a sewage treatment plant? The Elders didn't laugh. The Taliban were Kandahar fathers, brothers, nephews, sons, and friends.

Hull and Bauldaire's objective was to spread terror among the terrorists. They would take out the sentinels first then go to work on the stragglers. Selecting targets, computing ranges, verifying the kill; Hull's M40A1 put an exclamation point on Bauldaire's calculations. De-braining Taliban soldiers at midday in downtown Kandahar sent a message. The locals had far more to fear from the U.S. than the Taliban. By full dark, Hull and Bauldaire accounted for sixteen confirmed kills--all upper body and headshots. At 0200 when they appeared at the pickup point, the Taliban were still searching for their position.

The next morning, Haji Mukhtar, a Kandahar Provincial Council member said, "Instead of bringing people closer to the government, these type of Special Operations cause people to stay further from the government and hate the foreigners more."

"Damned if you do and damned if you do," Bauldaire observed.

The last time Hull drank Scotch for breakfast was the last time he returned from Afghanistan. He added two more cubes and poured a thumb-full of Glenfiddich into the glass. Hull knew the Scotch didn't agree with doses of Senor Mirtz and Gentleman Hal, but he feared the dreams.

He set the Scotch down, picked up the cordless phone and dialed the front desk. "Yes Colonel Hull?" the front desk clerk answered.

"I'd like to take the suite for another three days."

"Let me check if it's open," she said, "It is and the price for three nights, low season…with your discount, comes to $2250."

"You have my card number," he said.

He had slept six of the past seventy-two hours and could no longer fight the need to close his eyes. He only meant to lay down for five minutes but thirty seconds later he was asleep, his hands opening and closing, his legs jerking almost to his chest.

A 7.62 round ricocheted off the parapet wall. Hull was back at OP Seray. It was Hull's third tour--a full year before he would select Bauldaire for his spotter. Combat Observation Post Seray perched on a rocky spine ten kilometers from the Pakistan border. The valley floor was a mix of red dust and sharp boulders, divided by a single, pockmarked road that snaked west through high, red cliffs toward Kabul. The hills surrounding the outpost were a hardscrabble mix of dry scrub brush and blistered basalt.

Three tours had taught him the Moolies were creatures of habit. Searching the valleys that surrounded OP Seray was far too dangerous. The death rate was rising. The Coalition was losing the war. Blame the casualties on too few men spread across too vast, and far too dangerous terrain.

Another round hit the dirt-filled casements. Hajji Baba was up early. Hull held a pair of 10/40 Swarovski binoculars, his personal glasses. The Swarovskis hesitated as he adjusted the focus. A shepherd pushed his flock along the shadowy cliff edge. Danger haunted dawn in the Chowkay Valley and the shepherd hurried to reach the rocky defile that marked the red cliffs before the rising sun swept the valley floor.

Sergeant Walter Soderstrom climbed onto the parapet. Two hundred and thirty pounds, six five with size fourteen boots, Soderstrom was halfway through his third tour. Soderstrom's inability to compute distances had washed him out of Fort Bragg's Sniper School.

The week after his third posting to Seray, Soderstrom started to self-medicate with 15mg of Zoloft; four months later he had increased the dosage to 150mg of Remeron mixed with 25mg of Stetazine. He called it "Puff the Magic Dragon," a nod to the C130 Gunship that rained hellfire down on the Hajjis. The only problem with Puff was the psychotic side effects that shook the six and a half foot Minnesota Swede. As long as Soderstrom hated the Hajjis more than the 262's officers, and kept his M16A1 pointed outside the compound, he was tolerated at Seray.

But two months into his second tour, Soderstrom beat an Afghan girl half to death in a dry waddi south of Jalalabad. Near starvation had forced her to prostitute herself. The Taliban spared Central Command a court martial. The week before a military board convened, the extremists cut her throat. Soderstrom was subsequently returned to Seray, where he shot Abdul Mukin, the Taliban's Kandahar Province leader in the chest. In the months that followed, all references to the young prostitute were deleted from his record.

Hull also held the incident with the Pallas Cat against Soderstrom. The drought that gripped Afghanistan reduced the numbers of picas and rats the Pallas normally fed upon. Hunger had driven the cat into the open in search of prey.

The Pallas appeared at dusk, on a distant shale slide. A tiny adjustment brought the spotting scope to hard focus. Soderstrom slid his M16 onto a sandbag, took a breath, exhaled half and squeezed off a single round. It took a quarter second for the 5.56mm to fly 600 feet. Hit in the neck, the Pallas died without a shiver. Soderstrom watched it slide twenty feet then went under the wire to pace off the distance--six hundred feet. He skinned the carcass in the dark.

The stiff pelt now hung above the Sergeant's air mat in the hooch. Soderstrom acknowledged Hull with a vague salute and asked, "Anything of interest this morning, Sir?"

"Only the shepherd," Hull observed.

Soderstrom turned the spotting scope down valley. Six seconds passed. "That's no shepherd." He made a minute adjustment to the focus. "He's been there for the past two mornings. I'd bet a thousand afghanis he's Taliban."

"Twenty dollars?" Hull made the conversion. "Not much of a bet."

"And that shepherd ain't no fucking shepherd. Ten minutes after sunrise he'll be fully armed and hunkered down."

Lowering his head, Hull confessed, "I'm going to miss this place."

"Copy that Sir," Soderstrom replied without emotion.

Hull raised the binoculars. Give or take twenty meters, the rangefinder placed the turbaned teenager at 500 meters. His attire was SIA, Standard Issue Afghani. Taliban, al Qaeda, Mujahideen, Opium Lord, Village Baker, all dressed in manjammies—loose fitting pants, large shirts, vests, and gray turbans. His face was bare. He was still too young to grow a beard. The goats browsed on the run, grabbing dry stalks of grass as the shepherd lashed a sharp whip across their flanks. In Afghanistan the simplest tasks contained a base brutality.

Soderstrom settled the M107 LSR on the wall.

Hull watched the shepherd move toward a cleft where he would bed his sheep. Daylight was dangerous.

The M107 suddenly cut loose.

A second before the shepherd slipped into the cleft, his heart, lungs and liver exploded across his flock.

The report deafened Hull. "Fuck!" the Major yelled.

Soderstrom held the scope on the dead shepherd. The flock was scattering across the deep valley. "Where'd I hit him?" Soderstrom lifted his cheek off the M107. "This cold air made the bullet drop." The shepherd had merely served as target practice.

Hull worked his jaw. He could not hear over the ringing in his ears. "GODDAMNIT!" Hull grabbed Soderstrom by his shirt and drove the huge Sergeant back against the parapet wall.

Straightening to his full six foot four height, Soderstrom's showed a malevolent grin, "Sir...is this behavior sanctioned in the Unified Services Code of Conduct?"

"You stupid Fuck!" Hull's temper boiled over. "You just murdered a twelve year old boy!"

Soderstrom remained at attention. Officers far angrier than Hull had braced him. "Sir, I duly and carefully identified him as Taliban." A smile hung on his face.

"From five hundred meters?"

"His dress, his vigilant study of our defenses, his attempt to flee when he realized he was discovered," Soderstrom had studied the Marine Code of Conduct. "Sir, he was a spotter for the Sand Kisser mortar teams."

"Soderstrom, you shot a kid!"

"With due respect sir, his death will serve to warn the extremists to keep their fucking distance!"

Hull studied Soderstrom's drugged gaze. "You stupid fuck. You won't win Afghan hearts and minds by killing their children!"

"Sir, my intent was never to win hearts and minds. My goal is to help Hajjis attain paradise!"

In the distance an approaching Chinook hammered though the cool morning air.

Soderstrom was killed by a suicide bomber a month later while shopping for Remeron in Kabul. A twelve year-old boy pushed a wheelbarrow loaded with twenty pounds of high explosive RDX into the crowd. Soderstrom turned at the last moment. The explosion blew both his legs and one arm off. It stripped him to his skin, burned him black and left him sitting on the scorched pavement, screaming for his mother.

Chapter 14

Hull jerked upright. Twenty-fifteen. Quarter past eight. He'd slept for thirty-five minutes. Everything ached--ribs, shoulders, thighs, ankles. He crossed to the bathroom and splashed cold water on his face. Framed in the mirror's reflection, a purple bruise covered his right arm and chest. Deep scratches traversed his stomach and back. Hull thought of his father.

By the mid nineties, Phil Hull was twenty years beyond his final helicopter flight out of Saigon. If two decades helped bank the fires of Vietnam, Phil Hull still remembered the names, rank and faces of the 2nd Platoon, Baker Company, 101st Airborne who died. Ten years after the war ended, 2nd platoon held a reunion. Following half a dozen cocktails, the aging survivors of Dong Ap Bia Mountain, Lam Son 720, Tet and Quang Tri began to strip off their shirts and roll up their pant legs. Preserved in their aging flesh were the red dimples of shrapnel scars, badly healed breaks, waxy wrinkled burns and bullet holes.

A machine gun had stitched Roy Willis from nipple to hip in Quang Ti. When Willis lifted his shirt to the appreciative nods of 2nd Platoon, Hull saw that the wounds, and wounded, defined battles far better than the medals that followed. Eventually, long after the medals disappeared into a dresser drawer, the scars recorded courage, bravery and sacrifice.

Thinking about Roy Willis's wounds, Hull told his father, "I think I'd rather have the scar more than a medal."

The elder Hull looked over, "No you wouldn't," he promised.

CNN's Wolf Blitzer continued in the background, "Following bin Laden's death, crowds have increased at the Vietnam Memorial. It is unclear why."

Hull leaned on the bathroom counter and thought about the similarities. Vietnam was a muddy war with no clear objective and no decisive victory, but Afghanistan was worse. Too dry, too many deaths, no victories, no exit strategy, no memorial. Washington D.C.'s black granite tombstone offered a solemn, well-lighted place for relatives to honor Afghanistan's dead. People needed a touchstone…a place to mourn. Hull thought of Bauldaire, his last moments on the pass. Would the Lieutenant's name one day appear on a black granite wall? And would he live long enough to place his Colonel leafs and medals beneath the chiseled name?

Hull returned to the living room, added an ice cube to the rocks glass and drowned it with Glenfiddich.

The Alhambra's door locked automatically as Hull took the back stairs to Orange Street. The driver's side wiper pinned a ticket to the Hummer's windshield. He glanced at the time. Two hours over. In the Marines, if you couldn't soldier, you typed, if you couldn't type, you were an MP, if you couldn't memorize the codes, you caught dogs or took a job with the TSA. Traffic cops ranked below the TSA. He tore the ticket in half, then fourths and tossed the confetti in the gutter.

Hull drove north of Riverside, doing 70 in the fast lane of Highway 91. The speed limit was 65 but no one obeyed the limit—unless they had car trouble and were forced to the center divider where hubcaps, mufflers and drive shafts joined the baseball caps and newspapers that had either been deliberately thrown or accidentally sucked out of open windows.

In this, the Union's Golden State, "Golden" referred to the rush of 1849 and not the particulates spewed by the state's thirty-three million automobiles, each of which added twenty pounds per annum to the already salmon skies.

Colonel Dillard slowly materialized. Standing in front his blackboard, he had written in white chalk, "Fair Is Foul And Foul Is Fair: Hover Through The Fog And Filthy Air." Then below, Macbeth Act 1 scene 1. To this he had whimsically added, "Come what may, time and the hour runs through the roughest day."

Hull downed another Haldol without water. Colonel Dillard slowly faded.

How Hull found himself at the Kona Kai was a mystery.

The single story bar off Sierra Avenue in Fontana was once known as "Full House," a reference to the aces and eights-hand Wild Bill Hickok drew in Deadwood, South Dakota, the night he was murdered. After Western line dancing displaced disco, it became "The Buckin' Chute." The latest reincarnation was the "Kona Kai," which evoked images of frosty Mai Tais and statuesque girls in string bikinis wading slowly into a silvery ocean toward a setting tropic sun.

Hull parked the Hummer next to a rickety wooden fence, locked the door and started toward the entrance. He was twenty feet from the Hummer when a pit bull slammed against the wooden slats. He turned to face the snarling dog. The pit bull was short on time. Sooner than later, someone as vicious as the dog would kill it.

A decade of heavy lifting had sculpted the bouncer's striated chest and heavily muscled arms into tattooed blocks. A right cross in a bar fight had damaged his throat, and now, straining to be heard, he rasped, "We're over capacity. You'll have to wait."

Hull handed him a folded twenty. "Maybe you miscounted."

Pocketing the money the bouncer glanced over his shoulder, "You're right, I guess I did." As the bouncer stepped aside, half a dozen dancers focused on Hull's face and physique. The interested glances were instinctual, a reaction to determine if he was friend, foe, or worthy contributor to the ancestral gene pool.

To create an aura of tropic indolence, the Kona Kai's décor added tropical fish tanks, fishnets and green glass floats to bartenders in luau shirts and waitresses in strapless muumuus. On either end of the bar, two African Gray parrots moved restlessly around their brass cages, sitting on their wooden perches or hanging upside down. Given the right environment, African Grays could live as long as a man but following a decade of cigarette smoke, beer in their water trays, amplified music and salted peanuts the Grays had, at most, another year left before they toppled off their perches.

To the right of the bar a small stage held two guitarists, a conga player, a lead singer and a keyboardist. In front of the stage, a copper floor pulsed with dancers.

Standing three deep at the bar, couples smiled and flirted, their words muted by the music and the rumble of leather shoes on the gleaming metal floor. And as one hand grasped an elbow and another arm circled a muscled waist, Hull found a place at one end of the bar where he could see the wells filled with cubed ice and a rainbow of call liquor bottles, as well as the stage. He ordered a double Glenfiddich on the rocks.

A lead guitar's opening chord ripped from the speakers a second before the piano, base and congas triggered a unified twitching of buttocks.

Hull finished the Glenfiddich and nodded to the bartender. A fresh Scotch appeared and Hull pantomimed a twist, and held out a twenty. Circling the rim with the lemon peel the bartender took the bill and returned eight in change. Hull left three on the bar.

Los Angeles was populated by the beautiful and exotic; Anglo, Asian, Black, Latino and Polynesian hybrids that mixed the beauty of those diverse races. Hull's eyes moved down the bar, stopping at each person, studying their faces, expressions, how well or oddly they were dressed, until they focused on a cascade of silken black hair that fell onto a white silk blouse.

When she turned Hull knew how English sailors had felt when, after a year at sea, they watched Tahitian girls dance. Hull could only see her face, long neck and square shoulders as she faced the dance floor, moving in time to the music. Her face radiated the beauty of her Chinese mother and Castilian-Mexican father. Neither Chinese nor Spanish, she was an ancient mix of the warriors who swept out of Mongolia, served at the Emperor's court and built the Forbidden City. Her black hair, broad forehead and dark eyes reflected the glory of Spain's eighteenth century art and music, the exploration of the New World, the revolutions, wars, and the rise and fall of kings.

At five eight and a hundred and twenty pounds, she had inherited the best of her mixed parentage--her mother's narrow waist, supple hips and pale skin; her father's intelligent eyes, square shoulders, strong arms and legs. Her silk blouse was open to the second button, she wore little or no makeup, and her earrings were silver replicas of an Aztec death mask.

Beauty is rarely forgotten, and if a year passed before the woman returned to the Kona Kai, she still would have been recognized. If they never knew her name, the bartenders would not forget her figure, face or voice.

Rudy Navarra, however, would never forget her name. Grace Guerrera.

Grace was twenty-one when Rudy Navarra, an Assistant Manager for Neiman Marcus, offered her a full-time job in the cosmetics department. Leaning against the glass cosmetics counter, Navarra looked more like an Italian film star. Late twenties, with black hair slicked straight back he was five eleven, fashionably thin, with a black moustache beneath a slightly off-center nose. Young, grateful for the job and mildly attracted to Navarra's looks and passion, Grace's subsequent affair with him was short-lived and very destructive. When Navarra revealed an abusive side, Grace told him it was over and changed her phone number.

A month later, during a jealous rage, Navarra put her in the hospital with a broken right wrist and two fractured ribs. Grace refused to press charges. Hours after she was released, he appeared at her apartment door with flowers, a ring and a tearful apology. Inviting him inside she hit him with a ball peen hammer, and with the addition of a fractured skull, exactly replicated the injuries he'd inflicted upon her.

Grace knew Navarra was a man of false machismo and lasting grudges. Before he was released from the hospital, she quit her job and moved, first to Pasadena, then to San Bernardino, where she met Randy Hays.

"The Biggest Hearted Car Dealer in San Bernardino," Randy was fifty, and while standing in his air-conditioned office, he watched her long legs and the faint shift of her hips in tailored beige pants as she walked across the used car lot. "Take a break," he told his lead salesman.

Though Randy Hay's intentions were honorable, offering her a 2009 Camaro for half its sticker price did not reveal a particularly shrewd business sense. A month later he furnished her two-bedroom apartment, and gave her $4,000 a month for food and incidentals. He took her to Hawaii and to Santa Barbara, where they were seen in a secluded restaurant by one of his wife's closest friends.

Randy Hays was willing to take a divorce's financial beating to keep Grace, but when his accountant started going over the dealership's books and his lawyer told him to brace for a 50/50 split, Randy realized that his obsession for Grace Guerrera would cost him something more than three and a half million dollars. With profound regrets and a sincere confession that if there were another way, he would take it, he wrote a check for $15,000 and sadly returned to his wife.

Rick Rhone, a commercial real estate broker, who was also married, followed Randy. Having just turned sixty, Rick was mourning his fading youth at a San Bernardino club when he offered Grace $2,500 for a one-night stand. In answer, she hit him so hard he fell off his bar stool.

When Federal Express delivered a ruby ring the following morning along with a note of apology, Grace forgave his indiscretion. Rick was well aware of time's value, and spent a small fortune on appearances. He provided Grace with cash, paid her expenses, gave her lavish gifts and entertainment— all the while he was functionally impotent. Viagra helped, but did not cure the problem. In the midst of prolonged foreplay, Grace quietly assumed Rick Rhone was past his prime. The 11th-hour diagnosis of prostate cancer came as a devastating surprise. Rick weakened and within months, returned to his wife, who nursed him until the end.

Grace loved Rick and took his death hard. She knew she could have any number of wealthy, middle-aged men. Friends of Randy and Rick had made it plain they were available, should she be interested in a change of pace. Being handed from one man to another, however, stepped too close to prostitution and Grace broke the chain.

When Rudy Navarra failed to locate Grace on the Internet, he called her friends. When they blocked his number, he remembered Grace loved to dance and haunted the dance clubs around Riverside and San Bernardino. Navarra's humiliating three-year search finally ended when he saw Grace at the Kona Kai, standing next to the dance floor.

His move was cool and assured. Slipping between the dancers he appeared in front of her. "Grace, it's been a long time." His right hand took a bruising grip on her left elbow.

Navarra's sudden appearance terrified Grace. The past three years had not changed him. Grace had seen him lose his temper many times before and now feared if she cried for help he could pull out a knife or gun.

She looked toward the bouncer for help but he wasn't at the front door and she searched the surrounding crowd. Her eyes hesitated on a black haired man watching from down the bar.

Taking a grip on Navarra's hand, she tried to loosen his grip on her elbow. Her manner was calm, almost offhand. "Rudy, don't make a scene."

"Grace, where have you been hiding out? I've been looking for you." Navarra's voice carried a hard, angry edge. After three years, he would not lose her again. Taking a firmer purchase on her elbow, he steered her toward the exit. "We need to talk--someplace private."

"Rudy, you're hurting me!" She tried to pull free.

Grace Guerrera did not know the tall, square-shouldered man who suddenly stepped between them. His manner was calm, controlled.

Neither friendly nor unfriendly, Hull circled Navarra's wrist with his right hand, then squeezed. "Friend, the lady says you're hurting her. Do yourself a favor. Walk away." Unable to resist Hull's crushing grip, Navarra released Grace's elbow.

Navarra's temper boiled as he flexed his hand to return feeling to his fingers. Stepping forward until his face was six inches from Hull's chin, he demanded, "A favor? Is that por favor? Please?" He stood with his right foot slightly ahead of his left, his hands poised in front of his chest.

"Friend, you don't want to start this!" Hull had faced men infinitely more dangerous than Rudy Navarra. His breathing slowed as he waited for Navarra's first move.

"Who are you to tell me what I want and don't want?" Navarra's face rocked from side to side. "Grace… ¿quien es este pendejo?"
Keeping his eyes on Navarra, Hull gently moved Grace to one side. The music stopped, the lead guitarist abandoned the stage and the nearest dancers pushed back to give the two men room.

A large hand reached out of the crowd, grabbed Navarra's arm and dragged him backward. The bouncer had broken up a hundred bar fights. Recognizing Hull's relaxed Muay Thai fighting stance, he decided the Latino was suicidal. "Having a problem here?" he pushed between the two men.

His voice calm, friendly, Hull replied, "No, no problem. The lady's with me."

The bouncer looked to Grace for confirmation

She slipped her arm around Hull's waist.

The bouncer decided Grace was trouble but it was none of his business. Let the square shouldered dude she claimed to be with figure it out. The Latino was a different story. He would start a fight on the pretext of a look, a word, real or imagined disrespect. But not in the Kona Kai--not that night. "Dude, it looks like you struck out!" he pulled Navarra toward the door.

Ripping his arm out of the bouncer's grasp, Navarra confronted Hull. "Fuck you pendejo. No siempre estará rodeado de sus amigos."

"Amigos?" Hands opened slightly in front of his waist, weight balanced on the balls of his feet, Hull waited for Navarra's first punch. "Trust me, I won't need amigos."

Navarra's face flushed with anger, "Fuckwad, don't think this is over. We'll meet again…soon."

Grabbing Navarra's arm, the bouncer turned Navarra toward the door. "Time for you to go home and sleep it off." He dragged him through the crowd.

Pressed against Hull, Grace watched the bouncer push Navarra out the exit. Her hair brushed against his face and he smelled a perfume he could not name. It was one of the designer scents; "Poison," "Passion," or "Obsession" that filled magazines with scratch and sniff ads. The leggy models were years too young to wear the powerful, warring scents whose names spoke of death, violence and a struggle for sexual dominance. Grace removed her arm from around Hull's waist and turned to face him. "Thanks for your help."

"Not a problem." He offered his hand. "I'm Hull."

"Hull?" She took it, "Just Hull?

"Jackson--Jackson Hull."

"Jackson. That's unusual for a white guy."

"You get used to it," he admitted. "And if you don't, you shorten it to Jack."

"Jack, my pleasure, I'm Grace," she shook his hand and released it.

"Just Grace?"

"Guerrera."

Hull did not subscribe to the arcane sciences, astrology, numerology or the I-Ching. He did, however, believe in nominal determinism. If Grace

149

Guerrera's first name spoke of predestination, her last evoked war. He would later wonder if their meeting was part of a grand design--a plan in which Grace, Colonel Dillard and himself played unpredictable but related roles.

"Would you care to dance?" he followed her gaze onto the crowded floor.

Raising her face to his, she smiled.

He led her toward the copper floor where, slowed by his bruised shoulder and damaged ribs, he was not as quick as the black haired Latino men. Nor could he match the V-shaped black men whose shining shoes and designer shirts belied a natural athletic grace. The dancers had memorized the music and now gave life to the notes with the showy spins and feints of a pro receiver on a broken field run.

Hull took Grace's hand then spun her into his chest. For an instant her back spooned against him, the hard halves of her bottom pressing against his hips. Then she spun away, her breasts shifting beneath her top. They danced well together. Hull the anchor, Grace a fleeting mirage, her sensuality cascading around him. She interpreted the music with her feet and hands. When she spun against Hull, her expression was confident, excited.

The music faded, she took a breath, studied his face and said, "You're a good dancer!"

"You're a better liar."

He smiled.

She laughed as he led her to the bar and ordered her a Margarita, no salt. The bartender poured the drink with cheap theatrical flourishes, whipping the sweet and sour, lime juice, tequila, and Triple Sec into a battered mixer in long liquid arcs. He passed Grace the Margarita and took a sip from his Scotch.

Setting her drink on the bar, Grace claimed Hull with a finger through his belt loop. "Alright, so if I'm a good liar, you're not good looking and you can't dance." Taking his hand she led him toward the dance floor.

It was 1:00 A.M. when Hull led Grace out the entry, past the faded camellias into the Kona Kai's parking lot. The crowd had thinned and the night had turned cool. Hull slipped his arm around her shoulders to protect her against the chilled air.

Pausing next to her Mercedes, Grace hooked his belt again, "Tonight was ...well, sort of fun." She thought of Navarra. He would not stop until he found her. Next time Jack Hull would not be there to save her. She searched in her purse for her key.

Hull waited while she touched a button and the Mercedes lights blinked. "How about lunch tomorrow?" The squeak of an opening car door interrupted him.

Fifty feet away across the parking lot, Rudy Navarra stepped out of a Honda sedan and started to run. A blade flashed in the Kona Kai's mercury lights.

Taking a step forward, Hull moved Grace to one side.

Chapter 15

Rudy Navarra was five feet away, coming fast, his knife sweeping in a long, inaccurate arc. Watching the thin Latino run toward them, Hull regretted the evening had come to this. Navarra's knife swept past Hull's stomach and he reluctantly kicked him in the knee. A powerful right cross connected to Navarra's cheek and, in the half a breath it took the well dressed Latino to crumple onto the asphalt, Hull kicked him in the ribs, methodically inventorying the torn ligaments and ruptured muscles.

Navarra was laying unconscious at Hull's feet when Grace appeared at his shoulder. She opened her cell phone.

"Who are you calling?" Hull looked up from the prostrate man.

"The police."

"Not a good idea. This is more trouble than you need. The police will file a report. The newspapers will pick it up."

"But he just attacked us with a knife!" Grace objected. "He wanted to kill you...and cut me."

"He wasn't serious, or dangerous, only angry." Hull grabbed Navarra by his arms and dragged him to the nearest light standard. Slumped against the aluminum pole, Navarra looked like another drunk sleeping it off.

"He would have killed me," Grace said.

"No, he never intended to kill you. Just wanted to kiss and make up. Strange way of showing it but...there it is." Hull opened her door.

Her kiss was not unexpected. Hull circled her back with his right hand. Beneath the layers of silk, muscle and bone, he could feel the resonant echo of her heart.

"Call me." She wrote her number on Kona Kai matchbook, then slipped into the Mercedes, and started the car. With a single backward glance she pulled onto Sierra Avenue.

Hull was walking to the Hummer when the pit bull hit the fence. A board fractured and the huge head appeared three feet from his knee. White teeth snapping convulsively in the diffuse light, the dog struggled to force its shoulders through. His hand closed around the key in his right pocket and he pressed the button to unlock the H3. The board cracked and the dog broke free. Hull climbed in and slammed the driver side door behind him. Looking down, he saw the dog locked on the step, biting convulsively at the chromed steel.

Rudy Navarra lay propped against the light standard until 3:00 AM, when the bouncer from the Kona Kai locked the front door and crossed the parking lot to his car. When the bouncer failed to rouse Navarra, he called 911. The police cruisers and ambulance arrived five minutes later, their red, white and blue strobes lighting the Kona Kai's dry palm trees and the broken fence. The paramedics were lifting Navarra onto a stretcher when the pit bull returned. It had been trained to fight, and charged the paramedics and police at a fast, silent run. It bit the ambulance driver in the thigh and was backing off for a better purchase when a policeman unholstered his nine-millimeter Beretta. In the time it took the cop to raise his pistol, the pit bull bit the driver again, this time locking on. Kicking the dog off, the policeman blew a small, ugly hole in the brindle's skull. Unaware it had been shot, the pit bull snapped twice at the policeman's knee, then folded.

The dog's death spooked the bouncer and by the time the officers got around to interviewing him, he could not remember a face or a name.

It was 3:00 AM when Hull returned to the Mission Inn. He parked the Hummer on the street and took the stairs to the Alhambra Suite. Slipping the Colt Commander out of his waistband, he unlocked the room. The turndown service had placed a Godiva chocolate on the pillow. He slipped the M1911 into the nightstand drawer, poured a Glenfiddich, and flipped on CNN.

U.S. Marines had raided a Pakistan border compound. Hull increased the volume. "...the American Command called it a successful counter-terrorism operation. Coming shortly after the death of Osama bin Laden, the mission was intended to keep pressure on al Qaeda. Reports from Afghanistan claim that three civilians were killed and two wounded. Sources disclose that the raid occurred in the village of Kundi, in Khost Province." The beautiful talking head's mix of concern and regret was an act. Her personal connection to Afghanistan was limited to reading the teleprompter in front, and below her desk.

Kundi was a Taliban stronghold. ISAF troops would have swept the narrow streets, met sporadic resistance, and then retreated to base. The Taliban would return and attack the outpost. In two weeks the tactics would be repeated. ISAF troops would sweep Kundi, the Taliban would counter attack and villagers would be killed in the crossfire. Little wonder the illiterate, devout farmers preferred the Taliban and peace to the Americans and war.

"American-led AFA blasted open the front gate before dawn. A military spokesman claimed the father was armed with an AK-47 and showed aggressive and hostile intent toward the troops. A four year-old boy was bitten by one of the American's attack dogs and the ensuing exchange killed the father, mother and a male relative.

Hull moved closer to the HD screen. The added pixels enhanced the anchor's perfect eyeliner, foundation and blush; the more beautiful she looked, the more believable she appeared.

"Speaking before government officials and diplomats, Afghan President Hamid Karzai condemned the forced night time entry into citizens' homes. Karzai, whose supporters allegedly stuffed ballot boxes in the recent election, said, "This raid was an affront to the Afghan government."

Looking into the camera, the anchor reiterated that the Obama Administration was growing increasingly disenchanted with the Afghan president. "In a feat of political shrewdness, Mr. Karzai has surprised some in the Obama Administration by turning their anger towards him to an advantage," she said.

"Karzai is under enormous pressure to condemn the devastation that has occurred since the Americans occupied Afghanistan. The raid coincided with Karzai's demand that military forces show increased sensitivity toward the Afghan people."

Hull filled a glass with ice, added more Glenfiddich and changed the channel. The next four channels focused on wrecks, murders and rapes. In the four years since his first tour in Afghanistan, life in L.A. had become unremittingly violent. Late stage octogenarians were no longer the only ones who focused on death. Perhaps a quiet death in bed lacked the entertainment value necessary to make the evening news. Between the stabbings, shootings and ravages of AIDS, ICE and car crashes, L.A. news differed only by device and place from Afghanistan.

Hull changed the channel again. A local NBC news helicopter was circling the Kona Kai's parking lot. Two police cars, a fire engine and an ambulance were parked around the light standard.

"What was first thought to be the victim of a shooting appears to have suffered head trauma outside the popular Kona Kai Club," the news anchor reported.

The camera then focused on a uniformed spokesman for the Sheriff's department. "The victim was severely beaten and at this time has not regained consciousness. Police were also forced to shoot a Pit Bull that attacked the ambulance crew."

An on-the-scene reporter pushed a microphone toward the spokesman. "Any idea who might be responsible for the beating?"

"Two leads, but nothing concrete. We hope to know more by tomorrow." The Lieutenant brushed the microphone out of his face.

Self-defense or not, Hull hoped they didn't know more tomorrow. It was O315.

"On another note," the anchor returned, "word has reached NBC that the surviving member of the sniper team responsible for the deaths of Osama bin Laden and Siraj Haqqani was identified in Al Alam, an Iranian newspaper published in Tehran."

"Goddamnit," Hull quietly swore. He knew it was coming-- just hadn't expected it this soon.

"The unsubstantiated story was offered to Western European and American newspapers as well as television networks. Based upon U.S. Command's concern for the sniper team, all have refused to publish their identities. Al Alam bought the story for a reputed two million dollars. It has since been published online as well as in the smaller French, German, and

British papers."

Hull wondered how the story had traveled from Petraeus's office to Al Alam. The promotion and promises to protect his identity meant shit.

"According to details from the Al Alam story, Major Jackson Hull of the U.S. Marines appeared alone at Outpost Saker on the Afghani-Pakistan border. American forces defending the post reported Hull was on the run from an estimated three hundred Taliban insurgents. In the ensuing two hours the Taliban lost one hundred and twenty men. Saker suffered three wounded."

Whoever leaked had to have been at Saker. The Captain? Too smart. The Sergeant? He didn't like Hull but he was career Corps. Semper Fi. It had to be one of the Corporals.

"According to the Al Alam story, Hull accounted for one hundred and six of the number killed. While the U.S. Chain of Command has refused to identify the sniper team and have prevailed upon the international press to protect their identities, Al Alam reported it was a duty to the Islamic World to publish the name of the "assassin who martyred Osama bin Laden.""

"The story went on to identify Hull as a Marine Scout Sniper based in Jalalabad. The U.S. Command would neither confirm nor deny the information."

Hull's life had just gotten very complicated. Based on sketchy INTEL, al Qaeda would avenge Osama bin Laden. Hull crossed to the closet, opened the duffle and removed the SAW. He slid the bolt half open, checked the round then set the safety. In Afghanistan, he would have fired a test burst out the window. But this was L.A. not Saker or Seray and he knew testing the SAW would summon a TAC squad. He freshened his Glenfiddich. Assassin of OBL or not, Hull would have a tough time explaining what he was doing with a loaded SAW, an unregistered M1911 and a loaded Marine issue M30... and why he had just beat the shit out of Rudy Navarra.

Hull did not sleep or dream that night. Instead, between sips of Glenfiddich, he spent the early morning weighing his options. Drop off the radar...report to Camp Pendleton in San Diego...call a shrink and check into a mental ward--one choice was no better than the next.

When dawn filled the suite, he showered, shaved, and changed into a fresh blue shirt and dark pants. He ordered scrambled eggs, toast and black coffee in the Mission Inn Restaurant, and opened the L.A. Times. Below the headline "Sniper Hero Identified!" a smaller tag line continued, "Nation Waits to Honor Marine Scout Sniper." The copy repeated elements from the Al Alam story. A quote from Central Command closed the final paragraph "It is a great disservice for Al Alam and the Mirror to print inaccuracies that could jeopardize an American soldier's life. The U.S. continues to deny that any aspect of the story is true, and prevails upon the national news media to help us protect his identity."

The strong denials clearly identified Hull as the surviving Scout Sniper.

Hull paid the breakfast bill with a ten and a five then took the side exit onto Lemon Street. Someone had taken a can opener to the H3's driver's side. A dozen arrow-shaped scratches ran from the front and rear fenders to the driver's door where a precise, feminine hand had written, "HOW MANY DEAD AMERICAN SOLDIERS DOES IT TAKE TO FILL A HUMMER?"

Hull swore silently to himself. He wished he'd caught the vandal. But then, everyone wished that. Life in the L.A. Basin had mutated from simply strange, to unrelentingly dangerous. Before Iraq, "Hummer" stood for adventure. Now it took the blame for a failing war and a warming planet. Even if Hull had caught the vandals in the act, short of breaking their hands or wasting a call to the Riverside police, there wasn't much he could have done. "Fuck." He swore at the damage, then unlocked the door and climbed behind the wheel.

He needed to meet with Wardell Stone, Chief Executive Officer and Owner of Sun and Health Insurance. Stone had served in Vietnam with Hull's father. After the war, Phil Hull stayed in the Army while Stone returned to Los Angeles to take over his family's century-old insurance business. The two remained close. They called often, met for drinks, and commiserated about the dishonorable treatment of Vietnam Vets. Even with four sons of his own, Stone made it a point to be present for Hull's christening and every birthday afterward.

Hull was in his sophomore year at VMI when his father had a heart attack. Phil Hull was forty-six. Military Aid to Dependent Children paid for Jack's tuition to VMI, and Wardell Stone kicked in a thousand a month for miscellaneous expenses. In the years that followed, Stone served as Hull's surrogate uncle, hiring him one summer to work at Sun and Health, and taking enormous pride as Hull graduated from the Marine Corps Special Ops Command Advanced Linguist Course, the War College, and Sniper School. For those reasons alone, Hull never failed to call after each tour in Iraq and Afghanistan.

A wreck slowed traffic on Highway 10 that morning. Reading "How Many Dead Soldiers," on the Hummer, passing drivers revealed surprise, anger, or less often, disgust.

Hull was reaching for the radio volume when Colonel Dillard appeared. He was sitting in his office with a sheet of paper upon the desk's green blotter. The professor was writing. Hull watched his fountain pen form, "Tower'd Cities Please Us Then And The Busy Hum Of Men." Then, below that in smaller case, "John Milton L'Allegro!"

"Milton again?" Hull asked, above the ringing in his ears.

"Great rhymes evoke immortality," the Colonel punctuated the quote.

"Or speak of insanity?" Hull responded, keeping his eyes on the road and his foot on the throttle.

"Who spoke of insanity?" the Colonel looked up from the blotter.

"No one needs to," Hull countered. "Colonel Dillard, you alone are a fair symptom!"

"Me? When has poetry ever served as a diagnosis for mental illness?"

Hull tried to end the conversation. "Sir," he started, "With all due respect, what would it take to have you return to 1976?"

In reply, the Colonel returned to transcribing Milton.

Chapter 16

Located on Mountain Avenue, Sun and Health Insurance's red tile roofs, stucco walls, two hundred-year-old oaks and immaculate camellia gardens evoked an early California mission. Wardell Stone's office sat on the Administration Building's second floor, facing a broad, smoggy panorama of Upland's office buildings and beyond that, the mottled wall of the San Gabriel Mountains.

Hull hesitated outside reception as Dodo Dillard looked up from Shakespeare's "Henry VI." The professor quietly observed, "For many men that stumble at the threshold, are well foretold that danger lurks within."

Hull opened the door and walked to the desk. "Mr. Stone is expecting me," he advised the receptionist.

"Go right up," she smiled.

He climbed the stairs to the second floor and followed the hallway to the administrative offices. When he reached Stone's outer office, Darcy Wilkins, Stone's honey-haired Executive Assistant rose from her desk and kissed him lightly on the cheek. She was still pretty, a little older. "Jack--this country is so proud, and grateful...." She'd read the morning paper.

Grateful? Hull could not tell her how Adorean Bauldaire had died. Now that Justice had prevailed, the country would continue to observe the anniversary of 9/11 and, for a few years, Osama bin Laden's death. Only Hull, Bauldaire's father, his mother and classmates in Annapolis and Marine schools would remember Bauldaire's rank, name and where and why he died. "There was nothing to be proud of...we got lucky." Hull said.

"I understand." Her smile showed a trace of sadness as she touched

159

the intercom and notified Wardell Stone that he had arrived.

"Send him right in," Stone's voice rumbled over the speaker.

Buttoning his jacket, Hull opened Stone's thick oak door and crossed the expensive wool carpet toward the CEO's massive walnut desk.

Stone rose from his leather seat, circled the desk and pulled Hull into a powerful embrace. "Goddamn, son, it's good to see you!" he admitted.

Six-five and 320 pounds, Wardell Stone was not a handsome man. His head was a square granite block into which were chiseled a large nose and ears. He had buttresses for cheekbones, a lantern jaw, iron gray hair and dark brown eyes. Now sixty-six years old, his barrel chest and powerful hands still conveyed the impression of an aging linebacker who could come off the bench and stop any play up the middle.

Despite an inbred conservatism, Stone owed his size 54 long jacket, tailored pants, black slip-ons and silk tie to GQ's editorials. The August issue had featured Brioni suits, Kilgouras shirts, Ferragamo ties and Prada's custom-made shoes as fall's definitive fashion statement. If the elegant clothes would flatter a smaller man, they made Stone look like a Liberty Gun Safe wrapped in fine fabrics.

Stone gestured to a seat and cleared his throat, "I read the article about you shooting Osama bin Laden and that other son of a bitch Siraj Hag whatever. I won't hesitate to tell you how proud I am of what you've done." His voice rumbled like distant, muted thunder.

"Unfortunately, Al Alam uncovered my identity."

"Al Alam?"

"The Iranian satellite new channel. Fox, CNN--all of them are running the story. It's too bad that…"

"Too bad? Christ, son--hire a PR Agency and ride this all the way to the bank! Jack…you're a hero for decapitating that fucking terrorist rag head. I can't get enough of that fucking heroic shot! I never believed the SEALS got him. Too many men, too much loose talk, he was fifty miles away when Team Six came over the wall. Jesus, this country needed that to lift our spirits. Our fucking weak-ass president should give you the Medal of Honor. Not that he will. I'd start by calling a lawyer and suing the shit out of CNN. They'll settle without a fight."

There would be no Medal of Honor, not for Hull. Bauldaire, maybe, years from now when Afghanistan was just another forgotten war. Hull knew life was about to get far more complicated. "Tomorrow the story will make the front page of the New York Times."

"Those liberal bastards. You have no idea the scope of this nation's gratitude. Fuck knows why the President hasn't already called to promote you for packing a set of large brass ones."

"I missed his call. The promotion to Colonel came through in Afghanistan."

"Well, you goddamned deserved it."

"I'd trade the promotion for my spotter."

"Yeah, sorry Jack, I saw the CNN video. Those Taliban…well, they're fucking sadists." Stone shook his head with disgust. "The world's generally gone to hell. I thought after that blowjob foolishness in the White House, the younger Bush was just what the doctor ordered but Christ, that idiot fucked up the wet dream. The credit crunch, falling tax receipts, rising deficits…Sun and Health has got problems of its own. I just got off the phone with the State Insurance Commissioner's office."

Stone was given to angry outbursts and now his massive hand slammed onto his walnut desktop. "Goddamn the State of California! The Commissioner's office changes its rules to suit the exception. They've scheduled an audit first thing Monday morning." Stone disliked auditors in general and supervising auditors in particular. "Hull, I don't need to tell you that dissecting endless columns of figures in the hope of finding a single mistake, or contrived larceny, requires a missing chromosome."

Hull had filled in at Sun and Health during summer break in his sophomore year and knew that now, after eight years of little to no regulation, the insurance industry was suddenly under a high-powered Federal microscope. Stone had once admitted that the Commissioners were a tight-assed group--accounting's equivalent to a proctologist--probably good for your general health, but a pain in the butt once they got down to business. If such was their wish—and Stone was convinced it was--he wanted to make it as difficult as possible, without placing himself in the line of fire.

"How are your books?" Hull regretted having to ask.

"Fucked! Goddammit, it's not as if we can't pay our bills. It's the minimums!"

"Minimums? What about them?"

"It's a crime to leave those millions sit idle!"

Tampering with reserves was illegal. Hull waited for details.

Stone squeezed the bridge of his nose, and confessed, "I invested our minimums."

"Invested?"

Stone crossed his arms across his massive chest and looked toward the San Gabriels. "With the economy in the shitter, the rising market was too good to ignore. A hundred thousand a week, half a million a month, no one would have known the difference, if Bear Stearns, Goldman Sachs and the rest of those sons-a-bitches hadn't gotten greedy. Hell, it would have all worked out!"

"What's the shortfall?"

Stone did not immediately answer, "Eighty percent," he finally confessed.

"Your reserves are down to twenty percent?"

"A little less than that," Stone nodded. "We've got assets, but goddamit, most are underwater and the rest will take time to convert. There's no way we'll realize anything close to our costs."

"What are your chances for reorganization?"

"Reorganization?" Stone almost laughed. "Hell, I'll be lucky if I don't go to prison."

Hull felt an anchor drag. Bauldaire was dead, his marriage was over, now Sun and Health was slipping into bankruptcy and Wardell Stone was fighting to stay out of prison.

"What's your lawyer say?"

"I wish I had a dime for every dollar this company's spent defending pain and suffering suits. Those legal ticks will suck you dry, infect you with Lyme disease and still send you to jail!"

"Legal counsel could buy you time. At least until you get it figured out."

"The auditors won't shut our doors and make our policyholders eat years of installments, or hand off the policies to another company—not without the minimums. They're toxic. No one will take them, not unless California forces them to, and California doesn't have the resources to cover the losses! After AIG, the merchant banks, the investment banks' melt down--two hundred million dollars is big, big money! Sun and Health will have to convert assets, and the Feds will ratchet up their standards. Our minimums may go through the ceiling--but in the end, Sun and Health will survive. It'll be a dogfight. I'll end up in Federal prison." The bottom line overwhelmed him. When he continued, defeat filled his voice. "Jack, I've never asked you for a favor, but I could use you here Monday morning--to run interference." The CEO had nowhere else to turn.

Stone was facing years in prison. If he served the minimum sentence, he would be eighty before he was eligible for parole. His brow was deeply furrowed and his face was ashen. It was the first time Stone looked like an old man. "What kind of interference are you talking about?"

"Jack, you're a hero! Killing Osama bin Laden turned this country around. The auditors will pay for your autograph. Who knows? They may go easier on me!"

"Wardell.... you're dreaming."

"Jack, you just don't understand what shooting that son-of-a-bitch means!"

"I know exactly what it means."

Stone's voice deepened to an audible rumble. He was exhausted. Perhaps as exhausted as Hull. "How long before you return to Afghanistan?"

"Ten days."

"Don't count on it. I don't doubt I'll be watching you on Face the Nation, Meet the Press and the rest of those fucking liberal piranhas...after the Pat Tillman fuckup, you're worth too much to ship back to Afghanistan!"

"Talking to the press is the last thing the Pentagon wants," he disagreed.

Stone rested his weight on his elbows. "Goddammit...times have changed. And I'll be fucked if any of it's for the better. Jack, I need this favor..."

Hull rose to leave.

"Can I count on you Monday?"

"I'll call."

"I know you won't let me down," Stone put a massive arm around Hull's shoulder.

Hull exited Sun and Health through reception, climbed into the Hummer and dialed Grace Guerrera's number. He was surprised when she answered on the second ring--her voice calm, reserved. "Grace, it's Jack Hull."

Her manner changed, "I was hoping you'd call. You heard about Rudy Navarra?"

"On the news last night."

"He deserved a lot worse than a fractured skull." Grace's voice lacked remorse.

"The police are looking for witnesses."

"None of the Kona Kai regulars will come forward. And the bouncer, he doesn't want trouble!"

"You're probably right, but even so, I wouldn't go back to the Kona Kai. When he wakes up..."

"I hope he doesn't. We shouldn't talk about this on the phone--are you free for lunch?"

"I am. Can you come to the Mission Inn? There's an Italian Bistro on the ground floor facing the Main Street Mall called the Bella Trattoria."

Half an hour later, Hull took a table beneath one of the interlocking stone arches that supported the ceiling beams. The downtown mall was nearly empty. A waiter approached with water, bread and a menu. "I'm expecting someone," Hull advised him.

Long legs swinging in loose linen slacks and gray heels, Grace appeared in the gallery. She wore an emerald green blouse, pearl earrings, and light makeup. Hull stood and as they embraced, the firm pressure of her breasts, her perfume and sweet breath enveloped him.

He held her seat and took his own.

She glanced from the arches to the kitchen, and noted, "You have good taste." She moved her chair closer to him. "So, what's going to happen to that scumbag Rudy?"

"I doubt he'll have much to say when he wakes up."

"You think he will?"

"Wake up? Sooner or later."

"And then he'll come for me."

"I doubt it."

164

"But you can't be sure."

"Sure enough to promise you he won't!"

Studying Hull's expression, she slowly relaxed. Whoever Jack Hull was, whatever he did for a living, she sensed he could protect her.

The waiter returned. "Do you need more time?"

"I think we're ready," Hull looked at Grace.

She ordered a Caprese Salad and a cup of minestrone soup. Hull settled on a Grilled Chicken Paillard.

"And to drink?"

"Glenfiddich on the rocks." Hull waited for Grace.

"I don't usually drink in the middle of the day but what the hell, I'll have a Margarita, no salt."

"Scotch and a Margarita." The waiter studied Hull then turned toward the kitchen. "I'll be right back with your drinks."

Grace tore a slice of bread in half and appraised him. "So where did you learn to fight that way?"

"The Marines," he preferred not to lie.

"You don't strike me as someone who was in the service."

This time Hull didn't correct her. He never talked about Iraq or Afghanistan. Not even with a beautiful young woman. The waiter arrived with the drinks and set the Margarita in front of Grace.

Hull was grateful for the interruption. Raising his scotch, he said "To a new beginning."

"I never drink in the middle of the day," She told him. "But I'll agree with that." She touched his rocks glass with the Margarita.

Hull watched her dip the bread in a plate of olive oil and fig balsamic vinegar. "Aren't you hungry?" she asked.

In reply, he took a sip from the Glenfiddich.

When the food arrived, they ate slowly, avoiding any further reference to Rudy Navarra and the Kona Kai. She revealed a bit about her past, he very little about his own. They finished their drinks and Hull signaled the waiter for two more.

"No, no....one is my limit," Grace objected. "Tequila makes me crazy."

"Crazy is good," Hull said.

She laughed, returned his appraising look and nodded. "One more. That's it. I have to drive."

It was past two and the restaurant was empty when Hull paid the bill. Neither of them wanted to end the day and they moved to the Mission Inn's Presidential Lounge where they found a table on the level below the bar. The Presidential Lounge once served as an apartment and over the past century had been reserved by ten U.S. Presidents. That afternoon, the walnut paneling photos of those Presidents, exposed wood beams, the brass and leaded glass spoke to a more genteel era. A waitress took their order, Margarita for Grace, Glenfiddich for Hull. When the drinks arrived, Hull offered. "No sense switching horses."

"Good advice," Grace raised her frosty glass.

They did not rush. Both knew what the late afternoon held and drank slowly. When Grace finished her Margarita, Hull ordered another round.

"Hull, are you trying to get me drunk?" She leaned against him.

"Absolutely not," he placed his hand on hers.

It was late afternoon when Hull led her past the main desk to wide stairs that climbed past ornate wrought iron railings and devotional alcoves where lighted statues recalled Spanish cathedrals or catacombs--ancient sanctuaries where the holy spirit still held sway. Reaching the fourth floor, they followed the cantilevered walkway to the Alhambra Suite where he opened a leaded window that looked across the Inn's tile roofs.

Grace studied the décor and nodded. "Nice."

He told her what he remembered from a handout he'd found on the dresser. "The Mission Inn was built by Christopher Columbus Miller in the late Nineteenth Century, before Riverside was a town."

"Christopher Columbus? That was his name?"

"The Inn was left to Christopher's son, Frank Miller in 1902. Frank built this mix of Moroccan, Spanish and Italian Renaissance."

"You have a good memory...better than mine." She examined his right palm, "Your hands are hard," she looked up, "You never said what you did after the service."

"It's complicated."

"Investments?"

"No, not quite."

"You work for a company? Electronics? Or manufacturing?"

"Something like that." He rationalized the Marine Corps was a company. Not a private company, but nevertheless, well organized and disciplined. The difference was the number of casualties and a lack of concern about turning a profit. Someone, however, was profiting from the lousy war.

Grace was physically attracted to him and more than grateful for his help. She knew the impact she had on men and now stretched on her toes against him. He felt her lips touch his and her arms encircled his neck, her hard pubic bone brushing against his awakening manhood.

He had been celibate in Afghanistan and now the sexual drought broke within him. He wanted Grace and his hands sought her waist and the swell of her hard hips as he unbuttoned the tiny mother of pearl buttons on her emerald blouse. She crossed her arms and pulled it over her over her head, exposing her lace bra. He found her bra clasp and freed it, pulling the straps off her shoulders and down her arms, the sheer fabric falling as his hands skimmed across her full breasts. He unbuttoned her slacks and slid her panties down her long legs to the floor.

She kicked them away, momentarily losing her balance before she moved fully into his embrace. If Hull had been sixteen years younger he would have torn off his clothes, thrown her onto the bed and exhausted himself in a dozen deep thrusts. He now understood that time never repeats itself and forty years from now this moment would continue to flood, unexpectedly, upon him. He would see the planes of her face, her lowered eyelids and parted lips, the lift of her breasts and her athletic hips. By then he would have forgotten the Alhambra Suite's Persian carpets, antique wood and paintings and would only remember her smooth skin glowing in the soft, afternoon light and his desire.

"So, what exactly do you do," her breathing was shallow and quick.

"Odd jobs. Overseas. Afghanistan." He was fully aroused.

"Is that how you earned your body?" Her hand traced his erect penis.

He did not tell her his body had been hardened in Marine Corp's weight rooms and by hundred and twenty pound combat packs that cut into his shoulders and hips as it worked his thighs, calves and feet.

In reply, he picked her up and carried her into the bedroom, where he lowered her onto the king sized bed. Standing above her, Hull forgot about his lack of sleep, bruised shoulder and the dozens of cuts and abrasions that covered his chest, stomach and arms. He loosened his belt and stepped out of his pants, unbuttoned his shirt and tossed it to one side.

Grace blinked when she saw Hull's bruises. "Jesus!" she gasped. "What happened?"

Covering his right shoulder with his left hand, he lied, "I had an accident." The truth demanded too much time.

"In a car?" She sensed it was far more.

Lowering himself next to her, he caressed the inside of her leg. "No, not a car," he kissed her. He lost track of time. Ten minutes, an hour, he could not tell. Her eyes were dilated. Her chest wracked with rapid gasps as she whispered in Spanish.

Grace's recent lovers had been older--men who counted golf at their country clubs or an occasional visit to their dusty Bowflex systems as a way to preserve their youth. They were men in their late fifties or early sixties who were fighting time and age--whose chests, arms and abdomens had softened over the years spent behind their desks.

Their limbs entwined, Grace no longer noticed Hull's bruises, cuts and scars. Her hands explored his powerful thighs, stomach and chest.

In time, it was Grace, not Hull who could not wait. Her hips were moving methodically, her groans were deep and urgent. "I need you, now... please."

And then, as he started to enter her, his erection left him and he was filled with a desperate desire to rekindle his passion. He tried to focus on her beautiful breasts and hard belly. He tried to bed Grace with the ferocity that had carried him though six tours in combat. Instead he saw the cross hairs lock on Roxana's forehead. He felt his finger pressure the trigger and the heavy recoil against his right shoulder. He saw the jacketed bullets explode through Siraj Haqqani's hips and the head of Osama bin Laden swing in unanchored circles. He did not complain about his insomnia or describe Bauldaire's last minutes, or blame Colonel Dillard, the Haldol, the Mirtz, Scotch or that al Qaeda now had his name, rank, and if rumors were true, that Islamic moles were buried in the Pentagon and had his service records and serial number. The harder he tried, the more flaccid he became. When Hull finally rolled away from her he realized that along with bin Laden, Roxana, Bauldaire, and

168

now a part of himself had died as well.

Too young and far too fit at thirty-four, he wished he could think of something to say but the silence expanded to fill the large bedroom.

Grace was the first to speak. Lying naked on her back, she touched his bruised shoulder, "Look…it happens. You're young and strong…it's just a case of first-date nerves. You won't have a problem next time."

Even as she said it, Hull knew there wouldn't be a next time. Not with her.

Grace glanced at the clock radio on the night table, "Four o'clock!" She swung her legs over the side of the bed. "I have to go." She stood, looked around the room and picked up her panties, bra, emerald blouse and slacks.

She was dressed before Hull could summon the words to stop her.

Grace checked the room for anything she might have forgotten and said, "Thanks for your help…and today. Don't worry about this…" She did not put a name to his impotence. "It's not that bad," her eyes revealed an unexpected tenderness.

Hull tried to move beyond his failure. The word rang clearly, each permutation scourging him with images of Grace, naked, aroused, excited-- and his own, devastating, lack of performance. He ached for the smell of her perfume, her voice, her shape and touch, but was powerless to stop her and could only watch the door close.

After she was gone he stepped into the shower. Turning the water to full cold, he stood in the icy spray, remembering the look on Grace's face, gasping for breath until the cold turned his skin a chalky white. He didn't dry off, or even turn off the water, but walked naked into the living room and punched the remote control's power button. The volume blaring, CNN reported, "…suicide bomber killed fourteen children today in Khost, Afghanistan. You may wish to look away the following footage." A single-file line of children hurried down the rough sidewalk hard against a high wall. A communication tower stood on the far right. A military checkpoint blocked the road. Two men, local Afghanis loitered on the left beneath a green cypress tree. Fronting the checkpoint, massive redoubts and large circular culverts filled with boulders slowed traffic.

An SUV negotiated the serpentine route through the obstacles in front of the checkpoint. Left, then right. The size of the vehicle alerted the soldiers. Hull watched the children. They were young--eight or nine years old, on a field trip. The children were skipping. They stopped to look at something. The SUV skirted the third redoubt. The children hurried forward. A massive, silent orange and black blast filled the screen. Military grade-high explosive. Death was assured. Hull raised the volume until the commentary roared through the room.

"The toll stands at fourteen children dead, as well as an Afghan solider and a military security guard." CNN's talking head continued. "Fifty-eight civilians were wounded. Afghan officials said it was the last day of school and the children had just been given certificates of graduation."

Photos of the bombing's aftermath showed bloody, shredded books intermixed with small shoes.

The talking head went on. "President Hamid Karzai angrily condemned the attack, pledged to punish the bombers responsible for orchestrating the attack, adding they "will not escape God's punishment.""

"General David Petraeus, the top U.S. and NATO Commander in Afghanistan, offered his sympathy to the victim's families. He repeated his belief in the necessity of NATO's mission."

"Government sources claimed the attack was retaliation for the death of Siraj Haqqani."

A NATO spokesman read a prepared statement, "The brutality and disregard for human life by terrorists is unacceptable. We continue to witness innocent men, women and children being killed and maimed in the pursuit of this brutal insurgency, which demonstrates that our job here is not complete."

The station replayed the clip of a massive fireball enveloping small Afghani children in white hats.

If the VBED was indeed retaliation for Siraj Haqqani, Hull was responsible for the children's death. He squeezed his head until his nails dug into his scalp then started to sob, his chest heaving, as he fought down the sound.

Dodo Dillard appeared. The Professor was walking along VMI's Letcher Avenue in front of Preston Library. He quietly said, "The Gods visit the sins of the fathers upon the children."

A half hour passed before Hull rose, washed his face and dressed. He slipped the M1911A beneath his jacket and locked the door behind him.

Descending the five floors to Mission Inn Avenue, he crossed to the parking lot where the Hummer waited next to the curb, beneath a row of fifty-foot palm trees that swayed to a silent flute against the gray afternoon sky. Starting the boxy SUV he headed west on Mission before merging onto Highway 91, picked up 60, and headed east into the desert. It was late afternoon and the highway was jammed with eastbound commuters.

The Los Angeles daily commute from home to job dwarfed the great migrations--African wildebeest, Northwest Territories caribou or the swallows, humming birds and butterflies on their way to warmer wetter climes--Mexico, Costa Rica and the Yucatan Peninsula. Traffic had not moved in ten minutes. Hull turned off the motor and rubbed his eyes. Fuel injection and catalytic converters aside, V-6s and V-8s were inefficient at idle. The smog deepened when traffic ground to a stop.

Colonel Dillard reappeared. He was standing next to the VMI Parade Ground, watching the Cadets drill. As the formations squared left and right face, Dillard observed, "Idlers and cowards are here at home now, but the youth I love is gone to war far hence."

Taking a deep breath, Hull admitted, "I don't recognize it,"

Keeping his eyes on the marching Cadets Dillard said, "I'd be surprised if you did. It's a Kiowa Wind Song. But, Hull, we need to talk."

"A serious conversation with a hallucination?" Hull laughed.

"If not me, who can you talk to?"

The truth was, no one. Colonel Dillard offered perfect answers and, for Hull, perfect answers were becoming increasingly rare.

Shining through the H3's rear window, the sun looked like an over-ripe orange left to rot after the fall harvest. The fast lane began to move. Horns screamed in his ears and a fading woman in a new Prius stopped next to him and yelled, "HEY DUMBASS! DO YOU KNOW WHAT KIND OF MILEAGE THAT PIG GETS?"

Hull recalled the bumper sticker that read, "Keep Honking, I'm Reloading!" The warning included as many satisfying images for the aggressor as frightening ramifications for the victim. Hull started the Hummer and shifted into drive. Traffic inched forward toward Palm Springs, still sixty miles away.

In the distance and barely visible through the heavy smog that lay above the choked freeway, a traffic helicopter banked above a wrecker's flashing lights. Hull hit the seek button on the radio until it paused on a traffic channel then spun the volume to drown out the steady idle of the surrounding cars. A helicopter's pulsing "whop-whop" filled the Hummer's speakers. "Interstate 60 is at a standstill between Perris Boulevard and Moreno Beach Drive, where a double fatality accident is blocking three lanes," a traffic reporter viewed the intersecting rivers of commuters that flowed beneath the helicopter's transparent Plexiglas floor.

"The Highway Patrol reports that one driver is trapped in the cab and will have to be freed before they can clear the wreckage. At this point the most optimistic estimate is at least an hour delay."

"We're gridlocked," Hull observed.

"Not yet," Colonel Dillard replied. "It won't happen for another four years. Mid teens, maybe a few years later...we're still in pretty good shape. The average freeway speed is 20 miles per hour--a bit slower than in my day, but not that much slower."

A gray, heavily jowled man in a boxy, mid-eighties Pontiac suddenly slammed his fist onto the dash, threw himself back in the seat and ran a dirty hand through his long hair. Hull watched him for a moment then turned back to the taillights. He was no longer surprised by people who vented their frustration on inanimate objects; Iraq and Afghanistan had jaded him to all but the most overtly violent acts or those that threatened him specifically.

The mosquito sized helicopter hovered far ahead. "Traffic is, uh, backed up past Garey Avenue, about six miles," the reporter continued. "The surrounding arterials are also heavily congested. We're looking at an hour delay before traffic returns to normal. Anyone heading east is advised to take Highway 91, which is moving slowly..."

"Everybody has them!" Dillard said.

"Has what?"

"Bad days. Everybody has bad days. Even me. You'd think that great plays, novels and poems would offer an escape from the velocity of passing time." He paused. "Shakespeare described it best. 'And so from hour to hour we ripen and ripen then from hour to hour we rot and rot. And thereby hangs the tale.' It's from "As You Like It.""

Hull tried to focus.

"Psychiatrists believe..." Dillard started.

"Colonel, could we not talk about shrinks?" Hull interrupted. The left lane crept forward six feet then stopped. Above on the overpass, the cars moved a short distance and crawled to a halt.

"My apologies. I didn't mean to monopolize the conversation."

The setting sun colored the sky a deep red. Oncoming automobiles blinked their lights, sending a crude Morse code suggesting Hull turn on his lights. Timing was critical in the eyes of commuters. If he waited until the sun faded below the horizon, oncoming lights would blink again, laughing through their twin glare at his omission. Commuters blinked to say hello and to pass or not to be passed, or if his brights were on or one light was out. They blinked to turn and to warn other cars away, to pull over and speed up, until the blinking lights and the repeated doses of Haldol made him tremble like an epileptic dancing on the edge of seizure.

It took the CHP an hour to clear the wreck and even as the distant cars moved like the first trickle around a dam, miles back the drivers sensed the change and gripped their steering wheels with renewed purpose. It would be ten minutes before the traffic surrounding Hull moved, but watching the circling news helicopters and Highway Patrol motorcycles racing down the divider he felt the pressure change in this main artery as surely as if it was pulsing in his own wrist. And almost to the minute predicted, the traffic slowly crept forward.

The Hummer headlights picked up the silver reflectors leading out into the desert toward Palm Springs. Six tours in Iraq and Afghanistan bred a love of deserts in Hull. He tried to imagine what lay to the east beyond the sage and sand desert that stretched through Arizona and New Mexico. On the horizons, windowless remains of wooden shacks marked the historical progression west. He watched pioneers struggle across the plains to pull up short on the Pacific Coast. Los Angeles, Santa Barbara and San Francisco were eddies in that dying wave.

When the traffic thinned he pulled off the freeway and turned into a liquor store where he bought a quart of Glenfiddich, a bag of ice and a coffee cup that said, "Pray for Me, I drive Highway 93." He crossed to the gas station, purchased a gas can and filled it with unleaded. When he re-joined the freeway toward Palm Springs the H3 crushed a Blue-belly lizard that hugged

Interstate 10's fading heat.

Holding the cup between his knees and accelerating into the fast lane, Hull dropped a hand full of ice into the cup, covered it with Scotch and drank deeply. He meant to take the next exit but missed it and simply ignored the next. He drained the coffee cup, opened the Glenfiddich and splashed another shot over the melting ice.

He drained the coffee cup, added ice and two more inches of Glenfiddich, opened his phone, and dialed information. When the operator answered he said, "Boston, Massachusetts--Robert Everett Bauldaire."

The operator found the number and connected him. Bauldaire's father answered, "Hello?" His voice was intelligent, muted.

"Professor Bauldaire, my name is Jackson Hull…."

"I know your name. Adorean spoke of you…"

"I was the Senior Officer on your son's team."

"I don't need to hear your background. Adorean spoke of that as well. I read you were promoted. You're now Colonel Hull." Though the father tried, he could not strip the anger from his voice.

Hull could not avoid the call, and now that he was connected, could not hang up. "Professor Bauldaire, I wanted you to know how much I admired your son," he faltered, "He was an amazing man, a hero in the way he lived his life and how he…"

"How he died? Bauldaire interrupted him. "Colonel Hull, I saw the CNN tape. You've seen it as well?"

"Sir, yes I have--" he struggled for balance, "--I wanted to tell you how much I respected your son…"

"As well you should have, Colonel Hull. Do you have children?"

"No, I don't."

A half-minute passed before Professor Bauldaire continued. "Do you know how my son came by his name?"

"He once spoke of his mother..."

"It came from my wife's brother." The father's voice cracked, "It's a family name, from Romania. Transylvania. My wife's brother also graduated from Annapolis. He too joined the Marines."

"I was unaware…"

"Adorean Marcel also died in a regrettable place—Iran, in 1980,

174

during a raid to rescue Embassy hostages. He was one of the rescue team killed in a helicopter crash."

"I read about it," Hull confessed.

"Adorean Marcel's body was never recovered. Just as my son's has been desecrated in Pakistan. Yes, Major Hull, I know how he died. Osama bin Laden, Siraj Haqqani...do you think the deaths of either or both men traded fairly for my son?"

"No, sir. You're son was without measure."

"You said you watched the CNN travesty? Adorean's head was displayed like a trophy!" The Harvard professor choked then started to cry.

A grief-driven arrhythmia disrupted Hull's heartbeat. It started, stopped, then started again.

When the elder Bauldaire regained control he asked, "Colonel Hull-- why was my son left behind?"

"Sir...I tried to...."

"...I'm sure you tried, struggled, worked, you did your best...but your best fell far short. My son is dead!"

"Sir...I can only tell you that he died..."

"A hero? Colonel Hull, how he died, whether he was brave or a coward, whether he died for a cause or by accident makes no difference. All that matters now is that he suffered, and is dead."

"I want to extend my deepest sympathy, sir...."

"I don't want your sympathy Colonel Hull!" The Professor was now yelling into the phone, "I want my son. I want to wake up from this nightmare to find him alive and well. I want my wife to stop weeping, to talk again, to climb out of her bed, to feed herself. I want to pick up the phone and hear my son's voice, not the well-meaning clichés of a paid killer who happened to have known my son for a few months of his remarkable, unfulfilled life." Deep sobs choked out of him. The phone went dead.

Hull could not feel his arms, or chest. His mouth opened and closed as he fought to choke down a breath.

Colonel Dillard appeared. He was standing in a darkened classroom. His expression was distressed, his posture weak. He eventually said, "Show me a hero, and I'll write you a tragedy," and disappeared.

Chapter 17

I n late July the desert around Cabazon, California did not begin to cool until the sun settled into the Los Angeles inversion. True sunset was still twenty minutes away, but the afternoon smog was as impenetrable as Mt. San Jacinto's gray silhouette to the south, and minutes after the shimmering thermals faded, the western horizon flared blood red. Night followed soon after, cloaking the mesquite, dry washes and granite boulders with a palpable, smoky darkness, leaving only Cabazon's scattered porch lights, the orange headlights on Highway 10, and the Brontosaurus towering above it all.

A single spotlight cast hard shadows across its placid mouth, giving it a perplexed and confused expression. Two more spots lighted the long, arched neck that flowed gracefully into the massive chest and solid, muscled shoulders. Half a dozen more touched the trunk-like legs that supported an enormous, football-shaped body that in turn tapered down to a thirty-foot tail.

Its eyes seemed to study the east, searching for a sign of the brackish Salton Sea. Over the years the desert sun had boiled the moisture from its reptilian hide, fading it from olive green to a mottled chalk, yet so intent was its expression, it might have slowed on a spring migration. Soon, one of its front feet would take a single, plodding step, the opposite rear leg would follow and the Brontosaurus would start again, dragging its immense bulk deeper into the desert. From flaring nostrils to tip of tail two hundred and ten feet away, it was a soaring statement in balance, needing only ten pounds added to its brain to reach the equilibrium of an immense scale weighing the desert darkness against the distant, yet powerful glow of Los Angeles.

At half past eight, the Hummer skidded into the parking lot, spewing gravel and dust as it flat-spun 360 degrees beneath the Brontosaurus's pear-shaped head. Hull kept the transmission in low, the steering wheel cranked to the stop and the throttle on the floor as the heavy blue box spun in circles, one donut intersecting another. A dust devil rose around the Brontosaurus as the engine raged angrily above redline, its over-revved howl carrying far out into the desert. On the seventh three-sixty, the oil ran away from the pump, the pressure dropped, a bearing froze, and a metallic 'clang' changed instantly to a rough clattering as a shattered rod destroyed the camshaft and ignition. A second later, the crank locked and the Hummer slid to a stop, the sound of its mushy exhaust giving way to an uneasy silence as the dust slowly settled and the tinted headlights passed on Highway 10.

Chuck Berry's "Nadine" blared from the radio. Hull released the steering wheel and took his foot off the throttle. In the seconds that followed, he retrieved the Glenfiddich from the passenger seat, opened the door and climbed out into the cool night. He had not intended to blow the motor, but he was drunk and exhausted, and keeping his foot on the floor was the lesser of many evils.

"Well Colonel Dillard, what say you now?" Hull took a contemplative sip from the Glenfiddich and leaned against the front fender to consider his options.

For the first time in two days the question went unanswered.

Hull took a deep breath. "How does a sacrifice strike you?"

Colonel Dillard failed to appear.

"You of anyone would know the ancient, Romans used sacrifice as a way to celebrate a man's birthday." He took a second sip from the bottle and studied the Brontosaurus. "If you were very poor, you'd kill a chicken. If you were rich, you would offer a steer, a Christian, or a virgin.

No answer issued from the desert.

With a slight, drunken nod, Hull concluded, "Sacrifice works for me." Raising the bottle in salute to the Brontosaurus he noted, "The only problem is what? A virgin or a Christian? One is extinct and the other is running for Congress. The new century devalued heaven. Unless..." he paused, "You believe in Allah."

For a moment he tried to find the North Star. That night, however, the reflected light from Palm Springs obscured all but the brightest magnitudes, and he walked slowly back to the trunk where he removed the heavy duffle and the gallon of gas. He unscrewed the top, emptied the contents onto the Hummer's finish, and then flung the empty can into the back seat.

He paused in consideration, exhaled deeply to clear his lungs of the gasoline fumes, and took another pull off the Glenfiddich. "To you," he struck a match from the Kona Kai book Grace had given him and raised it to the SUV. "And to you," he turned to face the Brontosaurus. "A sacrifice to war. Iraq and Afghanistan, to the good and bad, living and dead, the whole and the maimed--and to the heroes."

The dinosaur's placid face stared down at him.

And then, unable to divine what came next, he said, "Let there be light!" and tossed the match onto the hood. A ruffled cape of flame swept backward over the roof and trunk and, taking a step toward the burning car, he watched a tiny red finger squirm from the rear quarter panel. The gas tank erupted, sending an orange fireball curling upward into the dark.

The Hummer was fully engulfed when a Ford Explorer with "L.A. Times," painted on the driver's door slewed off the freeway, roared into the parking lot and slid to a halt. The door flew open and a middle-aged, balding man pointed a Nikon camera at the burning sedan. "Hey Buddy! Look over here!"

Hull turned toward the blinding flash.

Checking the Nikon's digital screen the photographer said, "Great, that was great!"

Two other cars stopped. The occupants, notable only for the wonder in their expressions, edged quietly behind Hull. A moment later the attendant from the Wheel Inn, a Texaco Station near the off-ramp sprinted up. "What the hell happened?" he gasped.

"Probably something in the fuel system," the photographer volunteered. "Here, could you stand next to this guy? A little off center there?"

Hull ignored him.

"Buddy, you were lucky to get out of that," the attendant said

Traffic from Highway 10 continued to stop. "Anyone in it?" someone asked.

"A man and his wife," a spectator answered.

A second witness observed, "Jesus, that's awful." Invoking Jesus seemed to add an inviolate weightiness to the burning car.

"Anyone call the Highway Patrol?"

"They're on the way," the attendant said

"What about the fire department?"

"We're out of the district. It'll have to burn," he added.

"And what're you going to do about this wreck?" the attendant persisted. "You can't just leave it here."

Hull glanced at him, and continued to stare at the fire. "I'll have it towed," he answered.

"There's not much left to tow. It's burnt to hell!" the attendant pointed out. "The thing is, you'll need to get it out of here before the museum opens. This Brontosaurus is the biggest thing between L.A. and Palm Springs. The owners won't go for a burned Hummer cluttering up the area."

Black smoke swirled past the dinosaur's head. In the flickering shadows, its eyes seemed to move. Its tail twitched. The steering wheel caught fire, the exposed seat springs glowed and the windshield shattered, collapsing into the interior in an incandescent shower of granulated safety glass. A moment later the radial tires ignited, sending soft blue flames licking over the Hummer's fenders until they too slowly distorted, sagging down.

Gutted Hummers filled the Coalition's Afghan junkyards. Each had a story--recounted by the mechanics that cannibalized what parts they could from the twisted, burned hulks. The worst were victims of IEDs that blasted crews through the mangled sheet metal. Hull tried to think clearly. He had burned the Hummer as "A statement against...?" he struggled quietly within himself.

"What did you say?" the station attendant asked.

Hull did not hear him. He had burned the Hummer because? He tried to remember.

A California Highway Patrol Car pulled to a dusty stop twenty feet from the burning H3. Hooking their nightsticks on their hips, the two CHP walked into the crowd.

"Anyone know who owns this?" the taller of the two asked. Thirty years old, six feet tall with a black moustache and a gold nameplate that identified him as Thrall, B.M. The Patrolman raised his voice and repeated, "I said, does anyone know who this car belongs to?"

The attendant stepped back and pointed toward Hull. "This man here owns it,"

Hull glanced at the Highway Patrolman and returned to watching the Hummer burn. Afghanistan had taught him that Police--Afghani and Coalition alike, armed with loaded forty-five caliber Colts, were far more dangerous than an IED.

Lowering his voice, Patrolman Thrall asked, "What happened here?"

Ten seconds passed before Hull replied. "It started to miss a few miles back and when I stopped to check it out, it blew."

"If it was missing, why didn't you stop back there at the Wheel Inn?"

Hull looked from the burning H3 to Patrolman Thrall. Loaded on Gentleman Haldol, Senor Mirtz and Good Neighbor Glenfiddich, it wasn't wise to ignore the CHP. "I figured it was something simple…a loose plug lead."

Thrall held out his hand. "Can I see your license?"

Hull opened his wallet and handed over his driver's license and Military ID.

"I guess you weren't able to save your registration or proof of insurance," Thrall said, looking up from the license.

"Not in the four seconds before it blew."

Thrall studied his Military ID. "You active duty?"

"Home on leave."

"Where you stationed?"

"Afghanistan….Jalalabad."

"Shit…" the Patrolman's rigid professionalism cracked. "That's serious country. What's your mission?"

"First Marines…Interdiction."

"Goddamn, that's dangerous duty. I served in Operation Iraqi Freedom. Third Corps Support Command…"

Third Corps were truck drivers, assigned to deliver supplies. Thrall hadn't moved ten feet without an armed escort. "Hell of a deal," Hull managed to summon a shred of enthusiasm.

The Highway Patrolman studied Hull with new respect. "Dammit! I miss the service. I should have stayed in." He wanted to trade war stories.

"It has its good side."

Knowing Hull would understand, Thrall volunteered, "Being with Brothers in Arms."

Hull thought of Bauldaire, "That's it," he agreed.

"The Dinosaur complicates this fire." Thrall reluctantly turned from his memories of Irag. "Tourists pretty much ignore the Brontosaurus but this Tyrannosaurus causes more problems than it's worth. The vandalism and violence here makes me wish this Ferrocement piece of shit had never been built. But it's famous and private, which makes it doubly hard to demolish." He turned Hull's ID, "I'll need to run your license." Glancing toward the patrol car where the second patrolman stood behind the open driver's door, he quietly confessed, "If it was just me I'd say fuck it but my partner is a hard ass. My job is like yours--by the book."

The crowd started to thin. Hull listened to the engines start. A line of cars formed on the overpass. He had two choices. Hitchhike or call a cab--both sketchy prospects at night, twenty miles outside of Palm Springs.

Thrall crossed from the Black and White. Handing Hull his Military ID and driver's license, he said. "No outstanding tickets, no previous arrests. The Hummer is registered to Avis...except for your expired license, you're clear."

Hull wasn't aware it had expired. "Hell of a deal. When?"

"On your last birthday, April 28th. Why didn't you get it renewed? "There was no California DMV in Afghanistan."

"That would explain it."

"I'll renew it," Hull's promise, however, lacked contrition. During the past forty-eight hours, his life had spun out of control. An internal gyroscope had been brushed gently off center and CHP, Third Corps Support Command or not, now seemed to spin in tiny eccentric circles. Worse, the eccentricity appeared to be slowly increasing.

"Major, how much have you had to drink?"

"Enough," Hull noted Thrall's use of his rank.

The Patrolman studied him for a minute more. Brothers in arms or not, Thrall played by the rules. "Look Major, I didn't catch you behind the wheel so I won't cite you for DUI. You'd fail a breathalyzer." When Hull failed to answer, Thrall continued, "It's pretty clear you were drinking and driving, but that won't appear in my report. I talked to my partner. I'd say the Hummer burned, you were upset and had a drink." Without raising his voice, Thrall added, "If I were you, I'd count myself lucky."

"I've been that," Hull replied just as calmly.

"How are you getting home, Major?"

"A friend's on the way."

Thrall's partner signaled from the patrol car. "We got a jackknifed semi two miles east of Banning."

Thrall handed Hull's license back. "About the car…" he gestured toward the burning wreck.

Hull's answer fell short of a promise, "I'll have it towed."

"Major, Semper Fi," Thrall strode quickly to the Black and White, where he dropped into the driver's seat and swung expertly onto the freeway.

The flames flickered out as the flashing lights disappeared over a distant rise. The crowd drifted back to their cars. The last spun his wheels, adding dust to the black cloud that hung over the smoking Hummer.

Holding a notebook and pencil, the photographer hesitated beside him. He had been listening to Thrall. "Jackson Hull. Is that H-U-L-L?" he inquired.

Hull stared at the smoking Hummer and ignored him. He was drenched in sweat, whether from overdosing on Mirtz and Glen, the cold, or the realization that this was not a nightmare from which he would awaken; he was grateful that his sentence had been commuted. Hull could not stop shaking. If he could urinate or vomit, the shaking might stop.

He recalled a line from the Statue of Liberty. "Give me your tired, your poor, your huddled masses yearning to breath free." The smoke drifted into the dark night and he wondered aloud, "Where did we screw up?" Even as he said it, he realized that bashing America belonged to a distant and forgotten era. In the decades since the early seventies, the hippies had parented the Y people who had birthed the Me Generation who had been searching for a new identity when the price of oil went through the ceiling, the stock market crashed, and methamphetamines became the recreational drug of choice--a cheap taste of paradise that changed perky prom queens to toothless hookers.

Opening his cell phone Hull dialed the number for Classicab in Palm

Springs.

"Classicab," a flinty female voice answered.

"I'm at The Wheel Inn in Cabazon."

"Destination?"

"Riverside." he replied.

"Before we can send a cab, we'll need $200 in advance."

"Two hundred dollars?" Hull checked his wallet. He was down to four twenties. "I don't want to buy the cab, just…"

"Sir, I don't make the rules," The dispatcher interrupted. "I just follow them. The charge is two hundred dollars in advance."

"Do you take credit cards?"

"With two forms of ID…your cost to Riverside will be a total of $400.00. Do you want to me send a cab?"

"Please."

"Type of card, name on card, number, expiration date and code?"

Hull changed his mind. "Forget it." He said.

Picking up the heavy duffel, he walked the two hundred yards to where the on ramp joined the freeway and stopped beneath a quartz iodide lamp's bright circle of light.

Hull's jacket, cotton shirt, khaki pants and loafers offered little protection against the desert cold. A passing semi buffeted warm diesel fumes and dust. He watched the red taillights recede slowly west toward Los Angeles.

Standing on Highway 10's graveled shoulder he turned east toward Palm Spring's incandescent glow. Highway 10 was defined by taillights and to the north, beyond the smoldering Hummer, the desert's vast darkness. Traffic thinned. The single spotlight caught the Brontosaurus's tiny head and held it far above the Texaco Station. A vagrant breeze bore the heavy smell of Afghanistan--burned, super-heated metal, scorched insulation. The only thing missing was the sweet stench of cooked flesh.

Hull tried to remember why he torched the Hummer. He wanted to believe it was an important decision but he could no longer summon the conviction that helped him toss the Kona Kai match onto the sedan's volatile finish.

It came to him that he had sacrificed the Hummer to Fate and tried

183

to recall the myth. It came to him in pieces. The Greeks believed Themis, the Goddess of Necessity, and Zeus, had three daughters named Koltho, Lakhesis, and Atropos. All were skilled weavers. Koltho spun the thread of life; Lakhesis measured the thread's length; Atropos cut the thread at the assigned moment of death.

Hull tried to think but the Glenfiddich's alcoholic haze affected his memory. He needed to return to Riverside but, since he could not decide how, it was easier to focus on Greek mythology.

If the Fates only kept track of acts and time, life would lack terror. Existence turned interesting when the three weavers spoke to the Furies who sprang from the blood that had dripped upon the earth when Coronus castrated his father, Uranus. These three sisters--Alecto, the unceasing, Megaera, the envious rager, Tisiphone, the retaliator--were called the daughters of the night. With bat wings on their backs, fire in their eyes and the heads of dogs covered by writhing snakes, they avenged crimes of passion: torture, assault and murder. The punishment for murder was madness.

It was as good an explanation as any--as good as the Christian belief in a single, omnipotent accountant. Hull had seen too many lives wasted to blame death on anything but predestination. Allah, Christ, Buddha, Fates--it made no difference. The result was always the same.

A late model Cadillac stopped. Hull walked toward it. When he reached the rear fender the boxy sedan suddenly accelerated, filling the air with dust.

"Funny," Hull said aloud without humor. He felt the SAW's compact weight in his duffle bag. The driver was blessed to live in the United States where stupid, impulsive pranks didn't automatically appear on the obituary page. Afghan soldiers would have lit up the Cadillac's driver and passengers--innocent or not. A faint smile flickered across his face. Both sides, the Taliban and Coalition, knew full well that life was not a joke. He brushed himself off and returned to the highway light's incandescent circle.

A Ford station wagon passed him. Taking small amusement from Hull's upraised thumb, a child's face pressed against the rear window. He realized he might stand through the next day while a hundred thousand cars passed him. The desert sun would blister him as surely as if he were forced to cross Afghanistan's southern wastes without water.

"I must be going crazy," he whispered.

Colonel Dillard appeared. He was standing at a blackboard. Across it he had written, "L'homme est bien insense'. Il ne saurait forger un ciron, et forge des Dieux a douzaines."

Hull had not studied French since VMI and was able to translate man, God and the verbs, but the rest made no sense. After a minute of silence he asked, "Translation?"

"It's Michel Montaigne, from his "Essays." Underlining the chalk sentences Colonel Dillard recited, "Man is certainly crazy. He could not make a mite, and yet makes Gods by the dozen."

"It applies," Hull nodded. Reaching into his pants' pocket for his phone he felt the matchbook from the Kona Kai. In a clear, feminine hand, above the red sulfur tips, Grace Guerrera had written her number. He dialed the ten digits and waited.

Chapter 18

S eated on her apartment's linen couch, Grace Guerra ignored her iPhone through the fourth and fifth rings. On the last, a second before voicemail picked up, she uncrossed her legs and touched the green icon.

"Grace, it's Jack Hull."

"Hull," she replied without emotion.

"I'm sorry about this afternoon," he stared at his shoes.

"It happens…you needn't apologize. You saved me from Navarra--I'm grateful," she hesitated. "It's probably best we leave it at that."

Hull hated depending on anyone but himself but now faced west toward Los Angeles. "Grace, I need a favor. My rental car caught fire in Cabazon at the Wheel Inn under the dinosaur."

"Did you call the rental company?"

"Not yet." His voice lacked a defining confidence.

Grace recognized the change. "Hull…how much have you had to drink?"

"Enough. Look, it's a long drive out. I'm sorry I called."

Grace had known Hull for less than twenty-four hours and Cabazon was forty miles east. Other than his intervention with Rudy Navarra, she owed no dept to Hull. He was just another good-looking, impotent drunk. She was about to disconnect when his face appeared on CNN.

The silent image shocked Grace. The photo was an old one. Hull looked younger, less worn. She raised the volume. "The photo is attributed to al Jazeera," Wolf Blitzer reported. "A question remains how the story jumped from al Jazeera to the Internet. In the past four hours it has been downloaded two million times. As a result, and much to the distress of President Obama and the Pentagon, the name and photo of the Marine Major who killed the real Osama bin Laden is now public."

"The Obama administration has yet to explain how Osama bin Laden appeared to have been killed on a remote Pakistan ridge, a full two months after the Abbottabad raid. Photo analysis suggests that bin Laden may have used a body double. Unaccredited sources reveal that Major Jackson Hull, one of the Marine's most decorated Snipers, intercepted Osama bin Laden near Pakistan's North Waziristan region. While Lieutenant Adorean Bauldaire, Major Hull's Spotter, was killed during the ensuing firefight, Major Hull managed to escape to Firebase Saker. Al Jazeera reported he was promoted to Colonel for his role in the death of the two Islamic terrorist leaders. According to sources within the U.S. State Department, despite the fact he is on active duty, there is speculation that Colonel Hull may be entitled to part of the fifty million dollar reward the U.S. has offered for the capture, or confirmed killing, of Osama bin Laden."

Grace shut the TV off. "Jack, it's no problem to pick you up. I'm leaving now. The drive will take forty minutes, maybe a bit more but I'll be there."

"You don't have to, I'll wait for the cab."

"Hull, I'm on my way, where will I find you?"

He turned toward the brightly lit Wheel Inn. "I'll be at the Texaco station....thanks Grace." Hull closed the cell phone.

Grace left her apartment and crossed the brightly lit common area to the underground garage. Starting her Mercedes CLK550 Coupe, she waited for the V-8 to warm and wondered why she had just agreed to drive to Cabazon. The answer appeared in pieces. Hull was handsome, well built, smart, and if CNN was correct, a national hero who might make her rich beyond her wildest dreams. She slid the automatic transmission into reverse. The Mercedes moved smoothly back and she touched the brakes, moved the lever into drive and quickly exited the lot.

Reaching the Riverside Freeway she accelerated east up the on-ramp onto Highway 60--directly into the path of a speeding semi. There was the imminent scream of horns and the rhythmic, bouncing headlights from

187

tractor-trailer wheels locked in series. High double brights rushed toward the rear view mirror which focused the quartz iodide glare on Grace's calm eyes. For an instant the semi towered like implacable steel wall over the Mercedes' back bumper. Then the CLK's alloy V-8 soared into its power band. An extra thirty horsepower miraculously appeared, and caught between the desperate howl of 8-ply truck tires and the muffled screaming of three hundred-eighty-horsepower, the distance held. Like partners in a tango, the two circled but did not touch one another. The Mercedes arched seductively beneath the semi's chrome grill then slipped away, dipping slightly as its transmission slammed into third.

Grace was not oblivious to the effect of high-speed collisions between semis and sports sedans; it was more a matter of conditioning, of surviving the chaos of early life until now, short of her mid-twenties, it took more than a near-miss with a semi to lift her heart above a steady eighty beats a minute.

She watched the speedometer soar past 100 mph, but did not lift her right foot off the floor until the truck was far behind her and the desert loomed dark and impenetrable beyond. It was a measure of her past, a learned response to high stress situations and a remarkable coolness under fire.

Hull glanced at his watch. Ten thirty PM. If he had sacrificed the Hummer to Fates and Furies, he now doubted that the Greek's Pantheon of minor gods existed, or if they did, would have any knowledge of America's modern mechanizations of steel and plastic. The desert air cut through Hull's cotton jacket and he retreated from the highway across the parking lot toward the smoking SUV. The boxy four-wheeler resisted death, just as men were forced to endure beyond the point when common mercy dictates a painful end. A last fragment of insulation reached its combustion point triggering a spurt of flame from the Hummer's interior.

Grace's silver Mercedes turned left across the Highway 10 overpass to Seminole Drive. A second later she stopped in front of the Brontosaurus. Hull opened the door and the heavy smell of burnt Hummer followed him into the sedan's warm interior.

"Thanks for picking me up." Hull kissed her on the cheek.

"Count it as repaying a favor." She put her hand on his neck, looked at the burned H3 and inquired, "What happened?"

"It took a hit." His description was best left in Khost.

The Hummer's tires, seats, carpet, insulation and paint had burned away, leaving the steel exo-skeleton cooling beneath the towering Brontosaurus.

Grace studied Hull's profile. "You're him," she said. "You're that Sniper...the one who killed Osama bin Laden and that other Taliban terrorist...Siraj Haqqani." She pronounced both names correctly. Reading his surprise she added, "Al Jazeera outed you on the net!"

His expression hardened. If Grace knew, the world knew.

"CNN ran your photo. The major networks--FOX, ABC, CBS and NBC, are broadcasting your photo and name."

Hull knew the consequences of national exposure.

Grace massaged his neck. "Wolf Blitzer reported you're could receive a fifty million dollar reward for bin Laden and five million for Haqqani."

"Wolf Blitzer's wrong. I'm employed by the U.S. Marine Corps. Trust me, the Marines won't pay fifty-five million dollars for following orders."

"But--you are the Sniper who killed bin Laden?"

Further evasion would amount to a lie, "My Spotter and I were ordered to wait for a signal," he admitted..

His abbreviated answer disappointed her, "That's it? Wait for a signal. No name?"

"Just a signal...that's all." He skipped the seven days in Western Pakistan. "When we couldn't ID the target, we took out a tall Arab with a gray beard. We got lucky." He looked at her. "I found out later it was bin Laden. Haqqani was collateral damage."

"Blitzer says you're a hero."

"Blitzer is exaggerating. The shot wasn't difficult. The location was. Any Special Ops team could have placed those bullets. We were at the right place, at the right time."

"CNN claims your whereabouts are unknown!"

"CNN would never disclose my location."

"What does the Pentagon know?"

"Only that I'm on leave in Los Angeles."

"If the Pentagon knows, CNN knows. The press is going to find you and when they do, you'll be famous." She started the Mercedes and accelerated west on Highway 10. "Hull, you should schedule a press conference and save them the trouble."

"No, absolutely no press." He couldn't face a hundred reporters' cameras and microphones. Not while he was high on Haldol and Mirtazapine. He could easily confuse Colonel Dillard with a reporter and start babbling about Paradise Lost. They'd drag him off in a straight jacket. "No press."

"Alright, no press. But it's only a matter of time before they find you."

Grace was right. All resources, legal and illegal, credit cards, car rentals, hotel reservations, ATM withdrawals, ex-wife, friends, and contacts would be mobilized to track him. Phone records would be checked--the press would find him.

Grace followed Highway 10 to Cherry Valley where she joined 60 through Beaumont, then Moreno Valley and finally to Mission Boulevard where she pulled to the curb across the street from the Mission Inn. Putting her hand on his shoulder she said, "Look Hull, you're not thinking clearly."

"I'm fine, I just need sleep."

"Sleep's a good start, but like it or not, the press will find you and when they do, they'll crucify you. Your best hope is the Marines. They'll protect you."

The Department of Defense hadn't anticipated Hull would be identified. Not four days after the mission. Uncounted other missions had targeted Osama bin Laden and CENTCOM had little hope that Hull and Bauldaire would succeed. But Hull and Bauldaire had succeeded, and while CENTCOM had not planned on failure, it was unprepared for success.

Bin Laden was an Islamic hero, one of a rare few. Hull had made him an Islamic martyr. Hero or martyr, he was equally dangerous to U.S security. State could ill-afford to venerate Hull. Any more than the White House could allow him to be bludgeoned by the press. No medals, no parades, no photos, no interviews. Hull would simply disappear back into Afghanistan where a fifth tour would amount to a death sentence. One hero would follow another.

The U.S. State Department would strike a balance between the billions of dollars and thousands of dead soldiers lost in the pursuit of Osama bin Laden and deep regret over the half million dead civilians.

"Hull," Grace interrupted his thoughts. "The press and Marines are searching for you. You're in no shape to face either." She made a quick decision. "Look, you can sleep at my place. We have no connection, no history. They won't know where to look for you--at least not for a while. It'll buy you some time."

He was about to refuse her offer when an ABC News mobile satellite van made a left turn onto Orange. A moment later, a black sedan ran the red light.

Slipping the Mercedes into drive, she said, "Looks like the decision was just taken out of your hands."

Chapter 19

I n the thirty-five months since former President George W. Bush departed from Washington in the Marine One Helicopter, he had disappeared into a compound in Dallas' Republican enclave of Preston Hollow, where he worked twelve hours a day, seven days a week on his memoir "Decision Points." Published by Crown it had opened with brilliant sales. Two million copies pushed the ex-President's book onto the top of the Times' Hardcover Non-Fiction Bestseller list, where it stood for weeks. Laura Bush was proud of George, proud that he'd refused to write a pandering four hundred pages filled with sordid details. At first, Crown's editors didn't want to learn how the President accepted Jesus. Instead they'd pressed him about the personal things--his drinking, the wild years at Yale, the Air National Guard and campaigning for George Senior. Laura knew no one, not even the Crown's editors could force President George W. Bush to write about his weakness. From the very first, "Decision Points" was intended to expose George's strengths.

Driven by appearances on Oprah, with Matt Lauer on the Today Show, The O'Reilly Factor, Fox News, Hannity, and Greta Van Susteren, sales numbers for "Decision Points" had wildly exceeded all expectations. Of course, Bush was not surprised when The Huffington Post reported that chunks of Decision Points had been plagiarized.

Following the publication of "Decision Points," the ex-President focused on funding the Bush Presidential Library. With the costs expected to exceed $300 million, the Bush family made personal calls to long time supporters. In spite of the failing banks, epidemic real estate foreclosures and severely damaged insurance, car and housing industries, Bush's old supporters quickly stepped forward to fund a repository for his papers and presidential memorabilia.

It was Laura who suggested the Foundation Christening ceremony at Southern Methodist University, her alma mater. President Bush would extend personal invitations to Rice, Cheney, Rove, Rumsfeld, Ashcroft, Gonzales, even Tenet and Colin Powell. Bush was well aware that politics was one thing, but the judgment of history was quite another. George W. would spin it as a time for healing, a dedication for an institution of higher learning; a place where future scholars would come to unravel the complexity of the early 21st Century and in time, exonerate and honor George W. Bush as they had honored Harry S. Truman.

The news of Osama bin Laden's second death confused the ex-President. He wished he knew what the hell was going on and what to believe. Bush knew the killing of bin Laden belonged to his Administration--not Barack Hussein Obama's. Bush/Cheney could take credit for making the tough decisions and weathering the savage criticism of the last two years. Osama bin Laden, Siraj Haqqani—dead! He could not have paid for better news.

Bush immediately called Rush Limbaugh. Following the Republican Party's devastating loss in 2008, Limbaugh now spoke for the party faithful.

Bush had not communicated with the conservative radio celebrity in more than two years. "Hey Rush, how's it hanging?" The ex-President's tone was folksy, familiar.

Limbaugh, at first, did not recognize the voice and wondered how the speaker had gotten his private number.

"It's George," the ex-President was surprised he needed to identify himself.

"Mr. President!" Limbaugh replied with sudden enthusiasm.

Bush wanted Limbaugh to hit his fastball out of the park--into the upper deck. He pitched the radio star low and outside. Twenty minutes later, for a substantial honorarium, Limbaugh agreed to speak at the Bush Presidential Library Foundation Dedication. A blessing from Limbaugh's conservative audience would resonate through the Republican Party base. At least those who still had the means to fund the Bush Presidential Library.

The following morning, a blurb appeared in local papers, the RNC website and CNN. Ex-President Bush, along with members of his staff, would dedicate future site of the Bush Presidential Library. The ceremony was set for July 20th.

All but Colin Powell agreed to attend. Sandwiched between a two-hour lunch and an hour meeting to strategize about the future of the Republican Party and their own role in national political races, the dedication would take an hour at Southern Methodist University. None of the dignitaries would fly commercial. All would be back home by five o'clock that evening.

To avoid suspicion while he waited in Dallas, Rostislov took unskilled jobs; final dry in a car wash, landscaping laborer, fry cook, handy man. A job was a cover. No one suspected the hard-working multilingual illegal who held a job for a month. To keep him from moving on, his bosses typically offered him a raise, which he always refused. After a month, people would start to inquire about his background. He preferred not to tell the truth, nor to lie. Either one would reveal too much about him. The safest course was to quit.

The announcement detailing the dedication of Bush's library appeared in the *Dallas Morning News* Sunday paper. Details were sparse. The ex-President was scheduled to give a short speech at the site of his future library. Rostislov committed the two paragraphs to memory. Bush rarely left his compound. When he did it was in an armored limousine surrounded by Secret Service. Bush's agents were too thorough, too well armed, too prepared for a suicide bomb, an RPG or anti-tank rocket. Details of the ex-President's routes and schedules were closely guarded. Rostislov needed to catch Bush in the open, at a fixed point, where he would not attract attention. Southern Methodist University offered a perfect venue. Allah had blessed him again.

On Monday morning, Campus Security failed to notice the new security camera anchored to the chemistry building. It was a small, fixed unit, an exact replica of other campus video cameras, of which there were dozens. The new camera pointed toward the vast tent where the ex-President was scheduled to make his speech. Rostislov needed five minutes, no more.

The hardest part was waiting. Should the Secret Service notice the additional camera, the dedication could be cancelled. During those four days, Rostislov worked for an arborist, stuffing tree limbs into a diesel-powered chipper. One mistake and the chipper could turn a hundred and seventy pound man into a ten second jet of blood, flesh and pulverized bone. His boss had seen it happen.

That Friday, Rostislov found a white 1998 Ford Taurus on Craigslist with 104,000 miles on the clock and scratches on the right rear quarter panel. Like Rostislov himself, the car was virtually invisible.

He waited on a street corner that faced the main entrance of Southern Methodist for Bush's motorcade to pass. Dressed in black capes with white masks, a hundred protestors marched on the sidewalk opposite the entry to the University. A few carried signs accusing Bush of war crimes, others the names of dead soldiers. Rostislov knew how the old men and young women would be treated in Afghanistan but America was weak and the protestors marched and chanted while they waited for the ex-President.

The line of black Lincoln limousines appeared just before noon. The ex-President's limo was third in line, passing quickly while the Dallas police blocked the intersections. Rostislov caught a glimpse of Bush as the armored Lincoln passed. He looked older, worn and gray. Rostislov smiled at the change. He was pleased the past years had taken a toll. The infidel President had no idea of the pain he had visited upon Afghanistan.

Rostislov watched the motorcade until the limousines containing Condoleezza Rice, Dick Cheney, Karl Rove, Rumsfeld, Ashcroft, Limbaugh, and Hunt sped past. He then walked deliberately back to the Taurus and drove six miles to an empty lot where he pulled a transistor radio out of his jacket and turned to a news station that was broadcasting the ceremony.

Cheney wondered why the ex-President had to dedicate the Bush Library Foundation. He'd already dedicated the groundbreaking. What further dedications would he be forced to attend? Dick Cheney was the first to approach the lectern.

The ex-Vice President had lost weight since his eight years in office. An extended hospital stay to implant a mechanical heart pump had extended his life expectancy at the same time it stripped thirty pounds off his frame. In the past six months his face had changed from middle to old age. His face was waxen, shrunken but still fiercely determined. Though he used a cane to steady himself, he leaned it on his seat before he crossed to the microphone. The cane spoke of frailty, but heart pump or not, Cheney was not intellectually weak. The ex-Vice President's brief comments focused on Bush/Cheney's success in preventing further 9/11s. Cheney knew it was Bush's show, not his and quickly got to the point. Turning to face the ex-President, he forced a wise smile. "In the time since you left office, judgments have grown more measured than they were. When times have been tough or the critics have been loud, you've always said you had faith in history's judgment, and history is beginning to come around!"

Cheney's five-minute analysis of American Security, both prior to and following 9/11 weakened the ex-Vice President and he concluded his comments with a reference to "Decision Points." "The amazing response to Mr. Bush's book showed that the country has begun to reevaluate him!"

Then staring off into the distance, the Vice President felt compelled to compare President Obama's stimulus to the fully funded library's construction schedule. "This may be the only shovel-ready project in America," Cheney smiled before returning to his seat.

Ex-President Bush started with a joke. "Standing here on the future site of the George Bush Presidential Library and Museum, where hundreds of thousands of books and papers will soon be housed," he paused to allow the image to resonate across the crowd then continued, "A library may seem to be an unlikely place to reappear after my eight years in Washington D.C.," he nodded and smiled. "By now most of you know I've written a book. It's a tell all!"

The crowd laughed.

"In fact most of my critics were shocked that I wrote a memoir of my two terms in office. They didn't think I could read a book, much less write one."

The large crowd applauded his self-deprecating candor.

"It's been an interesting experience." Bush continued. "I'm not shilling for "Decision Points" -- aw, heck, you oughta buy a copy."

The faithful roared their approval.

"I want to thank the donors. The building was paid for even before ground breaking. Let the framing start!" His head bobbed delightedly.

Turning to a more serious topic, Bush raised his arms, "I'm sure you've heard the new news about Osama. But I'm confused! Was he dead then? Or dead now? Or not dead at all? I think Mr. Obama should get his story straight! What was it? Then or now?" Thunderous sustained applause, whistles and shouts greeted his thinly veiled criticism. Bush waved his hands above his head to quiet the crowd. "Whether in May, or two months later, I told you we'd get him!" The ex-President waited for the applause to fade. "It was our program, Dick Cheney's and mine that finally flushed him out."

When the applause finally quieted, Bush reminded the assembled crowd that the invasion of Iraq had been a necessary, but painful decision. In the future, a stable, democratic Iraq would lead the Middle East to a lasting peace. A democratic Iraq would become America's strongest ally in a dangerous corner of the globe. Bush continued with a synopsis of his accomplishments. He listed his efforts on behalf of Haiti, his contributions to fighting AIDS in Africa, his success in containing North Korea's atomic threat, as well as his long-standing efforts to keep taxes low and deregulate industry. He restated his firm belief that oil was America's life-blood, and that needless restrictions on drilling would cripple the economy. He mentioned the Deepwater Horizon catastrophe, but only as a failure of Obama administration to react quickly to the initial blow out.

"The decisions of governing are on another president's desk and he deserves to make them without criticism from me. But staying out of current affairs and politics does not mean staying out of policy," he told the crowd.

Then turning to the ex-Vice President, he recalled why he picked Dick Cheney for his running mate in 2000. Bush admitted, "As I stand here, there is no doubt in my mind he was the right man. He was a great Vice President of the United States, and I'm proud to call him friend."

The speech lasted ten minutes. Bush was never a commanding speaker but this one would be ranked among his best. Perhaps it would serve as a first step back. He concluded with "Thank you all and God Bless America!" The crowd went wild.

The faithful were waiting for Rush Limbaugh who crossed to the lectern and stood in the warm, Dallas sun. The sustained applause wrapped around him as he lifted his arms to embrace the praise. That day, only a Southern Methodist Professor of Modern History noticed the resemblance between Limbaugh and Italy's Mussolini, il Duce, when he too accepted the crowd's accolades.

Rostislov ducked into a thick stand of willows crowding an old irrigation canal. Six miles from the assembled crowd and hidden by the budding green whips, he aligned the mortar base plate to a north south azimuth then carefully assembled the 120mm tube. He anchored the tube to the base plate then consulted a hand held calculator to derive the angle from his GPS point to Southern Methodist. He'd checked and rechecked the coordinates a dozen times. Convinced his math was correct, he carefully removed a twelve-centimeter mortar round from the metal suitcase. The first of five was called Altai, for the Russian falcon that had been hunted to the brink of extinction; the second was Peregrine; the third, Barbary Falcon; the fourth Gyrfalcon, and the last, Merlin. All were birds of prey that relied on stealth and speed to survive.

The 120mm mortar shell had been developed by the American multinational corporation Raytheon. It had a range of eight kilometers, and with GPS guidance and laser homing, was accurate to within three-meters. Al Qaeda had paid dearly for the explosive payload. Rostislov dropped the mortar fins-first into the tube and covered his ears. Altai roared from the tube and soared to more than a kilometer over Southern Methodist University before it arced back to earth.

Pulling what resembled a garage door opener from his pocket, Rostislov touched one of three buttons. Six kilometers away, the security camera he had anchored to the Chemistry Building sent a single, green laser beam toward the tent's central high peak. The incoming Altai Falcon alone sensed the green light. The mortar's small fins adjusted, the course correction was made, and the projectile hurtled down through the tent fabric. It exploded seven meters above ground level, filling the tent with a loud BOOM. The blast shocked the Secret Service. Anticipating a second round, eight agents threw George and Laura Bush, Dick Cheney, Dick Rumsfeld and Condoleezza Rice to the ground. Flattened among the folding chairs, the crowd jumped to their feet and began to run. Three thousand supporters, young and old, stampeded for the exits.

The Secret Service jerked the ex-President, Mrs. Bush, Cheney, Rumsfeld, Rove and Condoleezza Rice to their feet and dragged them at a run to the armored limo that raced down pedestrian walkways. Less than two minutes after the concussion, the driver drifted sideways onto a main road that exited off campus.

Rush Limbaugh struggled to his feet behind the lectern. He hadn't finished his speech and would be damned if he'd run. Lifting the microphone, he yelled to the screaming, stampeding crowd, "Why the hell are you running?" No one turned to listen. Frustrated, Limbaugh continued to yell, "It was a dud!"

Six kilometers away, Rostislov returned the dismantled mortar barrel to the metal suitcase. He scrubbed his hands, arms and face with alcohol-wipes then threw the used towels into a garbage can. Obeying all speed limits, he returned to his studio apartment where he stripped and stepped into a frigid shower. For the next half an hour he scrubbed his body with antiviral soap. Developed by the Soviets, it was almost 100% effective. In this case, *almost* a hundred percent left far too much to chance. Rostislov wiped down with refined alcohol pads then repeated the process twice. He had four days to get out of Texas. Any longer and the faint margins of safety would vanish.

The Secret Service and FBI coordinated with the Dallas City Police and the Texas Rangers to establish roadblocks on all major freeways. During the following twenty-three hours, the roadblocks and overlapping investigations produced no evidence, no leads, and no suspects. Whoever mortared Bush had disappeared into the city of six million. With no leads, and no witnesses, the Secret Service and FBI grasped at possibilities.

The FBI grilled informants, searched recent firearm purchases, reviewed film from the campus security cameras—and came up with nothing. The Texas border with Mexico degenerated into chaos. The U.S. Border Patrol inspected every car, truck and pedestrian. The resulting traffic jam stretched eight miles north from all major and minor border crossings. Rural Texas Sheriffs ran surprise searches, profiling black-haired, brown-skinned drivers. Mexican, Mid-Eastern, Black--racial profiling was kicked into high gear. Anyone who resisted was arrested and held for further questioning.

More than ninety nine percent of those who were checked at the roadblocks proved to be illegals, U.S. citizens, and workers with Green Cards. A rumor circulated that the roadblocks were INS raids spurred by the attempt on ex-President George W. Bush's life. Caught in the massive traffic jams, many undocumented workers with invalid driver's licenses, expired proofs of insurance and false registrations feared deportation. Flight triggered pursuit and for the next two days, news helicopters chased Black and Whites following lawnmower-filled pickups. It was only a matter of time before a terrified gardener T-boned an innocent family. Eight fatalities occurred when two illegals made a U turn on U.S. 30, the Tom Landry Highway, right into the path of a minivan transporting a family of six to a wedding.

The FBI shook down Dallas informants, arrested members of radical groups, created profiles and offered a million-dollar reward for information leading to the mortar team. The reward prompted five thousand calls, all of which were checked. None revealed solid leads.

Rostislov used the ensuing chaos to slip, unnoticed, out of Dallas. Five days to the hour after the mortar exploded over the dedication ceremony, he simply disappeared. He sterilized his studio apartment. No fingerprints, garbage or scrap of clothing was missed. The apartment was swept clean, vacuumed, washed and disinfected, then triply inspected to ensure that even an intense forensic investigation would come up empty. Not a hair, thread, toenail clipping, toothbrush bristle or whisker in the bathroom sink was overlooked. Nothing. The absence of any clue was in itself, suspicious. Rostislov, however, was aware that a single overlooked fragment might lead the FBI to him.

Rostislov's impeccable planning and subsequent lack of clues, however, frustrated the FBI. With the Dallas freeways subject to rolling roadblocks, Rostislov kept to quiet residential streets where the white Taurus passed unnoticed. Once clear of the urban sprawl, he followed the back roads north through Celina and Pilot Point to Gordonville. He reached Madill, Oklahoma at four that afternoon, stopping only for gas and bottled water, picked up Highway 3 north to Ada, then the 377 due north to Prague. He skirted Oklahoma City east through Avery, and continued north until he crossed the Kansas border. It was late in the afternoon when he turned east toward St. Louis.

That evening, as the sun was setting, the car radio cut to George Bush and Dick Cheney's press conference. Bush sounded confident, more presidential than at any time in the previous ten years. "We were very lucky the mortar was a dud," he told the country. "I'm grateful that no one was injured and have every confidence that the FBI, working in conjunction with Texas law enforcement agencies, will capture the people responsible for the attack."

Rostislov listened intently.

"Vice President Cheney, do you have anything to add?"

Dick Cheney had returned to Wyoming immediately after the dedication ceremony. The station had patched in a feed from Cheney's home, and there was a brief pause before the former Vice President's familiar voice agreed. "Yes, I'd like to point out, in those dangerous years following 9/11, under the Bush/Cheney Administration, America remained safe. While President Bush and I weathered unrelenting criticism from those who would have had us lower our guard, the laws we enacted and the methods of alternative interrogation we endorsed, kept America safe. This attack represented the first serious security breach in more than eight years. During the recent past, President Obama's roll back of our hard work has made us less secure. Worse, it has encouraged the very terrorists we fought to defeat. I will let history decide who was right and who was wrong."

Rostislov had watched the Press Club dinner where Bush, in a joking mood, had narrated a photomontage that chronicled his years in office. In one, while looking under his desk, he ad-libbed, "I must be looking for Weapons of Mass Destruction." Rostislov smiled; the ex-President would know soon enough his statement had been prophetic.

It was late, past ten on the fifth day, when Rostislov stopped at a faded East St. Louis motel. Removing the metal suitcase from beneath the back seat, he rolled down the Taurus' windows to spare the glass from the neighborhood methamphetamine addicts. He told the motel owner he preferred not to be disturbed. Though she tried to remember his face, a minute after he left the office, she could not recall a single detail about him. Shrugging, she realized that some people were cursed that way.

Chapter 20

T he Federal Bureau of Investigation needed eighteen hours to identify four charred stainless steel fragments from the dedication ceremony. One had lodged in the lectern, another in the arm of a woman in the audience. The agents quickly determined the mortar was built by Raytheon, but had no clue where it was launched. During the first hours after the attack, while the Secret Service silently congratulated itself, the FBI agreed with Russ Limbaugh--the mortar had misfired. Bush was bruised, but otherwise uninjured. None of the other dignitaries had been hit by shrapnel. By the second day, both the FBI and Secret Service realized that the remarkable stroke of luck wasn't only luck.

An agent in Atlanta suggested an alternative scenario. The mortar hadn't misfired but had performed flawlessly. If it had been filled with high explosive, the detonation would have been magnitudes more powerful. The explosion served only as a propellant. The question was for what?

The FBI insisted the tent, seats and stage remain standing until they finished the investigation. A second sweep through the upended chairs revealed something more--a faint residue. The amount of trace powder on the stage and seats decreased in relationship to the distance from the lectern. The agent from Atlanta gathered a sample and sent it by courier to the Centers for Disease Control with a classified note requesting an expedited analysis.

At week's end, an otherwise healthy political science major who attended the dedication ceremony appeared at the Southern Methodist U's clinic, complaining of headache and fever. The examining resident noted it was early in the season for the flu. Aside from swollen glands, and a surprisingly elevated temperature, the student's symptoms were non-specific. The resident checked his throat for strep, but lacking identifying white sites, sent the student home with advice to drink water, take aspirin and rest. Following the doctor's orders, the student retreated to his dorm bed where his chills increased. By the following morning he was shaking uncontrollably. Without a thermometer he could not know his fever had reached a hundred and three and a half. Crossing to the bathroom for a glass of water and four more aspirin, he looked into the mirror. Framed by the young, handsome face, his eyes wept continuously. In the night, they had turned to blue agates floating in Bloody Mary mix.

Twenty miles away in Preston Hollow, George Bush rose unsteadily from bed and crossed to the bathroom. He felt like hell. He was coming down with something--probably the flu. For whatever reason, the medicos still couldn't figure out why the vaccine hadn't worked that season. Now he would pay the price for their incompetence, three, maybe four days, at fifty percent.

Even with the flu, he recognized that the dedication marked a brilliant peak in his career--right up there with the Trade Center speech. Bush had spent seven years in the office without a major terrorist attack. Now, after he handed Obama the keys to the Oval Office, his smooth-talking successor had flunked a mid-term exam. Bush smiled at the irony. The billions spent to defeat terrorism had protected the country. George Bush would be exonerated--far sooner than anyone expected. He looked at his face. A slight flush tinted his cheeks and his eyes were bloodshot. He definitely had the flu. He splashed cold water on his face, took four aspirin and reluctantly returned to bed.

At the same time, in his dark, Jackson Hole, Wyoming home, Dick Cheney arose and pulled open the drapes on the window facing Rendezvous Peak. The jagged summit was just catching the coming dawn's rose-colored light. No matter how many times he'd seen it, he never tired of the show. Further north, a storm was building over the Grand Tetons. The falling barometer was causing his joints to ache. There would be rain later in the day.

Since leaving Washington, he and Lynn had worked on their books; she on James Madison for Viking, he on his past forty years in Washington. Threshold Editions, an imprint of Simon & Schuster had released "In My Time: A Personal and Political Memoir" in August. The reviews for "In My Time" had been checkered. Not surprisingly, the liberal press had savaged the memoir. But Cheney could give a shit. "In My Time" was second on the New York Time's Best Seller List. Let the liberal bastards write what they wanted, history would decide what was the truth and what wasn't. He should never have admitted that his aggressive tactics had promoted an image of Darth Vader. He didn't need to hand the liberal press a comparison they wouldn't find themselves. But hell, he could not stand guard 24/7. He was there to do a job and eventually he had to let down.

The job had come at a price. His heart was shot to hell and he now feared further cardiac problems before he was able to put his life, his philosophy, and his victories on paper. In light of Obama's rapid revision of the Bush/Cheney's eight years' good work, the ex-Vice President hoped to pen the definitive last words.

Cheney was both glad he was out of the White House and pleased to have regained his political voice. The appearances on CNN, CBS, NBC, Fox, Face the Nation, and in the newspapers had helped him cast off the code of silence forced on him by Bush Junior. Hell, if he were younger, or if his ticker weren't shot to shit, he'd run for President. Considering Mitt Romney, Michele Bachmann, Herman Cain, John Huntsman, Ron Paul and Rick Perry and the ranks of potential Tea Party candidates, Cheney would have an excellent chance of winning.

Bolton would support him. John was a damned good man. But then Cheney had gone to the mat to secure his appointment as Ambassador to the United Nations.

Cheney knew he should never have flown to Dallas. The heart attack at thirty-seven sounded an alarm. The second in 1984, a mild one, was followed by the third in 1988. The coronary bypass led to his fourth heart attack--the one that almost killed him. He'd started to lose track of the procedures that followed, angioplasty, stents, and an implanted cardiac defibrillator.

The latest was a ventricular assist device—a euphemism for a mechanical heart. Cheney believe he could get used to anything but the mechanical heart had stripped him of a pulse. It wasn't as if he was dead on his feet. He just lacked a heartbeat. Some of his political opponents had been accusing him of that for years. In the end he'd have the last laugh. If the mechanical heart caved in there was always a cardiac transplant. Cheney didn't know how it would feel walking around with the heart of another man. Better, he guessed, than dead.

The mechanical heart was supposed to allow him to travel, golf, maybe hunt a few birds but the quick turns, even to Dallas and back, still knocked the hell out of him. Even though he was still angry as hell with George W. for leaving Scooter Libby to dangle in the wind, he owed a political debt to George H.W. Bush Senior and, God rest his soul, Ronald Reagan. For the past too many years he had been charged with counseling, protecting and guiding the unlikely heir to the Republican Revolution. Cheney should have listened to his friends and aides when they warned him the governor would be "the class clown in the White House." Considering Bush's unbelievably ill-advised decisions--the fires that had threatened to crown out of control, the gaffes and unbridled stupidity that he had been forced to call back before they went public, no wonder he felt like his bum silent ticker was sliding toward cardiac arrest number five.

Serving as Vice President was a thankless job. Cheney, however, could take pride in the fact that he'd always acted in the best interest of the country. Some day he would be judged by history. Knowing what he had learned in his forty years in Washington, he had no fear of how he would be remembered. The description came easily to mind.

Patriot.

Cheney was proud of the programs he steered through the President. After the Department of Justice bastards threatened to walk out en masse over the legality of electronic surveillance, Bush Junior had stopped answering the phone.

There was the other issue--capturing and killing al Qaeda operatives without due process. Cheney was nearly sick at the memory. Al Qaeda didn't afford due process to the victims of 9/11 and he'd be damned if he offered any quarter to international terrorists. Leon Panetta killed the program. Panetta was a coward who was unable to stand the heat.

Cheney's paramilitary teams were trained to pursue the "surgical" solution that Democratic doves kept cooing for. The Vice President would have increased the role of the remote-controlled Predators…even at the cost of collateral damage. An image of civilians killed by JADAMs flickered past. He wasn't saying Afghanis were expendable but, the fact remained, war is hell.

That's why he was so damned happy about the Scout Snipers who nailed Osama bin Laden and Siraj Haqqani. It was Cheney's program, Cheney's way of doing business, shepherded through the right channels. Even if he wouldn't receive credit, goddamn he was happy!

Cheney watched the clouds build above the Teton Valley. It was too early for a winter storm. His right elbow and left knee ached like hell and he felt feverish, a reliable sign of approaching low pressure. He noted a slight flushing on his chest and deep bloodshot tint in his eyes. He hoped it didn't signal more heart trouble. If the symptoms became more acute he'd call his cardiologist. Who would have known his sixties would have presented such physical challenges? As his mind was growing increasingly sharp, his body was falling apart. He swallowed the aspirin, sipped the clean, Wyoming well water and returned to the bedroom to dress.

Rush Limbaugh awoke in his Palm Beach, Florida home with a fever and aching joints. Kathryn, his recent bride, was asleep in her room. Separate bedrooms had not been his idea but Kathryn complained his snoring kept her awake. Not withstanding the difference in their ages, the marriage was proving to be the best of his four. Direct descendant of John Adams, daughter of an Annapolis grad, poised, beautiful, focused, blonde--she was a perfect partner. He preferred younger women and, at thirty-three, she was comfortable with older men... and though all marriages required compromise…David Letterman's late night cheap shot about the Viagra drip was below the belt. That part of the marriage was fine…just fine. Besides, sex was never perfect, not at first. All the shit on the Internet about his weight and penis size were untrue, absolutely untrue. As far as he could tell, Kathryn was satisfied, and not only because of the money.

Limbaugh hoped they wouldn't have to start a family. By virtue of damned good birth control and abstinence, he'd avoided the birth of children in his first three marriages. Bottom line was he didn't have time for children, couldn't see himself, diapering, reading "Three Little Pigs" or pushing a stroller around Disneyworld. So far, Kathryn had not pressed for children and, now that he was staring down sixty, he hoped she wouldn't insist on knocking the shit out of her damned fine body.

Mother Mary! He felt like death warmed over! He briefly contemplated canceling his radio show but the news that Osama bin Laden had been killed had hit the wire and he definitely wanted to bear witness. It would be an amazing show, three hours when Rush could draw a clear line between freedom and tyranny, liberty and dictatorship, government by the majority, and rule by terrorists. There were also other pressing issues. The Democratic majority had already rammed national healthcare reform through Congress, nationalized the four major banks, issued massive new loans to keep GM and Chrysler afloat, and taken on enough debt to sink the Carnival Splendor. Now that the Republicans owned the house, the agenda would change. He and Kathryn might even take time for a cruise.

In the past, before his marriage to Kathryn, Limbaugh always sailed for free on Carnival. For a brief speech on the Poop Deck, he was given the Presidential Suite, free food, free booze and, before he remarried, introductions to the lovely young Carnival hostesses.

It was a good gig, one he was sorry to lose. Rush blamed the Barack Hussein Obama Administration for trouble in the cruise industry. With the country awash in red ink, how could anyone afford to cruise? Not that Rush spent much time cruising during Barack Hussein Obama's rule. Cruising spawned too much indefensible press. Someone would always find a way to photograph Rush at the buffet table. It didn't make any difference whether he picked at the salads or piled on the roast beef and mashed potatoes, the paparazzi were always looking for the perfect shot: Rush lifting a fork of food to his mouth, Rush at the desert table, Rush overweight, flushed and unfocused. The Democrats and Liberal Press paid big money to splash those photos across national tabloids. The latest was taken when he was at his absolute heaviest. The caption predictably ran in heavy black font across the header, "Is Rush Limbaugh's Weight Out of Control?" It could just as easily have been the *New York Times*. They were all bastards.

The news about Osama bin Laden's second death had broken. The wire services now had the name of the Marine Scout Sniper who shot him.

Rush looked forward to the show. At the same time he rejoiced over Osama bin Laden's death, he would honor the sniper. His theme would be, "Attack the United States and there is no hole deep enough, no compound so isolated, no closet so dark, that we will not find you!"

Limbaugh felt like shit. He was working too hard. The mirror reflected his flushed cheeks and bloodshot eyes. "Damn," he surveyed his image. Terrible time for the flu. How was he going to survive a three-hour show? His brain wasn't responding. He downed six aspirin and took a sip from the mouthwash bottle. If he could manage the morning's heavy lifting, he could rest on Saturday and Sunday. He was rarely sick. If he were to tone down a notch, take more listener calls, save his voice and recycle some of his best lines, he would get through the show. He didn't have to produce fresh material for every show. No one could. Not even Rush Limbaugh.

Chapter 21

R ush Limbaugh settled heavily into his Palm Beach studio chair, adjusted the microphone and waited for his engineer's signal. As always, his show started on time. Fortified with vitamins, a mega dose of aspirin, potassium and zinc, for the first two hours it went extraordinarily well. He was in the zone, dancing the sweet line between telling the truth and actionable slander. He was surprised when in the middle of a long, brilliant monologue against the Obama Administration's bailout of Wall Street, the banks and the gang of lawyers who defended them all, he felt a need to use the men's room. It hit with such sudden urgency that Limbaugh frantically signaled his engineer to key a commercial and scurried down the hall. He was three feet short of the toilet when his bowels evacuated themselves in a powerful, prolonged flush. Rush Limbaugh had a deserved reputation for an obsessive, almost feminine focus on personal hygiene. Now he nearly fainted from the smell that boiled out of his cotton slacks. Much worse, his colon continued to contract in consecutive, prolonged spasms until he felt as if he was turning inside out.

His engineer knocked on the door. "Rush, you OK? I'm keying old clips to fill the dead air."

Resting his cheek against the stall's stainless steel panel, Limbaugh yelled, "Be out in a minute."

But he wasn't out in ten minutes. When he finally summoned the strength to wipe, the toilet paper was soaked with blood. Limbaugh screamed repeatedly for help, but still keying clips from some of Rush's more memorable monologues, the engineer didn't hear him.

Russ Limbaugh's bloody diarrhea alone would not have raised alarms. By that evening, however, George W. and Laura Bush, Dick Cheney, Donald Rumsfeld, Karl Rove, Ray Hunt, Condoleezza Rice and a dozen Secret Service agents exhibited symptoms of a severe, as yet unidentified flu. In addition to the politicos, nine hundred of the three thousand Bush Presidential Center groundbreaking attendees had staggered into emergency rooms, complaining of high fevers, aching joints and head pain. The number would double by morning.

The U.S. Centers for Disease Control was trying to keep a lid on what could quickly develop into a national panic. A day had passed since the FBI's hurried blood samples identified the agent as a filoviridae--an enveloped, single-stranded, unsegmented, negative-sense RNA virus. As with other negative-strand RNA viruses, surface spikes enabled links to receptors on the host cell, and that link allowed entry. Some of the individual thread strands were shaped like the letter U, others, the numeral six, and a few resembled a snail's spiraled shell.

The slide terrified the CDC. Marburg virus! The nightmare of biological warfare had become a reality! Half an hour after the CDC identified the virus, the agency head issued orders to quarantine all patients who expressed high fevers, severe headaches and atypical bleeding in segregated hospital wards. Caregivers were given detailed procedures on how to deal with the infected. The CDC knew that, if the virus became established in the general population, the death toll from 9/11 would pale to insignificance.

The origin of the Marburg virus was elusive. The most recent research pointed to an ancient disease that germinated in an unspecified East African animal host. One lead pointed to Kitum Cave, near Mt. Elgon; as few as half a dozen primary contacts triggered a zoonosis—an animal disease that infected humans. The biology was close enough for the disease to travel from an as yet unidentified species--perhaps it was Kitum's bats--to man. The puzzle was, naturally occurring Marburg had a lethality rate of 25%.

The CDC was completely conversant with the virus structure. Marburg contained 22 potential N-linked glycosylation sites on its surface. Viral replication took place in the cytoplasm, and envelopment was the result of budding, preformed nucleocapsids. Systemically, the virus targeted the liver, lymphoid organs, and kidneys. Of one thing the CDC epidemiologists could be sure; the Marburg virus used in the Dallas attack could be traced to the Soviet Union.

Marburg virus, like Ebola, was a Category A bio-warfare agent and all signs pointed to Biopreparat Institute. The Soviet scientists who worked at Vector, the huge, isolated, virology-research campus in the larch forests outside western Siberia's gray industrial city of Novosibirsk, called it "The System."

The Institute was created in 1974 to house a clandestine bio-weapons program. The public/political face of Biopreparat was charged with peaceful medical research. The clandestine face developed and produced sophisticated bio-weapon powders: smallpox, black plague, anthrax, tularemia and the Marburg virus.

A close relative of Ebola, weaponized Marburg could take as long as three weeks to run its course. Victims experienced massive hemorrhages in the skin, mucous membranes, internal organs, stomach, and intestines, as well as swelling in the spleen, lymph nodes, kidneys and less often in the pancreas and brain. Six to nine days after onset of symptoms, the victims' organs slowly emulsified; first the eyes, then the ears, nose and anus, and finally the skin itself.

The most famous case involved Dr. Nikolai Ustinov, a Biopreparat researcher who accidentally infected himself while injecting a guinea pig. As Ustinov slipped the needle into the large rodent, it fought back, forcing the needle completely through its body and into Dr. Ustinov's thumb.

Witnesses remember that Dr. Ustinov did not panic. Instead, he quarantined himself in a sterile containment ward, where everything, even the air, was sterilized. Medical staff and visitors were all required to take chemical showers before and after leaving the unit. All waste, including his feces, was burned in a designated, thousand-degree crematorium.

Married with two sons, Ustinov held no illusions concerning his fate. He said goodbye to his wife and sons and asked for a notebook. Two days later his temperature spiked. By the fourth day tiny hemorrhages had shattered the small capillaries in his eyes. On the morning of the eighth day the pain became unbearable as the virus slowly melted his internal organs. His body tried to eliminate the infection by bleeding it out from his eyes, mouth, ears, anus, fingernails and finally his skin. His colleagues said that at the end, he wept blood.

Sources later revealed that Dr. Nikolai Ustinov donated what remained to the Motherland. The scientists salvaged what they could-- blood, spleen, liver, that contained the new Marburg virus. In honor of Ustinov's sacrifice they named it Variant U. Nikolai Ustinov would have been proud. Variant U proved to be extremely virulent.

The Vector scientists kept the Ustinov virus alive and replicated in bioreactor flasks. They then dried Variant U into an inhalable dust and tested it on bio-isolated lab animals. Results showed a single inhaled viron of Variant U would kill monkeys.

Though no records of human tests survived, the CDC knew that an outbreak of Marburg Variant Ustinof would explode through a population. Weaponizing U Variant radically increased its lethality to 90%. The potential number of fatalities exceeded that of a hydrogen bomb detonating over a major U.S. city. Worse, by replicating the U Variant until their stockpiles exceeded a hundred pounds, the Soviets produced sufficient Marburg to kill every man, woman and child--not just in the U.S., but worldwide.

The CDC immediately realized the numbers in Dallas indicated a deliberate terrorist strike. The outbreak bore the mark of al Qaeda, who made no secret of their intention to obtain chemical and biological weapons to use against Jews and Americans. What the CDC did not know was where and how al Qaeda had obtained weaponized Marburg.

It would take a year to trace the source. Following the dissolution of the Soviet Union, the Russian bio-warfare factories were unable to pay the technicians and biologists. Many purportedly left Russia to work in other countries. Of those, half a dozen packed freeze-dried Variant U in hermetically sealed canisters in their luggage to offer it to the highest bidder for further experimentation.

The U Variant virus had cost al Qaeda twenty million dollars. Molding it into the mortars had taken a dozen lives, perhaps more--the scientists charged with tracking the victims had been among the first fatalities.

Of greater immediate concern were how many weapons the terrorists possessed. Dallas struggled desperately to quarantine the sick. Even more ominous, the medical staff that had treated patients in the earliest stages had also started to present symptoms.

It was early morning of the sixth day when Rostislov spread his prayer rug in the filthy East St. Louis motel room floor and turned to Allah for guidance. Thirty minutes later, when he finished praying, he loaded the four remaining falcons in the Taurus and turned northeast on Highway 55 toward Springfield. From there he continued north to Chicago.

Chicago offered a soft target for a mid-day, midlevel airburst of Variant U. The wind was blowing off the lake, colder to warmer. The viron cloud would drift for sixty miles blanketing the city with trillions of filovirus. Rostislov would wait upwind until the virus dissipated, then continue onto Boston, Philadelphia and New York. With luck, in three days he would explode the final Merlin Falcon over Washington D.C.

His only problem was wind. He had an alternate plan if it were to change. Denver, Seattle, San Francisco, and Los Angeles lay to the west. Allah would guide him. By evening of the eighth day, six million people would have inhaled Nicholas Ustinov's Last Will and Testament. By the morning of the tenth, America's Congress, Wall Street and ten million more Infidels would have breathed in the same microscopic viral whips. Osama bin Laden had a genius for revenge. Revenge for the killing of innocents, the impoverishment of the many for the gain of the few. America would soon grieve as it had never grieved before.

Rostislov tuned the radio to WTAD, Springfield's news-station. "A flu outbreak in Dallas is causing concern among local health officials," the announcer said. "Over fifteen hundred people, many of whom attended the dedication of George W. Bush's Presidential Library, have sought treatment at local hospitals for high fevers. The CDC is running tests to identify the virus."

Rostislov had less than a day to launch the second Falcon before Dallas hospitals were overwhelmed by the infected. Medical workers would abandon patients who would rapidly lose their ability to eat, drink, or crawl to the toilet; the city would quickly sink into an urban hell. The army would close the freeways, airports, high-rises, schools, sports venues--anywhere a large crowd could gather.

The newscaster noted that four members of the Illinois Republican

Party who attended the Southern Methodist University ceremony appeared at Chicago's Mercy Hospital complaining of high fevers, aches and recurrent bloody noses. Cell cultures had been flown to the CDC in Atlanta to confirm that the Chicago flu was linked to Dallas. The newscaster finished by saying that in spite of the recent health alerts, President Obama planned to give a speech to the Chicago Mercantile Exchange.

Rostislov knew the FBI was searching for a team, not a Lone Wolf. Rostislov's ability to act alone, keeping his intentions, activities and whereabouts to himself, made it triply difficult for law enforcement agencies to identify him. As the epidemic exploded out from the business district into the suburbs, Chicago would initiate a yellow, then orange, and in two days, a red alert. The airport would shut down. The state police and National Guard would man roadblocks. Traffic would grind to a stop. Rostislov could slip into Chicago, but now doubted he could avoid the overlapping security.

With the virus on the verge of devastating the city, Rostislov held the hood on the Peregrine Falcon. The mortar could not be wasted. His duty was to maximize each weapon's impact.

One other issue was of concern; the virus was extremely contagious and there were no guarantees that he would be spared. Rostislov had become an expert on the disease. The stages that followed the initial fever were lingering and painful. By the end, those victims who could still talk screamed for help. Rostislov did not fear death from a bullet, a bomb or even a knife but he refused to succumb to a microscopic strand of RNA.

The sun was rising. In the far distance, Chicago's skyline barely broke the horizon. Rostislov longed to fly the Falcons over Boston, New York and Washington--to finish the job that the martyrs of 9/11 had started at the Pentagon and World Trade Center. In four hours he could set Peregrine free. In three, he might be in a running battle with the Illinois State Police or the Federal Bureau of Investigation. For now, the FBI had no leads, no photos, no Judas. Infection, possible discovery, failure, death; the odds rapidly grew against a successful conclusion to his mission. Rostislov contemplated the distant skyline, then turned west.

He was a hundred miles out of Chicago, approaching Dwight, Illinois on Interstate 55 when he heard the name "bin Laden" on the scratchy Country Western station. He spun the volume knob.

"Following the recent killing of Osama bin Laden by Marine Snipers in the mountains of Western Pakistan, sources have witnessed a breakdown in Taliban cohesion!"

The Teacher dead? Rostislov knew the SEALs had missed bin Laden in Abbottabad. It was the first he'd heard about a Marine Sniper. The radio described how the sniper had shot the Teacher on a pass in the Hindu Kush. A sniper shot him on a pass in the Hindu Kush--an assassin, hired by the Coalition?

Rostislov pulled into the next service station. Bin Laden's face stared back from the cover of Time Magazine. An inside double spread showed the Teacher's head thrown back, his turban tipped awkwardly to one side as the bullet exploded through his vertebrae. Bin Laden had not been surprised. He knew it was only a matter of time before the drones, Infrared, Night Vision, Smart Bombs, Laser-Guided Rockets, superior technology killed him. In the end, none had succeeded. It had taken a Judas to betray him for a few thousand American dollars. The traitor would be taken and tortured when he tried to collect the reward.

Rostislov knew bin Laden had met his death with the same serenity with which he lived his life. He was now a martyr, a hero who would inspire future generations of holy warriors.

There was more. "Hull, a major in the U.S. Marines...multiple decorations, promoted to Colonel for his successful mission." Time claimed he was Los Angeles-born, educated at the Virginia Military Institute. The nation wished to honor him. The President requested patience. The press owed privacy to an American hero.

A scorching desire for revenge exploded through Rostislov. Osama bin Laden was dead! It was not within him to weep. Rage, anger, revenge, hatred were his only emotions. Fueled by all four, a new, simple plan took form. Rostislov would find the Marine Assassin Hull who martyred the Teacher. Then he would ensure that the Colonel died slowly. The KGB had taught him well. In the years following World War II, KGB interrogators had improved upon documents discovered in the Majdanek concentration camp near the Polish city of Lubin. When Soviet soldiers liberated Majdanek on July 22, 1944, they surprised two SS troopers who were burning papers. Neither of the Soviet soldiers knew how valuable the two-dozen surviving sheets would become. Most of the pages were scorched, but enough of the Nazi's research remained to serve as a foundation for further human experiments. The KGB added refinements that tripled the pain while prolonging life. Before they died, all prisoners confessed. It did not matter what they confessed. It was the strength of the process. All rushed to betray their mothers, wives, even children. At the end, Hull would beg for death.

Rostislov needed to pray for the Teacher, for Islam, for Afghanistan. He pulled off the freeway onto a dirt road that bisected hundred-acre cattle pastures where he stopped the Taurus and retrieved a folded rug from the back seat. Spreading it on the gravel next to the front bumper, he turned toward Mecca and sank to his knees.

He prayed for the strength, wisdom and courage of bin Laden. He prayed for the spirit of his Teacher, for the future of Afghanistan, for the death of all Infidels. Lost in prayer, he ignored an approaching pickup until it rushed past in a cloud of exhaust, dust and heat. The driver hit the brakes, skidded to a stop, then slammed the F-150 into reverse and backed up in a spray of dust and gravel.

He was in his mid-forties, hardened by working the land. Service in Desert Storm had crystallized his worldview and in the years since the rout of Saddam Hussein's army, he had continued to hate Iraq, Iran and Islam. For a man who topped two hundred and thirty-five pounds, he was remarkably agile. Throwing open the driver door, he came around the hood and demanded, "What the hell you think you're up to here?"

Rostislov's smile betrayed little surprise and no alarm. "Praying," he calmly replied.

"No you aren't! Not that kind of praying! Not here in America!" The ex-Army Sergeant looked forward to beating the shit out of this thin, dark Raghead. Clenching his right hand into a fist, the Sergeant realized Rostislov didn't really look like an Arab. He threw an overhand right that appeared to slow as Rostislov magically closed the distance and thrust the Karud dagger into his heavy belly and upward into the heart. The knife cut just deep enough to throw the rancher's heart into fibrillation. His heart barely beating, the rancher sagged. When Rostislov retracted the dagger, the rancher's face flushed with incomprehension. Putting his arm around the dying ex-Sergeant's waist, Rostislov guided him back to the driver's seat where he set

216

his heavy boot on the gas and the automatic transmission into drive. He then shut the driver's door and stepped away as the F-150 slowly followed the road down a distant, faint rise to the horizon. The pickup traveled almost a mile before the rancher bled out.

Rostislov returned to Highway 55 headed southwest to Springfield, Illinois, then on to St. Louis, where he picked up Highway 44 to Oklahoma City. Stopping for gas at a truck stop, Rostislov paid for a shower, bought a pre-packaged cheese and white bread sandwich and grabbed two hours of sleep in the back seat of the Taurus. When he woke, it was ten o'clock. Soon after leaving the truck stop, he was on Highway 40 to Amarillo, Albuquerque and Flagstaff, en route to Los Angeles.

The CDC contacted George W. Bush's doctor at 6:00 AM. Unlike many of those at the foundation dedication, who were dealing with nosebleeds, Bush's symptoms included a fever of one hundred and one, aching joints, a roaring headache and severely blood shot eyes.

Bush's doctor realized time was critical, and tried to be brief. "Mr. President, the CDC has issued a Health Alert."

The ex-President preferred to have the first word and interrupted, "Health Alert?" Despite his fever and aching joints, Bush joked. "It sounds like I need a second flu shot."

His doctor tried to soften the news and forced a smile. "No, Mr. President, you're up to date on all your shots. What you have is something different than a flu and far more dangerous. A Health Alert is the CDC's highest level. The agency typically avoids stronger wording to prevent panic. Sir, a second flu shot won't help. It's the Marburg virus."

Bush was puzzled. "Marburg? Sounds like a Wall Street banker. What is this, some hopped up strain of that Swine bug?"

"Mr. President," the doctor knew Bush's flippant responses were the ex-President way of handling stress. "No sir, it's not the Swine Flu, or any flu. It's a virus--but not like any other. It has infected the general population. You, the First Lady, the dignitaries, and three-thousand people at the groundbreaking were exposed. We need to isolate you and Mrs..."

"Isolate? Look Doc, I've got a full day tomorrow promoting my book. I need a flu shot, or adrenalin, or something to knock down this headache.

What is it you always prescribe? Take some aspirin, drink lots of water and go to bed early tonight."

"Sir, I'm afraid conventional therapies won't help. The headache and fever are only the earliest symptoms. Your blood culture revealed that you have the Marburg virus. The CDC does not have the exact timing but no matter what we do, your symptoms will increase in severity. The order varies from victim to victim, but the majority eventually experience liver failure and a resulting jaundice."

"Jaundice?" Bush asked.

"You turn yellow."

Bush frowned. "Well, what about one of those viral cocktails?"

"Such as are used for HIV?"

"My administration spent millions on African Aids victims."

"Sir, those drugs are HIV specific. I'm afraid they won't work on Marburg." He tried to return to the progression of Marburg. "The jaundice coincides with severe pancreatic inflammation. Within ten days of the primary infections, patients experience severe weight loss, delirium, shock and continuing multi-organ dysfunction.

"And then what?" Bush was beginning to grasp Marburg's lethality.

Bush's doctor gave him the worst case. "Mr. President, at that point, you can expect widespread hemorrhaging, pulmonary edema--in the final stage you will experience massive convulsions before you slip into a coma which may last a day….this variant of Marburg virus has a lethality of ninety-five percent within the first two weeks. And your chances of infecting any caregiver who isn't protected by multiple, viral-impermeable barriers is also ninety percent."

Bush's slack expression reminded his doctor of the moment the ex-President was advised of the attack on the Twin Towers. Accounts claimed he was reading the children's book upside down. The doctor didn't believe it.

"Of the five percent of patients who survive, recovery can take two months to two years." The doctor was almost finished. "That period will be marked by severe weight loss and amnesia. Further complications can include recurrent hepatitis, inflammation of the spinal cord, bone marrow, eyes, testes, and parotid gland, large organ dysfunction."

The ex-President was staring at a wall chart depicting a human skeleton. Turning to face the doctor, his glazed stare slowly turned to incomprehension, then anger. "What is this?" he demanded. "...April fools in July? I've got a headache! Not brain cancer!"

The doctor knew Bush's time was up. Hazmat technicians were waiting in the hallway. "Sir we have a room prepared for you, and the others who were infected at the ceremony. You need to enter a biohazard environment."

Bush's forehead wrinkled, "Biohazard containment? Like Guantanamo? No way, I'm not checkin' into a place like Guantanamo!"

"I'm sorry sir, you have no choice but total isolation. No visitors of any kind. Arrangements have been made to transport you to the Southwest Foundation for Biomedical Research in San Antonio. Moving highly contagious biohazard patients is extremely difficult. Marburg virus requires redundant barriers and isolated transfers."

Every minute of Bush's eight years in office suddenly showed on his lined forehead, and sagging jaw line. Tears filled the ex-President's eyes as he looked for an out, a way to deny the CDC diagnosis. Stripped of energy by the fever, Bush wondered, "If this Marburn is so damned dangerous, why aren't you all suited up?"

The doctor returned a quiet, calm reply, "Mr. President, it is "Marburg." I was infected when you first entered my office." The CDC was still culturing the virus when the doctor examined him. The rubber gloves and particulate mask would prove useless. In the fifteen minutes it took to check the ex-President's heart rate, weight, blood pressure, throat, take blood and urine samples, he had inhaled ten thousand virons. The disease was now replicating at an explosive rate throughout his body.

"I hate hospital food!" Bush attempted another joke. "Can I bring my chef to San Antonio?"

The doctor did not advise Bush that he'd eaten his last meal. No need to frighten him. At least not before the bleeding started in earnest. "Mr. President, your chef was evacuated earlier this morning. We'll all be together in the same containment unit."

Chapter 22

Hull woke with a piercing hangover and a flawed memory of how he arrived in Grace Guerrera's bed. He had not planned on sleeping at her apartment, but he was far too drunk to run the gauntlet of reporters and Marines who were waiting for him at the Mission Inn and quietly accepted her offer of a night's refuge.

Her ground floor single bedroom unit was clean and filled with modern art on the walls, brilliant Mediterranean reds, oranges and browns on one wall, cool beiges, rose and gray to the other. Beige, down couch, carved Chinese camphor chest, dining set...a single, unfocused glance suggested antique, Chinese...from Hong Kong.

Hull's prolonged sleep deprivation amplified the Glenfiddich and left him barely able to stand. "I'll take the couch," he said.

Instead she led him to her bedroom where she unbuttoned his shirt. Somewhere between removing his shoes and unbuckling his belt, Hull fell backward onto the bed where he lay without moving until Grace's shadow crossed his face. She had showered and slipped into a silk robe that clung to her breasts, the curve of her hips and her long legs. Coming instantly awake, he saw her face and black hair. Her eyes met his. She understood the impact she had on men and now, slowly undid her belt, slipped the silk off her shoulders and let her robe fall to the floor.

Hull inhaled.

Grace lifted the sheet and slid next to him. He felt he soft pressure of her breasts against his bruised ribs and smelled gardenias in her hair.

"We'll sleep," she whispered, gently draping her right arm across his chest. But they did not sleep. Hull was not overly aggressive, and she was not passive, and if they did not meet exactly in the middle, they started with a kiss that lingered, parted and joined again. His rough hands gently caressed the fair skin of her cheeks and shoulders. Her long, white fingers explored his large triceps and his bruised right pectoral. Their foreplay was long, creative and, for as little time as they had known each other, intimate. Despite prolonged sleep deprivation and torn muscles, Hull lost himself in the curve of her hips and her full breasts. She quickly forgot the previous day, and found herself drawn to this handsome, strong and now famous hero who had interrupted her life. She ran her hands through his cropped hair and across the powerful muscles in his chest, biceps, stomach and thighs.

That night, as her hips rolled like deep ocean swells and her heels raked his back, he drowned in the sweet musk and silky hair of her sex. Their desire covered them with salty sweat.

Framed between deep groans, she whispered an invitation that women had made to men for as long as language existed, "Hull!" she murmured in Spanish, "Por favor...te quiero dentro..."

In reply, Hull claimed her with a single, powerful thrust. They did not start quietly, or gently. He had returned from the killing fields, she from older lovers and each found what they needed in the other.

Clutching a pillow, Grace's eyes were closed as Hull stroked deep within her. Grace lifted toward an orgasm and he realized, despite its increasing strangeness, that life was still precious. He drove inside her with urgency, and she whispered, "Oh Dios, oh Dios, Jack, por favor, don't stop, don't stop." She locked her mouth on his and tightened her legs around his waist. After thirteen months of celibacy, Hull expected a single explosive orgasm. He was wrong. Physically damaged by his final hours at Saker, his hard-won endurance lifted her to successive orgasms, her hips driving over and beneath him until it was she, not he who finally slept.

Grace's soft breathing filled the silence. Their bodies cooled down. Still fighting sleep, he covered Grace with the sheet and blanket and tried to block the distant thunder of an unmuffled Harley Davidson on Highway 10. He closed his eyes.

One minute Hull was asleep next to Grace, the next belted into a Chinook over Granai in Afghanistan's Farah Province. Below, six craters were scattered through a dozen flattened compounds. The Chinook flared, dumped the ramp and dropped Hull, Bauldaire and ten regular Army riflemen in a wheat field west of Granai's bomb blasted alleys. Maintaining ten meters, the soldiers ran to cover behind a collapsed wall. "Stay alert!" Hull yelled down the line. "Watch for snipers and don't let civilians close with you. They could be packing BBIEDs."

Sending one soldier at a time across the open alley, the squad cautiously worked deeper into the shattered village. What remained of a body leaned against a wall. Taliban or farmer, he had been alive when he dragged himself into a sitting position. Left to bake in the hot sun, his corpse had blackened, filling the alley with the death smell.

The squad reached a narrow, rubble-filled intersection of four paths. The flow of battle was clear. The Taliban had forced two-dozen women and children into the village elder, Said Naeem's, compound. A second group of thirty was driven into the house of Mullah Manan where the Taliban opened up from the rooftop with heavy machine guns, RPGs and eighty-millimeter mortars.

Comprised of young conscripts from local madrassas, FATA tribal mercenaries, devout shopkeepers— the insurgents had come to sacrifice themselves, if necessary, even welcomed their martyrdom. In the end, neither the place of their birth, tribal loyalty, occupations, or the families left behind--ultimately mattered. All believed they were fighting for the complete independence of Afghanistan, and for a united, Islamic nation.

Colonel Watandar, the local police chief, radioed the ISAF quick-reaction force in Farah. Waiting behind reinforced positions, the Taliban's response was focused and furious. They drove screaming children into intersecting alleys then cut loose with AK47s and machine guns. The Afghan National Army held their fire and immediately took casualties. Twenty minutes into the firefight, the ANA's American advisors alerted Tactical Air Control.

Two F-16s roared over at 8 PM and dropped six, five hundred pound bombs. The high explosive reduced the block to shattered mud bricks. Only one woman and six children in the compound survived.

Hull, Bauldaire and the ten riflemen clung to the red mud walls of houses that fronted the debris-filled street. Red dust swirled above shredded blankets, splintered furniture and flattened pots.

The patrol followed screams to Mullah Manan's compound, where a hysterical crowd was frantically digging in the debris. When Hull's riflemen rounded the corner and stepped into the alley, two-dozen screaming villagers turned to face them. The surviving fathers, mothers and children blamed the Coalition, not the Taliban, for the slaughter.

An old man separated from the crowd and staggered forward, shrieking in Pashto, "Badstérgey balaa khuni!"

The riflemen established a defensive line.

Hull picked words out of the old man's thick dialect. "Shameless, monstrous, murderers."

"Dzhang atshawúnkey!" He was six feet from Hull when he threw a knot of shredded rags and pink ribbons that floated in a slow-motion arc toward the platoon. The bundle was still in the air when one of the riflemen put a round in the Afghani's chest. The jacketed bullet spun the bearded farmer in a spastic circle before he collapsed onto the dusty street.

Hull reacted by instinct. Arms jerking forward, he caught the rags. They were all that remained of the farmer's daughter. The blast had shredded her pink dress. The little girl's left leg and what was left of her right arm hung in broken, awkward angles. Her face and head were smashed. Her jaw was missing; one light eye was open, glazed by a film of dust. The rest had been blown away.

The dying father cried, "You, the Americans, are Satan!" he reached for the tiny body in Hull arms. "Heghwa dar zher leh na ped ad shol! The Taliban were gone!" he whispered in Pashto. "The bombs hit after they left...my daughter!" he only had seconds left. Summoning his final breath he cursed them, "Dzhang atshawúnkey; Warmonger, May Allah condemn you! May your sons and daughters..." he choked on his last words.

Hull kneeled and returned the dead child's broken body to her father. Her blood had stained his uniform and he tried to speak but could not find his voice.

The crowd surged forward. Bauldaire leveled his M4. The Geneva Convention prohibited troops from shooting into crowds. Murdering Afghan

223

civilians would end Bauldaire's career. His three shot burst was inches over the crowd's head. "Far enough!!" he shouted in Pashto. Another step and someone would die. "Do we have confirmation the Taliban retreated before the JDAMs hit?" Bauldaire asked.

Hull fought the bile rising in this throat. "None," he slowly stood. "Our Intel supersedes Bagram's." Hull's eyes remained on the dead father. "He was telling the truth."

The squad climbed over the rubble into the collapsed compound. The bomb had reduced the front room to a charnel house. What was left of two-dozen women and children littered the floor. Tangled legs, arms, heads and crushed torsos spread from the corner into a central courtyard. Splashes of bright reds, browns and purples were blasted across the lone standing wall.

A second before he lost his lunch, one of the riflemen whispered, "Goddamn motherfucker!" Infected by the smell of blood and vomit, a second rifleman began to wretch.

"Knock that shit off," Bauldaire quietly ordered.

A day later, Hull, Bauldaire and the rifle squad were helicoptered back to Jalalabad. Brig. Gen. Ray Thomas, a senior Army investigator, conducted an in-depth inquiry for General David Petraeus. Thomas pronounced the official body count at a hundred and seven. The wounded were double that figure.

Hull slowly opened his eyes. A black ache filled his skull. The clock in Grace Guerrera's bedroom read 6:00. Gingerly setting his feet next to the bed, he steadied himself against the nightstand and studied the photos on the wall. A formal wedding photo framed a handsome Latino man in a dark suit and a young Chinese woman in a white dress. In the intervening thirty years the print had faded, the colors washing out to a faint, sepia.

The walnut dresser held other framed photos. Brothers, sisters, cousins and grandparents--a mix of East and West--arranged upon a lace cloth. Hull rose, stepped into his briefs and slacks, and stood. He felt his cell phone in his pocket, flipped it open and checked his messages. None. Only Grace had the number. By day's end, the Pentagon would have it too.

Hull crossed the bedroom into the living room and turned into the kitchen. Grace was sitting at the kitchen table. Wrapped in her silk robe, she pressed a package of frozen peas against her face.

He walked over and reached to touch her. She recoiled. The bag of peas slipped down to expose a deep plum colored stain rimming her eye. In the second she took to adjust the bag, he saw the stain drained from her left eye, down her cheek, across her jaw and onto her neck.

Her damaged face approximated a shot to his solar plexus. "GRACE! WHAT HAPPENED?" He was shocked.

"YOU PUNCHED ME!" she shrank from him.

Hull remembered making love to her. Nothing more. No anger, no crushing blow to her cheek. He tried to regain control. "I couldn't have. I would never--" he started to say, but then spotted the fresh scrape across his right hand. A tooth had cut him--Grace's tooth.

"You were yelling in your sleep... when I tried to wake you, you hit me. I came to five minutes ago." Grace had been punched before...the first time when she was ten. Men hit her for punishment, for sex, to force her to obey until now, whether it was deliberate or not, whether it happened when Hull was in an alcohol-fueled coma or fully awake, she feared him.

"What the FUCK is wrong with you?" she yelled.

Hull struggled for an answer. Bauldaire, Dillard, Haldol...he searched for a reason. "I don't know, I couldn't have, I didn't mean...." The pink bundle in his dream floated toward him. He threw an arm to stop it, protect himself, catch it--he did not know. He had hit Grace. "I'm so sorry," his throat closed.

The slight pressure of shifting the package of frozen peas on her cheekbone caused her to wince. Lowering the bag to the table she looked him fully in the face. The bruise beneath her left eye grew darker. Her voice faded, softening her words that now joined in slow, deliberate sentences.

"Hull, you are dangerous." She ran her tongue painfully across her upper lip, "Not only to al Qaeda or the Taliban. I admit I loved it when you beat Navarra down—but I was stupid. I couldn't see that you'd turn on me."

Her eye closed and the muscles in her cheek spasmed as she touched the frozen peas to her face. The green plastic hid the darkening bruise. "No wonder the Marines picked you to kill bin Laden. Who better for the job?" Her cheek continued to spasm. "I unzipped your duffle. Why all the guns? To protect you? From what? Your nightmares? Those guns won't help any more than the Scotch or your blank prescription vials." Anger filled her dark eyes.

Hull could not excuse, defend or beg for forgiveness. He took a step toward her.

Extending her arm to stop him she warned, "Nothing you can say will make a difference. You've got one minute and then I'm calling the police. Take your things and get out!"

Hull collected his shirt, jacket, and shoes from the bedroom and his duffle from the front hall. He was crossing the living room when he stopped, "You need to know it wasn't deliberate,"

"It never is," she muttered. She watched him open the front door and close it quietly behind him.

Rostislov had taken twenty hours to drive nonstop from Oklahoma City to Los Angeles. The Monday morning commute traffic was building on Highway 10 when he exited onto the Highland Avenue ramp east of Redland and stopped next to a battered blue phone box on the side of a 7-Eleven convenience store. Rostislov knew cell phones were simple to trace. The newest included GPS transmitters. Once the FBI discovered his identity and traced a number, a single cell call would expose his location. It made no difference that the phone book had been ripped from the metal cover, the number Rostislov dialed was known to one other person--Osama bin Laden. No voice mail or caller ID was attached to the number. The man who owned the phone had been instructed to never use it for outgoing calls.

Rostislov's fingers pressed the pay phone's metal keys. He listened to the answering tones then waited. "Yes," an alert, but cautious voice answered. Until that moment the phone had not rung, and when it did now, the voice was surprised, but not reluctant.

"Our Prince blesses you," Rostislov greeted him. It was a key to the first lock.

"If that is true then I am, indeed, honored." The Voice opened the second lock.

"He prevails upon your hospitality...to aid his servant...at the same time you serve Allah."

"I have been waiting for his summons. And...my Prince is well?"

"By now, as you must be aware, our Prince was martyred."

There was a pause before the Voice replied, "Allah spared his life on the first assassination attempt in Abbottabad. On the second, he summoned the Teacher to his side. I mourn his passing from this earth at the same time I rejoice he has entered Paradise. Though he now sits with Allah, we remain his servants. I am here to help in any manner I can."

"Your help will be rewarded. I need information on the Marine assassin. You know his name."

"Hull. His face defiles the front page of the Los Angeles Times." The Voice belonged to a second generation Pakistani. Eleven years had passed since he was accepted to the police academy as part of the Los Angeles Police Department's drive for cultural inclusion. The LAPD's background checks failed to discover he was a devout Muslim who, following 9/11, was shocked when the Bush Administration invaded Iraq and Afghanistan. Watching as thousands of Muslims died in the streets of Baghdad and Kabul, the Voice prayed for guidance in a Los Angeles temple. In January of that year, he secretly betrayed the place and time of a planned Homeland Security raid against an Islamic cell, saving their lives. Six months later he was hand delivered the phone and a series of responses should it ever ring. He quickly committed the phrases to memory and destroyed the instructions. He had waited years for a call, and now, when the phone vibrated in his uniform's breast pocket, he was well prepared.

Rostislov fed another quarter into the coin slot. "I need what information you can provide about the assassin. Addresses, phone numbers, relatives, friends, license, arrest records--no detail is too insignificant."

"I understand," the Voice replied. "Call me in exactly one hour."

Waiting on the sidewalk in front of Grace's apartment for a cab, Hull glanced at his Seiko. Six thirty AM. Wardell Stone had been at Sun and Health for half an hour. Hull opened his cell phone, rapidly touched the keypad and pressed the green button.

"I appreciate you calling," Stone rumbled.

"I've been up for awhile," Hull replied. He turned to face Grace's apartment. The living room shade moved slightly. Grace was watching.

"I don't doubt it," the massive CEO coughed and got to the point. "The State auditors are busting my balls about that accounting glitch—could you come to my office?"

"How's half an hour sound?"

"That'll work--I'll be waiting."

Ten minutes later a yellow Chevrolet Caprice cab pulled to the curb. Dropping into the back seat, Hull remembered the unmarked military vehicles and network satellite trucks parked around the Mission Inn. He could not risk collecting his clothes from the Alhambra Suite. Nor could he call Avis. The press and military would have already contacted the car agency. His rental records would be deleted. The Pentagon would cover the cost of the H3.

The cab dropped Hull at Sun Health in Upland at six fifty-five. Hull waved off the driver's attempt to help him with the duffle, tipped him two dollars and crossed to the side entrance away from the parking lot. Stone had left it unlocked.

Before he opened the door, Hull dialed Grace. He was horrified by what he had done and waited impatiently for her to pick up--he needed to know she would, at least, seek medical treatment. He hoped she had driven herself to an emergency room and was, at that moment, having an x-ray taken of her cheekbone. On the sixth ring, her voice mail clicked on, and Hull hung up.

The stairs climbed three flights to the executive-level wing. The VPs and secretaries who occupied the eight offices had yet to arrive. Hull set the duffle in the outer office and knocked on Stone's half-open door.

Chapter 23

T he CEO looked away from a computer screen when Hull entered the office. He knew Stone's accounting was penny precise. His columns of numbers would total correctly. It was the subcategories, hidden within subcategories, veiled by deductions that would eventually be discovered. Once they were, a third-year accounting student could bring down Wardell Stone and Sun and Health.

"Son, you're looking beat to shit," Stone spoke to the dark circles around Hull's eyes. "You could stand some R&R."

"I'm on the mend," Hull promised. He could not take his mind off Grace.

"If what you say is true, it's gonna' take some time. You look about like your Dad did after he saved my ass in Hue," Stone observed. "He was a hell of a soldier--none braver. He settled down after he started his business and fathered you, but he was a warrior--fierce. You're clearly his son. Maybe even tougher...more of a hell raiser." He tossed the L.A. Times across the desk.

A half page photo froze Hull in front of the burning Hummer. His day old growth and short black hair filled the frame. He was exhausted, unfocused, and appeared a decade older than his thirty-four years. The flash overexposed his face, lending it a ghostly cast in front of the burning H-3.

Hull skimmed the copy, "Colonel Jackson Hull, recently identified as the leader of the Marine Sniper Scout team responsible for the death of Osama bin Laden, experienced car trouble last night in Cabazon. The police report revealed that Hull's rented Hummer developed a fuel leak on Highway 10 and caught fire twenty miles west of Palm Springs. When he stopped at the Brontosaurus Museum to investigate, the car exploded. Colonel Hull refused further comment."

"Sources inside the Pentagon revealed that Colonel Hull received a battlefield promotion in Afghanistan. In light of Colonel Hull's identification by Islamic language media outlets, CENTCOM has suspended his leave and recalled him to duty. When questioned about the Colonel's present location or how long it might be before he would be allowed to speak to the press, citing the threat to his life from suspected al Qaeda cells operating within the Los Angeles Basin, a Pentagon spokesman refused to comment. Further questions from reporters were deferred until a later time."

"At this moment Colonel Hull's whereabouts are unknown. Records note that the Colonel was registered at Riverside's Mission Inn. Hotel management refused comment."

The lower right quarter of the page noted that ex-President Bush and Vice President Cheney had contracted what was being described as a variant of the new swine flu. The CDC suspected the virus was passed by handshakes to the ex-President and Vice President at the recent Bush Presidential Center groundbreaking ceremony in Dallas. Rush Limbaugh, the keynote speaker at the George Bush Presidential Library dedication, has taken a week sabbatical from his radio show."

Stone warned him, "I'd say you've got another eight hours before the Marines declare you AWOL. Not publicly... but the Corps wants you to call home."

"I've got nine days of leave." Hull avoided mentioning the Combat Fatigue, Dillard or the double doses of Haldol and Mirtazapine he was using to wrap his memories in a chemical straitjacket.

"Putting a bullet in bin Laden and getting the film to prove it turned you into a six-star VIP," Stone stated the obvious. "CENTCOM took a huge fucking risk by letting you fly home, and now you're burning up Hummers on the front page of the L.A. Times? The Marines need to bring you in before the terrorists cut you into bite-sized bits on international T.V. If al Qaeda finds you first, all PR goes in the shitter. Terrorists ten, Coalition zero."

Stone was right about part of it. Once he was outed, the Marines would order him to report to Pendleton. No fucking way the Commandant of the Corps would approve a publicity tour...not that he'd ever agree to sit down with a hundred talking heads. There would be no rubbing shoulders at state capitols, talk shows, or meeting film producers to negotiate his story. Hull almost laughed. CENTCOM wanted him to disappear. New identity, new posting--a disguised life played out in pixilated interviews. Colonel Dillard was waiting off-stage for his cue. Gentleman Hal and Senor Mirtz were losing their punch. Hull's next year would either include a Veteran's Psychiatric Care Ward or, if the Corps Commandant was feeling generous, another tour in Afghanistan. Hull pushed out of the chair and straightened. "I'll give it some thought," he said.

"For now, that's fair enough." Stone rose behind his desk and offered his catcher's mitt of a right hand.

When Hull turned toward the door, Stone frowned, "Jack, this audit is going to get nasty. When the Feds discover the shortfall, they'll lock the doors." Deep furrows crossed his forehead. "That business with Madoff diced the rules. The auditors won't be satisfied with a quick look at the books and an expensive lunch at my club. They're empowered to dig. It may take a week before they discover the shortage, but they will find it." He took a deep breath, and exhaled in a soft wheeze.

"Shorting minimums is..."

"Embezzlement," Hull filled in the blank.

Stone nodded, "You were always brutally honest. Most times I liked that part of you...but not today." Silhouetted in the large window, he skipped to the bottom line, "Look son, I bought a new SL65 Mercedes. Before the Feds file some horseshit case and lock the doors, they'll impound my SL65. I need to store it until the audit is over and would just as soon not have it here or at my house. There's a warehouse on a Long Beach dock where I can store it."

Hull's expression didn't change. He thought of the bruise on Grace's cheek.

"I'm asking you to drive it there for me."

Hull almost said no, but knew he couldn't turn Stone down. "Where should I take it, exactly?" he asked, reluctantly.

Stone handed him the keys and the address. "You need to be there before nine." He glanced at his watch, "That gives you an hour and fifteen minutes."

Stone's Mercedes was waiting in Sun and Health's underground parking. Guarded by painted concrete pillars against dents from careless car doors, the Mercedes was hidden beneath a custom car cover. Hull rolled the cover back to expose an SL65 AMG Black Series. Hull had seen one in a dog-eared issue of Road and Track that had been passed around Fire Base Seray in Afghanistan. The SL65's hand-built, twin turbo, six point two liter V-12 pumped out seven hundred horsepower and slightly less than seven hundred and fifty foot-pounds of torque. The car had the muscular symmetry of a competitive body builder--if not Schwarzenegger, the Austrian Oak, who recently governed California, then Jusup Wilkosz who trained with him.

Designed for the German Autobahn, the SL65 could accelerate from zero to sixty in fewer than four seconds. It could top one hundred and thirty in eleven seconds and was capable of one hundred and ninety nine miles an hour before the electronic limiter cut the horsepower in half. Of the three hundred carbon fiber exotics produced, less than fifty were shipped to the U.S. The remaining two hundred and fifty disappeared into Saudi Arabia, Abu Dhabi, Switzerland, Russia, Southeast Asia and Australia. Those that reached the U.S. were reserved for the super rich or instantly recognizable. Brad Pitt ordered one in midnight blue. Mel Gibson preferred black. The Material Girl picked banker silver.

The SL65s driver's side door opened with a precise, nearly inaudible click then swung weightlessly out on shining German hinges. Hull was accustomed to fine machines; Sako rifle bolts or Mercedes car doors--mechanical perfection and survival went hand in hand. He stored his duffle in the trunk and slipped behind the steering wheel. The car smelled new. The carpets were still covered by the original shipping plastic. Gripped by the Napa leather seat, he touched the remote key and pressed the ignition button. The instrument panel came alive in a spectrum of white, blue and orange LEDs. The V-12 simultaneously woke with a startled, angry roar. Part whine of spinning cams and roller followers, part thrust of the twin turbo chargers, the engine's throaty response spoke of perfect balance, tight seals and precise electronic timing. Added to the SL65's inspired wind tunnel architecture, the twelve cylinders' brute horsepower could easily push the two-seat car against the double century.

In deference to the engine's new, tight clearances, Hull allowed the oil to circulate until the temp gauge rose past one-hundred-fifty degrees. He then slipped the gear selector into reverse and exited the empty parking garage.

Opening his phone he called Grace. Her voice mail clicked on after six rings. Her recorded voice was cool, detached. "This is GG, leave me a message."

"Grace, I need to talk to you. Please. Call me." He left his number.

The address belonged to a shipping company on Pier E Street in Long Beach. Hull followed Euclid Avenue to the Interstate 10 on-ramp where he opened the throttle. Not at once and not wide open, it was little more than an exploratory stab but the SL65's response was instantaneous and violent. Hull was slammed into the molded bucket seat as it hurtled up the narrow ramp onto the freeway. In a city ruled by automobiles, the SL65 attracted attention--too much attention. Hung over, worried about Grace, he ignored the signal indicator as the Mercedes darted between lanes in Highway 10's streaming traffic.

Rostislov did not waste the hour his contact, the Voice, required. Merging onto Highway 10, he continued west toward downtown Los Angeles. It was only a matter of time before he found the Assassin. The protocol was unassailable. Locate the coworkers first, then friends and finally, family. Each step closer meant greater resistance. Eventually, all would confess what they knew.

The Los Angeles skyline rose in front of him. Four Falcons were hidden beneath the back seat. If he set the fuse to detonate at a thousand feet, the morning's onshore winds would push the virus east across West Covina, San Bernardino and Riverside. Four million people would be infected. Of those, ninety percent would die.

Without doubt the viral net would snare both the Assassin and Rostislov. Rostislov studied the downtown Los Angeles skyline. He would delay the flight of the second falcon for the day it would take to find the Assassin. Rostislov anticipated the deep pleasure he would take from listening to the Assassin betray his God, his father and his mother. Before the Sniper Hull died, he would beg for mercy from the Teacher, then from Rostislov himself.

Exactly one hour after he disconnected from the Voice, Rostislov tapped a number into a convenience store payphone on Wilshire Boulevard, west of Highway 10. The Voice answered on the second ring. "Our Prince blesses you," Rostislov said.

"If that is true, then I am, indeed, honored," the Voice replied. His tone revealed he'd met with success. "The Assassin is a man with few friends and no family. His mother and father are both dead. No brothers or sisters. He is divorced. His ex-wife lives in Compton. The Assassin's father fought in Vietnam with Wardell Stone, the CEO of an insurance company, Sun and Health. The Assassin remains close to him."

"Home and work address?" Rostislov requested.

The Voice supplied the addresses, phone numbers, license plates, Social Security and driver's license numbers.

"His ex-wife's address?"

The Voice returned all but her home phone. It was unlisted.

"Women? Roommates? Close friends?"

"None." The Voice hesitated, "You will, however, find one valuable piece of information on the front page of the L.A. Times."

Rostislov advised the Voice he would call him back. Stepping into the convenience store, he bought the morning paper, memorized the photo and quickly skimmed the story.

Another story attracted his attention. Ex-President Bush and ex-Vice President Cheney had contracted an unfamiliar flu. Dallas Hospitals were reporting spikes in emergency room visits. Rostislov smiled. Health workers would be powerless to stem the growing plague. Another day, perhaps two, and Dallas hospitals would crumble under the weight of a million infected victims. The virus would jump from patient to doctor then explode out of the hospitals. Neither quarantines, nor available vaccines could contain it. Redialing the number, he dispensed with the greeting. "Do you have an address?" he asked.

"He is registered at the Mission Inn in Riverside, but did not return last night."

"A woman?" Rostislov said.

"Perhaps," the Voice replied. "But there is one other detail you can make use of....do you have a pen and paper?"

Rostislov did not betray his pleasure with the information.

He had no way of knowing that Hull was a few miles away, headed south on Highway 710 to Long Beach.

Hull pulled into the warehouse, where a hundred cars waited to be loaded into shipping containers and distributed across the Pacific. With credit locked tight, even zero percent interest and hefty rebates could not draw buyers into Porsche, Mercedes or BMW showrooms. The expensive German sedans were being shipped to China, Taiwan, Indonesia and South Korea--where wealthy Asian industrialists who had weathered the international economic collapse purchased them at bankruptcy prices. The Asians would store them until the market rebounded.

An agent appeared at the driver's window. Hull opened the door, slowly exited from the low interior and said, "Wardell Stone of Sun and Health Insurance said you'd be expecting me."

Dressed in a pressed white shirt, black pants and polished black shoes, the shipping agent studied his clipboard. "Stone? We were notified about the Mercedes but that was not the name attached to it. We have the name Hull... uh Jackson Hull...as the owner."

Hull was surprised. "Are you sure that's the name?"

"According to the waybill," the agent flipped the page, "A Mercedes SL65 AMG is scheduled to be shipped by its owner on the Nippon Yusen Kaisha freighter California Jupiter from Long Beach to Buenos Aires. Shipping time, two weeks. Total cost with insurance, thirty six hundred dollars. The insurance doubles the shipping price but the car is valuable. Since you've already paid the fees," he flipped to the second sheet, "That leaves three signatures on the Bill of Lading before we can prep it for the container."

Hull knew then that Stone had done far more than invest the minimums. He had been looting Sun and Health. As soon as the low-to-zero deposit mortgage loans soured, Sun and Health was within a month of bankruptcy. Stone had started to sell the company's assets. Not the largest.

Multi-million-dollar transactions would attract the attention of the California Department of Insurance. Stone would sell the stocks, bonds and futures--rapidly convertible, and legal, thus less likely to trigger an audit. In the last months, he would have converted the cash to the Mercedes, gold, jewelry, foreign currencies. With the auditors closing in, he was shipping the Mercedes to Argentina.

The agent misread Hull's hesitation. "I know shipping a car to Argentina is expensive. Too expensive for most. You probably already know about the thirty five percent Argentine Custom fee for the appraised cost of your SL65, as well as the cost of shipping and insurance. What most of our clients don't know about is the further twenty-one percent of the original cost for Argentine Federal Taxes and a final eleven percent for income tax--again on the original cost. The total comes to eighty percent of the appraised value of your Mercedes. Of course, we'll take care of customs, but you'll need a valid Visa and passport to claim your Mercedes in Buenas Aires. I'm not surprised you weren't aware of federal duties."

"No, I knew," Hull replied. "I was trying to avoid adding it all up. Two hundred and eighty thousand dollars may be the deal-breaker."

"It's a lot of money," the agent agreed. "But a new one won't cost any less in Argentina...if you can find one. They're rare anywhere. In Argentina, they may be nonexistent. If it's any consolation, I promise we'll take excellent care of it."

The Argentine custom service would impound the Mercedes but it was doubtful they would search it. Smugglers wouldn't risk both the cost of the car and the import duties. They'd load a Suburban or pickup. The Mercedes signaled a rich Americano industrialist...perhaps a Ted Turner interested in buying an Estancia and living out the remainder of his life surrounded by lovely Argentinean women.

While the California Department of Insurance Auditors struggled to make sense of Sun and Health's convoluted books, Stone would board a flight at LAX. Few would remember a big man with silver hair and a deep voice who took the aisle seat and rarely looked up from his newspaper. He would not talk to his seatmate or order from the beverage cart. The business class ticket would be written to the Dominican Republic. He would change planes in New York and arrive in Santiago at 12:02 the next day. There, in the back office of a small restaurant, he would pay five thousand dollars for a Dominican passport; the process would take two days. On the third, he would fly to Rome where he would pay an expatriate Russian forger ten thousand euros for an Italian passport and Argentine visa. From Rome he would fly to Buenos Aires, where he would pass through security without a secondary search. Three weeks later, he would appear at a Buenos Aires shipping office with a receipt for the container. Stone would pay the tax, sign the manifest and drive away.

Hull ran his hand over the glistening black roof. In his desperation, Stone had betrayed him. If Hull signed the papers, he'd become an accessory to embezzlement. If Stone would pay a quarter of a million to export the Mercedes, Hull could only guess at the numbers--millions, perhaps tens of millions. Whether Hull signed the papers or not, Stone would disappear. Hull needed to return the SL65 to Stone.

The shipping agent turned the clipboard toward him. The three places that awaited his signature were highlighted by a yellow marker.

Hull held the offered pen above the line, then handed the clipboard back to the shipping agent. "You're right," he agreed. "It's just too expensive. I'll have to think about it."

The agent shrugged, "You won't be the first."

Hull slipped the selector into first, touched the throttle and left two black scars on the concrete floor. He exited onto San Gabriel Street toward the Highway 10 interchange where soaring parabolic ramps balanced on tall concrete pillars. A more abstract eye than his might have realized that the interchange was in fact, a sculpture on the scale of Mt. Rushmore. Lacking Rushmore's stern presidential visages and thus unlikely to stir strong feelings of patriotism in those who traveled its interwoven byways, the interchange still spoke to America's greatness, the singularity of purpose, political unity and economic might needed to build an intercontinental system of which it was a tiny part.

Hull was in the fast lane doing seventy-five when the cellular phone rang. Grace and Stone had the number--no one else. The ID was private. Grace. He touched the green connect button. "Hello," he waited for her voice to answer. "Grace?" he asked.

237

He heard the click of a disconnect. He pressed the number one on the pad--Grace's speed dial. The call did not go through.

Colonel Dillard's sudden appearance shocked Hull. Six hours had passed since Hull last dosed on Mirtazapine.

The Colonel was standing in front of Scott Shipp Hall. "East and West will pinch the heart, that cannot keep them pushed apart: and he whose soul is flat--the sky will cave in on him by and by." The Colonel saluted a passing cadet. When Hull did not respond, Dillard said, "A woman wrote it, you will, almost certainly, know her name."

"Colonel, I'd prefer not to play this game."

"I don't see how you have a choice. Look at it as a form of literary Scrabble. A way to fill in the blanks. The answer would be last name, woman author, six letters across."

"Is it Sheema Kalbasi?" Hull guessed.

"No, that's seven letters. Who?"

"She's Iranian. I read her collection in Afghanistan."

"No, it's Edna St. Vincent Millay."

Hull nodded. "The first woman to win the Pulitzer Prize for Poetry."

"The quote is from "Renascence," Dillard reminded him. "She was twenty when she wrote it. It's her best work. Too often that's the fate of early genius."

"To be forgotten."

"It happens, even to the best." Colonel Dillard shook up a Camel. "Prose, poetry…speeches are judged not on what they say but how they sound. If people really listened to politicians, none would ever be elected."

"Depressing." The Mirtazapine's side effects now seemed preferable to Colonel Dillard's invocations.

Rostislov parked in front of Sun and Health at precisely 8:10. Dressed in a Los Angeles Police Officer's blue uniform, he wore a Sergeant's chevrons. The Voice had added a regulation belt, holster, cuffs and nightstick to Rostislov's Makarov. Along with the standard issue 12-gauge shotgun, the Voice had stolen a Browning .270 A-bolt fitted with a 3x9 variable scope from the L.A. Police evidence room, and locked both in a surplus Black and White that he parked on a residential street in West L.A.

Rostislov crossed the lobby to reception and identified himself. "Mr. Stone called in a report on a stolen car. I'm here to take a statement. He's expecting me."

The receptionist glanced at her message file. "Stolen car? Mr. Stone didn't say anything about that. I'll tell him you're here."

"No, that will not be necessary," Rostislov said. "I will find my way." He started up the stairs.

The receptionist came around her desk. "I should let him know. It's against company rules to admit unaccompanied visitors onto the Executive Floor...even a policeman."

Rostislov turned and walked back to her desk. As she lifted the receiver to ring Stone's office, Rostislov grabbed her jaw and skull and twisted sharply. Her neck rotated with a sharp snap. He caught her as she crumpled, wedged her body beneath the desk and pushed the chair in against her.

He climbed the stairs, stepped into the second floor executive wing and walked into the first office on his left. The secretary was young; an earnest woman in her early thirties who, that morning, had made a special effort to pick a conservative suit for the audit. She looked up when Rostislov entered. Her expression prefaced a question that switched to terror as Rostislov slipped his Markov PM from its holster. She started to cry out. The pistol's silenced report was no louder than a pellet gun. A bright red circle appeared on her forehead, the surprise faded in her eyes and her head rolled onto her shoulder. Rostislov opened the door to the inner office. Sun and Health's handsome Vice President of Institutional Accounts was perplexed by the L.A. Policeman's appearance in his office.

"Can I help?" he managed before the slug shattered his square chin. Rostislov's second shot destroyed his spinal chord. The Vice President tumbled backward behind his mahogany desk.

Rostislov walked to the second door on the left. The secretary's desk was empty. A middle-aged woman, dressed in a blue business suit, with natural gray hair and faint makeup sat at the desk behind the inner door. If Rostislov had asked, she would have identified herself as Sun and Health's CFO. He did not ask: he simply shot her in the face.

Methodical, remorseless, he opened the doors to each of eight offices and shot the occupants. He did not think about their families or friends. They were infidels, nonbelievers who worshipped only dollars. Let Allah judge their guilt.

The last door on the hallway opened to Wardell Stone's office. Turning to face the blonde woman behind the desk, he inquired, "Mr. Stone is in?"

"He is," she noticed the odd way the police officer turned a statement into a question. She wondered what an L.A. policeman might want from Wardell Stone. "But he's very busy this morning. Perhaps I can help you." The police officer was not handsome, but he was not unattractive. He did not look like a police officer but she could not say what he did look like.

Rostislov glanced toward Stone's office door. It was closed. "No, I don't think you are able to help. It is necessary that I talk to Mr. Stone."

Again, the odd syntax. The executive assistant tried to identify a single defining feature and couldn't. She lifted the phone. Rostislov could hear the answering ring behind the closed door. The attractive assistant caught the brief, peripheral movement of Rostislov's flicking wrist. She saw a glint and felt a terrible ache in her throat. It was her last thought. The force of the Karud's honed blade cut without resistance through her trachea and sliced across her third vertebrae. Darcy Wilkins had no sense of pain or dying. Rostislov lowered her into the chair, her head sagging onto the back of her right shoulder.

He did not knock on Stone's door. Twisting the handle he pushed it open and glanced from the CEO to the insurance auditors who looked up from open laptop computers. The Makarov PB P69 pistol slid smoothly from Rostislov's service holster. Stone recognized the silencer and started to move but Rostislov reacted with cold precision. The P69 spit twice. The 9x18 Makarov rounds hit one auditor in the throat, the second round split the second's nose, exploding his sinus and destroying the medulla. His breathing, heart and involuntary reactions slammed to a stop. He crumpled to the floor. Stone was reaching for Rostislov when the Makarov's third round hit him in the right knee. The shot staggered the massive CEO. The next bullet hit him below the clavicle, shattered his shoulder joint and blew a large hole in his scapula.

Stone's right arm was hanging limply at his side when Rostislov pushed him back into a chair, snap tied his hands to the chair arms and asked one, unaccented question, "Where is Hull?"

Stone took a deep breath and gritted his teeth.

"Heroics are futile," Rostislov assured him. He then put a bullet into Stone's left knee.

"MOTHERFUCKER!" the profanity exploded out of the CEO.

"Blasphemy will not save you. Hull is where?"

"Go to hell!" Stone roared.

"No, I do not think so." Rostislov duct taped Stone's mouth shut then pulled a pair of gardening sheers from a leather case on his black belt. He closed them once slowly in front of Stone's face.

Many men, much younger than the gray-haired CEO, would have confessed before the metal sheers clipped off his first finger tip. Rostislov casually took Stone's little finger off at the first joint. Eyes bulging, Stone fought to break the thick snap ties binding him to the chair. The plastic bands cut deeply into his wrists. With his mouth duct-taped shut, he controlled the pain with deep breaths, his cheeks bulging out, his nose flaring, as piece by piece, his fingers fell to the floor. With a bullet in each knee, one in his shoulder, and his hands pruned away, Stone should have begged to talk. Instead the gray-haired Vietnam Vet fought like a Cape Buffalo, rocking the chair and roaring inarticulately behind the tape as Rostislov applied the rusty metal blades to his ring, middle and index fingers.

Stone did not panic until Rostislov used the Karud to split the buttons on his shirt. He then slowly cut through the layers of Stone's belly fat into his peritoneal muscle. Stone's death was decided. His sole choice was to die quickly, or slowly. At the end with his small intestine pushing out of the growing knife cut, he finally broke down and begged Rostislov to take what he knew. Stone's information did not point directly to the Assassin but to his ex-wife, Cheryl. In Afghanistan, Rostislov had realized the sweetest revenge was to leave a man bereft of family, standing alone in the desert, desolate, as death appeared to claim him. And so it would be with the Assassin.

Chapter 24

H ull would not remember the exact instant he decided to return the Mercedes to Stone. It wasn't a difficult decision. His loyalty to Wardell Stone caused him to drive to Long Beach. He couldn't attribute the decision to fear of the law or the desire to do what was "right"—but he retraced his route back to Upland. It was a sense of balance. The four years in Afghanistan and three in Iraq had to mean something. Men and women had died by his hand, or by those men around him, in unpronounceable villages. The difference was, the Taliban had no doubt about what they were fighting and dying for...while Hull no longer knew. In the end, helping Stone ship the Mercedes to Argentina bothered him more than killing Osama bin Laden.

Hull parked the Mercedes in Sun and Health's front lot, close to the building's exposed aggregate facade. Glancing at his Seiko, he estimated the Insurance Commission had been at the audit for two hours. They had started with Sun and Health's profit and loss statements and, over the next week, would work their way down to individual accounts. They were in no rush. Upland, Riverside, San Bernardino or as far away as San Diego, the day rate was the same. Like investigative reporters, the auditors would search who, what, where and how.

Depending on how much they knew in advance, it would take as little as a few hours or as much as a few days to learn that Wardell Stone had diverted company reserves. The Commission's auditors would also discover that Sun and Health had been looted of its operating capital. Stone would eventually be charged with embezzlement, misuse of company reserves and fraud.

Hull switched off the SL65's engine and dialed Stone's office number. After five rings, the call switched to voice mail. He dialed the number again. Darcy should have answered. He looked up at the second floor offices. The secretaries might be busy retrieving files, but no one moved behind the large glass windows. He tried reception. The call was forwarded to Sun and Health's general voice mail.

A lone LAPD officer in a black and white police cruiser circled the parking lot then exited toward Highway 10. Hull briefly wondered if the officer was Mid-Eastern. Perhaps Pakistani--or Afghani, definitely thin, fit for a cop. Ten seconds later Hull remembered the cop had black hair and dark eyes, but no other details.

A gut instinct he had learned not to ignore alerted him. Something wasn't right. Stone, Darcy Wilkins, reception…someone should have answered. Sun and Health should have been busy with the audit, but the second floor administrative offices appeared deserted. Lights off. No movement behind the large windows. He walked to the Mercedes' trunk and unzipped the duffle. His right hand closed around the Colt Commander's black composite grip and he worked the slide. One round in the chamber, six in the magazine. He set the safety. Slipping an extra clip into his pocket, he eased the Colt into his belt, and slipped on a blue sports jacket.

He crossed the lawn to Stone's north-facing private entry where, using the key on the Mercedes ring, he opened the single glass door, and climbed the single flight of stairs to the second floor. The hallway lights were off. Hull tried one of the office doors. It was locked.

Hull slipped the M1911 from his belt and tried the next door. Locked. The halls and offices should have been filled with executives, accountants and secretaries shuttling paper records and computer discs to the conference room. Eight other doors lined the hall. Hull tried another office door. It too was locked from the inside. He stepped across the hall and tried the handle to Stone's office door. Also locked. Taking a step to one side, he hit it hard with the back of his fist. "Darcy!" he yelled.

No answer. Stepping across the hall he kicked the door. It held. Glancing down the hallway, he pointed the M1911 and pulled the trigger. The heavy .45 slug shattered the lockset. When he kicked the door a second time it opened, swinging slowly into Stone's outer office.

His eyes rapidly adjusted to the low light. Darcy Wilkins was sitting at her desk. Her head rested on her shoulder and her eyes were open. A knife had split her trachea to her spine. In the office's deep shadows, her white blouse was soaked with blood. A gaping black hole divided her neck. Hull had seen the same cut in Afghanistan. It was the Taliban's Halal stroke. Whoever killed Darcy Wilkins had come for him. Darcy was collateral damage.

The auditors were splayed on the floor just inside Wardell Stone's office door. One had been shot in the nose. The other's trachea and spine had been blown onto the wall. Blood- splattered files littered the room.

Stone was sitting at his desk--dead. Hull had witnessed many acts of torture in the isolated villages of the ascending Hindu Kush, but this exceeded even tribal revenge. The CEO had been snap-tied to his chair. Blood flowed from the chair's arms, down its legs, and onto the carpet where it pooled in two deep, coagulated circles.

Stone had been shot in both knees. His shoulder showed the blackening stain of a bullet wound. If the killer wanted to break the big man down, he had succeeded. Hull had seen men shot in their knees, elbows and hips. Exploding through cartilage and bone, the heavy slugs would set the strongest men screaming. The silver duct tape that hung from Stone's cheek had muffled his agony.

What appeared to be blackened Brazil nuts lay scattered around Stone's chair. Hull kneeled. Picking one up, he recognized the tip of Stone's left thumb. Starting at the little finger, the killer had cut the joints until only the palms remained. The killer had deliberately over-tightened the snap ties to prevent Stone from bleeding out.

Deep black circles ringed Stone's open eyes. The killer had asked his questions, while the Karud's sharp blade sliced through the massive CEO's peritoneal wall. Starting below the belly button, the killer had carefully exposed the layers of fat until he reached the abdominal muscle below. With his arms strapped to the chair, and his mouth taped shut, Stone couldn't prevent his intestines from spilling into his lap. When the killer finally removed the tape, the CEO had told him everything he wanted to know. It was clear that the killer had enjoyed the process.

Stone's mutilated body revealed that the Sun and Health CEO had betrayed names, addresses and any bit of information Stone could recall about Hull's ex-wife, Cheryl Birden, or any relatives, associates or friends. Hull soon discovered the bodies of the secretaries, accountants and executives behind the adjacent locked office doors. All had been executed. A single shot to the head ensured their silence.

He took the back stairs three at a time, crossed the lawn and dropped into the Mercedes. He did not notice the secretary sitting behind a first floor office window who watched the handsome, well-built man leave in Wardell Stone's expensive black sports car.

Hull called Cheryl's number. No answer.

Her message started, "You have reached 515...." He disconnected, shifted gears and pinned the throttle. Seven hundred horsepower slammed the small Mercedes through 110 mph.

Covina's Curtis Avenue appeared in the windshield. Hull downshifted and took the off-ramp at 100, then pressured the brake pedal until the ABS kicked in. Hanging on the edge of full lockup, the wide tires howled as the SL65 cascaded from one hundred down to forty. Hull glanced left, blew the red light, grabbed second gear and left two black arrows pointing north toward the San Bernardino Mountains.

Eyes flicking from the road to his phone, he dialed the three-digit information number and asked the operator to search for Fort Belvoir, Virginia. Belvoir was the home base of INSCOM, the United States Army Intelligence and Security Command. The Agency was responsible for the planning and execution of intelligence and security operations for the U.S. Army. Its research was available only to national military commanders, select members of Congress, and the President.

Ten years had passed since Hull and Lieutenant William Eilert had bunked together at Fort Benning. During five weeks of Sniper School, Hull and Eilert traded information about tactics, map routes and camouflage. When Eilert failed to hit the distance range's black bull's eye, Hull made his qualifying shot. The Range Master never believed Hull had entirely missed the panel with his second round. Eilert was a mediocre shot but a brilliant tactician and graduated from Fort Benning somewhere below average. Eilert, however, was not cut out for six-day missions on sweltering ridges. His strength was electronic intelligence.

Eilert had been eventually promoted to Colonel and transferred to Belvoir. Hull did not know what assignments had spurred his rapid advancement.

"I have a base operator," the operator replied.

"That'll do."

Five seconds later, a Southern voice answered, "Fort Belvoir, how can I direct your call?"

"Colonel William Eilert, please!"

"Could you state the nature of your business?"

"I'm a friend."

"And your name,"

"Triple X. He'll know me." Eilert would not forget the day Hull pin-wheeled three shots at a thousand meters.

"Please hold the line," the operator intoned.

The operator returned ten seconds later, "I'm connecting your call, Mr. X." Her voice betrayed scant humor.

Eilert's angry voice answered a second later. "Hull! Goddammit! Where the Fuck are you?"

"In Los Angeles, on leave…but."

"Look Hull, your leave was cancelled ten minutes after you cleared L.A. Customs."

"This is the first I heard about it. Eilert, I just left Sun and Health and..."

"Stop right now! Give me an address and don't move! The Marines, CIA and FBI have swept L.A. searching for…"

"No can do..."

"Hull, you better damn well listen up or you'll be facing a court martial for desertion..."

"No! Goddamnit. Eilert, you listen! I need credible INTEL! Now!" He described the murders at Sun and Health. "They weren't after Stone."

Eilert did not immediately reply. When he did, he said, "Let me get back to you." The line went dead.

Hull was headed west on Highway 10 when his cell phone rang. The caller I.D. was blocked. He touched the connect button.

Eilert rapidly explained the necessity for switching to his cell phone. "All INSCOM's phone lines are linked to digital recorders. Most of what we get is bullshit, but occasionally we stumble across something of value." He got to the point, "What I'm going to tell you is SCI." The acronym stood for "Sensitive Compartmented Information"--four levels above TOP SECRET.

"INSCOM traced you to the Avis rental, then the Mission Inn. There was the deal with the burning Hummer in Cabazon, the calls to the limo services in Palm Springs. After that you dropped off the radar."

Army Intelligence had been a half step behind Hull as he blundered from wreck to wreck in a Haldol and alcohol-driven haze. He did not volunteer information about Colonel Dillard or Grace.

"Jack, we screwed up. Communications broke down. House address, phone, email, none of your old contacts work. Either you've gone underground or have a shit load of luck but we need you to report to Pendleton."

"Sorry Will, not now." Hull said.

"You're officially listed as AWOL." Eilert said. "The Secretary of Defense is all over Petraeus for failing to hold you in Afghanistan. Petraeus should have been ahead of the curve. A Private First Class spilled your name to a BBC stringer. The Corporal is waiting in a Bagram stockade for as yet unspecified charges. No one considered that al Jazeera would out you this quickly."

"Eilert, twelve people were murdered at Sun and Health!"

"There's a link," Eilert promised. "The video of Bin Laden's death fucked up al Qaeda's command and control structure! Bin Laden's value to Radical Islam was inestimable. Without OBL's strong central leadership al Qaeda's role will shrink to harass and harry. What CENTCOM could not predict was the psychological impact Siraj Haqqani's death would have on the Tehrik-i-Taliban. Your chip held a full minute of Haqqani's shrieking pleas for mercy. He was reputed to be as tough as armor plate, but he weeps like a woman to Allah. It's clear Haqqani does not get an answer. Intelligence released the feed to al Jazeera and Freedom of America TV. It was payback to al Jazeera. The Iranians won't run it, but it's a wakeup. The Afghanis and Pakistanis can't resist it. They hate it, but it makes one hell of a statement."

Hull remembered Siraj Haqqani's tortured shrieks on the pass. Ducking incoming small arms fire, Bauldaire had the balls to videotape the scene.

"Both the Taliban and al Qaeda are in disarray. Ethnic divisions are resurfacing and CENTCOM now believes if we consolidate our holdings in Afghanistan, the Pakistan Tehrik-i-Taliban will implode in one hell of a big cat fight."

"The press has played every available political card to force a press conference. Since you were already outed, they figure talking to the press won't make you more vulnerable. The Marines are desperate to bring you in--under control. No interviews, photos or reunions."

This was the truth. Colonel Dillard, Haldol, the dreams, violence—a good shrink could rewire him, at the same time he took him out of the spotlight. They would switch the breakers, replace the old groundless circuits with GFIs, and then maybe, just maybe, he'd be used for another mission.

"...part two," Eilert was saying, "You heard President Bush and Cheney have the flu?"

"The story ran on the front page of The L.A. Times."

"It's not the flu--it's the Marburg Virus. Bush, Cheney, Limbaugh, Rice, Rumsfeld and three thousand others were mortared at the Bush Presidential Center groundbreaking. Bush and Cheney are quarantined in Level 4 biohazard labs."

"Goddamn! Where was the Secret Service? How did Bush's security break down?"

"Don't come down too hard on the SS. Bush's book tour offered far greater exposure. Half the former Administration was assembled at the groundbreaking. The FBI determined it had to have been a Marburg-filled laser guided mortar. Secret Service located a photo taken by a student that shows a man in blue maintenance overalls installing a security camera in the Southern Methodist quad. Computer enhancement made the image tack sharp--the problem is his face. Unremarkable. No way you'd pick this guy out of a lineup. We don't know why he hasn't launched the other mortars!"

"He? One operator? And more than one weapon?" Hull silently admired the brilliance of one focused terrorist with five biological mortars.

"A message from Kandahar arrived two days ago. A Taliban field commander was seeking to collect a million-dollar reward for verifiable information related to Osama bin Laden. But it wasn't bin Laden he wanted to betray. It was a close lieutenant--an Afghan trained by the KGB. This double agent betrayed the field commander's brother and a son to the Russians. Our boy carried a grudge ever since."

"The Afghani's all carry grudges." Hull informed him. "Some go back generations."

"This may be the credible exception. The informant called him Qari Azad. After the KGB pulled out of Afghanistan, Azad surfaced as one of the leaders in the Mazar-i-Sharif massacre. He became Osama bin Laden's bodyguard, then disappeared."

"Within days after Azad went off the radar, a lone Swiss businessman flew to Mexico City from London. We checked his records. No date of birth, schools, work history, relatives or friends. One of those human chameleons who doesn't exist." He took a breath.

"And you think this Azad mortared the Bush dedication?"

"He may have. Army Intelligence has information matching him to the same man who arrived in Mexico City from Delhi through London. The Mexicans say he never exited the country. He checked into a small hotel and spent three days in Playa del Carmen. Five days after he cleared Mexican Customs, the U.S. Border Patrol found two murdered Mexican nationals north of Arroyitos, Mexico. According to the Mexican Agencia Federal de Investigacion, the two were freelance drug and wetback smugglers. Rival drug lords may have killed them but one had his throat cut. Azad is a mass murderer who always takes credit for his work. Cut throats are his signatures."

Hull remembered Darcy Wilkins's gaping trachea.

"From Arroyitos, we believe Azad traveled north to Dallas where he went to ground. We're convinced he's behind the Presidential Center attack."

"This Azad is the only link you have between Dallas and Sun and Health? Eilert, this is fucking weak. Azad could still be shacked up in Cancun."

"The killings at Sun and Health fit Azad's profile. He tortures for pleasure. Information is secondary. When he finishes with his victims, he cuts their throats."

"It's clear the only reason he's in Los Angeles is to avenge bin Laden's death." Eilert took a breath and confirmed what Hull already knew. "Jack, he's coming for you."

Chapter 25

T en years had passed since Cheryl Birden married Jack Hull in Riverside's All Saint's Episcopal. Radiant in her white, sleeveless gown, even as the Marine Lieutenant reached to take her hand, she didn't trust him. During the exchange of rings and their kiss, it was not infidelity that she feared. Far worse than a fleeting sexual relationship, she questioned Jack Hull's black side, the violence hidden behind his dark eyes. What had turned a VMI Honors Graduate in Literature into a killer? In time, sooner than later, he would face a psychic disconnect. When he broke, and she knew he would, she did not want to be in the same room, house, or even the same city.

Cheryl soon realized that the true cost of the marriage was Hull's inability to truly get close to anyone. If asked to describe him in two words, she would choose "exciting" and "difficult." Following Jack's first tour in Iraq, he was just difficult.

Between tours, he drank too much, slept too little and showed little interest in her job, friends, or desire to start a family. They spoke infrequently, made love when neither could avoid it, had dates…a movie, a night on the coast, dinner with her parents.

Eight months after returning to Los Angeles, Hull received orders to report for a fourth tour in Afghanistan. As she embraced him a last time before he disappeared through security at LAX, she held no illusion that the separation would do them good.

Hull was six months into that fourth tour when Cheryl met Mark

Fitzgerald. The handsome, funny, ex-UCLA rugby player was the lead salesman for a medical supply company in Fontana. Fitzgerald was six foot four, gorgeous, bright, attentive—very attractive. After three years of fighting to close the distance to Jack she was ready for an honest relationship. Mark's interest in her past, her job, the books she read, her favorite movies, and their shared desire to start a family, convinced her she had found her soul mate.

Mark kept a separate apartment until Cheryl filed for divorce. The day after the signed documents reappeared from Afghanistan, Mark went down on one knee, produced a large diamond ring and with tears filling his eyes, proposed. Cheryl valued the tears more than the ring and though they hadn't set a date, she thought the following spring would suit both of their schedules.

The next time she saw Hull, his face was on ABC Nightly News, CNN, CNBC, Fox, the Internet, and newspapers. The photo was a decade old, taken the day Jack Hull had graduated from VMI. His youthful eagerness had faded in Iraq and Afghanistan.

The stories detailed how Jack and his spotter, a Lieutenant Bauldaire, had killed Osama bin Laden and Siraj Haqqani in Afghanistan. Bauldaire, the spotter, was dead. Hull had been promoted. She knew how her ex-husband would deal with the contradiction. One dead, one honored. He would drink. Glenfiddich. For a brief instant, she felt sorry for him.

She was adding final touches to her hair and makeup when the doorbell rang. Setting her brush on the vanity, she crossed to the front door and peered through the security hole. A black and white L.A. police car was parked at the curb. An L.A. policeman wearing dark mirrored glasses was waiting on the porch.

Cheryl Birden was late. She wondered why the policeman was alone, and frowned.

"Ms. Birden?"

How had he known she was there? "Yes," she reluctantly replied through the door.

Smiling slightly, he asked, "Would you mind opening the door?"

Unhooking the security chain, she opened it a quarter of the way, "Can I ask what this is about?"

"Colonel Jack Hull," the policeman replied. "I understand Colonel

Hull is your husband?" Taking a step back from the door, he smiled, a faint upturning of the corners of his mouth. Dressed in a pressed blue uniform, he was clean-shaven, of indeterminate nationality--his features revealing little more than perhaps a trace of European, South Asian, or perhaps Middle Eastern ancestry.

"Ex-husband," she corrected him. "Officer, to tell the truth, I'm late for work. Can we do this another time?"

"This will only take a second. Antonio Villaraigosa, the Mayor of Los Angeles, is hoping to honor Colonel Hull for his service in Afghanistan. He asked me to extend...."

"I doubt Jack will accept the Mayor's invitation," she wondered why a Los Angeles cop would be sent by the mayor all the way to her home in Covina.

"That's unfortunate…" the officer's disappointment seemed sincere. "Even if that proves to be true, Mayor Villaraigosa would very much like to meet Colonel Hull. Would you happen to have an address, or a phone number?"

"Can't you get that from the Marines?"

"We could, but in light of the recent events in Afghanistan, they are restricting his public communications...the Mayor really…" the policeman smiled as he pushed on the door, "You wouldn't mind if I came in?"

Puzzling over his odd syntax, she took a step back. "I'm running late," she reminded him.

Rostislov's glance noted her bare legs, her powdered cheeks and the lip-gloss on her mouth. Her hair was curled, he caught a scent of perfume and she failed to respectfully lower her eyes. Instead she appraised his uniform, hat and his service belt's leather holsters and pockets that contained a pistol, handcuffs, radio and can of mace. In that glance Rostislov saw the Assassin's wife was self-indulgent and sexually uninhibited—a casual plaything for men who worshipped no God, not even the Christian God.

Without warning, Rostislov smashed his right hand onto her left cheek, knocking her backwards onto the hardwood floor. Rostislov stepped inside and closed the front door. She was jerking spasmodically when he taped her mouth shut, grabbed her hair and dragged her into the dining room where he cuffed her to the table leg.

He was standing over her when her eyes fluttered open. In a voice stripped of emotion, he demanded, "Where is Colonel Hull?"

Shaking her head, the duct tape reduced her words to a series of muffled groans. Rostislov squeezed her nostrils until her eyes widened. He allowed her one, shallow breath before he repeated the process, watching for the cyanic blue to creep into her cheeks before he opened his fingers. The air rushed into her nose with a loud, desperate whistling. He repeated the process. After the third time, he held the Karud against her throat and quietly promised, "If you cry out, I will kill you." He removed his mirrored glasses.

It was then she saw his eyes.

Obsidian black, they fixed her with a cold stare. "I have questions that require precise answers," he said, slowly twisting her arm until her elbow reached its breaking point. A muffled wheeze blew from her flared nostrils as the muscles in her left arm resisted the pressure. Then the ligaments shredded and her left elbow rotated one hundred and twenty degrees. She was panting, her breath straining against the tape. She fought to keep from vomiting into her closed mouth.

A thin pursing of his lips served as a smile. "This is the first step in our interview. If you reply quickly and correctly, I will let you go. If you lie or delay...."

Cheryl rapidly shook her head as tears streamed down her cheeks.

Her dislocated elbow was ninety degrees from normal. The slightest touch was excruciatingly painful. Rostislov twisted it a few degrees then ripped the tape from her mouth. "You are aware of where Colonel Hull is staying?"

Cheryl screamed until Rostislov hit her. "Enough! You are wasting time. Where is the Colonel?" Cheryl knew she could not protect Hull. "I do not know!" she choked on the pain that seared up her arm. "We have not spoken since he returned to Los Angeles."

Rostislov revealed neither satisfaction, nor irritation. His right hand tightened on her right wrist. "His friends names?" he asked in a faint, lightly accented voice.

"His old boss, Wardell Stone; his mother and father died; his only friends are in the Marines!" The pain made her sweat. She focused on her wrist and Rostislov's pale hand. "He's a sniper...a loner!"

Rostislov's grip tightened, "At some point, would you not expect a call from Colonel Hull?"

"Yes!...no!" she whimpered. "He used to call when his plane landed, but I have not heard from him since our divorce."

"If not here, then where would he sleep?" Rostislov had not blinked in more than two minutes and his frozen eyelids terrified her more than her dislocated elbow.

"At a hotel," she guessed. "Here, or San Diego, next to Pendleton, the Marine Base. "I can't say. Not a dump. Close to the water...he was raised in Riverside...I don't know."

It took Rostislov three minutes to discover what little Cheryl Birden knew about the Assassin.

"You have answered my questions honestly," he said. "I will honor my promise."

Cheryl clung to this least hope. "I'll be quiet, I won't say..."

"A word...to anyone?" Rostislov finished her sentence. "No, of course you won't." Taking her left arm in his right hand, he smiled and slipped his hand along his belt.

On the edge of hyperventilating from the pain, Cheryl waited for Rostislov to unlock the handcuffs that bound her left hand to the dining room table. In place of the keys, he drew a knife. Cheryl forgot her dislocated elbow and jerked violently back. Rostislov renewed his grip on her wrist and slipped the razor-sharp Karud beneath her ribs, into her left lung and through her pericardium. Cheryl's bloodshot eyes widened and her rapid breathing suddenly stopped.

A key turned in the front door.

Rostislov shifted to face the entry. A second later, a large man in a gray suit walked through the door. He was in his early thirties, six foot four and carried the build of a college rugby player. Rostislov pulled the knife from Cheryl's chest and turned. He was a second late.

Mark Fitzgerald simultaneously saw the L.A. policeman, the cuffs binding Cheryl to the table, the blood on her blouse and the knife in the policeman's hand. A decade had passed since Fitzpatrick played blindside flanker for UCLA Rugby but at two hundred and thirty pounds he could still move with an athlete's speed.

Fitzpatrick's black brief case caught Rostislov high on the forehead, slamming his brain against his skull. An inch lower and half an inch to the right, and the blow would have killed him. Instead, as Rostislov's brain flattened against the fractured bone, he pitched toward a dark psychic well. His knees buckled and as he crashed onto the floor, he fought the concussion that closed his vision down to a gray, unfocused circle.

Lubyanka's martial arts instructors had trained Rostislov to clench his abdominals to force oxygen into his blood stream. His vision cleared as Fitzgerald raised his briefcase for the second, killing blow. Rostislov's years of martial arts in Lubyanka saved his life. Acting on instinct alone, he swung the Kurad upward into Fitzgerald's inner thigh. The surgically sharp blade sliced through the femoral artery. Fitzgerald's blood pressure immediately began to drop as a red, salty stream poured from the wound.

The cut was fatal. Death, however, would not come for two minutes. In a futile attempt to staunch the massive hemorrhage, Fitzgerald grabbed his thigh and without looking at the cut, brought the briefcase down in a powerful, final swing.

Rostislov jerked the Makarov from the police holster. Two simultaneous, hundred and thirty grain hollow points caught Fitzgerald as his heavy briefcase descended toward Rostislov's head. The first punched a hole just below his rib cage, mushroomed through the left ventricle and exited through the right scapula. The second slug was unnecessary. Breaking the temple mandibular joint, it blasted a three-inch exit through the anterior skull plate, splattering brains and bone across the ceiling's sparkling texture. The big man's legs buckled and with a single groan caused by the air rushing from his lungs, he crashed to the floor.

It took forty five seconds for Rostislov to drag himself out from beneath Fitzgerald's twitching corpse. During that precious three quarters of a minute, a torrent of blood soaked onto his uniform, painting his exposed arms and face bright red. Still dazed, Rostislov's reflection in the living room mirror resembled a survivor from the Mazar-i-Sharif cleansing.

Cheryl had crawled under the table where she now moaned in pain. Success depended on the next two minutes. Reeling from the blow and with blood dripping from his hair and face, he could not leave Cheryl Birden's apartment.

Staggering across the living room to the bath, he turned the shower to cold, and without removing his uniform, service belt or shoes, let the freezing water cascade over him. He scrubbed his shirt and pants with a back brush he found hanging from the spigot until the drain ran red with blood. In time, the bright arterial red faded to pink and eventually ran clear. The cold restored his equilibrium. He pulled a towel from the glass door, toweled off his hair, uniform and shoes, as best he could. Reflected in the mirror, his uniform's dark blue color camouflaged the soaked fabric.

Rostislov walked unsteadily into the living room where he unlocked the handcuffs binding the American whore to the table and rolled Fitzgerald onto his back. Rostislov retrieved his Karud, cleaned it on the dead man's jacket and slipped it back into a small sheath in his service belt.

He attempted to sweep the living room but moving his head triggered a massive headache. Unable to do more than wipe his wet footprints from the entryway, he exited Cheryl Birden's house and nearly fell down the front steps. He clung to the railing and vomited. Wiping his mouth, he appeared to be drunk as he staggered toward the blurred Black and White. He managed to open the driver's side door before his legs buckled and he pitched forward into the interior. It took a moment before he regained equilibrium and straightened behind the wheel.

He started the engine, shifted into gear and slowly followed Prospero to the next intersection where he missed a turn. He then missed another.

Hull hit eighty-five miles an hour on North Grand. He was within a minute of Cheryl's house on Prospero when the vertigo hit him. It was a side effect of Haldol: rare but dangerous for drivers. North Grand suddenly faded as Hull tried to hold the Mercedes between the curb and white line. When his vision cleared, he was following an armored Stryker in a lightly armored Humvee. Hull was on the passenger side, a SAW pointed at the floorboard. Gray dust billowed from the Stryker, forcing Bauldaire to increase vehicle separation to sixty meters.

A majority of Coalition troops traversed the most dangerous routes in MRAPS--Mine-Resistant, Ambush-Protected vehicles. Hull hated them. Slow, hard to maneuver, the MRAPS fortress on wheels philosophy signaled defeat. Invaders had built fortresses for a thousand years. All of them had been overwhelmed. Hull made a choice. The Humvee was vulnerable, but speed was safety.

INTEL rated that afternoon's mission as low risk, no more than an afternoon walk through flowering poppy fields. The four Coalition Troops and eight ANA had orders to secure a village in Helmand province. Once the village was subdued, the ANA would burn the fields. Hull, Bauldaire and two PFCs were ordered to offer support. None would help with the burn.

In the previous six months the ANA had destroyed more than 5,300 pounds, more than two and a half tons of raw product. To win the war, ISAF needed to disrupt Afghanistan's three billon dollar opium trade. Taxes on the raw opium financed the Taliban who controlled virtually all of southern Afghanistan's rural villages.

Four hours behind the wheel caused Bauldaire to volunteer to Hull. "I don't mind these burns. Not when opium kills more than a hundred thousand worldwide. Heroin kills more than twice that many."

"Bauldaire, burning this field won't keep the addicts from overdosing on junk." Hull watched the Stryker steer around an IED crater.

"Fucked up way to die." One of the PFCs agreed from the back. "Choking on your own spume."

"Where'd you hear that?" Bauldaire partly turned in the seat.

"Saw it in a movie." The PFC grimaced as the Humvee slammed into the crater. "Some chick was puking her guts out...from Coke."

"That wasn't that good looking bitch in..." the second PFC tried to remember. "You know with John Travolta and that black dude...?"

"Pulp Fiction?" Hull said.

"Thank you sir...yea Pulp Fiction."

"Uma Thurman was high on heroin, not coke." Bauldaire corrected him.

"All the same, she was a goner if Travolta didn't stick that needle in her tit."

Bauldaire didn't bother to reply.

There was a reason the eight-wheeled, General Dynamics IAV was leading. It packed a 50-caliber machine gun. Hull wished it was a M134 Minigun. Six thousand rounds a minute death dealing 7.62mm NATO rounds. The Minigun alone would keep the Moolies at a distance. There were limits, however, to CENTCOM's generosity.

The Stryker was carrying five Afghan National Army soldiers. Their leader, Captain Gulab Manhal, was thirty years old. Born in Kandahar, he had spent two years at the University of Kabul before the Taliban destroyed the lecture halls and drove the professors into exile. Manhal had a strong jaw, aquiline nose and dark, wide-set eyes. He spoke acceptable English, was a gifted leader, and was clearly in line for a promotion.

CENTCOM had far bigger plans for Manhal than burning poppy fields. U.S. Generals needed a warrior to lead the ANA.

Bracing his foot on the Hummer's dash against the dusty, rutted chuckholes, Hull had no faith in the Afghan National Army. Motivated by high pay, new uniforms, reliable weapons and helicopter gunships to cover their operations, the ANA soldiers were mercenaries in their own country. Fierce in a fight, the average Afghani boot was unreliable. Even Manhal could not call in artillery or air strike. Instead he depended on Hull and Bauldaire to transmit coordinates. When the Coalition finally declared victory, packed up and shipped home, Hull had no doubt the ANA would hand Afghanistan back to the Taliban.

CENTCOM gave Manhal the all-wheel-drive Stryker to guarantee survival and insure loyalty. The Stryker helped incentivise the Afghan Captain who behaved like a teenage kid with a new BMW. He ordered his troops to polish it until it shone. Then he had them polish it again.

Wind gusting across the road lifted a powdery dust that momentarily obscured the Stryker. Visibility fell to three feet. A second later the Humvee banged into another IED crater slamming Hull against the steel door. The two PFCs in back yelled at the shock.

Bauldaire said, "I lost the road. Anyone hurt?"

"Fuck Me!" One shaken PFC spoke for the other. "I thought that was an IED. Riding in this fucking pop can makes me jumpy."

Hull reached for a water bottle. The mission was a dangerous waste of men, time and material. Command knew there was no chance of replacing opium with tomatoes, lettuce or pumpkins.

"Idiotic," He commented to himself. Cultivating opium was stupidly simple. Add seeds, water and goat dung then wait. One opium poppy capsule produced a black tar that was simple to harvest, easy to store, and ignored by rats. Poppies thrived in conditions that killed wheat. Wheat required water, carts pulled by donkeys to reach markets where a buyer might or might not purchase the grain. The opium buyers came to the farmers who could store a season's harvest in two plastic bags.

In this land of scorched deserts and three thousand meter peaks, a hectare of opium was worth sixty times a hectare of wheat. The eight-year drought, remote fields, bad roads, poor markets and starving children left Afghanistan's farmers with little choice. Let Western politicians rail against the heroin trade, U.S. and Europe addicts drove the demand. Bottom line was opium accounted for forty five percent of Afghanistan's GNP.

Plow the poppy fields under? When forced to choose between feeding their families and betraying Coalition Soldiers, Afghanistan's farmers paid lip service to one and kept their hundred hectares of ripening poppies well-supplied with goat shit and water.

"Manhal just stopped," Bauldaire observed. The Stryker was sitting in the middle of the road where a single well-placed anti tank missile would kill the crew. The ANA Captain took too many chances. So far he had been lucky. If he continued to serve as a decoy for Taliban ambushes, sooner than later a 7.62 mm would rip the brave out of him. South of Kandahar, a holy death would lose much of its appeal when Manhal was lying on his back with black clots of coagulating blood filling his lungs.

"Fuck," Hull said. Safety lay in rapid movement, foot to the armor plate, blasting through ambushes. With luck, the IEDs would explode in the rearview. Stopping on an exposed road only invited an attack. Hull keyed his radio. "Captain…why have you stopped?" Afghanistan's unpaved roads enhanced concealment. Covering an IED with dirt and a light sprinkling of gravel erased its location.

"We find IED." Manhal's replied. "It take maybe a moment to fix all." IEDs were devastating Afghani police officers and soldiers. Extrapolating ANP and ANA casualties due to IED explosions alone, by year's end the total could top 6,000--up from 81 in 2003.

Two weeks before, four SAS British Reservists died when an IED blew their Snatch Land Rover into four pieces--engine, frame, the flattened body, and what was left of the rear axle.

"It looked like a tank mine triggered beneath a Ford Escort!" A British

Royal Marine described the burning remains.

Hull responded. "Captain, if the Taliban are watching with the detonator...." The Taliban was constantly adapting--IED design, materials and placement changed weekly. There was no telling what Manhal had stumbled upon.

Manhal forcefully disagreed, "No Taliban. Pressure trigger! We know fix."

Bauldaire watched the Captain. "Fix my ass." IEDs employed a variety of explosives...fertilizer and diesel fuel, mortar shells or old mines two decades of war had left scattered across Afghanistan. The triggers were stupidly simple to fabricate. Pressure plates, cell phones, the more primitive used a wire connected to a twelve-volt battery.

"Captain Manhal?" Hull triggered his mike.

"One minute please Major."

"Fuck," Hull shook his head. There was no use arguing with Manhal. Hull knew if the IED was pressure-activated and they detoured around, it would shred the next Toyota pickup truck loaded with women and children. He keyed the radio. "Captain, back away! We'll call in the EOD techs!" Keeping his eyes on the Stryker he told Bauldaire, "Call the 755th."

Bauldaire triggered the mike. "Sir, they figure four hours."

Hull heard.

Eavesdropping on the radio exchange, Manhal interrupted, "Too much time. Not need to take all day. We fight Taliban. Know how to fix." The 755th EODs had given Manhal's First Sergeant a basic training in bomb disposal. Blowing them was the safe choice. Manhal, however, was in a hurry and now stood above the IED. Hull listened to the rapid exchange in Pashto.

Forcing a calm he did not feel he said, "Captain Manhal! I suggest you back away!"

"This not big complex," the Captain objected. "Only simple pressure switch!"

Hull keyed the radio, "Captain, for the safety of your men, you need to wait for the 755th." The 755th would use robots to dispose of the bomb.

The Afghan officer waved. "Major, you see, this not take four hour." He admired the fact that the American Marine Officers spoke Pashto but was equally proud of his English.

Hull waited, then keyed his radio. "Captain, I'm the ranking officer and ultimately responsible for the safety of you and your men, I order you to back away."

The Captain was fifty meters out standing next to the Sergeant when he barked into his microphone. "Major Hull you order your men. I order mine!" He turned off his radio.

"Back up," Hull told Bauldaire. The Lieutenant shifted into reverse and slammed the accelerator onto the metal floor. In seconds the Humvee was a hundred meters from the Up-Armored Humvee and the two figures working on the road. Hull studied the Captain through his binoculars. Adjusting the reticule until the image sharpened, he watched the Sergeant squat on his heels. Dust drifted across the road as the mustached soldier used a twenty centimeter length of rusted rebar to scrape the compacted gravel away.

Bauldaire steadied his sixty-power Swarovski spotting scope on the steering wheel.

One of the privates in back asked, "See anything?"

"He's digging," Bauldaire replied.

"Those fuckers are crazy."

A minute passed before the Sergeant lifted a brass artillery shell above his head.

"Fuck yes!" the other Corporal exclaimed. "He got it! He should teach that trick to the 755th!"

Hull swung the binoculars to Manhal's Stryker. Three AFA soldiers climbed out and walked toward the captain. They were two meters away, raising their arms in celebration when a tremendous explosion obliterated the Stryker. A hundred meter pillar of dust erupted from the road. The Humvee was showered with fist-sized rocks. One shattered the armored glass a foot from Hull's face. The plastic core held.

"Everyone OK?" he yelled to the back seat.

"Clear!" The Corporals yelled back.

Hull jumped out of the Humvee and started to run. Bauldaire was a half step behind. Taking care to avoid secondary IEDs, Hull was within thirty meters of the crater when he passed the first body part. Manhal was still alive when Hull reached him. The bomb had quartered the Afghan Captain.

261

His legs had been blown off mid thigh, his arms high in the biceps leaving a blackened torso convulsing in the road. Kneeling beside the Afghan, Hull raised his blackened head from the dust. What was left of his body shivered. The stumps of his legs beat against the hard road. He tried to speak, but no sound came from his mouth. Hull watched the fear of his impending death wash across Manhal's burned features. His eyes fixed on Hull's face.

Bauldaire appeared at Hull's shoulder. The Lieutenant studied Manhal's corpse before he reported the casualties, "Including the Captain and Sergeant, four dead, two critical," he said.

Hull exhaled.

Manhal's blackened torso was convulsing with his final, choking breaths when Hull's vision cleared. The Mercedes was parked next to the central divider on North Grand.

Cheryl's address came to him in pieces; street number, town. Hull lifted his foot off the brake and pressured the throttle. The Mercedes surged forward. He reached the small house on Prospero in five minutes, parked the Mercedes and sprinted up the walk to the front door. He knocked, rang the bell then tried the handle. Locked. Cheryl must be at work. He knocked again, hard. A weak cry wavered from within the apartment.

He kicked the lock set from the wooden door jam. Mark Fitzgerald's corpse lay sprawled diagonally into the living room. Cheryl was struggling to rise next to the table. Rostislov's knife had punctured her heart. Her blood had pooled onto the hardwood. Taking her in his arms, Hull dialed 911.

"What exactly is the nature of your problem?"

"One shooting fatality and one victim in need of an ambulance."

The dispatcher repeated, "You said two victims?"

"Affirmative!" Hull yelled.

"A police unit is on the way. They should be there in three minutes. Please stay on the line until they arrive."

He held Cheryl in his arms and demanded, "Who did this?"

"A policeman." She coughed "From Los Angeles."

"Did you get a name...or badge number?"

Before she could answer, her heart faltered. It took a beat, then another--and stopped. In the seconds before she lost consciousness, her silent chest terrified her. The blood slowed in her arteries and in an attempt to set an anchor in this world, she dug her nails into his arm and fixed her eyes on his face. Her head rolled to one side.

Hull had witnessed far too much death in Iraq and Afghanistan and now, holding her in his arms, he wished that he and Bauldaire had never crossed into Pakistan. Even in death, Osama bin Laden exacted a harsh revenge. The shot that decapitated bin Laden ultimately killed Bauldaire and Cheryl. Closing her fixed eyes, he remembered the tenderness he once felt for her and mourned her death.

Sirens screamed at the edge of his hearing. Two Upland Black and Whites were within blocks of Prospero. Hull had no time to grieve. The police would hold him for questioning and when the detectives finished taking a statement, they would turn him over to the Marines. Hull needed to save Grace. To do that he would need to kill the L.A. policeman. He forced himself to his feet.

Colonel Dillard screamed into focus.

Hull was developing a resistance to the Haldol. Soon the powerful anti-hallucinogenic would stop working altogether.

"You can't leave," Dillard cautioned.

"I can't stay," Hull choked.

"The Brave man inattentive to his duty, is worth little more to his county than the coward who deserts her in the hour of danger." Colonel Dillard tried to stop him.

Hull heard the approaching sirens, "I have no time."

"You have no choice," the Professor replied.

With a single, backward glance, Hull looked at his former wife. She had contracted into a fetal position on the wood floor. The loss of blood had leached the color from her face. It now reflected the arctic white of a crescent moon.

Taking a last look at Cheryl, Hull closed the shattered door behind him.

Chapter 26

Nine hundred miles and a time zone away, doctors at St. John's Medical Center in Jackson, Wyoming had been warned that the ex-Vice President was exposed to Marburg. Lynne Cheney had begun to present symptoms, as had the housekeepers, a cook and the two Secret Service agents assigned to protect Cheney and his family. Able to track only some of Cheney's visitors and the people in the restaurant where he and Lynne had dined, as well as those who had come into contact with his drivers, the CDC could only insist on Cheney's immediate bio-quarantine containment. When Cheney resisted, they told him he had no choice.

Jackson, Wyoming is the gateway to both Grand Teton and Yellowstone National Parks. During summer, two million visitors pass through the small resort town on the way north into the parks. An outbreak of airborne Marburg would infect tens of thousands of tourists who would carry the virus across the nation.

Flying Cheney to NIAID Rocky Mountain Laboratories in Hamilton, Montana was out of the question. The NIAID containment facility would not be fully operational for another three months. A myriad of other dangers prohibited any transfer. Exposure to uninfected populations could trigger an epidemic that would rage across the west.

Jackson's St. John's Medical Center was a small hospital, unequipped to deal with more than births, injuries, and minor surgeries. With the CDC's technical help and biocontainment equipment, St. John's rushed to assemble a makeshift containment ward for anyone who had been exposed to the

Cheneys.

In an attempt to bio-isolate the ex-Vice President, the CDC quarantined Cheney in his home. Air Force C5A transport jets delivered Hazmat Suits, Level 4 oxygen and water filtration systems, portable chemical showers and state-of-the-art air locks. In less than eight hours, multiple, electronically secured airlocks to prevent more than one from opening at the same time guarded entry into Cheney's large living room. Medical workers in Hazmat suits subjected all air, water, body and medical wastes to rigid decontamination procedures. The Cheneys, their staff, and close friends who had happened to visit before the virus was identified were isolated in the living room's crude bio-containment chamber.

The CDC then turned to more pressing matters. Dallas hospitals were overwhelmed. New cases appeared in Miami, Atlanta, Dayton, Chicago, New York and Trenton--the implications were terrifying.

Grace Guerrera stepped in front of the bathroom mirror and stared at her left cheek. The deep bruise pulsed with pain. When she tried to close her mouth a searing heat flashed up her jaw and into her ear, before dissipating in a stabbing headache.

She had been struck by men before. Open hand slap or closed fist, she recognized the difference between a bruise and a break. The bruises could be camouflaged by makeup. She withstood the breaks as long as she could before submitting to the antiseptic claustrophobia of emergency rooms and interns who too often took more than a simply professional interest in her case. Bruises faded, bones knitted--both needed time

Her cell phone rang. Private number. Fucking Hull. She dropped the phone on the vanity where successive rings spun it in slow, concentric circles. The spinning was followed by a hard knock at the front door. On the third knock, she responded, "Who is it?" her words slurred out in the distorted cadence of a stroke victim.

"Hull."

"I'm calling the police!" she warned him.

"Grace, open the door." There was no mistaking the command in his voice.

She was still in the bathroom dialing 911 when the lockset splintered from the wooden jamb. Hull crossed to the bathroom. "Unlock the door!" he ordered.

"Get out!" she screamed a second before Hull kicked he lock from the jamb. Still screaming she threw a heavy crystal vase at him. Hull ducked and she swung a closed right fist at his jaw. He caught the punch, spun her into his chest and covered her mouth with his left hand. He picked her cell phone from the counter and slipped it into his pocket then dragged her into the living room.

"I'll take my hand off your mouth if you don't scream."

When she nodded, he released her. Gasping for air, she shrieked, "Hull—you fucking lunatic!"

"Listen to me!" He shook her then rapidly described the horror at Sun and Health and at Cheryl's house. "Cheryl lived long enough to I.D. an L.A. policeman, a Sergeant. Mark, her boyfriend, was already dead. Whoever killed them is hunting me. If he doesn't find me, he'll find you. You've got two minutes to grab what you need for a week!"

"Hull...you're completely crazy," she screamed.

Hull shook her again. "You won't recognize him until it's too late! He'll break you down, and after you give him the answers, he'll kill you." He was beyond wired. Sleep deprivation, massive doses of Haldol, Mirtazapine and straight shots of Scotch had exacted a harsh toll.

Grace needed to gain control. Forcing a calm she did not feel, she asked, "Jack, have you looked at yourself?"

He opened the front closet, grabbed a small suitcase and crossed to the bedroom. "I said two minutes." He opened her dresser drawer and grabbed a handful of bras and panties. From the closet he pulled out slacks, shirts and flat shoes as he barked, "Get ready!"

"Hull, you can't force me!" Grace started toward the front door.

Hull threw a small bag of toiletries into the suitcase and zipped it shut. "You have ninety seconds. If you call the police, he will be the first to arrive." He caught her as she was opening the front door. There was no bravado in his voice, "I'm the only one who can protect you."

"And how do you plan to do that? By screwing my brains out and then beating the shit out of me again?"

"You have seventy seconds."

CHAPTER TWENTY SIX

"Hull, you're fucking crazy. Forget it--I'm not coming!"

"If you stay, you'll die. Don't force me to drag you to the car. One minute." He looked around the living room.

"Goddammit, Hull, you're scaring me!" Grace sensed he was telling the truth.

"It's not me you need to fear. Get dressed!"

"Fuck," she crossed reluctantly to the bedroom and ripped a blouse and slacks off hangers.

"You've got half a minute. Or you'll dress in the car."

Hull held the SL65's passenger door. Grace was barefoot, her pants were unbuttoned and her blouse was open to her bra. Holding her shoes she dropped into the leather seat. Hull drew her seat belt out and locked it in the machined latch. He tossed her suitcase in the trunk next to his duffle and slid into the driver's seat.

"Where did this car come from?" she asked, but he was not listening.

Hull quickly checked the rear view mirrors as the V-12 ignited with the whine of spinning turbochargers. An L.A. Black and White appeared in the apartment parking lot.

Hull watched the Crown Victoria cruise slowly through the parking lot. In seconds the heavy sedan would block their escape. Shifting into reverse, Hull stabbed the throttle once, hard to the floor. Seven hundred horsepower catapulted the small coupe directly into the path of the L.A. Police car.

Unprepared for the violent acceleration, Grace pitched forward against the belt, then slammed back into the seat as Hull shifted the SL65 from full throttle reverse to full throttle first gear. Forced to bear the brutal reverse-first shift, any other transmission would have detonated. The Mercedes miraculously held together.

The SL65's tires churned smoke when Hull drifted onto Sunnybrook Avenue. The Mercedes could outrun Rostislov but it could not escape the L.A. police radio. Other L.A. Basin police cruisers would be closing on Sunnybrook. In two minutes news and law enforcement helicopters would appear overhead. Hull reached the 18th Street intersection, and with a quick glance left and right, blew the stoplight.

Coming hard on the throttle, he accelerated to eighty. At that speed, the crossing traffic repeatedly misjudged the SL65's closing rate and pulled

267

into the Mercedes' path. Hull repeatedly pounded the brakes or floored the throttle. Each maneuver slammed Grace against the belts. When the Mercedes reached North Euclid, the speedometer was a tick above a hundred. Hull glanced left, punched the shifter from third to second as he hit the brakes. The ABS engaged and the Mercedes drifted through a yellow light into the right lane. The tachometer touched the red line, and Hull shifted into third, then fourth, as the Mercedes hurtled north toward the San Gabriels.

The dash mounted GPS showed Mount Baldy Road's twists, turns, hairpins and short straights played to the Mercedes' strengths. Between the valley floor and the summit, the serpentine road climbed 4600 feet in 13 miles. The final five miles averaged over 8% grade with upper sections exceeding 15%.

Glancing at the rearview, Hull estimated the cruiser had fallen a half-mile behind. He calculated the time it would take to bring the Mercedes to a full stop, open the trunk, unzip the duffle and load the SAW.

With Rostislov pursuing at a hundred plus, Hull needed to increase the distance. The Mercedes accelerated through 110, 115, and hit 120 on North Mountain Avenue, devouring the long straights in brutal surges. The speed terrified Grace. Her eyes locked on the checked line which blended into a single white stripe.

Rock embankments, over-hanging Manzanita branches, towering fir and Ponderosa pine turned to a homogenous blue, green, and dun blur as Hull focused on brake points and exits. The speedometer wavered above one hundred miles an hour as a hard right approached. He ignored the mangled guardrail that offered a final barrier above a two hundred foot cliff. Pressing the shift paddle, he forced the transmission from third to second as the V-12 soared to redline. The ABS chattered on loose gravel, the SL65 settled, and Hull came back on the throttle, kicking the rear end loose, drifting the small car onto the next straight. A minivan blocked the road. Hull downshifted, flicked the wheel left, then right, as another sedan, horn blaring, swept past. The van faded in the rearview.

Hull held second gear to redline, and then let the V-12's enormous compression brake for the corner. It was more than Grace could stand. As the Mercedes dived on its front brakes, she yelled, "I'm going to throw up!"

"Roll down the window and hold it until the next corner!"

Grace fought her nausea until the Mercedes entered the sharp left then convulsed. She took a breath and wiped her mouth. The cold air revived her and she grabbed onto the leather bucket seat and braced for a dogleg right that bled into a short straight. Hull passed a Chevy sedan on a short straight. "FUCK! HULL--SLOW DOWN!" she yelled.

"HE'LL CATCH US!" Hull yelled back, his expression locked in a granitic focus. "LOOK IN BACK OF US!" he ordered.

Twisting in the seat she spotted the Cruiser a mile below, coming fast up the narrow road. The lights were off and she could not hear a siren.

The effort made her stomach turn. She rolled down the window. "Hold it until the left," Hull said.

She held her rising bile until the centrifugal force slammed her against the passenger door and emptied her stomach. Wiping her mouth with a tissue she slumped back into the seat. She took her eyes off the road for a moment, looked at Hull and said, "You didn't want me puke down the side of the car!"

Hull's glance neither confirmed nor denied. Instead he said, "We've gained time…"

"Time? For what?"

"I'm going to stop. When I do, run. Get far away from the car and find a place to hide. When the shooting stops…"

"Shooting?"

Hull focused on a rapidly approaching corner. "This is our best chance, while he is out in the open. I need to see him coming." The corner appeared as a sweeping left that offered a view of the summit. Mt. Baldy was a small community crowding the lee of the ridge. Hull slowed to avoid drawing the local police force's attention. Beyond the business district, he accelerated past Ice House Canyon Road then took a hard right up a dirt track that led into the Douglas fir and scrub oak. A hundred meters from the main road, he backed the Mercedes up a woodcutter's turnout, switched off the ignition and pointed to a white granite knob. "Run toward that rock outcropping." There was no compromise in his voice. "Don't stop! Find a place to hide. I'll come for you!" Exiting the driver's seat, he pulled the SAW from the trunk, fixed the drum magazine to the breech. Turning to Grace, ordered. "Move! Now!"

Grace stumbled uphill.

Hull sprinted back down the dirt road to a bluff that offered a clear view of Mount Baldy Road, and took position behind a downed fir log.

A Chrysler Minivan filled with a family of four pulled off to let the cruiser pass. Rostislov had killed the siren and lights. Speeding through Mt. Baldy would alert the small town's skeleton police force. If they tried to stop him and lived, they would radio the California Highway Patrol and L.A. Basin police departments for backup. Mount Baldy Road would soon be choked with interlocking roadblocks. Rostislov could not escape the Highway Patrol helicopters, nor could he disappear into the rocky forests that lined the twisting road.

The road continued to climb. Forests gave way to granite outcrops. Rostislov did not underestimate Hull. Concealment and firepower were the Assassin's greatest weapons. He had bought time and distance. Rostislov anticipated an ambush from the Scout Sniper. It would be precise, mortal. He had not passed the Mercedes. It was still somewhere ahead. He scanned the side roads.

The first dirt road revealed nothing. The third tributary dirt road bore a wide, low profile track in the dry, yellow dust--a sports car's tread--the Mercedes.

Rostislov threw the wheel to the left and floored the accelerator. The SAW's stream of 5.56x44mm rounds stitched into the right front fender, across the roof and out the trunk. The windshield exploded in a rain of glass popcorn. A dozen jacketed rounds ripped through the front seat, shattered the roof-mounted lights, and blew the rear window. Throttle hard on the floor, Rostislov swung the wheel right.

Hull's SAW tracked the Black and White as it swerved from left to right. The SAW's steady stream of bullets hit the rear door, ripped into the rear seat and steel pillar. From there rounds moved forward through the front passenger door and onto the engine compartment where they hit the transmission's torque converter, destroyed four vanes and slammed the debris against the converter housing. The transmission self-destructed.

Hull steadied his sight on the roof and triggered a burst. The cruiser roared from sight beneath the cut bank. Side hilling above the road, Hull followed the trail of raspberry colored transmission fluid around one corner. From the high ground, Hull could see the road ahead. The trail of transmission fluid stopped.

Hull risked a glance over the thirty-foot cliff that dropped to the road. The Cruiser blocked the right lane.

Rostislov's twelve-gauge shotgun shredded the tree trunk next to Hull's right elbow. The Scout Sniper owed his life to luck. Charged with double-ought, the pattern was erratic, scattering shot on both sides but not hitting him. The shot had come from his right. Rostislov would work to close on him-- the SAW's firepower would be matched by the shotgun's heavy loads.

Hull scanned the woods. A blue, uniformed pant leg was partially visible behind the three-foot trunk of a large ponderosa pine. Taking quick aim he snapped off a burst.

Rostislov spun and returned fire.

Hull saw an exposed sleeve, raised the SAW and touched the trigger. Two rounds later the SAW ran dry. Hull's last bullet hit the shotgun's stock. Two thousand-foot pounds of force ripped the shotgun out of Rostislov's hands. Three seconds later, a load of double-ought shot raked the trunk in front of Hull. Rostislov had recovered the damaged shotgun, and unable to raise the shattered stock to his shoulder, was now shooting from the hip.

A siren wavered into hearing--distant, approaching fast.

"Fuck," Hull whispered. The SAW was empty; Rostislov was waiting. Hull needed to return to the Mercedes, reload the SAW, find a defensible position and finish Rostislov. The siren grew louder. The Mount Baldy police were about to blunder into the firefight.

Hull faced a fear far greater than closing with Rostislov.

Death had defined his last dozen years. Bauldaire, Roxanna and the dozens of men, and women, who had died in his scope--two tours in Iraq, four in Afghanistan-- Hull was haunted by the dead. Overwhelmed by deep exhaustion, he struggled to summon the resolve to kill again. Hull had reached a limit...a point of no return. Another death, even the Afghani's death, could push him over the edge. What lay beyond that edge, he could not say. There was no doubt that the fall would ultimately be fatal.

Dillard appeared as Hull sagged against the thick trunk. In a deep voice, the Professor reminded Hull, "Theirs not to reason why, Theirs but to do and die."

Hull lowered the SAW.

Rostislov's shotgun was blown in half. The Assassin's last shot had shattered the stock, leaving the breech and barrel attached to broken, carbon fiber splinters. One 5.56x44mm round had hit his thigh. The jacketed bullet missed both his femoral artery and large femur bone. Rostislov was lucky. An exploded femur would ensure death.

Climbing carefully down the steep slope, Rostislov limped across the road. The SAW had raked the L.A.P.D. Black and White from hood to trunk. How he had survived the fusillade was a miracle. Allah had spaced the Assassin's bullets. The 5.56x44mm rounds had passed within an inch of his head, torso, arms and legs. The Assassin had missed the gas tank and the Falcons hidden in the trunk. Rostislov offered a brief, passionate prayer of gratitude.

He was reaching to remove the metal suitcase when the siren cleared the corner and came up the short straight.

Chapter 27

om Hamilton, Mt. Baldy's Sheriff, was halfway through lunch when
he received a call about an L.A. Black and White. No lights, no siren,
no radio response. Worse, the L.A. cop was far out of his jurisdiction.
Odd. Hamilton contemplated finishing his Mount Baldy Lodge hamburger,
but decided, "What the hell." His cholesterol was high enough. He left a
five and two ones on the table, started his cruiser and turned up the mountain.
He was half a mile from Ice House Canyon Road when a SAW's three round
burst punctuated by a shotgun blast brought him to full alert.

Hamilton had served with the Marines in the first Gulf War and now
wondered if an L.A. gun nut was testing an assault weapon. Los Angelinos
had the fucked up idea that the San Gabriels were still part of the Wild West.
Flipping on his lights and siren, he floored the Mt. Baldy patrol car.

Another burst. Whoever was shooting knew his stuff. No prolonged
automatic fire, just short, controlled bursts. Hamilton took the sweeping right
below Ice House and was hard on the accelerator when he swerved to miss
the shattered, colored lenses from a Black and White's roof mounted lights.
A hundred feet further on, a thick line of red transmission fluid led to a shot to
hell Crown Victoria. An L.A. police officer was standing next to the left rear
door; his leg bleeding from a bullet wound.

Hamilton skidded to a stop, jerked the shotgun from the dash rack,
unbuckled his side arm and ran toward the officer who was leaning against
the savaged Black and White. "What the hell happened?"

Rostislov pointed up hill. "The driver hit a bicyclist in Claremont. I pursued and when I came around the corner he opened up with an automatic weapon."

Hamilton nodded to his bloody right leg. "How bad you hit?"

"It grazed my thigh….," Rostislov glanced at his bloody pant leg. His arm and neck wounds were inconsequential.

"You need to have it looked at! And I didn't hear your 11-99," Hamilton said. "Where's your back up?"

"You're it," Rostislov replied.

"You transmit a Code Thirty?" he said, looking over the roof at the steep hillside.

"The reception was spotty."

"Not since the repeater was installed," he noticed the Sergeant's side arm. He didn't recognize the make. There was also something about the accent. It was close to American English. The L.A. cop might have spent time in England--but something wasn't right.

Hamilton was still trying to connect an L.A. police sergeant high in the San Gabriels to a shot to shit unit and an unreported hit and run, when the Makarov's heavy slug hit just below his nose. The bullet traveled through Hamilton's sinuses, then tumbled through his cerebrum before it exited through the skull. The Mount Baldy policeman collapsed into a sitting position. Their exchange had taken less than a minute.

Removing the metal suitcase containing the Falcons and the canvas duffle holding the rifles, Rostislov shoved Hamilton's body into the LAPD Black and White's back seat. Enough fluid remained in the torque converter to drive the cruiser to the far bank where Rostislov shifted the transmission selector to low and, reaching through the window, released the parking brake. The cruiser rolled forward, the front wheels bumped over the transition, the rear wheels lifted off the pavement, and the heavy Ford accelerated downhill through the boulders and scrub oak. No explosion followed. In seconds, the tumbling cruiser crashed over a transition. A wave of dust washed across the opposite hillside, followed by silence.

When Hull found Grace, she was wandering in circles through the Douglas fir. "We've got to go! Now!" He grabbed her right hand and dragged her down hill.

"What happened?"

"I missed. He got away." Hull cleared the barrow pit in a single jump onto Ice House Road 50.

"With all those shots? And you didn't kill him? How?" Grace stumbled a foot short of the road.

Hull yanked her to her feet "I don't know. He saw something—maybe the car tracks. He's hit, but not badly enough to stop him. He'll follow." Dragging Grace behind him, he sprinted the fifty yards to the Mercedes. Reloading the SAW, he turned toward where he thought the Afghani would appear. By now Rostislov would have replaced the shotgun with an automatic weapon.

Colonel Dillard reminded Hull, "It is a bad plan that admits no modification."

Grace was shaking. "Run? Where? Back down that road? He'll call the Highway Patrol. They'll be waiting." Fear lowered her voice.

"No way. He won't call!" Hull set the loaded SAW in the passenger foot well, drew the Colt from the duffle bag, slammed the trunk and guided Grace into the passenger seat. He sprinted around the hood and jumped behind the wheel.

The V-12 was howling at full song when the SL65 drifted out of Ice House Road onto Bald Mountain. Hull touched the brakes then cranked the wheel left. The SL turned sideways, then hooked up and accelerated back toward town. Slowing long enough to clear Mt. Baldy's downtown he aimed the Mercedes down a long straight and floored the accelerator.

Blood dripped steadily onto the pavement as Rostislov limped to Hamilton's patrol car. Sliding behind the wheel, he carefully inventoried his wounds. Butterfly bandages would close the gouge on his right forearm. The graze on his neck would require sterile tape, nothing more. The bullet wound in his thigh was far more serious. He needed to staunch the bleeding.

Rostislov had no hope of catching the Mercedes on Bald Mountain Road. He would pursue at a distance and wait for the Assassin to use his cell phone. Touching eighty miles an hour past Central Avenue in Mt. Baldy, he did not attempt to avoid detection. Baldy Mountain's lone surviving police officer would offer a momentary diversion. Rostislov checked the rearview.

No one followed.

He had just cleared an overlook that offered a smoggy view of the L.A. Basin when his vision darkened. A shadow slipped from the edge to the center. Slamming on the brakes, he managed to pull into a turnout. Then he blacked out.

Hull was three miles further down the road, shifting into third, when he glanced at Grace. Her hands were scraped. Her pants were dusty. He touched the shift paddles and the transmission sucked into second. The SL65 took the hairpin on the edge of adhesion. Tires howling, the sports car hung next to a mangled guardrail that bore a dozen deep dents.

Grace closed her eyes and braced for the next corner. If anything remained in her stomach, she would have vomited. Hull checked the rearview and eased off the throttle. The passenger window was down, and she held her head in the cool mountain air. Her black hair swirled in the wind and the color returned to her pale face. She opened her eyes. "Where are we going?"

"East. Palm Springs, then north toward Salt Lake City."

"Salt Lake City? Hull...no way I'm going to Salt Lake City!"

"Not as far as Salt Lake--to Nevada's Great Basin. I need...."

Grace interrupted. "Where did you say...the Great Basin?"

"I need space...separation, in the desert, to see him coming."

"Hull, you're not thinking. You need to call the Police, or Marines."

Hull didn't tell her about the Marburg. If he reported to the Marines, Rostislov would launch a mortar. Camp Pendleton, San Diego Tijuana, points east...five million people would die. Only the hot, uninhabited desert could neutralize the virus.

Grace knew then that Hull was crazy. The L.A. Policeman, his ex-wife, the killings at Sun and Health...all were hallucinations. The LAPD and Marines were searching for him. She knew Hull wouldn't give up without a fight. She needed to find a way out of the car and away from him. Forcing a calm into her bruised voice, she said, "Hull, he's lost us. We could drive back to my apartment, and you could call the Marines. You don't have to report, just give them a heads up about the cop." The purple stain had drained from her left cheek, down her jaw and onto her neck. The color of her navy blouse darkened the injury.

"Dumb idea." Hull said as Mt. Baldy Road's abrupt turns yielded to Padua Avenue's expensive homes. "If he loses us, he'll search your apartment for contact numbers and addresses…your brother, friends, all would be in danger."

"…. then leave me in Palm Springs. He'll chase you into the Great Bowl…or whatever."

"No, we stick together. It's the only way I can protect you." He would never forget Cheryl's face as she took her last breath, or Stone's mutilated body. Ahead, California Highway 210 crossed Padua Avenue. Hull accelerated up the concrete ramp into the right lane that skirted the mountain escarpment. Signs on the intersecting Baseline Road listed San Bernardino before it turned south to Redlands and a confluence with Highway 10.

"Hull, face it, you kidnapped me."

"Call it what you will, for your own good…I'm trying to keep you alive!"

It was two o'clock on Highway 210, and Hull held the SL65 to eighty miles per hour. Commute traffic was slowly building as nameless drivers of SUVs and semis, all headed to home or work. Ahead, a sign pointed to Interstate 10.

The Mercedes swept around the onramp toward Palm Springs. He hit the seek button. Talking over the Moody Blues' "Nights in White Satin," an announcer read an AP wire feed.

"Two bombings in the city of Karachi, Pakistan have killed twenty-five people and injured at least three dozen more. The first attack was attributed to a motorcycle loaded with explosives. The suicide bomber triggered the explosive a second before he smashed into a bus filled with Shiite pilgrims. The pilgrims were celebrating Arabian, a religious festival marking forty days of mourning for the Prophet Muhammad's grandson. The blast injured two-dozen people, who were transported to Karachi's Jonah Hospital. There, a second bomb exploded among the rescuers and victims, killing a further thirteen. No group has claimed responsibility."

"In a related story, the bombing forty days ago attributed to al Qaeda has now been blamed on Sunni Muslims. The blast killed twenty-five Shiva pilgrims. Pakistan's Prime Minister Sayd Yousuf Raza Gilani has appealed for calm amid growing tensions between Shias and Sunnis."

Grace reached toward the console and punched the radio off. "The world has gone insane!"

Hull did not disagree.

"People ignore the burned bodies that fill the news. Television has made us part of this insanity."

"Television, or not, the insanity exists." Hull told her how, halfway through his third tour, a link appeared in his email. "Bauldaire, my spotter, sent me a YouTube video that showed a woman in a blue burka. The Mullahs had buried her to her shoulders in a soccer stadium."

"Why would they bury her in a soccer stadium?"

"She was convicted of adultery. The extreme view of Sharia Law makes it a capital offense. There was no appeal to a higher court. The Mullahs shouted down her pleas for mercy as the religious guards used their AK-47s to push back the crowd."

"That's sick!" Grace turned in the seat to face him.

"A Mullah, one of her judges, threw a rock. It missed. He threw another, a little larger. It struck the crown of her burka. She started to scream. It only excited the crowd. Stones rained in upon her."

"Hull! Why are you telling me this?"

"To show you insanity. What the terrorists are capable...." Hull stopped. There was no need to further frighten Grace by describing the woman's ripped, blood-stained burka.

"No more...don't say any more."

He knew the Upland Police would cordon off Sun and Health. The FBI would soon take over the investigation. Hull had seen Wardell Stone that morning. He had called 911 from Cheryl's house. He'd left the scene.

"Alright...but we need to disappear."

"Disappear?"

"For a day maybe two," it was neither request, nor promise.

"To kill the Afghani?"

"He's coming." Hull knew Rostislov was close behind.

He was a Good Samaritan on his way to an afternoon hike in the San Gabriels when he rounded a hairpin and saw the Baldy Mountain policeman slumped over the patrol car's steering wheel. Gray haired, dressed in a USC sweatshirt, worn hiking boots, Levi's, and wire-rimmed glasses, he swerved onto the narrow shoulder and ran across the road. The patrol car's engine was running, the gear selector was set to park and the officer's hands clenched the wheel. Blood drained from a wound on his neck and the rip in the arm of his blue uniform was soaked a dark black. A bruise shadowed his forehead and he did not respond to the hiker's gentle shaking. He appeared to be dead.

The Samaritan attempted to dial 911 but the call failed to connect. The patrol car's radio emitted static-filled, nearly uninterrupted calls between L.A. Basin dispatchers and patrolling Black and Whites. The Samaritan was reaching across the unconscious policemen for the microphone when Rostislov's eyes opened.

The Samaritan jerked back out of the Patrol car. "Officer, you're bleeding. We need to call an ambulance!"

Rostislov rose from a dark psychic well and glanced at his watch. He'd been out for fifteen minutes. For Rostislov those fifteen minutes rivaled five days.

The Samaritan pointed to Rostislov's neck. "You've been shot!"

Touching his palm to the black coagulated blood, the Afghani slipped the Makarov from the LAPD holster and shot the Samaritan in the forehead. The wire rimmed glasses spun away.

Rostislov searched the hiker's pockets for his wallet and the keys to his car. Wrestling the corpse upright, he buckled the body behind the Mt. Baldy patrol car's wheel then removed the Falcons and scoped rifle from the trunk. Turning the wheel hard right, he slipped the gearshift into drive, and shut the door. The cruiser crept up a dirt berm, slowly leaned over the ledge then flipped end for end across the weathered boulders and tinder-dry mesquite into the deep ravine. On its fourth pitch pole the tank ruptured, spraying vaporized gasoline across the hillside. The patrol car rotated through a fifth roll, the rear quarter panel scraped a granite outcrop, sparks flew and the vapor exploded. A fireball swept up the sheer face, igniting the parched vegetation. Flames flashed across the steep slope. Pushed by a hot afternoon wind, the growing wild fire roared uphill.

Rostislov limped across the road to the hiker's silver Pontiac Grand Prix. Fast enough to close with the Assassin, anonymous in its design, it would raise no alarms. He carefully settled the Falcons on the back seat next to the Samaritan's duffle bag, and checked the shotgun's magazine. Five shots with one in the breech--full. He set the safety, laid it on the front seat and yanked the transmission into drive. With the fire now threatening to leap the road, he accelerated downhill toward Upland.

Following Highway 10 east through thinning subdivisions and gentrifying shopping centers, Hull bought space. There was no hope of losing Rostislov. One absolute truth remained. The terrorist would pursue him, until one or both of them died.

The Mercedes passed Calimesa, Beaumont and Banning where the freeway began to trade the Los Angeles Basin's interlocking grids for the desert's dry creosote, dusty washes and taupe foothills--all spider-webbed with tracks of ATVs, motorcycles and off-roaders.

Ten miles further Cabazon's Brontosaurus lifted above the Wheel Inn Texaco.

Wrapping a Hermes silk scarf across her bruised cheek, Grace said, "I need to use the ladies room. Stop at that gas station."

They still had a quarter of a tank. Fifteen hours had passed since Hull burned the Hummer and he exited the freeway and crossed under the overpass where he made a right onto Seminole Drive. Entering the Wheel Inn, he saw the Hummer had not been towed and now sat with a yellow citation fluttering from its bent aerial. Towering above the burned wreck, the dinosaur's head had been discolored by the black smoke.

Grace unfolded from the passenger seat and crossed toward the restaurant. Two deeply weathered Moraga Indians standing next to a new Ford F-150 pickup silently watched her long legs swing and her hips shift in the khaki pants. She hesitated in front of the darkened restaurant entry then opened the door and stepped inside.

Hull waited four minutes before he retrieved the M1911 from the map box and climbed out of the driver's seat. Slipping the .45 into the waistband of his pants, he covered it with his jacket and crossed to the restaurant door.

He found Grace at the cash register. "We need to eat," she said as the cashier rang up turkey sandwiches, apples, water and two large cups of coffee.

Hull paid the bill and followed her back to the car. Two minutes later the Mercedes circled the onramp onto Highway 10 and headed east toward Palm Springs.

Nine hundred miles northeast in Jackson, Wyoming the CDC medical staff assumed that with Cheney's history of cardiac problems, he would fail as the first violent fevers exploded through his body. It was a measure of Cheney's ferocious tenacity that he fought the bloody diarrhea, the maculopapular rashes, and the spontaneous bleeding from his ears, eyes and fingernails. His skin color changed from bright red to deep yellow as his liver and kidneys failed. The capillaries in his lungs and brain slowly collapsed, filling his last days and nights with episodes of pulmonary edema and terrifying nightmares. The nightmares were always the same; Iraq's civilian casualties would rise from desert graves, calling his name, seeking revenge for Operation Iraqi Freedom. Listening to Cheney's screams, the biohazard workers who, though protected by Hazmat suits, grew increasingly terrified of inhaling a single viron from the disintegrating former Vice President.

Chapter 28

Rostislov needed to treat the bullet hole that wept a continuous bloody stream onto the Grand Prix's leather seat. A Walgreens appeared on the right and he parked the Pontiac next to the loading dock and opened the duffle bag where he discovered a pair of Nike sweats, a fresh long-sleeved shirt, and clean cotton undershirt. Using his Karud to slice the undershirt into bandages, Rostislov stripped off the police uniform pants and bandaged the entrance and exit wounds in his thigh. He wiped the blood from the driver's seat, pulled on the sweats and stuffed the bloody uniform into the duffle.

In spite of the white-hot pain that seared up his leg, his expression remained calm...placid. His time in the store would be brief--long enough to purchase medical supplies. Leaning on a cart to hide his limp, he entered the store where he added four quarts of sterile saline to a pint of peroxide, surgical tubing, antibiotic cream, a bottle of acetaminophen, sterile gauze tape, alcohol, Betadine and two twelve-inch glass pipettes.

"Doing major surgery?" The clerk was half through checking Rostislov's purchases.

Rostislov kept his back to the security camera, "Nothing that severe." He handed him three twenties.

The clerk wisely avoided further eye contact. "Have a real good day," he said, automatically, as he handed Rostislov his change.

A minute later a customer pointed to a shoe print in front of the register. "Someone's bleeding," he warned.

The clerk leaned across the counter. "Damn!" A dozen crimson prints led from the aisle through the check out area and out the entrance door. "Looks like he needed surgery himself."

That morning a maculopapular rash appeared on George W. Bush's chest, back and stomach. Dressed in biohazard suits, the doctors, nurses and orderlies at the Southwest Foundation for Biomedical Research in San Antonio increased the morphine drip to ease his pain. During the ten o'clock exam, Bush's skin blanched under slight pressure of a doctor's double-gloved index finger. Equally alarming, the ex-President's nosebleed refused to respond to conventional therapies. There was no need to culture the blood. The doctor knew it would detonate across a culture medium in threadlike whips of hemorrhagic fever. Bush's bloody diarrhea returned that afternoon.

Sixty miles east of Los Angeles, on the low hills north of Interstate 10, windmill generators stood in precise, slowly spinning ranks. From there, Highway 62 cut north away from Interstate 10 toward Yucca Valley and Joshua Tree. Beyond that, the Great Basin lay, scarred by rough dirt roads and isolated ghost towns.

Stretching north to Oregon and Idaho, the Great Basin's creosote and cheat grass sheltered scorpions, brown recluse spiders and fire ants that bristled with stingers and spines. Above the insects, snakes and lizards, hawks, eagles and mammals--coyotes, mountain lions, javelinas and black bears--ruled the desert between the intersecting ribbons of asphalt.

The Mercedes was ten miles north of the Interstate when the rear end started to vibrate.

"What's wrong?" Grace asked.

Hull checked the mirrors. "Low tire." Pulling onto the shoulder he discovered a screw protruding from the flat right rear. Opening the trunk, he removed the spare and unlocked the jack and tire wrench. Kneeling in front of the flat, Hull realized a piece was missing. The tire wrench required a key to remove the lug nuts. He searched the trunk without success, then leaned across Grace and slipped the trunk key into the glove box lock. The glove box refused to open. Time was slipping away.

Grace said, "Let me try." Grabbing the tire wrench from Hull, she jammed it in the seam between the leather dash and glove box lid and with a swift, savage jerk, shattered the lock. The glove box slowly opened.

"That's one solution," Hull admitted.

Returning the lug wrench, she reminded him, "It's a car, not a woman."

He reached into the lined box where he found the lug key behind the owner's manual. Kneeling next to the right rear wheel, he set the jack on the frame, loosened the lugs and raised the wheel. He was tightening the spare when Grace opened the passenger door.

"Hull, there's something else! This was hidden in the glove box door." She held a thick manila envelope.

The tire iron had shattered the plastic back. No Argentine custom agent would guess that the deeply curved lid camouflaged a two-inch void.

Taking the envelope, Hull slit the top seam. Inside, a second envelope contained a bank wrapped stack of hundred dollar bills. A hundred times one hundred amounted to ten thousand dollars. A third, equally thick envelope, contained stacks of euros, Swiss francs and Argentine pesos. Sandwiched between the currencies he found a thin notebook filled with bank addresses, user numbers, passwords and account information.

Below the currency a velvet cylinder was tied with a black ribbon. Hull carefully unrolled it. The sleeve was sectioned into labeled pockets. Twenty held large cut diamonds in a spectrum from white blue to pale yellow. A dozen other pockets held Mong Hsu rubies, untouched by heat-treating. There were perfect Kashmiri blue sapphires and an assortment of emeralds, tanzanite, sapphires, spinels, peridots, all labeled, all the highest quality. Grace's eyes widened at a large green stone that dropped into her hand. Its twin fell from the adjoining pocket. They were green sapphires, extremely rare, from Sri Lanka.

Grace silently counted. Sixty total. She could only guess at the value. Five million dollars? Twenty? Over twenty million dollars? Hull opened a third envelope. The contents bordered on fiction. Ten U.S. Treasury Bills…three at five million dollars, four at three million, three at two million- -totaling thirty-three million dollars. The notebook recorded the registration numbers and identifying purchase information.

Grace turned the largest T-bill from front to back. "Five million? Five million…dollars?"

"Five million…exactly. They're Treasury Bills, guaranteed by the U.S. Government." Hull spread the notes into a fan.

"Dollars? Are you sure? Five million dollars?"

Hull continued to examine the Treasury Bills and stones. "More than five million dollars. Twenty-seven million more."

"How did he get this much money?" Grace turned the bill again.

"He looted it from Sun and Health's real estate holdings: the mortgages, houses, commercial property." Hull shook his head.

"But thirty three million and the stones…"

"I don't know the details, now no one ever will. My guess is that following 9/11, Stone knew that multi-million dollar transactions would attract the attention of Department of Homeland Security and ICC regulators. He must have started with stocks and bonds—small, rapidly convertible amounts, legal and unlikely to trigger alarms. He then converted the cash into U.S. Treasury Bills. No telling how much is hidden in the offshore accounts…"

Grace was shocked. "If you're going to steal, steal very, very big."

"It appears you and Wardell think alike."

"Everyone's got their price." Grace turned the treasury bill in her hand.

"Someone, maybe an old friend in the California Department of Insurance warned Stone of the impending audit. That's when he hid the envelope in the Mercedes glove box door, and planned to ship it to Argentina."

Lost among the nappa leather, carbon fiber panels and electronics, the void amounted to an insignificant detail. Hull thought out loud, "If someone tipped them off, Argentina's customs might disassemble the seats or open body panels, but no one would think to break the glove box door."

"Argentina lacks an extradition treaty with the U.S. so even if Argentine customs discovered the envelope, the penalty is a fine, not prison. The stones might present a problem."

"Hull, Stone had it all figured out. Forty, fifty, sixty million dollars, and no way to track it."

He nodded. "In a year, Stone would be back in business. In eight, the statute of limitations would expire. If all went according to plan he could return to the U.S. without fear of prosecution."

"Amazing. Simply fucking amazing." Grace's hand tightened on the Treasury Bill.

Small, missing details remained. Hull had no way of knowing that Stone was booked on a 1:00 flight to Bermuda when Rostislov walked into his outer office and cut Darcy Wilkins' throat.

Seconds were passing, each measured by a spindle's precise rocking, the measured decay of cesium isotope or just as accurate, the lengthening shadows. Before a Highway Patrol Officer stopped and asked for the SL65's registration, insurance and Hull's license, he needed to move.

Hull gestured toward the bill Grace was holding. "Let's keep them together."

"I'll hold onto this one."

"No."

"I found it. I'm entitled to one."

"Not five million dollars. Stop wasting time. Give it to me." He opened his hand.

Grace realized if she delayed for three seconds more, Hull would take it from her and reluctantly handed it back. He returned the Treasury Bills, cash, book and stones to the envelope and headed north into the Joshua Tree Monument.

It was mid afternoon when Rostislov checked into the Covina Motel on West Garvey Avenue. The Vietnamese desk clerk wisely refused to notice the red stain soaking his sweatpants. She took fifty dollars in cash, did not question the empty spaces on the registration form, handed him a key and disappeared through a bead curtain into the manager's apartment.

The Covina's dark corner room thirteen smelled of cigarette smoke, the bed sagged, and the faucet dripped. The window, however, offered a clear view of the Covina's intersecting wings. No matter that the Covina Motel would compete with Afghanistan's better hotels, Rostislov did not plan to stay for more than half an hour.

He took a deep breath and focused on his wounded thigh. An infection would disable him. Untying his bloodstained shoes, he dragged off his sweats then unwound the field bandage and studied the wound. Pressing the margins prompted a stream of bright red blood. He was lucky. The bullet had only cut veins and muscle. Had the SAW's 5.56x45mm ripped his femoral artery, shattered his femur, or both, he would be dead. Even more miraculous, the jacketed bullet had not fragmented or tumbled as it had scorched through his thick muscle. For the third time that day, Rostislov gave thanks to Allah.

He poured the Betadine into each of the four saline bottles until the liquid turned dark amber then, with a surgeon's precision worked the surgical tube onto the pipette. Lastly, he punched a small hole in the plastic saline cap with his Karud, forced the surgical tubing through the opening, and wiped it all down with an alcohol soaked pad.

Gritting his teeth, he tightened his abdominal muscles until the veins bulged in his neck then carefully poured the peroxide down the surgical tubing, pushed the pipette into the bullet hole and squeezed the saline bottle. A bloody spring poured from his leg. Taking a deep breath, he forced the pipette deeper into his thigh.

Weaker men would have fainted. Rostislov's expression never varied. A tic on his right cheek betrayed the pain that scorched up from his thigh as the pipette pushed deeper along the bullet path. The first saline bottle ran dry a quarter way through his quadriceps muscle.

Threading the tube into the second bottle, he continued until it too ran dry, and emptied the third. A quarter remained in the fourth bottle when the glass pipette emerged through the back of his hamstring. Pouring a stream of dark, yellow tinged Betadine onto the entry hole he pulled the pipette through. The antiseptic dripped from his leg onto the stained carpet. Rostislov packed gauze into the entry and exit wounds, poured more betadine on the bandages, then wrapped both with gauze. Lastly he used two spools of surgical tape to hold the bandages together.

Taking a deep breath, Rostislov tried to stand, but before he fully gained his feet, a black well opened in front of him and he crumpled to the rug.

The town of Yucca Valley's dusty tracts and roadside businesses slowly grew in the SL65's windshield. Hull craved sleep but could not stop. How many hours had he slept in the last ninety-six? A dozen? Sixteen? He couldn't remember. He did know that if he stopped to sleep, the Afghani would appear. If Hull didn't sleep, he would nod off behind the wheel. He knew how sleep deprivation played out. No matter how hard he forced himself to stay awake, one minute he would be watching the road, the next he would be slammed awake as the Mercedes flipped end over end into the desert.

Rostislov wasn't Hull's only problem. Grace had seen the gems and Treasury Bills and now believed that, without her, he would have never discovered the envelope.

Nodding at the driver door's map holder she asked, "What are we going to do?"

"With the Treasuries?" he kept his eyes on the road.

"And the stones?"

"I haven't decided."

"You haven't decided? What about me?"

"Grace, we've got more dangerous problems."

Grace glanced at her watch. "It's been three hours since you last saw your Afghan Cop."

"Three hours or three days, it won't make a difference. He's coming," Hull said.

"Then I should hold the envelope while you lead him into the desert. When you kill him, we'll take the envelope and run. To India, Malaysia, Australia, Tahiti—we'll lose ourselves."

"Not possible."

"Ok, give me half and I'll take my chances."

Grace would never submit to round-the-clock guards. The cost of survival would become a prison. In a month she would lower her guard. Not long…one evening dancing at a club. Rostislov would be waiting. Focusing on the road, Hull promised, "You wouldn't last a day."

The exhaustion he had held at bay since Afghanistan overcame him. Bone-weary, he hoped he could stay awake another eight hours. He glanced at his Seiko. It was 1600. If he drove to the absolute limit of his strength, he might outdistance Rostislov. For how long, he could not say. When he woke, he hoped it would not be to the scratch of a knife across his throat.

Grace turned in the seat to face him. "Hull, half of that envelope is mine!"

"What gives you that idea?" Hull floored the Mercedes. The sudden acceleration slammed her back into her seat.

"I found it."

"Grace, the truth is, it's not mine or yours or even Stones."

"When has the truth ever mattered?"

"Stone looted the company."

"Stone's dead."

"The money still belongs to the policy holders."

She laughed. "You've got to be kidding! Seriously! The policy holders?" Unable to strip laughter from her voice she repeated, "The policy holders! Hull, you can't be serious. Insurance companies have defrauded generations of hard-working men and women! And you're worried about the policyholders? The only difference between Stone and the crooks at AIG is scale! Stone's fifty million--or whatever, is spare change compared to AIG'S hundred and eighty billion bailout!" she shook her head. "You know what's funny?"

"I'm missing something."

"Those AIG crooks won't go to jail--ever!" Her laugh faded. "Jail sentences are based on a reverse scale. Steal a hundred billion dollars and the government will forgive and forget. Steal half a billion and you can trade a wing at an Ivy League law school for community service. Steal five thousand and you'll get twenty years. Shoplift a bag of groceries and you'll take a cop's bullet in the back."

Keeping his eyes on the road, Hull asked. "If you're that good at cost estimates, what's a soldier's life worth?"

"What?'

"You know all about AIG and Law Schools. "What does a soldier cost? No tears for the parents or wife and children he left behind, just dollars and cents?"

"Hull, what does this have to do with the envelope?"

Hull remembered the honors accorded to the returning dead, and the Pentagon bean counters that put a dollar figure on the flag-draped coffins. "You're the accountant, what's a soldier worth? As much as this Mercedes?"

"Hull, this is sick."

"Or a helicopter or an armored vehicle?"

"Hull, you're not making sense!"

"Aren't I? Treasuries finance those dead infantry sergeants, motor pool mechanics and ordinance bomb disposal specialists—the important, but anonymous, men and women!"

"Hull, I don't want to play this game."

"How much?" he demanded.

"Ok, this is fucked up, but alright." She guessed a round figure, "A million dollars."

"Half that. One hundred thousand, plus the optional four hundred thousand-dollar insurance policy. The subtotal amounts to half a million dollars for each of fourteen hundred U.S. soldiers who died in Afghanistan. Half a million dollars apiece totals seven hundred million dollars--less than one half of one percent of the AIG meltdown."

Colonel Dillard picked that moment to join the conversation. Across a black board he had written, "Endless Money Forms The Sinews Of War" (Cicero, Philippics, V.). Rereading his flowing cursive he noted, "I should add that Timothy believed money is the root of all evil,"

Hull quietly suggested, "Colonel Dillard, let's do this another time."

Grace shook her head. "Look Hull, I feel sorry for the soldiers killed in Afghanistan but returning the money to Sun and Health won't bring them back."

"No, you're right."

Colonel Dillard nodded, "Timothy doesn't rank with the major disciples, John, Matthew or Luke. In fact, he's been forgotten by all but Sunday's TV evangelists."

"For once," Grace said. "What are we going to do?"

"Grace, I don't know. Give it a break. I need to think." Hull's mind started to spin out of control. Blocking Grace, he wondered if Colonel Dillard possessed free will, if he inhabited a separate and distinct reality from the VMI Department of Literature. Hull risked asking himself who, or what was Colonel Dillard? Was he spirit or saint? Or a cerebral infection? A virus that spawned wild dreams while it killed the host?

"Think about what?" Grace persisted. "A lifelong struggle toward old age. Or travel, comfort, security …"

"Security?"

"How little security have we when we trust our happiness to others."

CHAPTER TWENTY EIGHT

Dillard agreed. "I'm paraphrasing William Hazzlitt's 'Table Talk."

Hull wondered if Colonel Dillard was divinely inspired, an archangel suited to the times? No matter how remote the possibility, if Colonel Dillard was sent by Jehovah, Allah, Brahma or Buddha, the Roman Jupiter, the Norse Odin, the Egyptian Ra or Chinese Chang Hsien, then the millions who daily turned toward Mecca, bowed their heads at dinner or proselytized for men's souls, were accumulating works of grace while he, Hull, was tumbling toward perdition.

He took a deep breath and said, "Colonel Dillard?" But the professor had disappeared and, while Hull tried to blame the apparition on a lack of sleep, his heart refused to return to its resting rate.

He felt Grace shake his shoulder. "Hull," she yelled. "You fell asleep! You're talking to yourself—who the hell is Colonel Dillard?"

"No one."

"Keep your eyes on the road. This is my damned life." She ran her fingers down her thighs. "And, my money."

Chapter 29

T he afternoon sun was streaming through the Covina Motel's faded Venetian blinds when Rostislov regained consciousness. Pushing himself off the floor, he inventoried his pain. His head ached, but not blindingly. A vein in his right temple pulsed at a steady ninety beats per minute. The bandage circling his thigh was stained red, but the bleeding had stopped, leaving his leg stiff but functional. Gathering himself, he settled on the bed and glanced at his watch. Four PM. Five hours had disappeared.

Using the night table for support, he eased his weight onto his right leg, limped to the window and raised a slat of the venetians. Other than a Chevy pickup and the Pontiac, the lot was empty. By now the California Highway Patrol would have identified the Mount Baldy Deputy and the Good Samaritan. Covina City policemen, San Bernardino County Sheriffs and CHP would all be searching for a cop-killer driving the dead man's Grand Prix. Rostislov needed to move.

Crossing to the bathroom, he rinsed the blood out of the sweat pants then squeezed them until a last rose-colored drip fell from the twisted cloth. Careful to avoid disturbing the bandage that circled his thigh, he slipped the sweats back on.

From his room he could see a pay phone next to the unoccupied pool and, with his eyes focused on the motel parking lot, he crossed to the receiver, deposited four quarters and tapped out the ten digits.

"Our Prince blesses you," Rostislov intoned when the Voice answered.

"If that is true, then I am indeed honored."

Rostislov detected a change in the Voice. An undefined alarm. It might be nothing--or it might signal a security breach. "I have lost the Assassin," Rostislov advised him.

"Not only lost the Assassin," the Voice projected the slightest anger. "You've inspired other, more serious problems."

"Mount Baldy?"

"The City servant's passing was," the Voice searched for the correct word, "...inopportune."

"His appearance was bad luck. The city servant left me no choice."

"His coworkers on the mountain and in the valley are distressed by his passing. They seek to question you."

"That will not happen."

"Do not underestimate their numbers and dedication."

"I will be doubly vigilant," Rostislov assured him. "No interviews will occur." He looked at the Covina Motel Office. The Venetian blinds were parted. The manager was watching. This would complicate matters. Seeking to end the conversation, he said, "The Assassin is traveling with a woman."

The Voice processed the information.

"You are aware of his location?" Rostislov waited for the coordinates.

Half a minute passed. "He is near Yucca Valley...north of Palm Springs."

"How long ago?"

"Twenty minutes. He is heading northeast. Toward Las Vegas.... possibly Salt Lake City. Both have international airports."

"His lead is two hours?"

"Twice that much. With traffic, four hours. Another hundred miles into the desert and we lose the signal. It will be difficult to reacquire his location."

"It is of critical importance that I start immediately!"

"Be advised, hundreds are searching for a Silver Pontiac. Lose it!" A final detail concerned the Voice, "If another servant is harmed, I will be forced to terminate contact. My position is critical to a greater good. Do you understand?"

"Yes," Rostislov assured him.

"Completely?" The Voice had no way of knowing about the Falcons. He would be infected as surely as the rest of L.A.

Despite the gunshot wound, Rostislov smiled. "I will protect you," he promised.

"My Prince blesses you."

Rostislov required a change of clothes, and he had to dump the Grand Prix. The time had come to flight another Falcon. He changed the TV to CNN. The Russians had identified the suicide bomber who killed forty commuters at Lubyanka Station. She was identified as Dzhanet Abdullayeva, a seventeen-year old Islamic Chechen woman. Abdullayeva was a black widow married to a thirty year-old insurgent leader who was killed on New Year's Eve by Russian security forces. Rostislov could ill-afford to be distracted, but dismissed the possibility that a small, separate annex in Paradise might exist for female martyrs.

Southern California's predicted onshore winds complicated his mission. A second Falcon required winds at his back. Onshore winds required flighting the Falcon in Santa Monica, then speeding north to avoid infection.

He considered launching on the run--a fast, unguided shot, fired from behind an empty warehouse. There were no guarantees that the virus would not infect him as he sat locked in afternoon commute traffic. The plan lacked precision. An unanticipated shift in wind direction would blow the virus into his face.

The Voice believed Hull was driving to Las Vegas. Rostislov wondered if America's brimming cesspool of prostitutes, gambling, drugs, adulterers, and thieves might serve in place of Los Angeles. Las Vegas had grown wealthy, not as a place of desert worship but as the Great Satan's Sodom and Gomorrah.

Of equal importance, Las Vegas was home to the Predator pilots who guided missiles into Afghanistan's village compounds. The Falcon would guarantee that the killers playing video games would share the ex-President's final agony.

A plan took form. He would first kill the Assassin, then launch the Peregrine Falcon over Las Vegas. A day later, the Barbary Falcon would arc into San Francisco's Financial District. Four days later, the Gyr Falcon would stoop above Wall Street. Rostislov would then head south to Washington D.C., where the fifth and final Merlin Falcon would fold its wings above Congress.

Blocking the pain that pulsed up from his thigh, Rostislov smiled.

The plan had faint chance of detection. Proper timing would produce massive casualties--far greater than atomic blasts. The virus would overwhelm the east and west coasts before racing inland. Wall Street, Congress, the White House, the Pentagon, hospitals, banks, airports, railroads, shipping--America would crumble.

With a last glance at the motel room, Rostislov shouldered the Falcons and .270 rifle, locked the door and exited.

There was one minor task that required his attention. Walking to the motel office, he rang the small silver bell. The Vietnamese manager appeared a moment later, shutting the door to her residence behind her. "You checking out already?" she inquired. "Something wrong with room?"

"No nothing is wrong," Rostislov replied.

She died from a single, surgical cut through her throat.

Rostislov merged into traffic on West Garvey Avenue. He was pleased when a thrift store appeared. He parked the Pontiac between two cars to hide the sedan from the street. The bored clerk watched him pick a pair of wool dress pants, two blue dress shirts, a tan blazer and a light blue tie. To this he added a pair of camouflage canvas cargo pants, a Gore-Tex camouflage jacket, a black ski hat and a pair of worn, but serviceable hiking boots.

He paid for the clothes with cash then slipped on the wool pants, dress shirt, tie and blazer in the dressing room. On the way out he passed a tool kit. He paid for it, accepted the change and exited.

The clerk forgot about him as soon as he turned his back. Two hours later she could remember what he purchased, but nothing about his face or build, hair color, identifying scars, or the fact that he favored his right leg.

Rostislov needed to dump the Pontiac but his bullet wounds severely limited his options. The leaking blood would attract attention and he could not walk more than a few blocks. A rental car required insurance, driver's license, credit card, home address. Buying a used car on a busy, commercial street where a passing police cruiser might ID him was not an option. The Grand Prix was too risky. He could not linger in one place for more than ten minutes.

Faced with shrinking choices, he chose a dangerous tactic. He parked the Pontiac in a busy shopping center, slipped the blazer over his dress shirt, adjusted his tie and waited. Five minutes later, his target appeared.

A thin woman in her mid-forties strode rapidly up the parking isle. Her plain face, lack of makeup and empty ring finger spoke of a woman who lived alone. She would not be missed for a day, perhaps two. He waited until she loaded her packages into the rear hatch of a BMW X5 SUV. She was just opening the driver's door when Rostislov appeared. Caught between the door and the seat, she did not feel threatened by the dark-haired man. Dressed in a brown jacket, casual shirt and tie, he was neither handsome, nor unattractive. His ethnicity might have been Persian--an exile, or perhaps Pakistani. She took him for a software engineer or a small business owner.

Smiling, he apologized for surprising her. "My battery died and I hoped that you could offer me a start?" His faint, unrecognizable accent and the way he turned a question into a statement gave her pause. He might have been born in the U.S. His parents might have spoken Urdu or Punjabi at home. She had no reason to be afraid of a Pakistani software engineer in the middle of a Covina shopping center.

The woman was within a second of insisting she was too busy when Rostislov said, "I called the Triple-A service, but they advised me it will take an hour before a tow truck can arrive. I would not ask for your help but my mother has been ill and she needs the medicine I have purchased." She looked at him, then down the line of parked cars.

"I would count it a big help." Rostislov smiled. "I possess the cables. It will start immediately."

She almost told him no but realized one day she too might be forced to rely on strangers for a single, important favor. She took a chance. "I'm in a hurry…you'll need to hook it up," she shut the door and started the engine. Rolling down the window she asked, "Where are you parked?"

He pointed, "Down the aisle. It will only take a second."

Waving her on with his right hand, Rostislov pointed to the Pontiac where reaching into the trunk he retrieved the suitcase containing the Falcons and the duffle with the .270. "The jumper cables are in my bag." She pulled up to the car and leaned forward to release the X5's hood.

While she was distracted, Rostislov opened the passenger door, tossed the duffle and suitcase into the back seat and drove the Makarov into her ribs. Color flooded into his face as his smile faded. "You will listen to me carefully," he said, the precise American accent giving way to the faint British pronunciation of his youth. "If you raise an alarm, wreck the car, or disobey my slightest command, I will kill you." He did not blink and this, more than anything he said, made her squeeze the steering wheel.

She started to say, "If you want money--or the car--"

"Please, do not waste my time." Rostislov shoved the barrel into her ribs. "All I want from you is to drive. At the limit, obeying all the laws--you will do nothing to attract the notice of passing police. Do you understand?"

Terrified, she quickly nodded.

"If you refrain from behaving stupidly, I will let you go. Now drive!"

Dark descended by degrees across the broad Mojave Desert north of Yucca Valley. The setting sun lit the distant, dry hills in a soft, rose hue, a color that evoked the western faces of Afghanistan's Hindu Kush. The Mercedes' Blaupunkt radio hesitated on a country western station. Hull needed the news and touched the seek button. It settled on a Fox Radio affiliate in Palm Springs. Though the signal was not strong the announcer struggled to pronounce a breaking news story.

"Earlier this morning, the U.S. Embassy and NATO Headquarters in Kabul was attacked by a combination of suicide bombers and rocket propelled grenades launched from an unfinished concrete building."

Struggling to pronounce the Afghan places and names, the announcer continued, "U.S. officials were quick to blame the Haqqani Network, a long time ally of al Qaeda. In a departure from earlier, carefully worded statements, officials expressed anger with Pakistan's ISI, the Inter-Services Intelligence Directorate. In the past, the ISI has been known to offer both support and direction to Haqqani fighters. An Embassy spokesperson insisted that, despite intense pressure from the State Department, the Pakistan military consistently refused to engage the Haqqanis,"

"Following the recent killing of Osama bin Laden and Sirajuddin Haqqani on a remote ridge inside of Pakistan, relations have turned toxic between one time allies Pakistan and the U.S. According to the State Department spokesman, in a clear attempt to protect the Haqqani Network, the Pakistan military has tried to disrupt over-flights by U.S. drones."

"Casualties number five Afghan police officers and at least eleven civilians including six children."

Grace reached for the volume. "This shit never changes. Bombings, attacks, dead and maimed children... no wonder you drink."

Hull pressed the volume toggle on the steering wheel. "The first bullet took out Haqqani. His screams identified bin Laden."

Confined in the car for hours, Grace was too exhausted to fight for a different channel. "Hull," she tried to reason with him. "You picked a Taliban soldier out of a dozen men. Bin Laden was deliberate. Haqqani was luck. He got what he deserved. Don't destroy yourself for a fucking sadist who detonated children!"

"It wasn't Haqqani..."

"Then who?"

In his exhaustion, Hull almost confessed, "Bauldaire."

Running at over 120 mph, the Mercedes closed on a minivan. Hull swung into the oncoming lane and passed. In seconds the van receded to a boxy silhouette in the rearview. Two miles ahead, beyond where the road crested a hill, the empty desert stretched north through the Great Basin into Southern Nevada. They would be in Las Vegas by ten.

"As long as the Afghani is alive."

"You've been watching too many Schwarzenegger movies," Grace looked at Hull without humor. "Your Afghan Cop is no Terminator. If he even exists, he'll be found and killed."

They were ten miles south of Twentynine Palms. "Grace..." Hull started to say. The radio interrupted, "...sources close to the Taliban claimed the attack was a first step to avenge the deaths of Sirajuddin Haqqani and Osama Bin Laden."

"Hull, listen to me!" Grace did not raise her voice.

He held up his hand.

The announcer continued, "Ambassador Rollings C. Crocker downplayed the insurgents' ability to strike directly at the heavily guarded U.S. Embassy. "This was, at best, a fleeting propaganda victory," Crocker said.

"The Ambassador neglected to add that Central Kabul was still at a total standstill as Afghan and Coalition soldiers fought to clear buldings surrounding the embassy."

"The death of Osama bin Laden impacted rival tribes in ways that are now beginning to be understood. Without bin Laden's leadership, ancient rivalries are dividing factions within al Qaeda. The Pentagon credits the Sniper Team responsible for bin Laden's death. While news organizations demand an interview, the Pentagon has consistently refused access." The announcer hesitated, "Our hope is this American hero will be allowed to talk to the U.S. citizens. The nation is waiting to honor his courage."

Grace's exhausted response was no compliment, "You're a hero," she turned to contemplate the broad desert valley. "Trust me, before this all plays out, you'll wish you weren't..."

"I wished that before I left Afghanistan." Hull pointed the SL65 at the horizon and buried the throttle. The speedometer soared through 120.

Rostislov sat straight-backed in the BMW X5 passenger seat. The Makarov was pointed at the woman's stomach.

Her California Driver's License told Rostislov she was Judith Lindle. Forty-six. Born in September. Address, 2208 Valley View, West Covina. Organ Donor.

Other receipts, letters, bills tucked neatly inside her purse revealed two telephone numbers; one business, one fax, and a cell phone. Four credit cards, health insurance; marital status, single. Judging from a recent birthday card, she had one close married sister, living on the East Coast, who had one daughter.

Rostislov opened the mail he found in the middle console. She had worked for Broad Horizons, a venture capital firm. Two years earlier, she had banked her profits and retired. Brochures and a trip itinerary told him she traveled--recently, to Bora Bora. In two weeks she was leaving for Machu Picchu. He scanned the address book on her cell phone. Call history revealed a dozen women friends. She had few male acquaintances and none she had called, or had called her in the last week.

Rostislov closed the cell phone. A highway sign for Palm Springs pointed to the approaching interconnect for Interstate 10. "Take the next exit," he instructed.

Judith Lindle knew survival depended on doing exactly what she was told. If she hesitated, disobeyed, or tried to resist in any way, he would shoot her. She had once read kidnap victims stood a good chance of surviving if they established a rapport with their kidnappers. Conversation was critical to closing the distance.

"No telling what you'll find at the mall," she started. "Here I thought I'd pick up a few things at a sale and, well, the next thing I know a nice looking man is asking for a jump start." Her smile bore the faint lines of a grimace as she forged ahead. "I want you to know, I'll do anything you ask. Just let me know what you need. I don't want to create problems for myself or for you. She managed a smile that he failed to notice. "I don't know anything about you. Your accent is different. Where are you from? India?"

Rostislov was not listening. Buying new clothes and kidnapping the woman consumed two hours. That would place him six behind the Assassin. Sooner or later, Hull would require gas, food and rest. When he slept, Rostislov would appear.

"Or perhaps you were born in Pakistan?" Judith persisted, "Did your parents come from there? I've always wanted to visit…"

"You would find it dusty, full of garbage…Third World," Rostislov cut her off. Her efforts to engage him were so incredibly feeble. Did she not realize he knew what she was thinking, what she had planned?

Merging onto Highway 10, the BMW confronted a line of brake lights. Far ahead, a tractor-trailer loaded with ten thousand gallons of 91 Octane had crushed a Honda sedan. Of greater concern to Rostislov was the time required to clear the jack-knifed gas hauler. Commute traffic was squeezed down to half a lane. Full dark was half an hour away. The hours were growing increasingly valuable. Even as he pursued the Assassin, he was being chased. A Highway Patrol Black and White passed on the shoulder.

"I've heard Pakistan is crowded and poor, but I think I would find the culture interesting…the food and people, the religion." The woman's eyes followed the blinking roof lights.

Rostislov right hand slapped her hard across the mouth. "Don't try anything stupid," he warned.

The outskirts of Twentynine Palms appeared as scattered porch lights surrounded by hundreds of acres of dry scrub, windblown dust and decomposed granite. Hull had almost convinced himself that he could stay awake for another eight hours. In the twenty minutes it took for dusk to bleed into dark, his eyes were open, but no signal reached his visual cortex. One minute the section of his rear brain charged with interpreting depth, color and movement functioned normally, the next it did not. The glitch did not last long. Two seconds at most. Long enough for the Mercedes to wander across the double yellow line.

"HULL!" Grace yelled. A pair of headlights rushed toward them. Hull pulled the wheel to the right. A semi missed by twenty feet. Too close.

Passing headlights flashed. Hull struggled to keep the Mercedes straight and level. Even as his head slumped forward his eyes remained open.

Colonel Dillard appeared. Standing on the sidewalk in front of Scott Shipp Hall, he turned to the east. It was early evening, the temperature was dropping, his breath condensed to cold vapor. "The woods are lovely, dark and deep...but I have promises to keep," he recited. "...and miles to go before I sleep...and miles to go before I sleep." Glancing over his shoulder at a group of cadets, the Professor turned and saluted. "That's Frost, of course," he said when they passed. "...his 'Stopping by Woods on a Snow Evening' is an American classic."

"That's it! This is far as we go!" Grace grabbed the wheel and held the Mercedes in the right lane.

Hull forced himself awake. "The Afghan," he said.

"Fuck the Afghan! We're stopping!"

Set on Twentynine Palm's western limit, the Harmony Hotel's lone vacancy was the Desert Suite. A silver nameplate identified the owner, Ash Maharaj, who handed the registration card to Hull, but Grace filled it out. She used Mr. and Mrs. Steve Jones for a name, and skipped the squares for license plate, home address and telephone number.

Ash Maharaj was an astute judge of how far his customers had traveled. Deep exhaustion haunted the man standing in front of the desk. He would pay whatever Maharaj quoted. "That will be ninety-two dollars," the hotel owner said.

Hull reached for his wallet. He knew the clerk was overcharging but if he raised hell over an extra thirty dollars, Maharaj could trigger a dozen alarms with one call to the Highway Patrol for a plate, address and phone verification. Hull needed sleep, not debriefing by CENTCOM Intelligence. Laying a hundred dollars on the desk, he accepted the change and room key. He parked the Mercedes between a cedar fence and a tangled hedgerow of mesquite and date palms that sheltered the last unit. Hull unloaded the bags and set his duffle in the closet, next to the double bed. Grace's suitcase he placed on a folding stand.

The room was small, but defensible. Layers of yellow adobe covered the original stucco walls. The three inches of dried mud and concrete would stop a jacketed round. The exterior turquoise door offered no better protection than paper mache. Two windows, one in the bathroom and one above the double bed faced Via Allegra Road. In an emergency, either would provide egress.

It was quarter to seven, but temperatures remained above ninety-eight degrees. Disregarding the heat, Hull locked the door and set the security chain. Crossing to the bedroom, he closed the window, then drew the shades.

"It's too hot for all this security." Grace opened the front window and turned on the air conditioning. The old unit slowly whirred to life and emitted a faint, cool breeze,

Hull started toward the window and Grace stepped in front of him. "Hull, your imaginary Afghan Cop won't look for us in Twentynine Palms. Not in the Harmony Hotel next to the main Highway. Take one of your chill pills and relax."

Hull sagged into a captain's chair. Under ideal conditions, bones intact, arteries untouched, the Afghan's bullet wound would buy them five hours. He glanced at the Seiko. Two hours of sleep…back on the road by ten. On empty highways it would take three hours to reach Las Vegas. They would disappear.

Grace unwrapped the Wheel Inn sandwich and held out half.

"No thanks." Hull raised his hand.

"Eat," she ordered him. "You can't live on coffee and drugs."

He ate mechanically. When he finished, she handed him a towel. "You need a shower," she said. "There's shampoo on the counter."

Too exhausted to object he reflexively stripped off his sweat-stained shirt and pants, set the water temperature to warm and stepped into the spray. He tried to order his thoughts. Experience dictated it was a mistake to stop. He should have kept driving until first light. The Afghan would have field-dressed his wound and kept coming. Two hours was optimistic. They needed to get back on the road. Another minute in the shower and he would dry off, shave and…

The shower door opened. Grace stepped in with him.

Chapter 30

Rostislov stared out the BMW X5's windshield at the jack-knifed fuel tanker. Red flares funneled traffic into the left lane where four highway patrolmen signaled the commuters with red flashlights. The BMW crept forward. One after another, three patrolmen slipped past the driver's window.

Rostislov pressed the Makarov's barrel into Judith Lindle's side and whispered, "Eyes front, keep driving."

The BMW approached the fourth and last patrolman who was standing next to a parked black and white. Lit by the blinking roof lights, Rostislov watched her rapid eye blinks; one, two …on the third, she yanked the steering wheel hard left. Rostislov's left hand also gripped the wheel. Except for a minute swerve, the BMW slipped unnoticed around the wrecked tanker.

The woman feared Rostislov. Sooner or later, he would punish her for trying to alert the Highway Patrol and tried to offer an excuse. "I almost hit the police car. That's why I swerved..."

"Don't insult me by lying," Rostislov cut her off. Under different circumstances, she might have succeeded in ramming the CHP vehicle.

"But we might have collided …" She started to cry

"You betrayed our agreement." Rostislov took no joy in anticipating the woman's feeble attempt to alert the CHP. He had no feeling for her at all.

"I didn't betray anything," she struggled to compose herself. "I was just afraid that…."

"No explanation is necessary. Stay in the middle lane and do not exceed sixty eight miles per hour."

Interstate 10 cleared beyond the jackknifed tanker and Rostislov and the woman drove in silence until he instructed her to take the Highway 62 exit, north, back across the freeway. As the X5 drove into the darkened desert, the fear she had held at bay gripped her. Unable to force the shake out of her voice, she asked, "Where are we headed?"

"North..."

The Voice believed Hull would fly out of Las Vegas. For the moment Rostislov would trust his instincts. Rostislov knew, sooner or later, the woman would need to stop. Desperation filled her plain face when she said, "I really have to use the bathroom." Struggling to keep from wetting her pants, she promised, "I won't take long."

Rostislov planned only to stop for gasoline. The X-5 tank was half full. The woman had tried to escape once before. A second scene in a gas station would create problems.

A waning moon closed the desert down to a strip of black asphalt running between dusty creosote bushes and gray windrows of sand. Rostislov told her to follow a dusty track that led away from Highway 62 into the desert. The road was heavily rutted and her discomfort grew as the X5 bounced from deep tracks to rock outcrops. She told herself that leaving the main road was her idea. She would quickly pee and then return to the paved road. He might rape her--the thought terrified her--but even rape was survivable. If she didn't resist--she now regretted the moment at the jackknifed tanker--it was stupidly impulsive, if she did not resist...if she did not resist. She clung to the hope that if she obeyed and did not try to escape, he would keep his promise and let her go.

The track narrowed to a single lane that combinations of off-road four-wheelers and desert rains had reduced to parallel trenches. Shifting the X5 into low, she followed the rough trail through dumps where abandoned, bullet-pocked cars and broken washing machines, bottles, beds and shattered lumber lay scattered among the dusty brush. After a mile the dumps ended, and the ruts narrowed, snaking between granite boulders and mesquite, dry washes and deep pockets of rose-colored dust that exploded silently around the car.

The odometer had added eight miles when the track reached a faint intersection. Instead of asking which fork, she hopefully inquired, "Is this far enough?"

"It will do," Rostislov agreed.

"I'll only take a second."

"Wait!" Rostislov stepped out of the car and almost collapsed. His right leg had stiffened during the ride and now buckled when he took a step. The feeling gradually returned and, without further display of weakness, he circled the BMW, opened the door and took her arm. Leading her off the track into the creosote, he said, "Here."

The interior light revealed a damp circle on his right leg. She realized his leg was bleeding. If he did not have the gun, she would have tried to out-run him. He would shoot her if she tried to escape. With no other choice, she lowered her pants and squatted.

The act of her emptying her bladder in front of him infuriated Rostislov. Following her attempted betrayal at the wreck, she had become a liability.

"Finished. " Her relief was obvious. She pulled up her slacks and started toward the driver's door. It was then she noticed Rostislov gripped a dagger in his right hand. In her life, she had never dwelled on the way she would die and now, the shining knife made her cry. She tried to think of something to delay the inevitable but at the end whimpered, "Oh no…"

Rostislov felt no passion for the woman. Voiding her bladder in the presence of a man had dishonored herself, and him. He could have killed her with a single stroke to her heart but believed she did not deserve a quick, painless death. Instead he ensured she lived for five thrusts of the dagger. On the sixth, he stabbed her deeply enough that the light slowly ebbed out of her eyes and she slumped into the dust.

Touching her carotid artery he felt the final flutter of a pulse, then nothing. He wiped the Karud clean on her shirt and slipped it into the sheath he wore on his belt. He grabbed her wrists and dragged her thirty feet from the track where he dumped her body in a thicket of creosote. In the morning, the circling buzzards would betray her location but no one would waste the time or gasoline to follow the large black birds to her corpse.

Rostislov limped back to the BMW and slipped into the driver's seat. He eased his wounded leg onto the throttle and reached for the ignition.

The key was missing! He tried to remember the sequence after the woman turned off the ignition. He had circled the SUV, she had stepped out, they had walked into the desert, she had voided herself. She must have deliberately hidden it!

Without a flashlight he was limited to the interior lights. He checked the console and ripped out both of the floor mats. He forced his fingers beneath the driver seat, explored the metal frame and electric motor. He searched the glove box for a spare then gingerly stepped out and searched around the SUV. Nothing!

He then retraced his faint, moonlit footprints to Judith Lindle's dusty corpse and searched her pockets, her shoes, and her blouse. Still nothing.

An hour later he had still not found the key. He could neither abandon the Falcons nor drag the suitcase eight miles back to Highway 62. A deep rage at her betrayal filled his lungs.

"ALLAAAAAH!!!!" he screamed to the empty desert.

Thirty miles ahead, the Harmony Motel shower smelled faintly of desert snows and Bristle Cone Pines. The indigenous Chemehuevi Indians called Twentynine Palms "The land of little water." That was before 19th century engineers tapped into the deep aquifer, lifting the ancient, precious river to the surface from the sand and rock strata where it originated.

The cool well water washed over Hull and Grace as they stood naked in the pink tile enclosure. At another time passion would have driven them into each other's arms, but Grace's bruised cheek and Hull's aching exhaustion now left them standing with closed eyes, baptized by millennia-old water pumped from a thousand feet beneath the ancient oasis of Marah Springs.

Hull slowly opened his eyes and studied Grace. The deep Marah Spring water changed her silky hair to black ropes, falling first to her shoulders then down her back. He could not look away from the honeyed lift of her breasts or her nipples rising to dark parasols. His eyes swept the curve of her hips, strong thighs, knees and calves. Cupping the Harmony's soap in his right hand he gently lathered her belly.

He kissed her ear then her right cheek. "I'm so sorry I hit you," he started to apologize.

Grace grabbed his hand. "We'll deal with that later." She took the soap and passed it front of her nose. Distaste wrinkled her bruised cheek, "This smells like Drano!"

Stepping from the shower, she returned with an elliptical bar that smelled of gardenias. "Try this." She placed the soap in his hand and guided him to her left breast.

Grace was never sexually aggressive--uninhibited, no doubt, predatory, never. Her sexual history was limited to men who pursued her with a single-mindedness they too often could not duplicate in bed. That night, for reasons she could not divine, she was drawn to Hull. With past men her passion built slowly or not at all. That night sliding her soapy breasts against Hull's chest in the Harmony Motel shower, for the first time in her life, she initiated sex. Hull's powerful body fired her desire and taking the soap from him, she washed his muscled chest, arms and legs, and raised her mouth to his.

In turn, he used the gardenia-scented bar to explore her muscles and mysteries. Grace stepped out of the shower, dried him with a rough bath towel and led him to bed. There, with the failing air conditioner pushing a faint cool breeze, she fanned her black hair across the cotton pillowcases. Laying skin to skin, their mouths met as his hand slipped past her hard stomach to the union of her firm hips and muscled thighs.

Her breath came in desperate gasps. Tossing her head from side to side, she licked her lips and bucked and thrashed while the sweat speckled across her breasts, honeyed belly, hips and thighs. Hull thrust above her until it seemed as if the tendons in his back and legs would rip from their anchors. In turn, she clenched her teeth between parted lips and groaned.

Afterward, lying naked on the bed, the sweat cooling upon them, he remembered a line from John Dryden, "She hugged the offender, and forgave the offense. Sex to the last."

Turning her dark eyes upon him, her right foot found his leg and slid slowly up toward his knee. "Sex is nature's physical therapy," she whispered. "You'll sleep now."

Hull, however, did not sleep. Instead, sex imparted a heightened vigilance. The Afghan was coming. Taking time for rest and sex at the Harmony Motel tempted fate. Mobility was the Marine's heart, soul and conscience. Still holding Grace's breast, he said, "We need to move. I'll pack the car."

Grace whispered, "No, not for two hours. You need sleep."

"Half an hour, no more," he reluctantly agreed.

Grace was still fully awake, "What do we do with the envelope?"

Pulling her gently closer, he replied, "Return it."

She lifted his hand off her breast and turned to face him. "I have a better plan."

"Lose yourself in South America, or China?"

"China, there's an idea."

"Grace, you speak Mandarin but you won't lose yourself… not among a billion people." He paused, searched for a credible way to warn her, "You'll need to hire body guards, arrange bribes, install security and when it's all in place, you'll be forced to escape to the next corrupt sanctuary. If you're very careful, it might take ten years before the money is gone. If you're very lucky you'll still be alive."

"Skip the drama," she said. "Fifty million dollars will buy a lifetime of protection."

"Until a body guard falls asleep."

"We can't give it back!"

"We have no choice."

"Hull…this is our chance! We could turn south and be in Mexico tonight! We've got our passports, the car and the envelope. Mexican customs won't check us."

"Grace--guaranteed, they'll check the Mercedes."

"Then we dump it and buy a cheap truck in Palm Springs! We drive to Guadalajara. Or Acapulco."

"Grace, they'll follow us."

"Who're they?"

"Army Intelligence. The State Department. Mexico won't work."

"What about Argentina? I speak Spanish. You could pass as Italian. All we need is our passport and a clean criminal record. We could book a last minute cruise to Buenos Aires.

"How do you plan to slip the stones and treasury bills through Argentine customs?"

"Hide them in my purse. They won't search me."

"Walk fifty million dollars into Argentina?"

"Who will know? Nothing will go wrong..."

"And if it does?"

She sat silently upright, her back against the pillows, her arms crossed over her breasts "It's worth the risk!"

Hull heard the finality in her voice.

Grace slipped off the bed, shook out her hair and crossed to the bathroom. An instant before she closed the door, Hull watched light play across her breasts, stomach, hips and legs. The room faded to full dark. In the second before he fell asleep, he remembered a phrase and tried to recall the author--perhaps Blake? His lips moved slightly as he recited, "The wrath of the lion is the wisdom of God. The nakedness of woman is the work of God."

Ten seconds later he was sound asleep.

Lacking tools and a wiring diagram, Rostislov could not hot-wire the BMW's ignition without triggering the alarm and eventually draining the battery. His wounded leg prevented him from packing the Falcons and the .270 rifle eight miles back to Highway 62. The key was his only hope. It required an hour to meticulously search the X5's interior. The key had not fallen between the seats, slipped under the floor mat, or been hidden in a map, envelope, visor or crevice. It was past midnight when he realized the interior was clean, stepped outside and carefully searched the pool of light thrown by the interior and door lamps.

The first eastern light appeared by degrees. Deep indigo gave way to a spectrum of purple and gray, until it grew bright enough to see. Even then he feared he might miss the faint, steel glint among the desert sand. If he stepped on the key and buried it in the sand, it would be lost.

He found nothing under the car, next to the wheels or on the bumpers. He circled outward until he reached the damp spot in the sand where the woman had squatted. An hour later, he was thirty meters away from the BMW. The woman could not have thrown the key that far without his notice. The sun had just crested above the distant hills when he retraced the drag trail to her body. Four crows study the corpse from the surrounding creosote. Beating their wings into the morning breeze, they did not go silently. He had heard similar screeching in the streets of Mazar-i-Sharif.

He rechecked the woman's pockets. Nothing. He then methodically stripped the corpse. First the blouse, followed by the pants and bra until the woman was clothed only in her turquoise briefs. The color and clingy fit marked her as wanton...a woman who, though she had no husband, still prayed for sex. Looking at her small breasts and flat stomach he grabbed the bikini strap and ripped the lacy fabric to her knees.

The key fell into the dust between her legs. Judith Lindle hoped to trade the key for her life. The five hours her deception had cost him was a Pyrrhic victory. By now, the Assassin would be in Las Vegas.

Dawn was breaking above the eastern horizon when Rostislov inserted the key into the BMW's ignition and twisted. The X5 started and without as much as a backward glance at the woman's naked corpse, he slammed the shifter into low and bounced through the creosote. Seconds later he was speeding down the dusty ruts back toward Highway 62. Intent on driving, he did not notice the crows had returned to the corpse.

The boldest, an old male, hopped onto Judith Lindle's chest. The Crow had fed upon men twice before. Human carrion was much to his liking and cocking a quizzical black eye toward her dusty face he tentatively pecked at her eye. He waited for the corpse to move and when it didn't, he turned his attention to the knife wound in her neck. His powerful beak tore into her thin skin. In time, half a dozen other subservient crows joined him on the corpse. In two days the birds and insects would reduce Judith Lindle to a circle of white bones and brown hair.

It was six AM and Highway 62 was still a mile away when the ruts improved to gravel and Rostislov shifted into fourth. Reaching the pavement, he glanced to his left and accelerated toward Twentynine Palms. Early morning traffic was limited to semis delivering freight. Keeping one eye on the road, he keyed the GPS. Twentynine Palms was twenty miles due west. The fastest route to Las Vegas followed Highway 62 to 95 North. Or—he increased the resolution--he could take Amboy Road from Twentynine Palms north to Route 66, and from there, 95 north through Searchlight into Southern Nevada. With luck, he might cut an hour off the drive.

Retrieving the woman's phone from the console, he dialed Los Angeles.

310

"Our Prince blesses you," Rostislov said, when the Voice answered.

"If that is true, then I am, indeed honored," the Voice replied.

"Any news of..."

"Your quarry has disappeared," the Voice interrupted him. "The signal died outside of Twentynine Palms. The reception was insufficient, the battery may have failed, or he may have turned the phone off. The last is a guess. He may now well be in Las Vegas or Salt Lake."

"Las Vegas," Rostislov promised.

"How can you be sure?"

"His whore chose."

Chapter 31

F ull daylight was streaming through the Harmony Hotel shades when Hull slowly opened his eyes. The bedside alarm had failed! A glance at the clock radio told him it was 0630. He had slept for ten hours. He threw off the sheet and bolted out of bed. Grace was gone! Vertigo swept through him. He felt drugged. An empty Lunesta box in the bathroom wastebasket betrayed the reason why he'd slept. Grace had spiked his water bottle! Two ten-milligram doses were more than enough to knock him out.

Grace's suitcase was gone. He opened the drawer in the nightstand. She had taken the envelope. He grabbed his pants and checked the front pocket. The key to the Mercedes was gone! He grabbed the Colt, opened the motel room door and checked the brushy alley beneath the palms. The SL65 tire tracks led from the dusty lot onto Highway 62.

Back in the room, an envelope bearing the Harmony logo lay askew on the desk's scarred wooden top. Written on a blank sheet that served as motel stationery, her goodbye was brief, her style stripped of emotion; the Treasury Bills helped boost her self-confidence. He skimmed from his name down.

Jack,

I know you'll be angry with me for taking the car and envelope but you left me no choice! PTSD, Combat Fatigue, or whatever name you want to attach to it, you've been whispering to yourself! At this point, I don't know if the L.A. cop was truly a terrorist or one of your hallucinations, but I can't risk sticking around to find out.

The cash and stones are real--and untraceable. You're crazy to think about giving them back to Sun and Health. If you don't want the envelope, I do!

The Treasury Bills will allow me to disappear! They will guarantee you won't find me! Don't try! If ever the time feels right, I'll find you.

It's been crazy! Too crazy for me!

Grace.

P.S. Those pills you're taking aren't helping! I got rid of them.

Hull crumpled the letter and dropped it in the trash. He knew the Treasuries and stones would seduce her but hadn't expected that seduction to occur so quickly. Fifty million dollars...the total was irresistible.

Slipping the Colt into his belt, he searched the room for any detail she might have overlooked. She had been both silent and thorough. Hull shouldered his heavy duffle and crossed the shaded courtyard to the office.

Ash Maharaj looked up from behind the front desk when Hull entered.

"That F-150 yours?" he gestured in the direction of a white Ford truck parked at the back of the motel.

Maharaj looked past him at the dusty pickup and nodded.

"I need to rent it," Hull said, dropping five twenties on the desk.

"Your wife is not returning?" Maharaj's curiosity was not entirely professional.

Hull ignored his question.

"She departed at first dawn." Maharaj raised his hands, palms up in a conciliatory half apology.

"What about the truck?"

"That would be difficult," he confessed, sincerely. "I cannot see how I could rent it. My insurance would not cover you and I have no guarantee it would not be damaged."

Hull counted ten more twenties onto the desk. "One day, three hundred dollars. I'll return it with a full tank."

Maharaj hesitated. "Your wife was very, very beautiful...but my old pickup does not stand a chance of overtaking your Mercedes."

"That's my problem. I'll pay for any damage," Hull counted five more twenties onto the desk. Three minutes later, he twisted the pickup's ignition key. The engine ground, then slowly fired, one cylinder picking up the next. Hull was in second gear when the F-150 reached Highway 62. He bounced once hard, then turned north toward Las Vegas.

He powered up his cell phone and dialed Washington. Eilert answered on the third ring. His voice was atonally calm, "Hull, turn around...the desert around Twentynine Palms..."

"How did you know I'm in Twentynine Palms?"

"You know the technology! We searched the national database for a cell phone with your name, Social, driver's license, old address. When none came up, we tried private listings. Verizon coughed up your number last night. Your cell sends a GPS signal. You turn it off the signal stops. Right now you're headed north on 62."

"I wish you'd told me earlier." Hull needed Eilert's help.

"We didn't know until four this morning. Do you have a weapon?"

"Three. A SAW, an M40, a 1911. Fuck, I don't have time—have you been able to track the Afghani?"

"Since the firefight on Mount Baldy?"

"You knew about that too..."

"Look, Hull, an L.A. Black and White shot to shit with a SAW left a pretty clear signature. The dead Mount Baldy patrolman surprised us. One shot to the forehead. No resistance--it was an execution. He commandeered the patrolman's car."

" I didn't know about that one. Any further information?"

"A name--Rostislov. Russian-trained during the Soviet occupation. Sources place him in Lubyanka. And there's a definite connection with the Marburg attack at President Bush's Library. CDC is starting to panic. Altanta, Dallas, Chicago, Seattle, local hospitals can't keep up with the victims."

"Bush, Rumsfeld, Rove are all fighting midcourse symptoms, diarrhea, severe headaches, joint and abdominal pain, vomiting...their doctors are reduced to antivirals, intravenous fluids. Cheney and Woo have started to bleed...details aren't necessary...of greater concern are secondary infections. The CDC's quarantines are crumbling. Isolation is the lone viable treatment. Hull, this could kill five million people before it burns out."

"Five million?" Hull was stunned.

"If it burns out! Our source claimed Rostislov had five mortars. If he targets a major city the potential kill-ratio is ninety-five percent. How al Qaeda secured five weapons needs to be worked out--but five total--one down, four left. We have one chance to stop him. Rostislov was bin Laden's bodyguard...number one, fanatically devoted. Before you killed OBL, Plan A was the virus. You're a distraction. As long as you're on the run, you buy us time."

"Any way to track him?"

"Only by the victims. He shot a second man."

"When?"

"Twenty minutes after he killed the deputy--same style--bullet to the forehead. Cold blooded. He dumped him in the deputy's patrol car and steered him off a cliff. It started a major brush fire. Twenty thousand acres and counting. Responding fire units found the car and his corpse at the point of ignition. Burned beyond recognition. If his wife hadn't called in a Missing Person's when he didn't return home he would have gone unidentified."

"What else?"

"He took the guy's car, a silver Pontiac Grand Prix."

"That's a break."

"He dumped it in a Covina shopping center."

"Fuck. Anything else--plates, car, contacts?"

"Only you as bait. Rostislov can only be tracked by his victims. If Army Intelligence, the FBI or any other state, local or federal law enforcement agency throws a ring around you, he'll disappear. If he knows we've ID'd him, he'll hit four cities in as many hours. You need to avoid population centers. Las Vegas, Palm Springs. And don't return to L.A.!"

The silence lasted twenty seconds before Eilert admitted, "The debate reaches all the way to the President. We bring you in, Rostislov disappears. You stay out, he kills you, he still disappears. Five days later a million people swamp emergency rooms with an atypical flu. Game over. I hate this mano a mano duel in the desert shit but it may be our only and best chance. Hull, what are your chances of taking this guy out?"

"I'll get back to you," Hull said and turned north toward Amboy and the old Route 66. The desert was already beginning to hold the rising sun's

315

heat.

"Don't shut off your phone!"

Hull didn't reply. He couldn't. Colonel Dillard was sitting in the passenger seat. He was looking ahead, his elbow on the open window, a Camel in his right hand.

Turning to Hull, Dillard smiled, showing yellow tobacco stains on his teeth. He now observed, "In the desert I saw a creature, naked, bestial, who squatting upon the ground, held his heart in his hands and ate of it."

Grace had flushed the Haldol down the toilet. His defenses now gone, Hull gathered his courage. All similarities to an apparition had vanished. Colonel Dillard was now as real as the truck, the road and the enveloping desert. Without the Haldol, the Professor would have his say…how, what, and when he pleased.

Forcing a false calm into his voice, Hull inquired, "Dante?"

Colonel Dillard glanced over, "No," he replied. "Stephen Crane…. from the Black Riders." He flicked the smoldering butt out the window and hooked another out of the pack. Bringing a worn silver Zippo to the tip, he took a deep drag off the unfiltered cigarette and studied the passing desert. "The poem was not well received. The Chicago Daily Inter-Ocean observed that "Poetic Lunacy" would be a better name for the book."

Hull continued to drive.

"But that's beside the point. Tell me, what is your objective?" When Hull failed to answer, Dillard said, "It's not necessary to talk. But conversation does help pass the time."

Hull finally replied, "To find Grace!"

"For what? Reclaim the treasuries? Punish her? Apologize?"

"To save her from Rostislov."

Colonel Dillard nodded as if he had known as much. "So it is that the gods do not give all men gifts of Grace," he said. "It's from the Odyssey."

Twentynine Palms residential streets ended and the desert rolled north into the Great Basin.

Grace was holding the Mercedes at 120 miles an hour across the desert north of Twentynine Palms. At that speed the desert flowed around the

SL65 in a rapid stream of blue sage, gray creosote and the distant, sun-baked hills. If she could dodge the Highway Patrol she would be in Las Vegas by 10:00 AM. She wished she could keep the SL65 but the black sports car attracted far too much attention. She would dump it in a parking lot on the Strip and take a cab to the airport. Compared to the envelope, the car's three hundred thousand-plus-dollar sticker was expendable.

Reaching over to the passenger seat, she released the clasp of her purse and retrieved the envelope. The Treasury Bills made the impossible suddenly very possible. For all their beauty, the stones would present a problem. She doubted she could smuggle twenty million dollars worth of emeralds, sapphires, rubies and diamonds through airport security.

The TSA would insist, "All purses through the scanner." Arranged in their velvet pockets the stones would erupt onto the computer screen.

Grace was thinking on the run. She could rent a safe deposit box in Las Vegas. Later, after she found a buyer, or figured out how to smuggle the stones out of the country, she would return to close out the account. She might risk one Treasury Bill--a single check for five million dollars in her billfold. The rest she would leave in the safe deposit box. Alternately, she could make flight reservations at a travel agency and have them send a FedEx package to a five-star hotel in Buenos Aires.

And she had her passport--thanks to Hull, she would catch a flight to New York. There she would pick an international destination; Rio, Hong Kong, Zurich, Buenos Aires—she'd find a way to deposit the Treasury Bills without a wide paper trail. Details such as where, how much at one time, withdrawals and statements needed to be worked out. Until then she would use the Swiss francs, dollars and euros.

Now she had a plan, she needed to make time. The speedometer had dropped to a hundred. She pressured the accelerator. For the first time the Mercedes failed to respond. For a second Grace hoped she was mistaken, but in the next instant, the SL65 began to buck in protest as the electronic fuel injectors ran dry and the V-12 quickly starved. When the engine quit, the speed plummeted through a hundred, eighty and sixty miles per hour before Grace slipped the transmission into neutral and nursed the car to the side of the road. She pressed the ignition button. The engine spun, tried to fire once, then nothing. Glancing at the gas gauge she saw the yellow, low fuel light warning and realized it was empty.

Rostislov had just entered Twentynine Palms when the amber fuel gauge flickered on the X5's dash. Intent on finding fuel he gave the Harmony Hotel a passing glance. The lot was empty. He quickly filled the X5, then bought a sandwich and a large coffee, and returned to Highway 62. Five minutes later, he turned into the rising sun on Amboy Road, following it west out of town toward Bush...a name that caused a thin smile to flicker across his face. Thirty miles out of town, the BMW was holding a steady hundred and twenty miles an hour when an anomaly appeared on the empty road. Sharpened by war and desert distances, from a mile away, Rostislov could make out a small, black car. At two hundred meters, he recognized the driver standing next to it. A woman. Tall, dressed in pants and blouse. The wind rustled her black hair.

For the second time that day, Rostislov praised Allah.

Stranded thirty miles north of Twentynine Palms on Amboy Road Grace wondered how she could have been so stupid? Hull hadn't gassed the Mercedes in Cabazon!

Stepping out of the driver's seat, she looked to the north where the asphalt crested over a distant rise. She turned south, back toward Twentynine Palms. Thirty seconds passed, then a minute. Nothing. Neither the sound of a car, truck or plane disturbed the desert silence. She waited impatiently. She had no doubt she could hitchhike to the nearest town. A gas station attendant would give her a lift back. If someone would just come! She raised her hand to her eyes. In the distance a small spot moved on the black thread that was Highway 62. A car was approaching. She watched it grow in size and shape until it was a hundred yards away and closing fast. At first she feared it would pass by, and she held out her hand and waved.

The driver hit the brakes and the nose dropped as the car rapidly decelerated to a stop next to her.

The driver lowered the passenger window and asked, "You are having car trouble?"

When Grace bent to answer, her blouse fell away from her breasts. "I think I ran out of gas," she smiled. She was relieved to see the driver was dressed in camouflage--obviously a Marine from the base at Twentynine Palms.

Looking north, the man said, "Amboy is forty miles. You could purchase gas there."

Grace could not return to Twentynine Palms. The Lunesta would have worn off. Hull was awake. "If you wouldn't mind?" she smiled for a second time.

The dark haired Marine reached across to open the door "No, it will be a pleasure," he replied. If Grace believed she was a good judge of character, she would have had trouble describing the man who stopped. Neither handsome nor unattractive, he was pleasant looking, almost innocent.

Hull scanned the F150's gauges. Water temperature a tick above normal, oil pressure two ticks below. The speedometer and gas gauge didn't work. Hull couldn't calculate how much gas was left in the tank. Full or empty, he had to stop. Pulling into a station at the edge of town, he punched his credit card into the reader. It instantly dialed a central office computer that checked Hull's records and verified the account was still open. Returning a clearance number, it could have revealed a great deal more about Hull, his age, address, telephone number, place of employment, income, marital status, number of children, if any, past purchases, payment record and credit rating. The computer could also generate both personality and purchasing profiles as well as his travel itinerary, breaking each down into subheadings and probabilities. Only the past purchases were accurate. INSCOM had erased the rest.

A clearance number appeared on the digital screen. He lifted the unleaded regular hose and slipped it into the tank until it was filled.

He crossed to the office, where a young pregnant woman, the wife of a Marine stationed at the base, watched him set a five gallon steel gas can and a case of bottled water on the counter.

"You can buy that gas can cheaper down at the Napa Auto parts," she said.

"Thanks--I'm in a hurry," Hull looked at the shelf containing the drugs. Nothing approximated the Haldol. Colonel Dillard would continue to ride shotgun.

"You expecting trouble out in the desert?" she said.

"You can't tell what you'll run into between here and there," Hull said, paying for the gas can and water.

"No, you never can," she nodded.

Hull filled the can then roped it into the pickup bed. Tossing the water on the cracked bench seat he slipped behind the wheel and when the old engine fired, shifted into second and let out the clutch.

Hull did not vacillate over whether to return to Los Angeles or drive to Las Vegas. Grace had no ties to Los Angeles. No close family, job or lovers. She would not think small. She would head north to Las Vegas, board a flight to the East Coast, Europe, possibly Asia, and try to disappear.

Colonel Dillard studied the early sun as it filled the desert hollows with a golden light. Prospectors claimed the desert springs from the Chemehuevis Indians, and it was the prospectors who labored in dusty silver mines for the bonanza that would pay their way out of those blistering valleys. The Mojave was hard on men. It was little wonder why, as a measure of their suffering, the prospectors named their camps Cadiz, Baghdad, and Siberia.

Hull was five miles north of Twentynine Palms when Dillard observed, "There is no cure for birth and death save to enjoy the interval." He paused and gave the attribution, "That's Santayana, from his Soliloquies."

Chapter 32

G race climbed into the BMW, double wrapped her purse strap around her right arm and buckled her seat belt. The Marine put the X5 in gear and accelerated north toward Amboy. He said something. His voice was soft, almost inaudible. To hear better, Grace raised her window. It shut with a slight, hermetic wisp. The car was now silent. No radio, no road noise. "Excuse me?"

"You are headed to Las Vegas?" he turned the statement into a question.

"How did you know?"

"It must be Las Vegas or Salt Lake City. The road forks and your Mercedes is not suited to Nevada's small towns or gravel surfaces."

Raised among L.A.'s diverse accents, she wondered if was born in the U.S. to foreign parents. His use of "one of either," "suited," and "surfaces" made him sound as if he'd studied English, not spoken it from birth. She noted his camouflage shirt. It lacked insignias of rank, his name, or other identifying badges. Glancing in the back seat she could not see his cap. He wore black shoes, not boots. She asked, "Are you a Marine?"

He nodded.

"In Twentynine Palms?"

Again, a nod.

The BMW's speedometer climbed through eighty miles an hour. Fear crept into Grace. "Have you served overseas?"

He appraised her with a single glance. "Why do you ask?"

She hurried her answer. "I have friends in Iraq and Afghanistan." It was a small lie that omitted only the proper tense. Hull had been in Iraq and Afghanistan.

"Afghanistan," the Marine admitted.

"It's a dangerous posting."

"Of course," he nodded. The BMW continued to accelerate.

"A single tour?"

He remained focused on the road, "A little longer."

She knew it was unfair to judge the Marine Corps by Hull's behavior alone. She did, however, know men. She knew what drove them--their goals and self-image. It occurred to her that no Marine NCO could afford a fifty thousand dollar BMW. If the driver could make the payment on an expensive SUV, it would not be a BMW. The X5 was an executive's or a woman's car.

Without looking away from the road, the Marine asked, "How did you acquire the bruise on your face?"

For the third time she noticed his odd, formal, speech. "I tripped."

Rostislov admired her deception. With thirty miles separating the SUV from the nearest town, he had time to prolong the charade. Information was more reliable when it was not extracted under torture. "It seems such a bad injury," his observation lacked compassion.

"My face hit something…"

The friendliness faded from his voice "Hit something?" He studied her for a second, "Or was hit by someone? I have seen women bruised in this way before."

He'd said, "Women" plural instead of "Woman." There'd been more than one. Grace wondered how many.

"The purple stain such as yours does not necessarily result from a man's right fist. A fall into a table edge might produce such an injury…but most often it speaks of an angry husband. Or a betrayed lover…"

Her attention was drawn to a damp circle, high on his right thigh. Blood was dyeing the camouflage browns and beiges a deep maroon. He had been shot--on Mount Baldy, by a Scout Sniper! Grace knew then the driver was no Marine. Hull had been telling the truth!

Rostislov recognized Grace's parted lips, her wide eyes and the protective crossing of arms over her chest—both surprise and aching fear--

he had seen the same expression on a dozen Hazara women. Their disbelief lasted until his Karud pierced their belly's pale skin.

She had recognized him, imperfectly perhaps, from a brief glimpse on the mountain road but she was now afraid and that fear would make her dangerous. Slipping the Makarov from the map case next to the driver's seat, he pointed the muzzle at the base of her left breast, midway up her rib cage.

"You know, of course, who I am."

"You were driving the L.A. Police Cruiser on Mount Baldy…"

"Very good," Rostislov smiled as if he were encouraging a child. More than his admission, that smile frightened her. "Please do not force me to harm someone as observant…and beautiful as yourself." The compliment made her skin crawl. "It would be a shame to damage a woman with such rare physical gifts." Again, the foreign formality. "Despite what the Assassin Hull may have told you--if you do exactly as I say, I will spare your life." He glanced at her. "Do you believe me?"

For the first time Grace looked into his eyes. Black, impenetrable, unblinking, they offered a window to a dead soul.

Rostislov did not demand an answer. Taking a blood-tinged cloth from between the seats, he pressed it against the growing stain on his upper thigh. Though the pain was intense, his expression did not change. "While we travel together, there are a few rules you will obey. Do not think for yourself. Listen to my every instruction and you will live. Hesitate and you will die. Is that understood?"

She took a deep breath and tightened her arm around the purse. The BMW accelerated through a hundred miles an hour--far too fast to jump. No one was there to help her if she did.

"You will answer--yes or no!" There was nothing pleasant in his command.

"Yes," she lied a second time. She first needed to distract him, then she would take the gun.

"Good. We have an understanding," Rostislov said. "I will need your cell phone." His expression told her that once the rules were established, she would hesitate at the risk of her life.

She opened her purse. Her smart phone had slipped below the envelope. Her hand pushed past the bulky currency and stones then closed around the

Blackberry. She reluctantly handed it to him. Placing the Makarov on his lap he touched the phone's glass panel. The menu lighted to life. The signal was weak but serviceable. He scanned her incoming calls. Eighteen were from a private number. One dialed immediately after the other. Rostislov knew they were from Hull. Handing the phone back to her, the Afghan ordered, "You will dial him!"

Grace did not argue. Hull had a blocked number. She dialed and waited for the first ring.

Rostislov reached for the phone.

Hull was thirty miles behind, struggling to hold the F-150 at sixty miles an hour. The oil pressure sank and water temperature climbed. Any faster and the old engine would shake itself apart.

His cell phone rang. The caller I.D. read Private Number. Touching the green phone icon he expected to hear Grace.

"Colonel Hull," the caller carefully pronounced his name. "I am in possession of something you value." Holding the phone out to Grace, he said, "You will tell him to do exactly as I say."

Grace's voice barely rose above a whisper, "Jack, there's a problem."

His left hand on the wheel, Rostislov's right fist smashed into her lips. "Speak louder!" he commanded

Grace tasted blood. She caught her breath and started again, "Jack, I'm sorry I took the car. I ran out of gas. Guess who came along?" She did not laugh.

Rostislov took the phone. "Major, or should I call you Colonel, Hull?"

"Hull will do fine," he said. "And your name?" He did not reveal he knew the answer to his question.

Rostislov's voice was calm, a shade soft, "It is of no importance. I believe the phrase 'we've leveled the soccer field' applies."

Hull refused to cede him the high ground. "Get to the point," he returned.

"The woman..." Rostislov looked at her.

"Grace." Hull said.

"Your woman, Grace."

"I've known her two days. She's not my woman."

"If you do not know her well enough to save her life," Rostislov's left hand caressed the Makarov's ballistic grips, "there is no need for further communication."

The Afghani would spare Grace only as long as she was of value. Hull alone could postpone the inevitable. Without betraying emotion, he said, "You're calling the shots, what's next?"

"That's better, Colonel Hull. If you have an interest in seeing her alive you will join us in Amboy."

"Amboy," he repeated.

Grace's cell phone disconnected.

Colonel Dillard looked over. Flicking the ash of his unfiltered Camel he said, "Once to every man and nation comes the moment to decide. In the strife of Truth with Falsehood for the good or evil side."

Hull floored accelerator and the old pickup slowly accelerated into a freshening southerly wind.

Rostislov sought high ground that offered an unobstructed three hundred and sixty degree field of fire. He needed isolation, a place removed from the jurisdiction of the police or Marines. Such a place existed outside of the small town of Amboy. The GPS claimed Amboy offered gas and groceries. Rostislov could not know how far Hull was behind him. The hunter and hunted had exchanged roles. Now it was Rostislov risking the CHP's attention. He needed to buy time. The Assassin would not blunder willingly into his sights. He may have taken pleasure from the whore, but his training would not allow him to trade her for his own life. He would need to be forced into taking suicidal chances. He would come, carefully. Rostislov would be waiting.

Holding at one hundred and twenty north along the broad valley, they would reach Amboy before 9:00. Grace did not dare ask what Rostislov planned. She could not show her fear and she sat with her legs crossed, her arms holding herself together.

Hull mercilessly beat the F-150. At seventy-five, the engine would last until Amboy--no further. Colonel Dillard sat straight back against the bench seat. Turning to look at Hull's duffle lying on the rusted bed he recited,

"Once more into the breach, dear friends, once more;
Or close the wall up with our English dead
In peace there's nothing so becomes a man
As modest stillness and humility:
But when the blast of war blows in our ears,
Then imitate the action of the tiger;
Stiffen the sinews, summon up the blood,
Disguise fair nature with hard-favor'd rage;
Then lend the eye a terrible aspect."

When he finished, Colonel Dillard admitted, "I love that passage. It speaks clearly to a soldier's duty! You'll recall…"

"Colonel, even a Rat could recite Henry V. We memorized Shakespeare's 'Into the Breach' soliloquy."

Dillard nodded, "For moments when men 'rush to glory or the grave!'"

"Thomas Campbell, 'Hohenlinden,'" he remembered.

"You surprise me, Hull."

"Some things stick." A road sign passed. Amboy was fifty miles--at seventy-five--forty minutes away. Rostislov would be waiting on high ground.

Lighting another Camel, the Colonel inhaled, "Priorities determine success or failure. You need to be clear about your objective."

Hull waited.

"Your primary duty is to the nation."

Hull stared to where the Amboy Road bisected the distant horizon. "I'll kill the Afghani and, if I can, I'll save Grace." He glanced at the Seiko. Forty minutes.

Rostislov was ten miles from Amboy, when a half dozen abandoned scattered buildings rose out of the flat desert. A century and a half old, Amboy had thrived on salt mining until Route 66 brought tourists to the dying town. Roy Crowl opened "Roy's" restaurant, motel and gas station in the late 1930s.

326

Roy's served good burgers and cold water--necessities in the empty Mojave Desert.

When Rostislov slowed for the intersection of Route 66, he had a choice. Turn west toward Barstow, or east and north through Amboy to Las Vegas. Rostislov would run only until the terrain favored his plan. He made a right toward Roy's. Only the store was open.

Stopping beneath Roy's canopy, he turned to Grace. "Give me your hand!"

His demand surprised her. Cautiously extending her left hand, she watched him encircle her wrist with a white snap tie and cinch it to the steering wheel. "Don't try anything stupid." He opened the driver's side door and limped into the store.

The clerk was a seventy-two year old desert miner who had spent much of his life working a gold shaft that was slow to prove out. Gold was there--just a hundred feet further into the mountain than he had dig left in him.

Rostislov placed two bottles of water on the counter.

"Those plastic wrapped sandwiches are fairly fresh," the prospector nodded to the cooler. "They was delivered on Monday. Today's Wednesday. They're still good. I could knock a couple of bucks off the price."

Rostislov shook his head, "The water is sufficient." Turning toward a black cone that rose to the west, he said, "That is Amboy Crater?"

"Sure is...unless it's moved in the last couple'a hours and I sorta' doubt that since it's been there for maybe ten thousand years. The Bureau of Land Management geologists figure it last erupted five hundred years ago... how they know is a mystery." He paused, "Sure you don't want to try one of them sandwiches?"

Grace had nearly severed the snap tie with a nail file when Rostislov returned to the BMW. "That was stupid," He almost punched her but decided she was damaged enough. He need her awake and able to walk. He pulled the Karud from the camouflaged pants' pocket and sliced through the last plastic thread. Rostislov had less than an hour before the Scout Sniper reached Amboy. It would be sufficient time to prepare.

Hull held the F-150's throttle to the floor while the miles flowed beneath the worn tires and the temperature gauge climbed. If the gauge was accurate, the radiator would soon begin to boil, pinning the needle against the H. As the temperature climbed, the oil would thin, driving the pressure gauge to zero.

In the distance, a car was parked on the shoulder. Hull was a half-mile away when he recognized the SL65. Stopping behind it, he checked the driver's door. Locked. Grace had kept the key. She had intended to return.

Hull shifted into low and forced the F-150 north on Route 62.

It was 10:05 AM when the BMW turned into the Amboy Crater parking area. At one time a rough Jeep trail fought through the lava flows to the Crater but the U.S. Park Service had closed the old track with four large boulders. Rostislov could not waste time hiking across the flats. Nor would his leg last the extra mile. Shifting the BMW into low he followed a faint road that exited the south end of the parking area and wound through the sandy hollows. Three hundred yards into the lava flows, the road rejoined the old track.

The BMW climbed over ten thousand year-old lava flows that now lay one upon the other like a haphazardly shuffled deck of stone cards. The old road followed the Park Trail for more than a mile before it encountered a deep, eroded gully. In front, the Amboy Crater vaulted upward in a rose and black cinder wall that was scarred by an ascending, diagonal path. Rostislov studied the crater rim and then glanced over his shoulder at Highway 66.

"Get out," he pointed the Makarov at Grace's chest.

For an incautious second, she almost ran. Rostislov's leg would slow him down. Fifty feet of open ground stood between her and the volcanic hummocks. The fifty feet could have been fifty yards. He would shoot her in the back before she managed four steps. Grace's only hope was Hull. "Come soon," she prayed.

In a soft voice distinguished only by its odd syntax, he said, "The Assassin will come to save you but I now own the high ground. We, you and I, will test his courage." He grabbed Grace's left hand and limped to the BMW's rear hatch where he pulled the scoped, bolt action .270 Browning from a padded case. The gun was sighted to within a click on the scope. At a hundred yards it was accurate to an inch on both the X- and Y-axis. Slipping ten .270 Nosler silver-tip rounds in one pocket, he returned the Karud to its leather sheath. Gesturing with the Makarov toward the path that climbed diagonally across the cinder cone, he said, "Leave the purse!"

Slipping the strap over her shoulder she said, "We'll need it."

"Walk!" Rostislov shoved her toward the trail.

"To carry the water!" Grace knew Rostislov would keep her alive as long as she was useful.

He hesitated, then slipped the two bottles into her purse and pushed her toward the looming cinder cone.

Hull reached Amboy an hour after Rostislov. The SAW was on the F-150's bench seat, its magazine full--a round locked in the breech. It took two minutes to scout the ghost town. No detail escaped Hull's attention. Roy's white cabins were deserted. No cars were parked behind the gas station or across the dirt road at the old Café.

For as far as Hull could see to the east and west, nothing moved on Route 66's shimmering blacktop. He did not know what the Afghan was driving or whether he had reached Amboy. He might have found it too exposed and continued on. Stopping in front of Roy's, Hull hefted the Squad Automatic Weapon and entered the small store.

The prospector stepped back from the counter. Keeping his eyes on the SAW, he admitted, "I don't have much but you can have all of it. I'm sure as hell not gonna die for fifty bucks and a couple of chicken sandwiches."

Hull scanned the store. Other than four thinly stocked shelves and a bank of coolers down one wall, the room was empty. "You can calm down old man, I just want information. Has a car stopped in the last hour?"

"One or two did." Nodding to the SAW, he said, "I guess you don't plan on plinking cans."

"This one had a black-haired woman."

The clerk relaxed when he realized Hull wasn't going to rob him. "The black-haired girl stayed in the car. She was real pretty."

"And the driver?"

The clerk thought for a moment. "Now that you ask, I can't remember a thing about him. Hell of a deal. He wasn't in here more than an hour ago."

As Hull turned to leave, the Clerk remembered, "He asked about the

Crater. I figured he'd take a photo and keep drivin'."

Hull looked out the door at the black cone.

"A storm's building. I wouldn't be on the rim when it hits. You won't believe the way the wind will whip things up!"

Hull dropped the SAW on the seat and started toward what looked like a charred stump in the crumpled expanse of black pahoehoe flows.

The approach to the Amboy Crater was from the north, down a dirt road off Route 66. The Bullion Mountains rose to the southwest, the Bristols to the northeast. Hull took the left turn, then slowed. He sensed Rostislov was watching from the crater. The distance was a mile, maybe a mile and a quarter. Rostislov would be a good shot, but his maximum range would be four hundred meters...and even then he would miss three out of five.

Surrounding the crater for seventy square miles, the intersecting lava flows mixed sand bottoms with sheer basalt walls. There was no easy approach--and no cover. Locked in four-wheel drive, the F-150 could force three hundred yards through the lava field. Beyond that it would high center, break an axle or follow a blind alley into a ten-foot lava cliff.

The pickup rolled into the empty parking area. The wind rose out of the southeast enveloping the pickup in a cloud of dust. Hull opened his cell phone and dialed Grace's number.

"You have found us," Rostislov answered.

"It wasn't hard. You leave a wide trail."

"Only because your woman is weak--a plaything," Rostislov laughed, a sound devoid of humor. "You need to approach closer."

"Soon enough," Hull promised, studying a lone set of tracks that skirted the barrier and wound toward the crater. The wind had erased all others.

Judging the distance at a mile, Hull shifted the F-150 into compound low and started into the black lava field.

Hidden by the crater's black pumice, Rostislov tracked Hull's progress. The F-150 was still a mile away when he lifted the .270 to his shoulder. At that distance, even with the advantage of a ten-power scope, details disappeared. He could see the truck but nothing more. He needed to draw the Assassin closer. He glanced at Grace. Holding out the water bottle, he pointed the .270 at her. "Drink!" he ordered.

Rostislov's sudden generosity frightened her. She feared any gesture. "I'm not thirsty..." she tried to smile.

"I said drink!"

"OK, I'll drink." She raised the bottle to her lips.

Watching her tilt the bottle to expose her unlined throat, he thought, "Beautiful, but stupid." Rostislov needed Grace to be hydrated for her role. Soon enough, the Assassin would come at a full run.

The wind was sweeping sand across the truck's hood as Hull closed the distance to the crater. It was still twice the distance the Afghani needed for a minimum accuracy. Dividing his attention between the rough track and the distant crater rim, he searched for a depression that would allow Rostislov to see, but not to be seen. Cresting over a rise, he saw the X5. It was half a mile away, parked against a lava outcrop.

Hull continued to force the F-150 deeper into the Amboy flows. The wind dragged the dust from the surrounding dry lakebeds in sinuous skeins across the pickup, which slowly wallowed through the sand washes and labored over the lava outcrops.

Hidden among blocks of ejecta on the crater rim, Rostislov watched the approaching truck. Hull would soon reach the same basalt cliff that had blocked the BMW. From there Rostislov knew the Scout Sniper would cut cross-country and assault the crater from the rear.

On foot, Hull would lack cover among the lava flows. Rostislov would let him close to a point where a crippling shot was assured. And if that failed, there was Grace. He would make excellent use of her assets.

Holding out the water bottle, he ordered, "Drink."

Grace realized any resistance, even refusing to drink, was dangerous. She took the plastic bottle and sipped.

"Drink more! Half of it!" he commanded. Watching her raise the bottle to her mouth, Rostislov made a second call. Touching the cell phone's green icon, Hull's number appeared. The truck sat just beyond the Afghani's maximum range. He did not want to kill the Assassin. Not immediately.

The number autodialed then connected. Hull opened the phone but did not answer.

Rostislov said, "This is progressing too slowly."

"I have more than enough time," Hull estimated five hundred yards across broken lava to the crater. "First condition--You release Grace and I'll give you a half hour head start."

"First condition?" Rostislov objected. "Non negotiable...I own the high ground. Did your trainers not teach you a thing? You cannot shoot for fear of killing your whore. To save her you must climb through descending fire."

"Let Grace go..."

Rostislov's voice was silken, "If you want her, you must fight for her." The phone disconnected.

The crater rim towered above the pickup when Hull set the throttle with the cable-operated choke, cracked open the door, and slipped out. Running at a crouch next to the F-150 Hull grabbed the duffle and sprinted for a lava outcrop. The snap from super compressed air warned him that a high power round had just passed close to his stomach. Two inches less lead and he would now be gut-shot. Hull had underestimated Rostislov. The Afghani had missed by inches from four hundred yards on a running target.

Hull dove on his stomach behind the lava outcrop a second before the next round showered his face with basalt splinters. He was lucky--none of the razor-sharp shards entered his eyes. In the millisecond it took to blink, Colonel Dillard appeared above him. Surrounded by the Amboy flows, Dillard stood in a pressed uniform, a pair of eight-power Zeiss binoculars raised to his eyes.

Hull rolled on one shoulder and cautioned, "Sir, you may want to seek cover."

"And ruin my uniform? Your enemy is no threat to me." Adjusting the binocular's focus, he said, "He's with the girl, next to the large rock outcrop on the ridge."

Fifty yards away the driverless F-150 pickup wallowed forward, until it finally crashed into the BMW. The collision crushed the X5's right rear quarter panel. The pickup's tires spun in the soft dirt, then the engine lugged under the load and quit.

Hull had underestimated Rostislov's marksmanship. From the crater rim, the Afghani had a clear shot. The three-foot block of lava offered cover, but no chance to return fire. Hull was trapped. If he risked a shot, he had a minimal chance of hitting Rostislov. The Afghani was using Grace as a shield. She would take the bullet.

Dillard interrupted Hull's analysis, "Though I have not worked as a spotter since basic training, I do remember how to calculate wind speed, distance and bullet drop."

"I'll have time for two shots. Give me inches of drop."

The Colonel raised the Zeiss. Spotting a bullet impact at five hundred yards was almost impossible. Dillard could not see Rostislov, only the rock outcrop.

Opening the duffle, Hull pulled the M40A1 sniper rifle from its padded case. He had shot ten thousand 7.62mm match rounds through the bolt-action, heavy, bedded barrel. Hidden behind the basalt boulder, he slowed his breathing. "Distance?"

Colonel Dillard held the Zeiss steady on the crater. "Five hundred and thirty yards. Wind, ten miles an hour with gusts."

Swinging the M40 on the basalt block, Hull squared the 10-power Unertl scope on the rock outcrop. He caught Rostislov's silhouette. The Afghani raised a rifle to his shoulder.

"Target is exposed," Dillard said.

Hull squeezed the trigger. A puff of dust appeared in the ejecta.

"Twelve inches low, eighteen inches right!"

Hull racked a fresh round into the breech, adjusted and squeezed the trigger.

Rostislov was lowering his face to the .270's stock when the 7.62 round hit a foot in front of his face. The impact blasted the granular black pumice into his eyes, momentarily blinding him. Swearing in Pashto, he rapidly blinked to clear the grit from his corneas. "The water!" he swore at Grace. "Give me the water!"

Watching him claw at his eyes, she tipped the open bottle toward the red pumice. The liquid poured from the plastic bottle. Spinning on his knees, Rostislov ripped the bottle out of her hand a second before the last rivulet drained out. He splashed the remaining drops in his eyes, and his vision slowly cleared. When he next looked through the scope, Hull was gone.

Chapter 33

H ull had not waited to see the match 7.62 round connect. He knew it would miss. The shot was a diversion. Hull was on the run a second after the jacketed bullet left the heavy barrel, sprinting the eighty meters to a black cliff face that ran diagonally toward the crater. When he turned, Colonel Dillard was standing next to him. Other than a faint sheen of perspiration on his bald forehead, he showed little sign of exertion.

"A+ job, Colonel," Hull thanked him.

"An excellent shot. Unfortunately it failed to score a kill."

A bright flash appeared in the southeast sky. Twenty seconds later, deep thunder rolled across the crater. Hull waited until another lightening bolt arced above the dry lakebed that extended southeast from the toe of an ancient lava flow. Pressed against the warm rock, he watched the Seiko's sweep hand. Fifteen seconds passed before the thunder rumbled over. Divided by five, the storm's leading edge was three miles away. Dry desert lightening storms generated wind. Hull watched half a dozen dust vortices lift from the dry lake. He estimated fifteen minutes before the first lightening strike forked onto the rim. Rostislov would be forced to seek a less exposed position. Hull's phone rang.

"My compliments to your skill--and luck," Rostislov voice was stripped of emotion. "But if you wish to hold your woman's hand again, I suggest you start climbing. Now!"

Rostislov would wait for a shot that would drop, but not kill, the Scout Sniper. A high-caliber bullet to the stomach was a torturer's tool. In the hours following, stomach acid leaking onto small and large intestines would drive Hull to pray for death. The Afghani would take his time. Hull would suffer far greater agonies than bin Laden. In the end, the Scout Sniper would beg for any death--even the slow, painful gift of the Karud.

Two hundred and fifty feet below, the wind strengthened across the rough lava flows. A thirty-foot gap separated Hull from a wall that cut toward the crater cone. He took a breath and ran.

Rostislov's crosshairs tracked Hull mid-waist, eight-inches ahead as he sprinted through the break in the lava flow. At that distance it was a high percentage shot--square in the stomach on a running target. Badly wounded but alive, Hull would drop. Intent on tracking the Scout Sniper, Rostislov did not see Grace lift a sharp-edged lava boulder. A instant before the .270 recoiled, the boulder crashed down upon his right leg. The wound ripped open.

A searing pain exploded out of his right thigh and he jerked the trigger. The bullet snapped a foot behind Hull.

Gritting his teeth Rostislov snarled at Grace, "That was a mistake." Anger radiated from his black eyes. In a tone he might use to beat a dog, he commanded, "Here!"

Grace took a step back. Six feet separated them. If she tried to run, he would shoot her in the back.

Rostislov reached into the camouflaged cargo pants pocket and withdrew the rusty dikes. Locking his eyes on her face, he yelled, "COME! HERE!" Grace glanced from the dikes to the rifle and turned to run. Rostislov was a step quicker. Lunging across the space that separated them, he grabbed Grace's left hand and spun her around. Before she could resist, his dikes circled her left ring finger then closed on the second knuckle in a single, sure bite. Rostislov twisted the dikes and the tempered steel blades crunched through cartilage, ligaments and skin. The finger dropped onto the red pumice.

An agonizing scream ripped from her chest. Grace collapsed to her knees where she nearly fainted. The Afghani picked the pale digit out of the dirt. The red nail polish only confirmed her wanton nature. With a faint smile playing across his dry mouth, he flipped the slender finger downhill where it came to rest in a pile of black rocks.

Blood pulsed in a deep red stream from the stump. Grace clenched her left hand and continued to scream.

"Too bad you wasted the water--it might have kept you from bleeding to death." Racking the .270's bolt open he checked the round and warned her, "Pray the Assassin comes soon." He opened the phone, waited and stated, without remorse, "You need to talk to your woman."

Hull listened for Grace's voice. Nothing.

Rostislov voice returned. "It's a shame you delayed. Time is now doubly precious. A delay will bear tragic consequences. But, I will allow the whore to tell you…"

Grace fought rise on top of the pain. She did not beg him to save her. Instead, she hissed, "Hull…the animal cut off my finger!"

"Enough," Rostislov jerked the phone away. "People can function quite well on nine fingers." He paused, "The loss of all ten, however, presents problems."

Hull calculated time to the crater rim. Two hundred and fifty vertical feet, a quarter mile total. Three minutes across the flats. Four to climb the steep, pumice slope.

Rostislov read his mind, "Two minutes from now and she'll be down to her index finger and thumb. Lose those and all fine motor skills disappear…"

Hull listened to Grace retch and fought to control his temper. "Killing children, torturing women--defined the coward Osama bin Laden."

"Don't be obvious, Colonel," Rostislov laughed. "I have no temper." He swept the lava fields with his scope. "Bin Laden? You are unworthy to speak his name. And your Coalition? Seven innocents die in Afghanistan each day. Seven days a week. Consider the wounded: the amputees, the brain damaged, children shot through their stomachs and lungs." He searched for the Scout Sniper in his scope. "However, we have more important matters to discuss than blame, or politics, or religion or the innocent dead." He searched for color among the black basalt flows. "Let's speak of your woman. By my count, she now has nine fingers. If I take one per minute, in nine minutes her hands will be barren. Show yourself, or she will learn to live with eight fingers…then seven." Flanked by Grace's hissing breath, Rostislov promised, "Once her fingers litter the ground, I will work upstream. Her wrists, forearm, elbow….you, as a soldier, have seen Marines without arms? They function quite well. As long as someone brushes their teeth and

337

performs other necessary personal functions." A deep cough traded for his laugh.

"I will confess to you honestly," the Afghani continued, "I've never been privileged to work upon such a beautiful subject. I will very much enjoy the coming process." The phone went dead.

Any doubt Hull had about killing Rostislov evaporated. He would take pleasure in shooting the Afghan. More than once if he could. He sprinted along the basalt cliff until it faded against the cinder cone. From there he continued west until he cut a game trail that climbed diagonally across the Crater's west face. A harsh gust swept around the cone, dusting Hull with the saltpan's fine gray dust. Lightening forked from the black cloud base. Deep thunder rolled above the crater three seconds later. The squall line was five hundred meters away.

His feet dug into the soft pumice as he fought uphill--twenty-five meters of the hundred to the crater rim. His heart rate and breathing soared, sweat poured into his eyes and lactic acid filled his thighs. Running up hill through the rising wind and deep volcanic ash pushed his heart rate above 195 beats per minute- forty above an accurate shot. Hull could see the summit. Driven by violent winds that were rolling across Amboy's salt plane, black thunderheads boiled above the crater's black pumice. The rising wind drove him to his knees. Memories of Bauldaire, exhaustion and Saker flooded upon him. He remembered the two Marines running down hill to save him. Rising to his feet, he clenched his abdominals and churned uphill through the soft pumice

Colonel Dillard was running at his side. The rim appeared above as a curved red line against a towering black wall. "Hull," the Colonel tried to get his attention. "Before an Apache youth became a man, he would take a sip of water from a gourd, hold it in his mouth and run through the blistering heat to the top of a high mountain. When he returned hours later, he would spit the water on the ground. "Deserts and discipline...they're one and the same."

Standing just below the crater's crest, Rostislov looked at his watch. The sweep hand touched twelve. "Time is up!" he announced.

Grace had vomited once, violently. She was wiping her mouth when Rostislov wrapped his right fist in her long hair and jerked her onto her back. He stepped on her throat, extended her left hand and before she could stop him, cut off her middle finger. It did not come easily. She felt the dikes tear through the meniscus. The tendons resisted, then separated. Held by skin alone, the finger dangled. Rostislov rocked the side cutters until the middle digit finally fell to the ground. Hyperventilating against the pain, Grace fought to her feet and swung blindly. Her right hand hit Rostislov in the left temple, above the bruised frontal lobe.

Luck or fate, her fist aggravated the concussion from Mark Fitzgerald's briefcase. Grace's punch triggered a second, deep cerebral explosion. Rostislov staggered, took one unsteady step and folded. Grace clenched her bleeding left hand and tried not to faint.

Rostislov lay unmoving at Grace's feet. She could not know how long he would be out. Fumbling for her phone in Rostislov's coat pocket, she touched redial.

Hull answered the cell phone's first ring.

Grace was screaming. Not terrified, enraged, the screams of woman fighting for her life. Her screams pushed Hull beyond his limits. Running uphill through the soft ash drove his heart rate above two hundred beats per minute. Twenty years of training allowed him to hold that rate for a dozen seconds. No more.

He reached the crater rim just as Rostislov's left hand locked around Grace's belt. She hit Rostislov with a roundhouse right matched by a bloody left as the Afghani slowly dragged himself up her thin body. Eyes unfocused, a faint smile playing on his face, Rostislov found his knees.

Ignoring the pain in her bleeding left hand, Grace hit Rostislov with combinations of lefts and rights, painting his head with her blood.

Rostislov gained his feet and hit her hard, once in the jaw. The blow dazed her and she stopped struggling. His hand found the Karud's scabbard on his belt. In one fluid move he circled her chest with his arm, slipped the knife free and brought the sharp blade to her throat.

When Rostislov's vision cleared, Hull was running toward him along the crater rim. Out of breath, his heart rate screaming above two hundred beats a minute, the Scout Sniper stopped, raised the rifle and tried to steady the cross hairs on the Afghani. The scope danced across the Afghani's skull, hesitated on Grace's neck, lifted onto the Afghani's jaw, back to Grace's eye, his arm, her breast.

Hull could not take the shot. He needed to lower his heartbeat. It was ten seconds he did not have.

Yanking Grace between himself and the Scout Sniper, Rostislov yelled, "Our moment has arrived!"

The scope circled around Rostislov's forehead. He could not shoot. Dillard appeared.

Out of breath, Hull gasped, "I cannot help but hit Grace!"

Dillard calmly advised him, "Churchill believed 'Nothing in life is so exhilarating than to be shot at without result.'"

Hull lifted the scope a click above Rostislov's head and touched off a round. The 7.65mm passed within a quarter inch of the Afghani's left ear, close enough to make Rostislov duck. "Kill Grace and you'll die!" Hull racked another round into the breech.

"I don't think that is true." Rostislov jerked Grace in front of him. She was off balance, helpless. A thin trickle of blood traced the course of his blade across her throat. "Lower your rifle!"

Hull watched the cross hairs drop from Rostislov to Grace's face.

"Do you think the thought of death frightens me? Your Christian God condemns murderers but when I die, Allah will welcome me to Paradise." The wind pushed his words across the crater, "Colonel Hull! How many men and women and children have you killed? Can you count them? Hundreds? Your spotter--the young Lieutenant--the Taliban soldiers who found him said you shot him in the heart. Colonel Hull, did you watch his eyes when you pulled the trigger?"

Images of the last seconds high on the pass above Firebase Saker flooded upon Hull. Bauldaire's hopeful smile, his clear eyes, the intelligence in his young face, his acceptance of the inevitable. Bauldaire's honorable escape ran through Hull. Taking a shallow breath, the young Lieutenant said, "Major, only you can help..."

"Negative."

"Sir, you have no choice. You cannot stay--and you cannot leave me alive. Major--I'd count it an honor."

Hull reached to lower Bauldaire's lids.

"Don't close my eyes!" Bauldaire managed to move his head. "Not here, not now...don't turn this into an execution. Leave my eyes open.

Remember what we accomplished. Please, Sir..."

Hull raised the .45. Tears filled his eyes. He did not hear the report. The bullet tore through Bauldaire's heart. Ever curious, the Lieutenant looked from his chest, to Hull. Then the light faded from his eyes and his head slowly rolled to the side.

"The young Lieutenant was brave. You--not the Taliban fighters--killed him," Rostislov yelled. "And the innocent Afghan girl, Roxana? You are surprised we knew her. She was young, beautiful and innocent! It was our informer who called Chapman security! And you, Colonel Hull...you the honorable, obedient, soulless soldier followed orders precisely and shot her in the face..."

"Do you remember the others? Osama bin Laden, the great leader--a father and a teacher--a religious man who fought against oppression. It was bin Laden who called for devout Muslims to distribute food and water to victims of the Pakistan floods. You shot Siraj Haqqani, a good son, a faithful husband and a brave warrior. Both died without having the chance to face you. Bin Laden, Haqqani cowards? For fighting to free the world's oppressed poor?" His laugh turned bitter.

Hull's breathing slowed. His heartbeat fell from two hundred beats per minute, to one ninety, one eighty. The Unertl scope steadied.

Holding the Karud to Grace's throat, Rostislov demanded, "What do you fight for? Medals? To protect your country? Money? All lies! You fight because you're a killer--a predator, born without a conscience. To you, men, women have all become numbers, each one added to a total..."

The Unertl's crosshairs settled on Rostislov's forehead.

Rostislov sensed Hull had locked on and shifted Grace directly in front of him. Grace's long hair whipped across his face.

Hull's shot evaporated.

"Colonel Hull!" Rostislov yelled. "This whore's death will stain your soul. I kill her, you kill me. I ascend to Paradise. You live with her memory until you can no longer live with her memory. When you kill yourself, your God will bar you from Heaven."

The storm's leading vortex spun above the crater driving dust into Hull's face. In the same way Bauldaire had known the only way home was through Hull, the sniper now realized the only way to Rostislov was through

Grace. Colonel Dillard moved quietly next to Hull and said, "Conscience is but a word that cowards use, devised at first to keep the strong in awe." The professor took a deep breath. "At the risk of your own sanity, you cannot allow Rostislov to live. If you and Grace die, it is a small price to pay for millions of lives."

Hull raised the M40. At a hundred yards it was a simple, offhand shot. The target was clear. The cross-hairs settled on Grace's chest. He blinked away tears.

"Colonel Hull!" it was Rostislov. "Our time has come to settle this." He moved the Karud against Grace's throat. "Drop your rifle--throw it into the crater!"

Hull squeezed the trigger. A millisecond later the 150-grain match round blew through Rostislov's left hand. It hit Grace above her right breast and passed through her lung and shoulder blade. Smashing into Rostislov, it simultaneously blew a large hole in his lung, clipped his liver and broke two ribs.

The impact drove Grace into Rostislov. The 7.62mm's ton of force ripped Rostislov's blade back off her throat. Grace crumpled down and to the right. Rostislov was blown backwards, into the crater.

Hull racked another round into the chamber and swept the rim with the scope. Lightening forked above. The crack of thunder was instantaneous. The storm's fierce winds dragged an opaque powder curtain across the crater. The final sight picture Hull recorded was of Grace sprawled face down in the red pumice. Rostislov had disappeared.

Bending into the wind, Hull sprinted through the blinding dust. Visibility dropped to six feet. Lightening forked around him as he fought forward. He had lost track of distance when Grace's arm appeared. She was lying face down, blood staining the back of her blouse.

Rolling her onto her back, he touched her carotid artery. A pulse answered. Slinging the M40 across his back, Hull removed her scarf and wrapped her hand to staunch the blood flow. She needed immediate medical attention.

Dillard appeared. "How do you know the Afghani is truly dead?" Turning a single glance toward Grace, he said, "You must do your duty!"

The wind was rising, visibility dropped to four feet. The bullet that hit

Grace high in the right chest below her collarbone, exited her shoulder, and slammed into Rostislov's lower ribs, liver-level. The Afghani was bleeding out. Rostislov's life was now counted in minutes. Hull knew, when wounded, all species run down hill. He dropped into the crater, away from where Grace lay unconscious on her back.

Shielding his eyes against the blowing pumice, Hull searched for Rostislov's body or a track. Nothing. Torn between saving Grace and confirming Rostislov was dead, Hull turned uphill. He would notify Twentynine Palms. The Marines would locate Rostislov's corpse before dark.

Summoning T.S. Eliot, Dillard advised him, "I will show you fear in a handful of dust."

Hull found Grace, gathered her carefully in his arms, and turned down hill. "Rostislov is dead," he promised Dillard.

"For a moment, the lie becomes the truth," the Colonel warned.

"The bullet destroyed his liver," Hull yelled, "He's dead!"

Hull's 7.62 round took Rostislov by surprise. He would not have believed the Assassin would shoot his whore to kill him. But the shot had not killed him. When Rostislov stopped in the deep pumice, he used his Karud to cut bandages from his shirt. One he wrapped around his hand. Once again, the jacketed bullet had missed bone. The other, he stuffed into the bullet hole and tried to breath. Badly damaged, he estimated his right lung would function for two hours, perhaps three. His right hand and liver, he did not know.

The blowing dust saved him. Lying face down in the pumice, separated from the .270, he went undiscovered by the Assassin who passed a few feet away. The storm intensified. Compared to what Sacha had endured, the bullet hole seemed inconsequential. He lay in the warm pumice and allowed the dust to settle upon him. Soon, when he was sure the Assassin was gone, he would gather his strength and descend from the crater. The majority of gunshot wounds were survivable. He had been trained to tense his abdominals, slow his breathing. He needed a minute to rest before he started to walk. He remembered Sacha survived fifty-seven minutes and thirty-three seconds. For her sake, he would match that time. With luck, he might even double it. Closing his eyes, he tensed his stomach and took shallow, slow breaths.

Hull carried Grace downhill through the blowing dust. Two hundred and thirty vertical meters --a half-mile to the truck. Blinded by the swirling pumice, Hull ran through the ash until, free of the steep slope, he renewed his purchase on Grace's back and legs and awkwardly sprinted across the lava flows to the pickup. He was out of breath when he belted her into the passenger seat. Jumping behind the wheel, he twisted the ignition and when the engine caught, ripped the shifter into reverse and back-tracked through blowing dust to the parking area and Route 66.

Missing badly, the old pickup truck struggled to seventy miles an hour. The engine temperature rose and the oil pressure dropped as Hull pushed the F-150 through the junction to Twentynine Palms. He was twenty miles south of Amboy when the rod knock started. Faint at first, the clatter rose to a heavy death rattle. Dust from the salt plane clouded the road but Hull could not slow down. Danger in the desert appears in many forms, and he knew he could not hail a ride holding Grace in his arms. No one would stop for a man carrying a bleeding woman.

The rod knock grew louder. Grace had less than hour to live. The F-150's life expectancy was counted in seconds when the Mercedes materialized out of the blowing dust. Hull slammed on the brakes and skidded into the barrow pit. Praying for a miracle, he jammed his hand into Grace's purse. Under the envelope, his fingers closed on the key.

The driver's door lock clicked open and he hit the key's start button. The V-12 spun, stuttered then died. A yellow light showed from the dash. The SL65 was out of gas. Hull grabbed the gas can from the pickup bed, opened the gas tank door and turned the five-gallon metal can on end. It took fifty seconds to drain. Lifting Grace from the truck, Hull carried her to the Mercedes and lowered her onto the passenger seat. He set her feet on the floor, crossed her hands in her lap and pulled the shoulder strap across her chest. For a moment she remained upright then the belt slowly unreeled out of the doorjamb and she slumped forward. Pushing her back, he lay her head on the rest. Throwing the duffle into the trunk, he started the V-12, cranked the steering wheel and stabbed the throttle. The black coupe switched ends.

Easing into the throttle he watched the speedometer rise to a hundred miles an hour. At that speed a semi creeping through the blowing dust could kill them both. Better to risk rear-ending a tractor-trailer than watching Grace bleed out. A mile passed, then two, and suddenly Highway 62 broke from the salt plane and the creosote-carpeted hills. The dust faded, the visibility jumped and Hull punched the throttle. The small coupe vaulted to one hundred and eighty mph. With the V-12 screaming in full song, the SL65 devoured the narrow, desert road in one savage howl.

Hull was five miles outside of Twentynine Palms when Grace started to gasp for air. Her skin was a translucent white; plasma and immediate surgery were essential if she was to survive. Grace coughed again, then slumped forward against the shoulder strap. Hull pushed her back into the seat. Her eyes opened. She looked at him and tried to focus. Her chest heaved, she coughed again and her jaws suddenly clenched. She tried to speak.

"Grace, breathe!" Hull tried to coax more speed from the Mercedes.

A desperate whistling filled the interior when Grace inhaled. "Where are we?" her voice was faint.

"Two minutes from a hospital." Hull backed off the accelerator as the Mercedes drifted around the sweeping left east of Twentynine Palms.

Grace looked at her bandaged hand. Her lips barely parted, she said, "He cut off my fingers!"

"He won't hurt you any more." Hull pushed the speed to a hundred and thirty on Amboy Road. "Help is close...just a few minutes," he promised. Convulsions wracked her. Her eyes rolled back into her head and she shook violently.

"GRACE!" he shouted. "Open your eyes!" Twentynine Palm's Marine Corps Air Ground Combat Center appeared on the horizon. Hull took the corner in third, drifting the small Mercedes then flooring it down the long straight toward the base.

Grace fought for each breath. Her chest wheezed with the effort. Placing his hand over her upper breast Hull applied pressure. The wheeze subsided. He was driving with one hand, weaving in and out of traffic toward the Marine Base. A small Mercedes traveling at a hundred miles over the posted limit was a threat. The Main Gate would be alerted to his approach.

The Marines would react with force.

Grace strained for breath. Panic filled her eyes as she fought for air. Grabbing his arm, she cried, "Help me!"

"GRACE!" Hull's anguished roar filled the small car as the Air Combat Center's Main Gate rose in the windshield. Two Humvees blocked the road. Half a dozen Marine MPs trained their weapons on the Mercedes. Closing at over 130 miles an hour, Hull, shifted into fifth, fourth and third, the speed cascading off, as the ABS disc brakes hammered violently on the four corners. Fifty yards short of the roadblock, the Mercedes skidded to a stop. Any closer and the MPs would open fire. Throwing open the door, Hull climbed out, his hands in the air his Military ID held between his left thumb and forefinger. "I am Colonel Jack Hull, Scout Sniper, First U.S. Marines, 3rd Corps, assigned to Afghanistan. I have a badly wounded woman in the car who needs immediate medical attention!"

Dressed in a ballistic vest, helmet and desert camo fatigues, an MP crossed the distance, his M16 leveled on Hull. Grace wheezed desperately. Hull was losing her.

Pointing the M16 barrel at Hull's chest, the MP took the ID, studied the picture and ID number, then looked in the car.

Hull was desperate. "Marine, there is no time, the girl in the car has been shot in the lung, she's dying. If you need confirmation, call the base commander. Now--Goddammit!"

A second later the Marine made the connection.

"Colonel Jack Hull?" the base commander asked. "The Scout Sniper who nailed bin Laden?"

"Yes Sir, his ID confirms it!"

"Everyone, including the Commandant of the Marine Corps is looking for Colonel Hull!"

"Sir, he looks beat to shit and the woman's hemorrhaging out. She doesn't have much time!"

"Leave the car! Evacuate the woman to emergency. I'll alert them she's coming in."

The MP stepped forward, "Sorry sir, I've got to do this." He patted Hull down, and then hurried around the car to the passenger door.

"I'll do that," Hull said, picked her up and walked toward the

Humvees. One accelerated to meet him. Hull loaded her in the back seat then jumped in next to her. The Humvee accelerated to Robert E. Bush Naval Hospital where a trauma team was waiting outside the Emergency Entrance. Running next to the gurney, a surgeon who had served two tours, one in Iraq and one in Afghanistan, examined her mutilated hand, bruised cheek, shallow cut across her throat and upper chest bullet wound.

Grace fought for breath as the trauma team sprinted to an operatory. She tried to speak but could only cough. Blood drained from her mouth.

The surgeon grabbed Hull, "Colonel! This woman has been tortured! Where are her fingers? What the hell happened?"

"There's no time to explain. Her fingers are lost."

The surgeon looked toward the gurney. Grace's black hair hung down as she disappeared around a corner. "Damn, Colonel!" Turning he ran down the hall toward the OR.

Boots ringing on the polished floor, three Marine officers entered the emergency receiving room. Saluting Hull, the tallest identified himself, "I'm Colonel Kassanner. I've been asked to debrief you," he said. "I understand the young lady was shot?"

Hull nodded.

"Any idea how it happened?"

Hull stared down the hallway. "I know exactly how it happened. But this is not the time."

"I'm sorry to do this Colonel Hull, but there's a protocol for gunshot victims. Especially in the company of Marines shortly returned from theater. We need to ensure this isn't a criminal case. Do you know who shot her?"

Hull thought of the past three days. The dreams, Rostislov, the Amboy Crater, Dillard, the sight picture as his scope locked on Grace's chest. "I did," he finally said.

Kassanner glanced at the other officers. "Colonel Hull, we'll need to ask you a few more questions. If you wouldn't mind following us."

He led him to a conference room where he directed Hull to a chair at a long table, then sat erectly in the chair opposite. "Do you care for water?"

Hull shook his head. "How is Grace?"

"They're operating now. They'll tell us when they close her up. Colonel, in light of your service to the country, I'd like to make this as painless as possible. If you could start at the beginning."

Hull glanced to his right. Colonel Dillard was sitting ramrod straight in the chair next to him. His uniform was cleanly pressed. Studying the three officers, he asked, "What is life? A madness. What is life? An illusion, a shadow, a story. And the greatest good is little enough: for all life is a dream, and dreams themselves are only dreams."

Epilogue

T rained in Iraq and Afghanistan on traumas from IEDs, rocket-propelled grenades and high power rounds, the Marine surgical team deftly closed the bullet hole in Grace's upper chest. It took two tries before the lung reinflated. At the same time they were working on her chest, they reconnected the veins in the remaining finger stumps and covered them with flaps of skin. Following the initial salvage operation, the missing ring and middle fingers would serve as an annoyance, but not a disabling handicap.

Colonel Kassanner struggled to prove Hull's account of the past three days. At best, Grace was an unreliable witness. Suffering from blood loss, emotional trauma, shock--when she emerged from the OR, her memory of the events leading up to her shooting proved to be faulty. Selective amnesia blocked the worst of the events. She thought she remembered Rostislov, but could not recall his face, how he was dressed or how she had lost her fingers. She did remember that Hull had shot her. Beyond that, she could not say why.

She remembered to ask for her purse as soon as she came out of anesthesia. During her week in Robert E. Bush Naval Hospital, she never let it out of her sight, not even when she went to the bathroom.

Eilert, in Army Intelligence, contributed details about the Marburg attack on the Presidential Library. He recounted the phone call with Hull following the Sun and Health massacre, but he had no way of physically placing the terrorist Rostislov in L.A., or, lacking a body, confirm Hull's statement that Rostislov resurfaced at the Amboy Crater. The deaths of the Mount Baldy deputy, the Good Samaritan, the Covina Motel clerk, Judith

349

Lindle, Cheryl Birden, Wardell Stone and the secretaries and vice presidents of Sun and Health went unsolved. Only Hull had seen the L.A. Police Department Sergeant, Cheryl, Stone and Sun and Health's employees. A secretary at the insurance company had watched Hull steal Wardell Stone's SL65 from the parking lot, a few minutes after the murders.

The old hard rock clerk in Amboy had no memory of an Afghani customer. He did remember Hull, "That SAW was hard to forget," he admitted. He also remembered the beautiful girl. He thought for a moment, and confessed that his memory was slipping. He believed the girl was with Hull.

The rare fall windstorm had raged across the Amboy crater for the better part of a day. When the storm died, two hundred Marines scoured the Amboy lava fields but found no evidence of a BMW X5. The Marines worked hard to prove Hull's innocence.

Following a three day intensive search, the Marines never found Rostislov's body. No tracks, no blood trail. Nothing. The winds had erased his tracks. One officer on the investigating team postulated the Afghani might have disappeared into one of the ancient lava tubes that laced the flows. The Marines returned with one spent .270 case and Hull's 7.62-millimeter cases. Nothing else.

When no physical evidence was discovered, one of the search team officers quietly wondered if Hull was suffering a seriously shit bad case of Post Traumatic Stress Disorder. Following a call to General David Petraeus in Kabul, he was ordered to stow it. Hull was a Marine hero. He would remain a Marine hero.

Massive organ failure preceded Dick Cheney's death. The virus had reduced his liver, kidneys, stomach and intestines to mush. Blood wept from his tear ducts, his ears, skin; virtually every orifice. Death came hard for Cheney. He cried bloody tears as his mind rid itself of classified secrets and begged forgiveness from both political adversaries and old friends. During his final hours he returned to his days on the gridiron, where he consistently fell short of the goal line.

His lungs and heart were the last to succumb as he fought the blood rising into his throat and nose. At the very end, he reconsidered his support for waterboarding terrorists. As the blood reached his larynx he faced the terror of drowning.

Cheney's body, bedding, clothes and anything he had touched were immediately cremated in a portable biohazard kiln.

When the disease burned through Lynne Cheney, the two house keepers, the cook, three Secret Service agents and half a dozen other friends and family who had visited before Cheney's primary diagnosis, the house was burned. Any fragments that survived the fire were loaded into biohazard containers and trucked to nuclear waste facilities. The remaining ash was then soaked with gasoline to inhibit dust and buried beneath six feet of sterile soil.

In Texas, pulmonary edema finally overwhelmed ex-President Bush. In his last lucid moments he marveled at the pain's enormity. He understood what it meant to float on a lake of fire. In the depths of his delirium, George W. Bush became his mother's boy, constantly seeking his absent father's approval. At the end, he tried to tell George H. Bush that he had done his duty and had no regrets. Before he could utter the first word, he vomited a quart of bright, arterial blood.

Further east in Florida, Limbaugh, like Cheney, began to massively bleed out. Watching from behind multiple glass barriers, Hazmat workers listened to him beg for help.

Quarantined in a crude, Level 4 containment unit, at one point, it appeared as if Carl Rove might survive. His temperature dropped as his renal function and lung volume improved. He was even starting to take fluids when his heart stopped.

Rumsfeld lasted a few hours longer. Gripped by end-of-life hallucinations, he denied responsibility for the soldiers who died while he was Secretary of Defense. Ashcroft took two days more before he died from combinations of renal, liver and pulmonary failure.

One unexpected side effect of the virus was a final psychological breakdown. During the disease's closing stages, a few victims regressed to their childhoods. Limbaugh reverted to a school-ground bully, disliked by all, including the smaller sycophants who curried his attention. None died well; none managed the strength of Nikolai Ustinov, whose virus now choked their blood.

Two months passed before the Marburg virus burned through Dallas. Anyone who expressed a low grade fever was evacuated to Cowboy's Stadium in Arlington Texas, where they were quarantined according to the stage of their infection; days one through seven were confined to the broad concrete ramps leading to the seats; seven through fourteen on the playing fields. Of the sixty thousand people who were infected during the initial outbreak, roughly fifty-seven thousand died. Two-dozen health care workers were added to that total when their Bio-containment suits failed. The behavior of Dallas's uninfected mirrored the worst years of Europe's Bubonic Plague. Bloodshot eyes served as death sentences and, in an attempt to avoid Cowboy's Stadium and its hellish mix of bleeding victims and dense viral air, the infected often locked themselves in their basements until the disease ran its inevitable course.

The CDC canceled all flights in an out of Dallas. Roadblocks were erected on major and minor highways and infrared predators were used to track those families who attempted to escape on foot.

Before the virus was identified, victims managed to fly to Saint Louis, Denver, Atlanta, as well as a half-dozen other cities. The CDC quickly isolated all those who came into contact with what were subsequently referred to as "The Couriers." Before they were evacuated to bio-containment sites, the Couriers managed to infect another twenty thousand, of whom eighteen thousand expired within the expected fourteen days. Hot spots continued to burn for two months after the Dallas attack but by then the CDC had organized rapid response teams. Their tactics would later be described as effective, but brutal.

Of Bush's Cabinet, only Rice survived, but at a terrible cost. She would live another year, but wish she hadn't.

Hull was not immediately ordered back to Afghanistan. Dr. Harlow Rogers was flown back from Bagram to lead the debriefing. While the Marines continued to search for physical evidence, Doctor Rogers administered every test at his disposal. The results proved inconclusive. Hull matched a killer's profile. Only the knife didn't fit. By nature and training, snipers preferred to stand off at a distance. Whoever cut Stone, Darcy, Cheryl and the rest of the victims, rejoiced in the closeness and took pleasure in inflicting the pain.

Rogers encouraged Hull to relive the three days after he landed in LAX. Hull gave him the basics--Pakistan, bin Laden, Bauldaire, Saker, Stone's and Cheryl's deaths—Rostislov, the Amboy Crater. He admitted that he'd shot Grace to kill Rostislov. Without Rostislov's body, Rogers' notes were filled with underlined question marks. No one--Grace included, would understand. Hull did not speak of Dillard, the Treasury Bills or the stones. Rogers knew the Scout Sniper was holding back.

General David Petraeus backed Hull to the limit of his vast influence. The President also weighed in. Not completely. In light of his crashing polls, he held certain options in abeyance. It was enough. Rogers believed only intense psychotherapy would reveal what had transpired in those three days. Hull's leave was extended three months.

In late September, a man known only as Esmatullah contacted Burhanuddin Rabbani, the head of Afghanistan's High Peace Council. Rabbani was charged with negotiating peace terms with the Taliban. By then the Coalition was willing to underwrite any peace process, as long as it accelerated a withdrawal. Claiming to have a critical message from the Taliban leadership, Esmatullah was welcomed into Rabbani's home. Esmatullah immediately crossed the room, embraced the venerated leader and detonated a kilo of high explosive hidden in his turban. The blast beheaded both men. The attack confirmed the Taliban's ability to reach into the highest levels of the Afghan government. A U.S. Embassy spokesman confessed that Mr. Rabbani's killing dismantled Kabul's efforts to negotiate peace with the Taliban. The following day, in a rare agreement with Hamid Karzai, President Obama described Rabbani's assassination as "A tragic loss."

The national press continued to clamor for a televised conference. None of the three-dozen writers assigned to the story doubted a series detailing the Scout Sniper's killing of Osama bin Laden and the string of murders that had followed him across Los Angeles would qualify for a Pulitzer Prize. To ensure they did not get that opportunity, the Marines kept Hull sequestered in Twentynine Palms before he was transferred to Pendleton in San Diego and the Mountain Warfare Training Center in Bridgeport.

Five days after the assassination of Burhanuddin Rabbani, the Taliban attacked an out building in the U.S. Embassy complex. An un-identified embassy spokesperson revealed the building housed the Central Intelligence

Agency in Kabul.

A short time later, the embassy received a message from Maulvi Haqqani. Delivered by a young boy to an embassy guard, the letter both bitterly mourned the death of Haqqani's son Sirajuddin and promised the fragmenting Coalition that the attack on the Embassy, CIA and mosque bombings served as a beginning. In the coming year, Sirajuddin Haqqani's assassination would cost the Coalition dearly.

A week after the attack on the embassy, a CIA drone launched a Hellfire missile into an SUV carrying Anwar al-Awlaki, the head of Yemen's al Qaeda across the Yemeni desert. An American citizen known for his fiery calls to jihad and terrorist attacks, Awlaki and four other high ranking al Qaeda operatives died when the Hellfire reduced his SUV to scorched fragments of mangled sheet metal. In Washington a debate erupted over the legality of assassinating a U.S. citizen. The American Civil Liberties Union filed a suit claiming the killing of Awlaki violated the al Qaeda leader's First Amendment rights. Washington studied the suit, then declined to respond. After Osama bin Laden's death, Awlaki marked the Obama Administration's second high profile assassination in five months. The coming year would witness a dozen others.

Two days after Grace's release from Twentynine Palms she had hired a bodyguard...an ex-Marine Sergeant in Special Ops, whom Hull had contacted. The Marine surgeons were confident that Grace's chest wound would heal. The bullet left a small scar above her right breast and a larger one in her back but it was her left hand that caused problems. Rostislov's rusty steel dikes had introduced antibiotic-resistant bacteria into the crushed bones.

During the month following her initial treatment at Twentynine Palms base, in an attempt to limit the infection to her middle and ring finger stubs, hand surgeons at the Harbor-UCLA Medical Center operated half a dozen times. If the bacteria were to become established, they feared it would take her left hand. If it took her hand, she might lose her arm.

Six weeks passed before Grace felt strong enough to take a vacation. She had booked two flights to Argentina when her hand began to throb. The middle finger stump was infected. The operation to reopen the flap and flush the wound took an hour. She spent the rest of that day and night in the hospital.

"Hull called from Bridgeport when she came out of surgery. "How are you feeling?" he asked, quietly.

"The surgeon irrigated the infection, he thinks he got it."

It was the first good news in weeks. He brightened. "I'm looking forward to Argentina."

Her tone softened. "So am I."

He was waiting when a nurse wheeled Grace out of Harbor-UCLA Hospital on an early winter day. Her left hand was heavily bandaged. Her purse sat on her lap, her left arm double looped through the shoulder strap. The sun stood behind him and she was forced to squint up at his black silhouette. She could not see his face but knew he was waiting to escort her back to her rented house in Brentwood.

He asked, "You are ready to return home?"

There was something familiar about his syntax--turning a statement into a question.

About the Author

Andrew Slough's work as a writer/photographer has taken him around the world. In his travels Andrew has chased the legend of Dracula to Romania's Borgo Pass, skied the Haute Route across the Alps from Saas Fee Switzerland to Chamonix, France and ridden a bicycle over four Swiss passes in a single day for a total of 15,000 feet of vertical and 106 miles. He skied Mutnovsky and Achivinsky, the Kamchatka Peninsula's active volcanoes, circumnavigated Italy's Monte Rosa Massif, skied New Zealand's Southern Alps and captured deep powder days in Japan, Quebec, Argentina, Austria, France, Italy and Switzerland.

In the course of Andrew's travels, he has contributed stories and photos to Esquire, Outside, Men's Journal, Rock and Ice, Sports Afield, Sports Illustrated, National Geographic Adventurer and others including "The Washington Post", "Toronto Star," and "Christian Science Monitor," as well as numerous newspapers, inflight, trade, and foreign periodicals.

Andrew Slough has two books in print and is presently working on the sequel for "High Value Target."

CPSIA information can be obtained at www.ICGtesting.com
Printed in the USA
LVOW08s0003260115

424182LV00003B/4/P